Archdeacon
(Full of bright ide

By J. Ewins and L. Telfer

CREATE EMPOWER COMMUNITY

WordHive Ltd: London

Published by WordHive Ltd, 2020

The right of J Ewins and L Telfer to be identified as the authors of this work has been asserted by them in accordance with the Copyright, Designs and Patents Act 1988.

This book is a work of fiction. The characters manifested in this book are purely in the authors' imagination, and any resemblance to actual persons is entirely coincidental.

This book is sold subject to the condition that it shall not by way of trade or otherwise, be lent, resold, hired out, or otherwise circulated without the authors' consent in any form of binding or cover other than that in which it is published and without a similar condition including this condition being imposed on the subsequent purchaser.

First published in Great Britain in 2020 by WordHive Ltd, 77 Victoria St, London, SW1H 0HW

www.wordhive.co

WordHive Limited Reg. No. 105153310

Bible quotations from THE MESSAGE. Copyright © by Eugene H. Peterson, 1993, 1994, 1995, 1996, 2000, 2001, 2002, 2018. Used by permission of NavPress. All rights reserved. Representations by Tyndale House Publishers, Inc.

WordHive Ltd: London

A hilarious story starring A.D. the Archdeacon, as in changed times, he reflects on the previous year's progress of his mission to revamp religious broadcasting and take the church out of the building with the help of his outstandingly funny team of long-suffering assistants.

Archdeacon goes Live (full of bright ideas and only 46!), is the first in the series of the amusing exploits of A.D. as he prefers to be known by those who love him. And he believes there are many!

In his side-splitting way, the Archdeacon thrives on life, love and God's faithfulness. He has no doubt as he motors through his calling that his instantaneous prayers, his "Smith Wigglesworth moments," as he calls them, will be answered. Full of humour but at times a tender struggle for him and those around him, the story tracks the progress of A.D. and his team and family in changing circumstances, in this lovable, entertaining story.

Excerpt;

'What?' spat out A.D. He stepped back, initially seized with panic. The whole concept of being related to Paul Downing, if this young man before him became his son-in-law, was testing. Prayer required, he told himself: possibly counselling. He breathed and closed his eyes.

Storm waited as thirty seconds went by, watching him with some concern. A.D. opened his eyes, calmer now. He tried to look pleasant. He set his face to the expression he always wore with the Purley Flower Committee.

After all, thought A.D. having Paul as an in-law was not the lad's fault. Trying to smile between praying for strength he gave Storm a once over.

A.D. said: 'How do you know my daughters? Which one is it?'

Dedication

This book is dedicated to all key workers.

Characters:

Archdeacon Mark Wilkinson (A.D)

Louise Wilkinson

Eve, Charis and Judith (Jude) Wilkinson

Zack

Great Aunty Elspeth

Wills

Chris Duncan

John and Maureen Duncan

Marie

Jenny

Aunty Gladys

Lucya

Stacy

Laurie

Adeniji

Bishop Rob

Uncle Colin

Storm Downing

Paul Downing

Stefan

Gareth

Millie

Sophie and William

Lesley

Mary

Cheng

Amy

Ellie Beech

Joel Rivers

Ravi Acharya

Mike Briggs

Rafe

The Honourable Letitia Simpkins-Blythe

Rev. Deirdre Pullman

Paula.

One

Busy as he was Archdeacon Mark Wilkinson stared through the window at his wife in the garden. On the desk in front of him his mobile gyrated with a call from Sarah at the BBC. Panic seized him: what to say, how to start?

He knew he had missed his slot and that he was late, which was why Sarah was calling. As he reached for his phone his eyes switched back to Louise, his wife of twenty-six years, who had put her laptop with the spreadsheets to one side, pulled a small mirror from her case and positioned it against her empty coffee cup. Next, out came a pair of kitchen scissors. Slowly she lifted them to her head and took a strand of hair from the top and held it between two fingers. Then she started to cut. Fascinated at such unusual behaviour from a woman who had a hairdresser's appointment every five weeks the Archdeacon froze as his phone went to voicemail.

'A.D. it's Sarah, are you alright? Oh, he's not answering. Ring off.'

A.D. was his preferred title. A term of affection he was sure and "Archdeacon" was such a mouthful. He hit the number and waited for Sarah to answer. It was engaged. A.D. peered out at Louise again and saw that she had moved the scissors to one side of her head.

It had been a challenging morning trying to do an outside broadcast from his study. Jude, his youngest daughter, had put her head round the door several times, and then gone on the wi-fi, despite a strict discussion over breakfast that no-one

—

was to use it that morning. A.D. was trying to use an ISDN line, whatever that was, and was supposed to be on air bringing what Sarah had described as an "ebullient" aspect to the issue on every one's minds. He still needed internet apparently, hence the ban on the family using it. That was why Sarah had called him on his mobile as she couldn't get a message through on screen.

The door crashed open and his two spaniels invaded the room. Max and Gus became entangled in wires connected to one of the laptops. It died. A.D. chased them out and set up again.

He did a check on Louise. One side of her hair was short, the other long. Should he go out to her? Sarah was ringing again and A.D. took the call: 'Sarah, I'm sorry, I froze.'

'Family on the internet, are they? Do you remember A.D. we said one screen for emails the other with the agreed points to prompt you? I can't get through to you without calling and my messaging should be instant. You've done this before, A.D. no need to be nervous. We agreed the script and you can always message me.'

'Sorry, just my daughter I think, the rest of the family have stayed off it, as far as I know. The dogs got in and got tangled in a wire so one of the laptops went down. Wife's working in the garden, so it's not her as she's just cut her hair. It's a bit odd, really.'

'Managing the social isolation! Can't get out to the hairdresser. *Perfect,* start with that,' said Sarah. 'You've got five minutes before you're on. OK?'

'Seems a bit facile,' said A.D.

'Not to a woman, it's real,' said Sarah, curtly.

'I mean in comparison to … look, I was a bit late last night … one of the members of the church here passed away in hospital …'

'You didn't go in?' asked Sarah.

'Tried to, they wouldn't *let* me in,' said A.D. morosely.

'Thank goodness for that. Now, A.D. just focus as this should be straightforward. Reflect back on those two stories but keep it ebullient, remember, ebullient.'

That wretched word again, thought A.D.

'We'd wondered if you'd like to co-present this morning instead of just doing the five minutes?' Sarah asked. 'I can email you a draft script. Just keep the family off the internet and keep the interaction natural. The figures are up, so well done.' Sarah hung up.

'All *morning,'* said A.D. into the phone. 'I can't, Louise has a senior management meeting in half an hour. She'll lynch me if she can't get onto the internet. Are you there? Oh, she's gone.'

'Who's gone,' said Louise, appearing in the doorway rubbing freshly washed hair.

'Sarah from the beeb. I, er, oh, hair looks nice,' said A.D. surprised.

'Yes? Good, like I used to wear it and should buy me time before the grey shows through,' said Louise. 'That's the good think about curly hair, it bounces up and hides the grey. And a really bad cut. I reckoned I'd got three weeks before everyone knew what my real hair colour was.'

'Would it matter?' asked A.D.

Louise gave him the look she used before she shut down a division. 'Two tone hair? I don't think so.'

'Couldn't you wear a scarf?' asked A.D.

'Don't be ridiculous. How can the F.D. wear a scarf? Are you done with the internet?'

'Hold on, I'm on,' said A.D.

'Twenty-five minutes before I need to be on zoom,' hissed Louise through the crack in the door. 'How on earth did you get sucked into all this?'

Good question, thought A.D. but he knew the answer. As he adopted the expression he usually reserved for the Purley flower committee the Archdeacon would be live and there on screen would be his study. That source of memories from the last year since he had responded to the BBC flooded back. How much they had all taken their freedom for granted. Five, four …. His mobile went off. It was Storm's number. A.D. had to take it.

'Storm, where are you?'

'Hang on, A.D. Dude, I was waiting outside. Sorry A.D. give me a minute will you, my lift is here and I've been trying to find the man. The name's Downing.'

A.D. could hear the response in a thick French accent:

'There's two of you?'

'There was,' Storm answered. 'She didn't make it.'

'Sorry,' said the French accent.

'Amy isn't there?' asked A.D. Sarah's message on screen was in red. He'd missed the link again.

'Where are you Storm?' asked A.D.

'Geneva. The airline's only putting twenty people at a time on the flights and as that doesn't make it worth their while flying they've reduced the number of flights to one a day. I'm on the 9.25 tonight to Heathrow, A.D. but no Amy. She's stranded until April twelfth as the lights failed on the runway. She's in touch with her embassy apparently.'

'Right, I'll come and get you at Heathrow. I think that's a pretty essential journey,' said A.D. making up his mind. Wear the dog collar in case the police questioned his movements and he should get through to the Short Stay car park. 'Can't have you trying to get home on the trains at that time of the night. Not everything's running. I think we're the closest to Heathrow as well. You can hole up here. You probably want to be near Heathrow anyway for when Amy gets here. How was West Africa?'

'After seven weeks it was good to leave. It was pretty basic on the rig. Any word from Chris?' asked Storm.

'Not since last night,' said A.D. 'Like you they're trying to get back. No flights I gather. He said they'd volunteer if they get stuck and keep in close touch with the British Embassy.'

****

A year ago, it had been very different. It was always the same in a half term holiday as the numbers at the store entrances were high. The previous summer the Archdeacon had waited on the first floor for his assistant, Chris Duncan, to arrive. He caught a glimpse of the tall young man as he passed the gaggle of Americans deep in a discussion about their itinerary. It was the length of their regulation raincoats and strong accents that gave them away. The women were immaculately made up, not a hair out of place but he was always amazed at the trainers and socks worn regardless of the rest of the outfit. It was as if the fashion consciousness stopped at the knees.

The clouds that morning had been lined up like guardsmen advancing slowly above the store. It was a veritable palace of luxury. Knightsbridge on a wet day and a briefing for Chris Duncan. A.D. could tell from the despondent expression on the young curate's face that his cup definitely did not run over. The London drizzle continued to fall in visible waves on Knightsbridge, and the young man's shoes were soaked.

The way the day had started might have deterred Chris Duncan from his decision to walk but after all he was a Duncan from East Devon, recently returned from Africa, and rain in London was as nothing in comparison to a downpour in Colyton or the rainy season in Sierra Leone. Chris had set his course to walk up Sloane Street for the exercise. His shoes, however, were regretting it. He had needed the exercise, but also the time to think about the phone call from the Archdeacon.

'We'll meet for a drink and discuss "it" then,' the Archdeacon had said. 'I have a little shopping to do.'

As usual Chris Duncan's antennae was twitching when the Archdeacon had come through on his mobile. "It," he surmised referred to religious broadcasting.

14

Sometimes now A.D. woke in the middle of the night, a sense of panic seizing him at the invasion of his home.

Nearly a year ago when Chris had taken his current post his boss had jovially suggested that Chris call him "A.D." The Archdeacon viewed the shortened version of his title as a term of affection that he was sure all felt for him. True he was a character and occasionally Chris felt a warming to his boss but most of the time the man's ideas terrified him. He suspected that he really should have walked the other way when he had read the job spec. It was that little addendum that did it about:

"Assisting the Archdeacon as required."

That day in Knightsbridge the message had not been a call out of the blue. There had been hints over the previous week coupled with sotto -voce references to: "It" at Langham Place. After his first confused reaction, mistaking "Langham" for "Lambeth" Chris had fought off the panic attack. He had opened his mouth to reply, hoping to clarify what the "It" was but too late, the Archdeacon had moved on.

Chris had the expectation therefore, that he was about to be landed right in it.

Ah there it was, thought A.D. the tell. Chris glanced at his reflection in the mirror near the escalator to check the effect of the damp on his hair. As a result, he missed the opportunity to avoid being caught up in a Chinese tour party busily negotiating the available space. Two-thirds his height, they did not appear affected by the crowds and he was absorbed into their number like an amoeba. Nowhere to go and unable to escape, Chris entered the department as part of them. Once inside, he decided to stand still and the tour party peeled away from him like a skin and were gone, doggedly following the inscrutable tour leader, moving towards "shoes." It was clear Chris had doubts about the direction from there. Did he want the bit in the middle? Or was it to the right? This always happened in the palace of luxury and his sense of direction, which was fine outside, failed him.

A.D. waited. He would give Chris five minutes and then go and find him. The instruction had been very clear:

'Meet me in Black Robin on the first floor.'

Chris had even googled it: the place specialized in gin. 'When,' Chris had said to his reflection, 'had A.D. acquired a penchant for gin?'

Pondering on why he like the 'Palace of Luxury' as he called the store, so much A.D. knew how easily seduced he was by the smell of the perfume as immaculately attired men and women lined up to spray fragrances under his nose. They had no other expectation of him than that he would buy for the love of his life.

'Good job I don't come too often,' he said, smiling at the girl on the Chanel counter.

Pulled out of reflection A.D. saw a courteous shopper pointing Chris towards the right direction but he still had not seen A.D.

A.D. knew that Chris had left his storm jacket zipped up with the slight embarrassment that he had not yet overcome in

---

16

some settings when in his dog collar. The young man's hand went to his neck to subconsciously check it.

At last Chris had arrived at the entrance of "Black Robin," Taking in its 1920's black and white photographs. Before him a deferential waiter offered a menu, and then walked him across the room to where A.D. was sitting waving at him.

'The Archdeacon explained another gentleman would be joining him, sir,' said the waiter, as he pulled out a seat for Chris and remained, hovering, for his jacket. Chris did not remove it, feeling even more embarrassed at being in a cocktail bar in his dog collar. Why A.D. had insisted they meet here dressed as they both were, was beyond Chris. It was a gin palace. The heat flooded his cheeks.

'Well done dear boy, bang on time!' called A.D. loudly. Yes, heads turned, or was it Chris's imagination? A.D. took a sip of his drink, a dark concoction with two straws and just like a good host said: 'Do have one of these, delicious!'

Despite the tension he felt Chris turned down the offer of a drink at ten o'clock in the morning.

'It's a bit early for me A.D,' said Chris, feeling his Baptist upbringing creeping up behind him.

He was never comfortable with his colleague's propensity to briefing meetings in bars or gatherings in pubs after the evening service. London, he thought, it's different because its London. A.D. however was oblivious to his discomfort as he sucked up the glutinous substance, wiping his hand down his immaculate beard to ensure no drops took root.

'Ha, good one. It's the Blackberry, the non-alcoholic version. I really like the atmosphere in here. You would never know you're in a store it's so well done. Also, we're not going to bump into anyone from work here, so we can chat freely without the idea going viral.'

Chris glanced at the woman at the corner table taking the photo of A.D. Instagram, thought Chris. She'll call it "Reflections of my sightseeing today in London."

The waiter was back.

"Water," said Chris.

'Nonsense, try this one, it will do you good,' said A.D.

'I'll have the same,' Chris said to the waiter for a quiet life. The man receded backwards, bowing.

A.D. laughed and nodded towards the entrance of the bar. He said: 'Ah that group is out of menswear now.'

The Chinese group were entering "Black Robin." It was a cacophony of sound as chairs scraped on a tiled floor.

A.D. carried on: 'No sign of a slowdown in the Chinese economy given their propensity to spend.' He pointed to the bags they had acquired and Chris looked at his watch noting how little time had gone by since they had entered the store.

'I just wanted to say ...' Chris cut in again.

'No need, dear boy. Having seen you giving my Eve the once over I know where your heart is.' A.D. chuckled.

'What? You know?' Chris slipped slightly sideways on his chair. The waiter was very attentive.

'I'm sorry A.D, I didn't realize that you knew. I mean, I do apologize, it's just that she's so....' Chris struggled to find a polite description for the woman's father.

'And feels the same about you,' A.D. interrupted, wheezing slightly as he laughed. 'But when are you going to do something about it? You've been making cow's eyes at her every time you see her. Right, that apart, the main reason we're here, rather than in the office, where Jenny absorbs everything like a sponge, is to have a confidential chat about an approach I've had from the BBC.' A.D. drained his glass and made the universal hand gesture for the bill.

'Let's go,' said A.D. doing the touch routine with a card. 'I need a tie, and I can fill you in.'

'We're shopping?' Chris dropped his mouth open and his guard down.

'Of course,' said A.D. 'That's the other reason we're here. Come on, there's just time before we need to get back to Church House.'

The waiter had brought the bill and Chris's drink at the same time. Chris had a couple of sips and pulled a face but it was lost on A.D. who was off through the exit of the bar and across the floor into Menswear.

****

Chris Duncan sighed as A.D. led him at speed through the "Pink" section towards the ties. Lanvin, Hugo Boss, Christian Dior; all the big names were there. He wondered where the

Archdeacon was going to land. His boss moved, clearly on a mission, his eagle eye checking out the range, the colour and the quality. A.D. was a man of medium height, coming up to Chris's chest. His personality though was that of a giant and he was absolutely unstoppable. When convinced of the right way forward he would set his course and move incrementally onward. It was the case of quality not quantity in him. Watching his superior's determination and energy made Chris feel tired. A cold hand tightened around his vitals as the Bishop's Enforcer ran a hand over the ties by Lanvin. Such scrutiny, Chris felt, would also be directed towards him.

Chris nervously checked his jacket again to ensure he had not absent mindedly opened it to reveal his collar. Under his breath he muttered: 'This is so embarrassing…' His hand anxiously went up to his hair, a nervous reaction that surfaced when stressed. Chris found a mirror and checked his hair was still in place. It was so full of product that a nuclear explosion would not have dislodged it. He realized that A.D. was turning ties over and lifted one for Chris's opinion.

Chris acknowledged it as A.D. was explaining: 'I just must find the right tie for the firm's do tonight. Louise doesn't want me turning up amongst her city colleagues looking like a vicar so I shall be going in 'mufti.'

'Shame you didn't wear the suit you'll have on tonight so we could have checked the tie out properly,' said Chris.

A.D. looked impressed. He said: 'Yes, good point Chris. I didn't have time to change before I came in here though. Just feel the silk, look at the sheen on it.' A.D. flipped it over and against the Lanvin label was a £95 ticket.

Chris could not help himself: 'Goodness, the price!' he said loudly. 'You wouldn't want to drop your soup! Will Louise be alright with the price?'

A.D. peered over his glasses at his curate. 'I doubt there will be soup. Louise will always spot quality so we're home and dry with it. A Finance Director of a FTSE 250 company won't want me turning up in any old thing.'

'Yes, I suppose so,' said Chris, weakly.

Chris liked Louise Wilkinson. She was always calm in the middle of her husband's storm. She had qualified as a Chartered Accountant while A.D. had studied theology, accepting her role as the bread winner for them both as her lot to release her husband into a calling they both firmly believed in. At a time when her husband's initial placements in voluntary positions before his first curacy she had moved quietly and resolutely up the career ladder. Three daughters had followed as A.D. progressed to vicar and then Louise had re-entered business when their second child started school. Yes, Chris admired her. The investment strategy had rejected the allocated house that went with the role of vicar, choosing instead for them to buy their own home. Now the size had grown. He thought he had got the wrong address the first time he went to Purley. The house turned out to be a five-bedroomed mock gothic place up on the hill with about four acres. Three daughters and two Spaniels helped to fill it, as did the endless number of parish "do's" A.D. held in the garden.

A.D. delighted in telling everyone that he was a kept man. He had introduced Louise to Chris as: "my very clever wife."

Chris had spontaneously responded, 'And like how!'

Louise had warmed to him and laughed. She had also noticed the effect of their eldest daughter, Eve, on the young man.

A.D. was across the sales floor to the cash desk to pay. Chris joined him and in an aside A.D. whispered: 'What I've been trying to say is I've set up a meeting with the BBC. It's huge and we have to tread carefully.'

Chris could feel the heat in his cheeks, his brow furrowed. 'Here it comes.' He thought. He knew the sweat was starting.

A.D. noticed it too and put it down to a modest humility. A lack of confidence that would go with experience but which he had seen quite a lot in this young man over the last six months.

'Take a breath you're going pink! That's right. Keep breathing,' said A.D. He took the bag from the sales assistant and they moved a short distance away from the counter. With one hand on Chris's arm he steered his assistant towards the escalators. Irrespective of the state Chris was in, or because of the moment of weakness, A.D. explained:

'The Beeb have approached us, Chris, trying to stop the decline in the viewing numbers with the religious programming. Apparently, their strategy to date hasn't worked. As you will know if you've watched it lately. But they're stuck with this brand image with which they've saddled themselves.'

Chris looked down at his hands and unclenched them. His knuckles were going white. They were a good contrast to his face.

Weakly Chris asked: 'What image would that be A.D? I don't understand why they would approach us.'

'Because we have a series of successful church plants in venues that were about to be demolished and they're always happy to bring in what they perceive to be "experts." They just see religious programming like they did baking, and countryside programming. So, in their eyes, they can get us involved two weeks out of four and it's likely we will change things up and increase the viewing figures. Attract younger viewers.... It's all about ratings. Now, it's full of ugly vicars and terribly calm people. The average viewer is in their 80's and about to peg it. So, the viewing numbers are literally dying on their feet.'

A.D. raised his voice to the shock of a near-by assistant. 'Get it up, they said.' Chris glanced at the assistant. The pink colour of his face increased. He turned his face away. Perhaps the woman would disappear if he did not look at her. A.D. was oblivious and carried on: 'Match Bake off, Country-file and we're home and dry. Of course, that's not our objective.' He dropped his voice and noticed that Chris's brow was furrowed again.

'Isn't it?' asked Chris. 'I don't actually watch religious programmes.' Chris shook his head while he continued to allow his eyebrows to hit his hairline.

'Exactly, of course you don't! Who does? The timing of when they go out is all wrong for us anyway,' A.D. said. 'Have to record them on I-player all the time and with limited space on my contract I can't be bothered.'

'I'm not sure why you keep saying, they've approached "us" A.D? They haven't contacted *me*,' said Chris.

'Ah,' the silky, persuasive voice was back. A.D. continued: 'but your role is to assist me, so in a roundabout way they have. I'd like you to write me three proposals, one to submit now as a gentle lead in, and the second we'll put aside until our feet are under the table. The third can be the "reaching for the moon" scenario. And make a focus on leadership, which is very trendy now.' A.D. glanced over his shoulder, Chris automatically looked too. There was no-one there.

A.D. continued quietly, out of the side of his mouth: 'Attracts a lot of funding. So! It's a question of seeing if we can change it up, or save it, or get a new viewing public - Imagine getting ratings of seven million viewers. However, you look at it, it's just like being invited in to a service with a team. They'll leave what they have in place two weeks in four. Easy!'

A.D. paused and stared at Chris. It was the focused, penetrating stare, close range, through the glasses. Chris was learning to fear it.

'You get the team together Chris and let's go get 'em!' said A.D, enthusiastically.

'The team?' said Chris, thinking he had missed something. 'Who are you thinking of as the team, A.D?'

A.D. examined his nails while reflecting. He said: 'Oh, Mike, that youth worker with the skateboarders, the one with "work in progress" on his hoodie, who moved in with you recently didn't he? Wasn't he homeless or something? Then there's Dr. Ellie for brains...your other lodger, Ravi, would be good too, lots of energy there. And I thought of that surfer friend of yours with the Christian Surfer Church in North Devon, the one with the funny name. Smash cat or something....'

Chris stifled a laugh. It would be good to laugh, psychiatrists said one should. However, if he started he might become hysterical.

'His nickname is actually Storm. It's surfing stuff, you know.'

'It wasn't really my scene years ago, too wet and cold,' said A.D. 'Still it's got a strange appeal now. He's probably free tomorrow so get him up here. Maybe an overnight train. I think we're done, aren't we?' The Archdeacon checked his watch. By now they were at the bottom of the escalators and as if by arrangement with Chris's immanent departure the Chinese tour party they had last seen in "Black Robin" were suddenly between A.D. and Chris. It was like a river that could not be crossed. Chris called over their heads to A.D. above the tour party's chatter.

'Tomorrow? Why tomorrow?' Chris held his hands out, his face contorted.

A.D. however, stared at the Chinese tour group now blocking the escalator. 'Good grief, they have no spatial awareness at all!' He switched back to Chris and said: 'Yes, it has to be tomorrow. The meeting at the BBC is at 2pm. The weather's apparently rubbish for surfing tomorrow – your friend is bound to be free. Jude, my youngest, checked for me on some surfing app she's got. You know what thirteen-year olds are like. It's all digital stuff. Very taken with his photos she was. Might be a good opening shot riding the waves, nice scenery and all, North Devon. I think Storm's church will be keen and it links him up with Mike and the skateboarders. Maybe, we could go with a connection with Ellie's church in Melbourne. I think they'll be quite interested. They're very innovative, Melburnians, and she's such a modern Australian, completely fresh in her unpredictability. I see potential with Ravi's link too, he's so entrepreneurial. Anyway, we're meeting at the Beeb at one forty-five tomorrow and we'll go in together. Thought a breakfast meeting at Westminster would be good around nine-thirty tomorrow morning.'

Chris was lost trying to follow the tack A.D. was on but then his boss was off the escalator, walking through the exit doors. Chris followed in A.D.'s wake.

Outside A.D. wheeled round to look for Chris, yet again checking the time. Chris arrived grateful there had been no international incident.

'Come on, Chris, I have to get back to change.' A.D. said.

'Just picking up the idea of the meeting A.D. I'm not sure everyone will be free. It's not much notice.'

'Well that's the way the Beeb operates, forty-eight hours if you're lucky,' said A.D. 'I once was asked to review scripts, twelve they gave me over two days and no relief of other duties. Forty-five quid a script they offered. I told them I couldn't do it with all the work I had on and I wouldn't have been allowed to keep the money anyway. Hopeless really, but that's their world dear boy! There is no choice.'

'But everyone you mentioned works for other people!' Chris said.

A.D. sounded exasperated. 'Try and see it as a major outreach opportunity, it's your future you know, and the way people will view you as a vicar.'

Chris was feeling first hot and then cold. His face contorted as he said: 'I'm afraid I don't see where me as a vicar comes into it, A.D.'

'What a statement! You'll front the programming, and you can change the stereotype - which you don't fit anyway, I mean look at your hair! The very fact you have hair. That's why you're perfect for this, Chris.'

Chris stopped his hand going up to his hair again but A.D. saw the reflex gesture and grew a little softer at the expression on his assistant's face as the nerves were so evident. Thinking it would be encouraging to a twenty-seven-year-old curate he added, 'Just think how the ladies will love you, and you'll get the message across.'

Chris felt his mouth open but nothing came out. He eventually managed: 'But I don't know if the others are free Archdeacon. I can't make them come.'

'That's right, you don't until you make the phone calls. Listen, I have full faith in you. And if necessary I will make phone calls. However, I would prefer not to have to spend my time calling their bosses. But, if you have problems get a message to me.' A.D. was moving off down the street.

'Send them a WhatsApp or something, then get along home now and chances are you'll catch them before tonight. Full-team, Chris, full team. I shall expect everyone at nine-thirty tomorrow morning for breakfast.'

****

Two

Looking at the sky as he left the department store it became clear to Chris that it was in an undecided mood. Rather like him about the job he had taken. He walked past the busker playing a guitar, and paused to listen, deciding it was not bad. The case on the pavement in front of him showed a respectable number of coins. Chris wondered why there was a toy dog placed next to it. The guy was advertising a link for his recordings. Chris bent down and put £3 into the guitar case. The guitar riff was good.

'Thanks Mate,' the busker gave him a chord.

'S'good,' Chris gave him a thumb's up. He headed along the Brompton Road towards South Kensington, moving to the edge of the pavement to avoid the crush. It was coffee time and the Café on the Corner was beckoning.

Summer half-term in London meant that it was impossible in the tourist areas to walk in a straight line. Chris weaved through the crowds finally resorting to walking on the kerb. Just in time, he avoided decapitation by the wing mirror of the number 74 bus as it moved into its stop.

The meeting with A.D. troubled him. Having that kind of exposure was not something he wanted. Again, Chris regretted not staying in Africa. He felt like a seven-year-old again learning to ride his new bike and forgetting how to brake - the crunch that followed as he had collided into the stone flower urn in his parent's garden had left a lasting weakness in the left knee. Like that weakness, he feared the exposure the BBC work could bring. He did not want it.

He turned into Thurloe Place. It was part of his village that he had created for himself in London. The daily routine, of places and people, had helped when he had first come to the city and it was a way he survived in a place.

'Use your security zone.' His father's advice came back to him. After he found his faith and fell in love with God, prayer had added to this. His father, John Duncan, had survived the vagaries of successive governments as a senior civil servant with his "security zone" training from the 1980's. Whereas his mother believed in giving oneself a treat.

So, at the Cafe on the Corner, with its portal to the square, that was exactly what he would do. There was however a short queue. Chris joined it and forgot he was wearing his dog collar. He unzipped his jacket and then Marie was there with her brilliant smile that she had for him every day. She looked at the collar and Chris felt the blush again.

'You're late today. Do you want your usual?'

'Please, latte macchiato. I had to meet my boss.'

'God stops you getting coffee?' She laughed and Chris managed a half smile at the joke as he paid and collected his drink. Sipping it he walked through the pedestrian area and ran the gambit of dodging the buses to cross towards the Lamborghini shop.

'Not that kind of a treat!' He spontaneously laughed to himself and then remembered his Aunty Gladys's question, when she had first visited him in South Kensington six months ago.

'What do they sell?' Aunty had said as she and Chris had stood outside the show room and stared through the window at the one car. 'Bit of a waste of space in there,' she had added.

'It's the shop where you shop for Lamborghinis, aunty.' Dear lady, she was his favourite, but not just because of her help with a loan for the deposit on his flat in exchange for a chunk of the equity as an investment. She was the most positive person he knew and the most encouraging at each stage of his choices. How would she view this BBC business? Probably very positively. He must call her later.

He had made one mistake though with Aunty Gladys. He had agreed that her prayer circle could pray for him regularly. So now he was bombarded by her group who had all done the IT course at Age UK and were into digital. They had found him on WhatsApp. He received copious requests for updates on his love life (non-existent), work issues (dare not share those on social media), and his sense of calling (full of doubt that he had one any more).

Still, he thought, she meant well. She's definitely my favourite, apart from Uncle Colin.'

Chris had reached the corner of Rosary Gardens. He passed the blue plaque on the side of a house announcing that "Herbert Beerbohm Tree, Actor, Manager, had lived there. For the umpteenth time, Chris thought that he must google him. As always, he questioned the name of the road, with the five storied, red brick properties lining it, there was not a garden in sight. Edwardian expansion mopping up the green, he told himself. Feeling calmer, he was through his gate and down the steps to the basement flat. Putting his key into the front door he was home. Home in this big bad city, miles from Colyton, miles from Africa, but home, thanks to a benevolent relative's support, and to the three people with whom he shared it.

****

Chris put his bag down on the floor, and added his damp shoes to the those already accumulated there. His wet socks needed to come off too. The pile of coats on the stand implied there were more people than his flat-mates inside. Throwing his coat on the top, he watched the stand rock, then steady, and finally settle. From the pavement outside came the noise of a couple of drunks. There was little light in the hall and he flicked on the only spot light. Chris attempted an adjustment of his hair in the mirror, and noticed the trail of black bits on the cream carpet plus one set of newspaper fingerprints on the edge of the white door.

'Mike's in and Ravi,' he thought, and then smirked, 'Alias the "black sock gang" and "FT" man.' Mike's bitty socks and Ravi's Financial Times were well-known for the traces they left around the flat.

He bent down and picked up the worst offending bits. The newsprint would come off with a scrub. He opened the door to the lounge and facing him were three teenage girls, sitting on

32

his settee. He stopped in the doorway in momentary panic, going no further and stared in surprise.

'Hi, I'm Chris, is Mike here?' Chris asked.

'Kitchen!' said the one with the mobile who did not take her eyes off the screen. The girl in the middle was busy chewing her nails and the third one produced a sandwich from the bag on her knee and took a bite. Chris watched the mayo drip onto his cushions. All girls were identically dressed in jeans and short jackets. There was a small colour variation in the grey they wore but that was all. They had their shoes on, in his lounge, on his carpet. Two pairs of white trainers and one pair of Doc Martins!

'Mike!' Chris shouted, not moving a step from the doorway.

The answer came from the direction of the kitchen: 'Hi, be out in a minute.'

A bedroom door opened and Ravindra Acharya, known as Ravi to his friends once he had taken on board the propensity the British had to shortening names, came into the lounge with his "hard copy" of the Financial Times. Ravi had a daily download too so Chris never saw the point of the paper as well.

'Hey, OK?' Ravi sat down at the table and slightly cocked his head towards the three wise monkeys on the settee.

'Sort of Ravi. Can you spare me half an hour in a bit if the others are in?' Chris asked.

'Of course.' Ravi said. 'Are you coming in?'

Chris and Ravi exchanged glances about the teenagers and Chris nodded at one of the doors opposite him. 'If Ellie's here?'

'Yes, she's in her room, Mike wouldn't have opened the door otherwise.' Ravi gave a reassuring smile.

Chris's brain had just started to go through the fact that three female, underage teenagers, were sitting on his settee with three male church workers in the flat. Chris breathed deeply to control the panic.

'I've been in the bedroom.' Ravi added just in case he needed to. 'Mike's in the kitchen with the boys.'

'There's more?' Chris said, his eyes going to his carpet. Then he added before he could help himself. 'Any chance you could read the FT just online?'

'You know it's not quite the same feeling as holding the newspaper.' Ravi said and returned to the article.

Chris glanced at the headlines over his friend's shoulder. 'You would think they could do something about the newsprint coming off given its market, it's really the worse one.' He glanced at the white doors in the lounge but could find no trace of fingerprints. Ravi chuckled knowing his friend's compulsion and changed the section he was reading. Chris walked to Ellie's bedroom door with as much distance as he could put between himself and the girls.

'Ellie, could you give me a minute?' called Chris.

The Reverend Doctor Ellen Beech was an unexpected addition to the flat. She had arrived on placement to the Diocese for a year and found that accommodation in London in anything other than a hostel was beyond her personal means. Her supervisor, the Rev. Deidre, had not come up with enough money with Ellie's Melbourne supervisor, so she faced either sharing with Deidre or moving into a backpacker's hostel while in London. Neither was attractive as an option partly as Reverend Deidre, known for her mystic persuasions, had not moved on since the "seventies" and a backpackers' hostel was completely out of the question as far as Ellie was concerned. Chris had offered her the second bedroom off the lounge a month ago.

There were three bedrooms in the basement flat, a previous owner having converted the outhouse which ran off the kitchen, so there was a third bedroom with an extra bathroom. The complication occurred when Mike Briggs, a youth worker from the Southbank Skateboard church, became homeless as his grandmother's flat was returned to the council on her death. Ravi had come through on the issue and had been happy to share with Mike.

Ellie was as far from old stereotypes of Australians as one could get. She did however have a straightforward approach and her intellect had a punch. In Melbourne, she had piloted a venture out of her church facilities as a brunch business. From the income, her church had started a homeless drop in. Ellie had also formed a relationship between her Diocese at home and the London Diocese on their homeless work with a lecturing role thrown in. She was part way through a placement in London as a result.

Ravi had returned from India and now was also in London for a year's placement. He was a tall North Indian from New Delhi with a ready smile. Sadness tinged his face at times as his family had disowned him on his conversion. His FT, and his

Bible, were never far from him. Chris had "seen" a paper Ravi had written on the:

"Re-organization of the Indian Postcode System and the future of online shopping in India." He had managed to collect enough information from the opening paragraph of the paper to sound like he understood the issues. The comparisons with China were, however, over his head. He could see why A.D. viewed his friend as being useful in a start-up situation.

Ellie stuck her head out of the door.

'Chris It's supposed to be my day off and I'm not supervising youth,' said Ellie.

'What do you mean, Ellie?' asked Chris.

'Just what I said. It means that we had an agreement when you let Mike move in here that no youth meetings were allowed,' said Ellie.

'OK. I somehow don't think this visit is down to him. I'll sort it. Just help us for five mins, will you?'

Ellie persisted. 'I told him the flat was off limits.'

'Yes, it is, but as we have them here can you help by being in the lounge 'til the girls go?' Chris asked.

'How long?' Ellie gave Chris a look.

Chris suppressed the irritation with his flat mate, 'Five to ten minutes.'

Ellie placed herself on a dining chair, crossing her arms and her legs in a clear closed posture, glaring at the girls. They, however, were oblivious.

Chris opened the door that led into the kitchen in search of his friend and the boys. It sounded as if they were taking his fridge apart. Inside, Mike Briggs was in full youth worker mode and three boys, about fourteen in age, were noisily enjoying the food he had dug out from the fridge. The boys were enormous. Chris thought that it looked like Super Dry had become the trend as it was being well advertised in his kitchen today. He wondered if a sponsorship deal had been done as the brand name was on everything he could see that the boys were wearing. From the smell in the kitchen "Superfry" may have been more appropriate.

'Hi Chris,' said Mike enthusiastically. Chris gave his friend a meaningful look. He doubted Mike had initiated the visit. It was the one potential cloud that the other two flat mates had flagged up when he suggested that Mike move in. To Chris, Mike was one of the best youth ministers he had ever met. A.D. had christened them "Little and Large" as Mike was a short guy, chunky and perfectly built for skateboarding, whereas Chris was tall and lanky. Even A.D. had confirmed how good Mike was, describing him as the most inspirational youth minister he had met.

Mike spread the peanut butter on the toast. "This is a spontaneous visit by some new skateboard church members."

'Right, I thought it might have been. Hi, where are you from?' Chris asked.

'Purley, the Archdeacon's village church. That's how we got the address. I'm Zack, a friend of Jude's.' He was about fourteen, going on thirty-five and Chris estimated from his manner potentially a future Chief Executive of a multinational.

'I was explaining to Mike how I do a meal with my friends,' Zack continued. He took three seconds to assess Chris and then turned back to Mike. 'I organise my friends to do a course each and then bring it round.'

Mike asked. 'How?'

'That's my skill,' said Zack.

'Middle name?' asked Mike.

'John, why?' answered Zack.

"Thought it might have been Boris," said Mike.

Mike and Chris swapped grins. Mike offered Chris the plate of toast and said to the boy, 'That's the absolute opposite of who I am!'

Chris picked up a piece of toast. 'Guys I need to talk to my flat mates about work tomorrow. Are we pretty much done here today?'

The boys nodded and with mouths full they picked up the rest of the toast in handfuls.

'So, see you Friday night Mike.' Zack patted Mike on the back and opened the kitchen door to start herding his friends out. Chris flinched at the bang against the wall and made a mental note to get a door stop fitted. There was no end to his neurosis as he watched the toast bits trickle down on the carpet.

Mike followed them out into the lounge, while giving them a few reminders for Friday. The girls reluctantly stood up as the boys came through. The nail biter turned to Mike and said. 'Us as well?'

'Sure!' He responded. 'You'll be our First Lady Skateboard team.' Here was Mike, the salesman.

Zack stopped his progress through the lounge and turned back to Mike. He asked: 'Can we do some biking instead? We could start at the old country station at Box Hill and Westhumble. Everyone's doing it now.' Having got so far with getting Mike's agreement for them to go skateboarding he was now cutting a deal for what they really wanted.

Mike gave Chris a look. 'Well, Chris here is the biker, so we'll have to talk to him. I think we're due out next week at Purley for a service, aren't we Chris, so let's chat then.'

'Box Hill's great,' one of the other boys said as he gave Chris a punch on the arm. Chris flinched slightly, and then gave a punch back, which he assumed was a youth work method for bonding.

The girl with the mobile had been looking at Ellie and sizing up her hair and what she was wearing. Distracted by trying to work out how Ellie got her hair to shine like that she said, 'Yeah and the kestrels are there! Your hair's nice. Will you be there on Friday?'

'No, I don't work with Mike. I'm on placement here at a college,' said Ellie.

'You just live with him?' The question was from the girl in the Doc Martins. The giggling started from all the youth and Ravi had joined in, seeing the funny side of it. Ellie's face was set and Ravi soon stopped. Slowly he lifted his FT higher so that it hid his face.

Firmly Ellie said: 'I'm a lodger here like he is, and my boyfriend is in Australia.'

Mike intervened to avert the start of hostilities.

'OK people, let's head for the front door, and I'll just step out with you to make sure you can find your way to the tube.' The lounge door closed behind him as the gang of six went down the hall.

Ravi emerged from behind a wall of grubby pink. 'At last! What were they doing coming in from Purley?'

Chris crumpled onto the settee sprawling his legs out. 'Sounded like A.D.'s youngest was involved somehow and they want a youth worker.'

'You're kidding me, how pushy,' Ellie was incredulous.

'Or full of initiative,' said Chris. 'You haven't met the youngest of A.D.'s daughters.'

Mike was back and climbed over the back of the settee, flopped down putting a cushion over his face. He took the cushion away and started to work it through.

'If A.D. sent them I can understand it. I just wished he'd called me first and I could have set something up down at the Southbank so they didn't turn up here.'

Ellie got up before Chris could stop her and went into her room, closing the door with a firm click. The three men looked at the closed door for a few minutes. Then Chris stared at his carpet. Mike followed his gaze.

'Oh sorry, I did take the socks off but the bits are stuck to my feet.'

Chris bent and started picking bits up from the lounge carpet. 'Maybe if you changed the make?'

'How long do you wear your socks Mike?' Ravi asked.

Mike looked sheepish, but his eyes were starting to brighten with amusement. 'I throw them at the wall and if they fall off I put them back on, if they stick, I'll change them.'

Ravi looked astonished. 'Seriously?'

Mike grinned. 'No, do you mind if I put the sport on?' He picked up the TV remote and put the headphones on.

Chris walked into the kitchen and threw the bits in the bin and filled the kettle. 'I'd better get it over with,' he said aloud. Pulling mugs down from the cupboard he stuck his head round the kitchen door and made a wobbly hand signal to Ravi and Mike, meaning a drink. Ravi nodded but Mike shook his head.

Chris waited for the kettle to boil and thought he should speak to everyone now and then he could call Storm. He braced himself to try and get the other three on his side to help with A.D.'s idea. He made his tea and one for Ravi and walked back to sit in the lounge. He checked on the App: "Surfline," for the areas that Storm could be working in today: Croyde, Woolacombe, Putsborough and Saunton. Yes, A.D.'s daughter was right, there would not be much surf tomorrow.

Chris paused as a shout went up from Mike: 'Yeah, come on!' Mike made punching actions in mid-air to the football. Ravi and Chris waited but Mike settled back down as the goal was missed. Ravi got up and went into the bedroom. Mike turned off the match and said to Chris, 'Are you alright if I do some guitar practice?'

'Sure. You can borrow my room Mike, as the others won't hear it in there. Before you do, I need to talk to you all about something A.D. has dreamed up. I'll get Ellie and Ravi in too.'

'I'm due out in an hour Chris, will it be long?' Mike said.

'What I have to tell you will take about ten minutes, the shock will take longer to wear off,' said Chris.

He tapped at Ellie's door and then stuck his head into the bedroom Ravi was in. They heard Ellie's determined footsteps coming towards the door. She whipped it open. 'Don't tell me those kids are back!'

Ravi stood in his doorway and said, 'Did you know that Germany spends almost $9 billion a year on chocolate? Makes you think.' Ellie's look said reams but not to Ravi.

'I need to talk to you about an idea A.D. has dreamed up with the BBC.' Chris sat on a dining chair, positioning himself, so that he could see them all at once. Ellie looked at him and sighed.

'I'm trying to remain calm. All week-long people at church want a piece of me. I must have a day when I can know that there is no youth, no idiot colleagues, and no A.D. If I must leave here, Chris, to get some peace, I will. I've got another 6 months in this cloud covered, claustrophobic little island off the west coast of Europe before I can, before I can...' The sniffing became audible.

Ravi gave her his hanky. 'You're missing Joel.'

Ellie looked at the hanky dubiously. 'Have you used this?'

'Only a bit.'

'Aargh.' Ellie dropped it on the carpet and went into the kitchen. They heard the loud nose blowing with the banging back of a cupboard door on its long-suffering hinges. A mug hit the work surface and the kettle clattered into action. The Reverend Dr. was making herself a cup of tea.

Mike exhaled, taking the risk of an opinion. 'This bloke she's going out with, do you think we could call him for some pointers about how to communicate with her? I haven't had a proper conversation yet, and I don't usually have problems with people.'

Ravi stared at the closed door. 'He's an Investment banker. His life is one of negotiation.'

The three men thought it through for a few moments and then Mike nodded. Knowing that Ravi and Mike had to leave shortly Chris tried to take them back to the Archdeacon. 'I know we're short of time from your angle guys so I'll try and get her back in here.' Chris got up and went into the kitchen.

'I've never met an investment banker.' Mike said.

Ravi sucked in air through his teeth, thought about Mike's comment and said, 'No, neither have I.'

Ellie came out of the kitchen with a large mug of steaming tea, closely followed by Chris. She sat down next to Mike on the settee. Mike hooked an arm across her shoulders, hoping it would soften things, slightly. She gave him a look, and he withdrew the arm.

'I'm fine, thanks.' Ellie said, and sipped her tea. 'Come on Chris, what's this about?'

'A.D. has got us involved with the BBC.' There, it was out and no one had yet left the room but Ravi was looking confused.

'I don't know what that involves yet until you explain more. I'm not sure why it would involve the word 'us' either.'

It was Mike who provided a type of explanation and he carried on staring at Chris, but there was no hint of humour left in his eyes. 'Do you mean some sort of religious programme? Not the one I'm thinking of I hope?

Chris stared into his mug. 'Yes. Religious programming Mike.'

'I'm with Ravi about the "us" bit. I'm finding it confusing mate.' Mike twisted round in his seat, giving Chris the type of stare, he reserved for kids who offered him a spliff. He said: 'What do you mean us? We don't work for him. *You* do.'

Ellie put her mug of tea down onto the coffee table in front of her. 'I'm not sure why I'm in the room actually as this clearly has nothing to do with me.' She started to get up but Chris held up a hand to stop her.

'No, Ellie, please stay,' said Chris. 'A.D. has included you in what he said to me this morning. It's his new strategy to use it as a vehicle to do outreach, change the way the church is viewed at the BBC, change up the stereotyping of clergy. There's a whole load of reasons and I'm not sure I get where he's going with this. All I know is that he's either assumed that your supervisors will agree, or he's prepared to square it with them, for you to form part of the team he's putting up to the BBC.'

Ellie struggled for words again. 'You must have misunderstood, Chris.'

Chris pressed on. 'You're young clergy Ellie, a woman who has the word Doctor in front of the name and in your case Mike, the skateboarding will be of interest. From what he said this morning, he sees us dynamic people. Who knows what's in his mind? There's a meeting tomorrow over breakfast with him first and then we all go to the BBC for 2pm.'

'I guess A.D. thinks the Beeb will see it as a strong team.' Ravi said and glanced at the time on his mobile.

'I have nothing to do with this diocese.' Mike's face was set. Chris looked at his friend and gave a rueful smile.

'You're a youth minister licensed by a Bishop. You know how this works. A.D. will just make a phone call and you'll be reassigned. Imagine what publicity this will mean for the Skateboard church. You on TV preaching, reaching the kids, doing your tricks. Camera, action…. "A Backside, a Caballerial while riding Fakie!" All that stuff you do.'

Ellie looked at Ravi and screwed up her face. Ravi shrugged. She flung her arms out and asked, 'What are you on about Chris? What's a backside got to do with it? And that other "stuff" you just cited?'

Mike was still staring at Chris. 'They're skateboarding terms, Ellie.' He was starting to think the situation through but was not yet on board. 'Chris, you sound like him.'

Chris stared out of the window and noted again that there was little light into the small patio at this time of the day at the end of May.

'It's because he thinks we can change things, be dynamic, self-starters, that sort of thing.'

Mike nodded, slowly Ellie was turning red. 'You're kidding, right?' she said. 'By the time this gets off the ground Ravi and I will be gone.'

'Don't bank on it, Ellie.' Chris, the nerves finally dissipating, was starting to understand the strategy which he was sure would be international.

Mike had developed that far-away look. He said: 'No, wait. It could be good - we get young people in it – skateboarders, link up with Australia and India.'

'You see,' Chris gave a sad smile. 'You're already on board. That's the irony of this. That's exactly why he wants the five of us.'

Ellie barked out, 'Five? We're four. Who's number Five? And if you said breakfast meeting tomorrow I can't do it.' The colour was draining from her face.

It was bordering on a strop, Chris thought. He answered her question: 'Number five is a mate at a Surfer Church in Devon, Ellie,' explained Chris. 'A.D. wants us all there by 9.30 am. It's a priority. Really screws up my day too,' Chris said as he flicked through his diary on his phone. 'Probably we've all got arrangements tomorrow.'

****

46

Three

Chris stood up and went across to where Ellie was sitting. He dropped down on his knees and picked up one of her hands in his. She stared into his eyes as he gave her an uncertain look.

'We grew up together. My mum and dad sort of fostered him really and we were like brothers when we were kids. Same school, we both learnt to surf together and roamed across the beaches in our early teens. He taught me to fight at school when I was bullied and he was always there to back me up. Then when we were University age he went to the LSE and I went overseas for a gap year with my uncle. By the time, I was back he was into his second year, and I went to Oxford. After he graduated he had a gap year down in Devon and then became involved in the surfer church. He stayed.' Chris looked at the time. 'Actually, I've got to call him.'

Mike asked, 'Name? Does he have a name?'

'Yes, of course, it's Storm.'

Mike looked sceptical. 'That's not original, but I can't remember where I heard it. I meant his real name.'

Chris gave an apologetic grin. 'Mum christened him Storm because she said he would brew on the horizon and then hit without any warning. I'll go and make the call,' Chris got up.

Ravi said as he stood up, 'Look Chris, I have to go to work. I'll check this out at Church House.'

Chris nodded distracted by the dial tone that was now ringing on his phone. He went to his own room off the kitchen. Ellie went into her room to start to make calls. Mike's boss was so keen Mike had to talk him out of turning up to the BBC meeting himself. Ravi went to change for work. Ellie found when she called her office that she had been reassigned as A.D. had called Rev. Deidre.

'Bye Mike,' said Ravi, passing through the lounge. 'Why this Archdeacon wants me involved I can't imagine.'

'You're the one with the FT, mate.' Mike said and grinned.

'Well, I'm not sure what difference that makes. But I remember what Karl Barth said about reading a paper through your bible,' said Ravi. He looked out through the lounge window into the small patio garden. One half of it was in sunshine now and he would enjoy a glimpse of sun on his way to the tube. He said: 'You know, this seems such a funny thing to do. Part of me wants to laugh but part of me is so much more aware of what it feels like to be a minority as a Christian that I'm starting to think, let's do this, yeah good for the Archdeacon.'

'Do you mean in Delhi, Ravi?' Mike had put his phone down and stared at Ravi.

Ravi nodded and aware of Mike's silence he said: 'Chris hasn't said how he feels about this.'

Mike said: 'Frankly? Knowing him he'll be terrified of the profile. He's bad enough when he's preached and gets the queue of women who want to speak to him on the way out.'

Now that it was all out on the table, Chris was feeling more relaxed. He had got through to Storm and he had heard the background platform announcement.

'Hey Storm, sorry are you travelling somewhere?'

'Yeah, mate. Don't worry I was going to ring you anyway. I'm just at Exeter.' The announcements continued and momentarily Storm and Chris waited for them to stop.

'How's work?' Storm asked.

'It's gone crazy. That's partly why I'm calling. Before I get onto that are you up for a weekend at Colyton next week?' Chris asked.

'Sounds good. Aunty Mo and Uncle John will like us both being there. We could get some wind surfing in at Exmouth.'

'Yeah.' Chris said.

Storm paused, 'So. Are you finally going to tell me why you've called in the middle of the day?'

'It's a bit difficult. It's my boss.'

'Shall I make it easy for you? I know about the Beeb. Gareth and the team are really up for it especially if they do some shoots down here.' Without waiting Storm carried on. 'You can hear I'm already on the platform. I'm getting the London train from Exeter. Gareth's hoping to meet the Archdeacon before the BBC get down here. He's got a mate working in London who says we can expect them to move pretty fast after the meeting tomorrow. Look, I should get into Waterloo in time for dinner. Any chance we can go for a meal down in the Cut and kick this disaster around?'

'You already know?' Chris said exasperated with A.D.

'There's so much excitement down here it's all I could do to stop the whole team coming up with me. Apart from what it does re the church it will be good for the businesses in the area if it happens.'

'Well, if A.D. has anything to do with it, it will happen. Yeah, I'll come across to Waterloo and meet you and we can do dinner somewhere. Good you're coming.'

'See ya later, bro. I've got five minutes before the train will pull out and I need to board before they lock the doors.' Storm was gone.

****

In his dream Chris was banging his head against the pulpit in church. He was dressed in a wet suit and the words up on the screen which was suspended in the centre of the aisle were of one of the more suggestive surfing songs that he and Storm had learnt when they were teenagers.

 In a corner of the church the flower committee were slowly killing the new Curate, Rafe Ackland, by beating him with withering Lilies. The worship leader played a guitar riff but it was drowned out by Ellie playing a didgeridoo.

Reality dawned with the alarm. Chris sat bolt upright and his hand went out for his mobile to switch the alarm off. It was set to be the guitar riff, from the busker. The didgeridoo existed though and Chris realized it was Storm's alarm. The shrub outside his window had partially blown over in the night and was banging against the glass. Chris swung his legs out of his bed and slipped his feet into the leather sandals he usually wore around the flat. The mound on the floor which was his guest snoring and he threw a paperback at him. Storm Downing surfaced with an offended expression and a grunt.

'Coffee?' asked Chris.

'Green tea,' said Storm.

'I don't have any. English breakfast tea I can run to but that's all,' said Chris.

'Water. This is too early, man!' Storm lay down again.

'Yeah I know we were late but we need to be at the Abbey by 9.30 this morning.'

'Not sure that place we ate in in South Ken wasn't a bit dodgy. My stomach is complaining. We should have gone to the Cut.'

'Your train was late remember so we didn't have time. We should have called it quits after the meal instead of visiting all your old haunts. It was 2am by the time you unrolled your sleeping mat. What is that sleeping bag you've got now?'

'Ascent,' said the mound and Storm had disappeared from view into a shapeless mass again. 'Breakfast,' the mass said.

'Water I can do but breakfast is at Westminster. What is that smell?' Chris stepped over Storm and opened a window. A chilly early summer morning entered the room. There was an air of disinfectant about his friend and Chris sniffed it audibly.

'What are you doing?' Storm emerged head first. If he had been standing he would have matched Chris for height but the build across the shoulders was broader. Like his friend, he had a lot of hair but, whereas Chris worked to make his hair look as if he had stepped out of a magazine, Storm's hair was bleached by sun and seawater and looked like thatch. His skin already had a look of age and although he was only in his late twenties it tended in the early morning to resemble a desert dying of thirst.

Storm paused briefly, sniffed the sleeping bag and said, 'The bag's been in storage at the office. The cleaners must have left the top off the bleach. That means I'll stink of it. I'll hang it out in the garden.' He rolled out of his bag and asked, 'What was it with that alarm this morning?'

'Which one, there were two?' Chris asked.

'Rock guitar is not the greatest way to greet the day, Chris.'

'I can live with it instead of a didgeridoo, mate,' Chris said.

'How about the rain stick?' Storm's arm emerged from the bag for the bamboo rain stick which was propped against the wardrobe. The gentle sound of rain filled the room. As an answer, Chris went into his bathroom. Standing with the water pouring over his head he became aware of a bass and drum in the background. His average shower time was twenty minutes so the background noise continued to blend with the pulse from the shower. When he came out Storm had climbed out of the window onto the patio after opting for a steaming mug of liquid from the kitchen. Putting his head back into the room through the open window Storm said: 'I feel like I'm in a steam room in here! Your flat mates have made you a coffee but it's probably cold by now.' He pointed to a mug on the bedside table. 'They're a bit nuts with the music though.'

'Where's the music coming from?' asked Chris.

'It's your lounge,' said Storm, grimacing. 'You must have very tolerant neighbours.'

'Is that Delirious?' Chris said, turning his head to one side as he listened.

'What else?' said Storm, grinning. 'Shades of our youth!'

Ravi had found Chris's supply of music and had selected which was on at full volume. Chris came through to the lounge from his bedroom and indicated to Ravi with his thumb and forefinger to turn down the volume, using his other hand to point to the ceiling.

'They're out.' Ravi shouted, also pointing with his finger to the ceiling. Chris gave him a thumbs up.

'I thought we could get some inspiration.' Ravi yelled into his ear. 'And I thought it was time to initiate Mike to the flat mix!'

Mike and Ellie were joining in by bouncing on the settee. By the time the song was half way through Storm had appeared and was conducting with his mug.

'Team building!' shouted Storm.

****

Chris stared into a blue sky. South Kensington through the pollution haze was lit by a watery sun. He compared it to the parts of Kenya he knew at this time of the year and recalled the dry periods when the sun would crack the ground. Nairobi knew a thing or two about pollution. He thought of the place his uncle had rented in the compound on the Argwings Kodhek Rd in Nairobi, and the birdsong that began as the sun came up.

He half smiled at the thought of the delinquent monkeys running across the roof in a raiding party. Uncle Colin would scare them off with a broom. Once again, he wished he was still there.

The new team had been silent as they travelled to St James's Tube. Ravi, read his FT of course. Ellie had whipped out a paper from her bag to mark despite the brief journey, such was the pressure with her deadlines. Mike had nodded off and his head was lolling around.

Storm stood and had his earplugs in trying to shut out the commute in London. He nudged Chris with his foot and leant forward. Removing one earplug he said: 'I'd forgotten what this was like. It's bringing back the claustrophobia. How do you cope with this every day?'

'I don't do it unless I have to. I walk instead. You must have got used to it when you were at the LSE?' said Chris.

'I didn't do it in rush hour: Student life.' Storm shrugged and smiled. Thinking for a few moments he leant forward again. 'Any sights around where we're going Chris?'

'Of course, I was preoccupied and forgot it's ages since you were here. We've got time to go along Birdcage walk if you'd like to?'

Storm nodded.

Getting off the tube at St James's Park meant they all went with the crowd shuffling towards the stairs for the exit for Queen Anne's Gate to satisfy Storm's desire to play tourist. There was time to go up Birdcage Walk, past the Churchill War Rooms and down Storeys Gate, towards the meeting with A.D.

---

and breakfast. That sightseeing completed and Storm satisfied for the moment, they crossed Victoria Street at the traffic lights and went under the arch, into Dean's Yard.

Chris kept up a running commentary for Storm's benefit: 'Dean's Yard used to be a farmyard. Now it has a different sort of animal.' Chris pointed to the school boys on their way into various buildings across the green. Storm smiled at the joke and took the area in, turning a complete circle to do so.

'Where's A.D.'s office?' Storm asked.

'Down there.' Chris pointed to the building at the bottom of the green. 'That's Church House.'

'Is that where you work as well?' Storm asked.

'When I'm in London, yes. I've been going out to Purley most of the time for the last six months, but now the church there has got a new Curate who started this week and he's going to be there instead of me. I'll be here most of the time now.'

'Do you have a secretary?' Storm asked.

'A.D. has. Do you remember Jenny in Colyton, one of mum's friends? Well she works for A.D. now as his secretary. I vaguely remember her leaving to come to London when we were small. She and her husband moved and she apparently started working here. She's still the same as I remember.'

Storm looked at Chris for a few seconds as a memory came back, his face moving between recognition of the woman from his childhood and then horror at a memory. 'Wasn't she the one we threw soil at over the hedge? Poor woman.'

'Yes. Fortunately, as six-year olds she forgave us. But yes, it's her. She will know by now you're involved with this idea of

A.D.'s so your sins will find you out.' Chris slapped his friend on the shoulder.

'That's the woman I spoke to yesterday then. It's a small world. How weird is that, Jenny from Colyton working with you here?' Storm stared round the courtyard taking in the age of the buildings. 'I like it. It's nice. I can hardly hear the traffic outside. Good there are places like this still in London. I don't think I could cope with the amount of people there were on the tube every morning any more. I'm too used to Woolacombe now with wide open spaces and a lack of tall buildings.' Storm pointed to the side of Church House. 'What's at the back of that entrance?'

'There's a street beyond the arch at the bottom which reminds me of Diagon Alley out of Harry Potter. That way would take you round to Millbank and Victoria Tower Gardens. I can show you later if we have time. St John's Smith Square is down that way and it has a good café too.' Chris nodded towards the area.

Ravi interrupted them and pointed to the left where tables and chairs were set up around a kiosk. 'If A.D. said to meet him in the yard I guess that is where breakfast is going to be.'

'Or maybe not,' said Ellie. 'There's also a "Closed" sign.'

'Here comes A.D.' Chris said. 'That's all the sightseeing for now Storm.'

And indeed, the Archdeacon was coming down the steps of Church House, walking towards them across the green, rubbing his hands together with a broad smile through his beard.

'Good morning, good morning, good morning all of you!' A.D.'s enthusiasm at seeing his new team waiting for him spilled over into a warm greeting. 'Well done, you all made it. And this must be the famous Smash from North Devon?'

Storm tried to control his reaction, but couldn't stop the eyebrows going into his hairline as he extended his hand. 'It's actually Storm, Archdeacon, and calling me that is fine. And you must be the famous A.D!'

A.D. laughed as they shook hands. 'Where these names come from! Good of you to come all this way. How are things at the surfer church?"

'Busy and a lot of excitement at this potential venture. It was all I could do to stop my boss Gareth coming with me. You both spoke I think?'

A.D. was clearly delighted with this. He took in the surfer gear and the general look of being washed up on a beach. He said: 'Good, good, glad they're enthusiastic. I suspect we shall be down in Croyde before we know it after today.' A.D. was moving on to Ellie and gave her a kiss on both cheeks while he asked, 'Dr. Ellie, how was Melbourne?'

Ellie had been assessing A.D.'s ability to "work a room" as he moved along them all. She half smiled wishing she could do it but somehow there was always something false about it to her. Pulling herself together she said: 'Warm and I was tempted to stay. I've been shivering ever since I got back.'

'And how is the man in your life?' A.D. caught her by surprise with that question. 'Our gain to have you here, but he must be sorry that you've returned.'

Despite herself Ellie smiled broadly. 'Oh, you are informed. Joel was fine, thanks, and he'll be here soon for about three weeks, and then we have a break out in Spain together. So now, A.D. you are fully briefed on my love life, which is far more than I had told this lot.'

A.D. chuckled and continued to shake each of the men by the hand and to show his personal interest.

'Ravi, I love that paper of yours about the changes for the Indian postcode system for digital deliveries.'

Ravi smiled, and took the proffered hand. Even if A.D. had only had a briefing on it he took the compliment as it was meant. Ravi said: 'I'm amazed you've had the time to look at it.'

A.D. shrugged and said, 'Well, the economics did go over my head but Louise, my wife, was very impressed with your conclusion.'

Finally, A.D. had reached Mike. They were a similar height and there was a softening in A.D's eyes for someone who was experiencing personal difficulties. He said: 'And Mike, good to get to meet you. Your minister speaks very highly of you. I hear you've had some accommodation problems recently?'

Mike had already registered as he listened to the greeting with the others that A.D. had obviously done his homework on them all before the meeting. He took the outstretched hand and pumped it up and down.

'And good to meet you, A.D.' said Mike. 'Yeah, losing my Gran was one thing but I didn't expect to lose my home. It's sorted now thanks to Chris, and Ravi too, for putting up with me sharing the same room.'

A.D. persisted. 'I've got a suggestion about the accommodation side of things so we must have a chat later after the BBC. It's a serious long-term issue so we can't have your work disturbed by needing a home. It's a priority. My youngest daughter, Jude, is a big fan and showed me a clip from You Tube. How do you do those tricks, do you call them tricks? Yes? You may get a visit from some of her friends soon at the Southbank.'

Mike was taken aback at the empathy but pulled himself together. He said: 'They came yesterday, A.D.'

A.D. was surprised and said: 'Bit quick off the mark! Jude's been away in Paris with the school. She must have told her friends about you and the skateboarders before she went. I do hope it wasn't inconvenient?'

Mike shuffled his feet, not wanting to drop the daughter in it, but the man had to know. 'It was actually Chris's flat that they came to.'

'What?' exclaimed A.D. 'That means Jude's gone into files and found the address. Little Madam! I'll have to get Jenny to have a look at that.'

'You have your files password protected presumably?' Ravi asked.

'Yes, of course.' A.D. paused and then realization dawned. 'Ah! That's how she did it.'

Storm grinned at him and put a hand on A.D's shoulder. 'You've used her name and date of birth, haven't you?'

'Yes. It helps me remember passwords.' A.D. looked a little sheepish.

'You could mix up family names if you tend to use them A.D.' Chris suggested.

'It won't work,' said Mike, 'she's that age where she'll work it out. That generation are the problem solvers of the future and digital is all intuitive to them. Chances are she'd hack into anything.'

'What are your other children called?' Storm asked.

'Eve.' Chris spoke it like he was breathing out. Storm looked at him and registered that he had a dreamy look in the eyes. A.D. saw it too.

Storm exchanged a barely susceptible wink with A.D. and said, 'Ah, there you are then A.D. you could use Eve's name with something else added onto it. How about a play on words?' Storm fixed Chris with an enquiring, innocent, gaze.

'No, you couldn't mess around with Eve's name.' Chris answered his friend with a slightly furrowed brow.

'No,' said Ellie, joining in the game. She had seen the exchange of looks between A.D. and Storm. 'It's too beautiful a name, isn't it Chris?' He did not respond. Chris looked like a trapped animal.

Storm continued with a straight face speaking directly to A.D. 'How about this. You need to use a mix of upper and lower-case letters, I'd suggest. How about, "ChristenedEve" as a password.' However, the way he pronounced the words sounded as if he was saying "Chris 'n Eve."

A.D's mouth twitched but he managed to control the enormous laugh that was building in his chest. He turned it into a cough, glanced at Chris who was staring, shocked, at his boyhood friend, and took pity on his assistant.

'Well, thank you for your suggestions,' A.D. said. 'I'll get things changed so it's more secure. Now let's get back to the reason why we're here and see about that breakfast.' A.D. started to rub the palms of his hands together.

Storm was sniffing the air. 'Wow - check out the smell of that grub! I wonder where the cooking's being done. I can smell soup, then there's the gravy. They are playing with our *minds*. Where do you think it's coming from?'

Mike nodded at a school building. 'It's that posh school over there, like the one you went to, you Toff!'

Chris looked at Mike with a wistful smile. 'Ah, the years of school dinners and baked puddings.'

'Yeah?' Mike laughed. 'You mean they fed you? We just escaped at lunchtime to the local chip shop down the road. My arteries must be like congealed fat.'

Storm looked at Mike with concern trying to work out the background, but Mike grinned and gave him a playful punch. Unused to this sort of thing unless it meant a fight was brewing Storm took a step back.

Ellie interrupted the establishment of a relationship by Mike. She said: 'OK, if the male bonding behaviour is over can we please get some food, or my low blood pressure is going to become a problem and you'll be picking me up off the floor. As you see, A.D. the kiosk here has a big closed sign for us to contend with.'

'The café is inside the cloisters,' explained A.D. 'But they've started putting tables and chairs out here as the spring has gone on. I'll go and see if I can raise anyone.' And with that A.D. walked to the corner of Dean's Yard and disappeared inside. The group could hear banging. A few moments afterwards A.D. reappeared and shrugged. He was followed seconds later by a man wearing a black waistcoat and trousers with a white waiter's apron tied round his waist.

A.D. turned to him, smiled a welcome and said, 'Good morning, surprised you're not open by now, hospitality, etc. We wanted six breakfasts, thank-you.'

The man was struggling with the request and was clearly uncomfortable with the English for anything other than a straightforward order from the menu.

'No breakfasts, not open. Ten o'clock.'

A.D. pulled his scarf away from his neck to show his clerical collar. He said, 'Perhaps you can make an exception. There's only fifteen minutes difference.'

The waiter picked up a menu and thrust it at A.D. 'No breakfasts - menu.'

A.D. took the menu over to the tables while the others stood still unsure of their ground. He sat down at a table next to the "Closed" sign. A.D. turned the sign round as if it were offensive and wore the expression that indicated only a bomb would move him. The waiter looked exasperated. He dropped the menu onto the table in front of A.D. and reiterated, 'Not open!'

Chris went across to A.D's table and smiled at the waiter. He picked the menu up and sat down next to A.D. Chris said: 'Thanks. We'll have a look.'

The waiter walked away towards and the cloisters. Ravi slowly followed him, while Chris looked through the menu, turning it over in case he had missed something.

'This is a franchise, isn't it?' Chris asked A.D. 'I thought the principle of hospitality was the aim, you know, linking it back to the middle-ages and the Benedictines. There's not much on the menu. Maybe it's the time of day?'

Mike picked up a menu and joined A.D. and Chris. Ellie peered over his shoulder to see what was on offer.

Mike was not impressed. 'It's a bit odd,' he said. 'Funny sort of menu for 10am.' He passed the menu back to Ellie. She too sat down and turned the menu over looking for something that was not there.

'There's only cake on the menu he's given us.' Ellie wrinkled up her nose. 'Cake and cream teas. I don't want a cream tea at ten in the morning. What is it with the obsession with cream teas in London now?'

Ravi re-emerged from the cloisters and shrugged. 'He's locked the door. I got a foot inside and was forced back as he closed it. It looked a lovely place but they need to sort the food. Reminds me of a College cafeteria with half empty shelves. Do you remember Chris the one down in the basement in the faculty library?'

'Oh, yes, they never carried a stock.' Chris nodded at the memory and smiled at Ravi.

63

Storm leant half over the counter of the kiosk and rummaged in a shelf below. He straightened up and turned around triumphantly brandishing a croissant. He exclaimed: 'Ha! A lone croissant on the shelf, maybe there's more underneath or it's yesterdays. I could do with a good fry up frankly.'

Ellie looked at Storm and said: 'I bet you know great places where you live, by the beach I mean, for breakfast.'

Storm looked wistful. 'Yeah, there's a few, like the Barn in Woolacombe, or if you're feeling flush there's the Woolacombe Hotel. Then there's places in Croyde, like Hobbs Hill. If this BBC project gets off the ground and you come down to North Devon I'll show you. The surf won't be what you're used to in Australia though.'

'I must hook you up with my boyfriend Joel when he gets here. I've done a bit but he's the surfer of the two of us.'

'Got any photos?' Storm asked Ellie. She pulled her mobile out of her bag and the two of them looked at her screen as she scrolled up and down for him. Storm nodded and grinned at her. Ellie smiled and put her mobile away.

A.D. looked completely deflated at the way things were turning out. Chris decided it was time to tell him about one of his special places.

'Look, A.D. I know a place I've been going to for years that my dad showed me when he was working up the road. It's not posh or scenic but the food is brilliant and the welcome warm.'

Ellie put her hand on A.D's shoulder to try and cheer him up. 'I don't care where it is, A.D, I need *Breakfast,* not cake.' She looked hopefully at Chris and said: 'this place you know, is it alright or just grease?'

'Any eggs you want just name it. Lovely Italian stuff too as well as a good fry up. It's on the concourse at St James's tube.'

A.D. was up at last; the cloud of gloom having moved on elsewhere. 'Lead on, dear boy,' he cried, ' and we will follow.'

Ellie and Ravi linked arms and purposefully strode towards the exit of Dean's Yard. A.D. took out his mobile and gave his secretary, Jenny, a call to say that he would be back for his laptop later than expected. Chris and Storm did a quick run towards St. Margaret's church so that Storm could play tourist. Then Chris got him back to the doorway of the Abbey, braving the unfriendly usher on the door. Storm just quickly got a look inside. They ran past Central Hall, into Tothill St, dodging taxis and to the tube station at St. James's. There was excitement amongst the group as the smell of full English breakfast captured them.

****

Chris was a valued customer at Cafe Lucya, he was always so appreciative of everything they put before him. Inside on the counter were small cubes of rustic bread that had been cut up as it was cooling from the oven. The team descended on the plate while Chris leant over the counter, peering into the kitchen on the right.

'Lucya!' Chris called.

Two ladies came out of the kitchen. Smiling, as they always did when he arrived, they were introduced to everyone as Lucya and Stacy. Lucya laughed at the way her bread was being devoured. She said: 'I can't afford for you to bring your friends too often Chris.'

'We could smell your cooking half way here Lucya. Meet new devotees of your grub!' Chris swept a hand around the group and greetings were made by everyone.

'Did you want your usual Chris?' Lucya asked him.

'Yes please, times six. What does everyone want to drink?' There was a general chorus of tea, latte, white Americano. Somehow, Lucya noted it without writing anything down and started putting together the drinks order.

Stacy disappeared to the kitchen to start the cooking. A.D. looked around and spotted some tables that were free in a corner, under the window. He said: 'I've been walking through the tube for years and can't believe I've missed it. What a find!' He was rewarded with an appreciative look from Lucya. Storm and Ravi started to move six stools around two tables.

A.D. called over to Lucya: 'What do we get in the breakfast, Lucya?'

Lucya ran through the list. 'Bacon, sausage, tomato, beans, two fried eggs, hash brown, two rounds of buttered toast, and the tea or coffee is included.'

Ellie took a stool and sniffed the aromas deeply. 'Of course, I wouldn't normally eat all this but it sounds a "Genius" breakfast!' She exhaled audibly and Storm and Ravi were in complete sympathy with her.

'Bring on the hot buttered toast,' Storm said.

'Oh man!' Ravi exclaimed and started taking photos on his mobile of the group, the counter, the staff, pausing briefly to ask, 'How does your dad know these places Chris?'

Chris looked round at his friends, enjoying their pleasure. 'He told me a colleague brought him here when he first joined the Civil Service. It kept changing hands and then Lucya came and has been here for about twenty years. It's all about finding your village in London for me so different places around the city start to feel like they are my home.'

'That's what you meant about a security zone. OK, I get it,' Ravi said, as mugs of coffee and a green tea were brought over, followed by hot buttered toast while the rest of the food was cooked. The team sipped, some added sugar to their taste, and there was silence briefly, followed by the crunching of the toast. From the kitchen came the sound of frying and then the smells intensified. A.D. paid for everyone while they waited for the cooked breakfast to appear. He pocketed the receipt and smiled at Lucya for the good value and the friendly service.

'Louise, my wife, would love this. I'll have to bring her,' A.D. said.

****

Four

Stacy came out of the galley kitchen carrying four plates of breakfasts. She put them down in front of the team and disappeared to get the other two servings. A.D. gave a meaningful thanks for the food to the amazement of other patrons. He said: 'Do start, everyone. We'll create ideas later.'

They all went to work on the food before them. Storm and Mike added ketchup which was the only exchange as one asked for the bottle and the other said: 'There you go, mate.'

When the initial hunger was satiated Mike mopped up the remaining egg on his plate with a slice of toast and looked at A.D. He asked: 'So, what's the game plan this afternoon A.D?'

A.D. signalled to Lucia for more toast for everyone before he answered. He mouthed: Marmalade?' to her and Lucya nodded and disappeared again into the kitchen.

'Do we need a team builder?' A.D. asked. 'Storm I hear you're good at team building activities.'

Storm flinched and gave Chris a look. 'Me? Who told you that? I need sea for mine. The team builder here is Ravi.'

Chris had his mouth full but stifled the laugh without choking. Ellie reached over and nabbed a slice of Chris's toast. Mike gave the back of her hand a gentle tap with the flat blade of the knife. In response, she gave him a look and dropped three sugars in his coffee. Mike raised an eyebrow at Ellie but he was not to be defeated so he gave it a stir and took a sip. He turned to A.D. to make a suggestion. A.D watched their interactions and smiled to himself. Food had built the team and

—

68

he had a group that would work together. Just as well, as Ellie said: 'As we're short on time could we just make breakfast the team thing? I've got to get off at eleven to make some appearance at work.'

Lucya appeared with six more rounds of toast, butter and marmalade. A.D. took the plate from her and could barely get it down on the table before hands came across for the toast. He looked over his glasses searching for the sugar amidst the debris on the table.

'Right, let's stay focused everyone. I believe, according to my youngest daughter, that the phrase is that I'm "stoked" to have you join this venture. Is that the phrase? Sounds odd to me.' A.D. confessed.

Ellie jumped in to affirm A.D's use of the word in his attempt to be up to date. 'Spot on, A.D. it just means thrilled.'

'Great, thanks, for that. Alright, I want you to be mentally prepared for the BBC today. The strategy is to try and impact the religious programming that is currently in train. I think it's being stereotyped, and we can affect the quality and the reality of it. We have a message to get out and the BBC will have their ratings in mind. We can help with that as you are a young dynamic team. If they can change up their viewing ratings on bread baking and countryside programming, we can be part of a presentation of the reality of the church today. I know through the projects you work on that you are full of energy and drive. The stereotype of church that the religious programming presents is one type. You don't need to be anything except yourselves in the meeting. I must trust you, and you me, in what happens this afternoon, as apart from Chris and Ravi I don't know you very well. And you don't know me either. Try and leave anything difficult to me, and take the long-term view. We develop the programme, not try and take it over. No matter what happens today look at the project as a long-term situation that we can influence. The BBC are looking for development two weeks out of four.'

Ravi applauded: 'Taking the long-term view is very Chinese A.D.'

Mike put up a hand to get A.D's attention. 'Just want to clarify exactly how far we're letting the BBC in on this plan. Will you be discussing this at the meeting today, A.D?'

'This plan?' A.D. adopted the face that he used for the flower committee when he did not want to give his real objectives away. His voice went up a tone slightly: 'No,' he said. 'I should think they will want to size us up and get cracking. Their approach will be: "what are the major four things happening in the world today and how do we present it," type of meeting. We know we have a message to get out there. They will probably not think like that. They will be looking at a product, which will pull in an increase in viewers. We'll no doubt encounter a sceptical approach from them as far as our beliefs are concerned. That's why I'm saying we must take the long view. Is that alright, everyone?' A.D. looked round the group.

There were a few doubtful faces in the team, mainly Storm and Ellie, which was as A.D. had feared as they were the two members that he knew least. He made a mental note to sit by them in the meeting. Mike was nodding, as was Ravi. Chris looked anxious, but that was nothing unusual. His experience of Chris was he was always fine when he had to think on his feet.

No one spoke.

A.D. decided to take silence as agreement and wrap their time up. 'Alright then, everyone, let's run with going through with the meeting. I'll see you all outside the Langham Place entrance at 1.45pm. Just a thought on what we all wear. Ellie and Ravi, if you could look more casual this afternoon I think we can present in real ways. Not too many dog collars around the table. Chris and I can both conform to potentially the stereotype of what the BBC is expecting and turn up in our "medieval costume" as my daughter, Jude, calls it. Storm and Mike, you are fine as you are. One more thing. As I think we need to celebrate afterwards, I've booked afternoon tea in a hotel near the BBC. It's on me as a thank-you for allowing me to disrupt your lives.'

'Oh, more food,' said Ellie, laughing. 'I wish you'd told us before I ate that breakfast. But thank-you A.D. that's very kind of you and you're being a good host to us and very caring. We'll enjoy celebrating.'

A.D. beamed at her: 'I generally think people do better if they're looked after,' he said. He leaned over towards Chris and said: 'I need to collect my laptop from the office, Chris, walk back with me and we'll chat. I realize you need to go home to change, so I won't take too long.' He looked round the group as they started to move and thought it still felt hairy that the whole project would work. Still, he did feel now that he had a team.

A.D. and Chris took the "Broadway" exit of the St James's tube complex towards the Abbey and Church House. Ellie and Ravi turned for the Circle and District line to get some time back at Rosary Gardens before their appointments at eleven.

'What are you wearing this afternoon Ravi, apart from the FT?' Ellie asked.

'I had debated about a three-piece suit, actually Ellie. How about you?'

'Cocktail dress and heels I think. Seriously though Ravi, I think I *am* going to put a dress on for a change and some heels. It's not every day I get to go to the BBC, or a central London Hotel.'

'A.D. did say more casual didn't he. Maybe just smart without the suit. For myself, Ellie, I will leave the heels off.' Ravi grinned and avoided a thump.

Mike and Storm had gone for the tube and were both checking the map so Storm could refresh his memory. Mike was due at the Southbank but Storm had nothing in particular to do before the BBC meeting.

'Do you want to come down with me to SE1 and see the base?' Mike suggested.

'Yeah, that would be good,' said Storm. 'I'd like to see what you do. Can we walk across Westminster Bridge rather than take the tube? It's some time since I stood on the bridge. We can chat about you coming down to Croyde if you like the idea. I was thinking about teaming up with groups so that our kids get a taste of the city and your kids try the surfing. What do you think Mike?'

****

The central green square of Deans Yard and the variety of trees contained within it softened the imposing structure of the Abbey. A.D. and Chris Duncan walked up the steps of Church House and in through the main entrance where they were greeted by a familiar face to Chris.

'Laurie!' exclaimed Chris to the Porter on reception.

'You know each other?' A.D. asked.

'Yes, Archdeacon, sir.' Laurie replied, proudly displaying his huge smile.

'Laurie and I were in Sierra Leone together ten years ago,' Chris explained to A.D. 'We lost touch. I was there on a gap year with my uncle.'

'Yes, I remember from your C.V.' A.D. said, watching with interest the transformation in his assistant with an old friend from Chris's time in Africa.

'How is your uncle, Chris?' Laurie asked.

'Uncle Colin? He's in Mali at the moment. I haven't seen him for ages. He doesn't come back to the UK that much. Prefers to take his rest times in warmer climates.'

Turning to A.D. Chris explained: 'Laurie was the head driver on the public health project I worked on with my uncle.' Chris smiled at Laurie. 'We did some long runs from Freetown to Bo and Kenema.'

'Do you remember Chris the delay we had with the handover when we changed vehicles. That trip where we had to wait in a bar because the vehicle coming out to meet us had already put its spare tyre on to replace a flat and couldn't drive without a spare.' Laurie turned to A.D. as if he had to explain it in full for him. 'The driver could not travel from Freetown all that way without a spare tyre so he had to go back to replace the spare. The drive took four hours longer than it should have done.' Laurie let out one of his high-pitched laughs, which echoed round the reception. He continued: 'Do you remember Chris, the one-legged man who bought us a coke as a thank-you for helping his village?'

'Yes, I do. We should have bought it for him.' Chris was beaming at the memories.

'No, no, Chris, we would have taken his pride away. It was right to accept the drink.' Laurie, with a broad smile, went into Krio. 'How da body?'

Chris responded with a smile and pumped Laurie's hand even more, answering: 'Da body fine, tenki!'

A.D. looked from one to another. 'What does it mean?'

'It's how are you, then the reply means I'm fine,' Chris said, still smiling and it all registered with A.D.

'Ah yes,' said A.D. 'Like Black Country dialect, where I grew up.'

'Where is that, Archdeacon, sir?' Laurie asked.

'In the Midlands, Laurie. I have elderly relatives who will talk to me using Black Country dialect.' A.D. smiled at the thought.

'I didn't know that you were from the Midlands?' Chris said, looking at A.D. with interest.

'Oh yes, it's supposed to be linked to Early Middle English. I've still relatives who have never been out of the area. We joke about Uncle Amos, in his eighties, and still working in his work shop at the bottom of the garden. He's never been the other side of the Cradley tunnel except to parties at our house in Purley. But this is all of no interest to you both. You catch up and I'll see you upstairs Chris.' A.D. turned as if to go but Chris called after him.

'I did Chaucer, A.D. I'd be really interested to have a look at the dialect.' Chris was genuinely enthusiastic.

'Well, we will then. Now I'd better leave you two and get upstairs to the office.' A.D. turned again to go.

Laurie said, 'Archdeacon sir, I have to start the security check.' He proudly held his scanner aloft ready to check their bags, and maintained his broad smile.

'Laurie, I've been in once this morning and I don't recall having to be scanned before.' A.D. was starting to sound impatient.

'It is a new system, introduced today, sir. I came on duty five minutes ago following training. Everyone now has to be scanned, sir.' He waved the scanner aloft again looking apologetic.

A.D. opened his satchel and Chris saw the brand name "Fossil." Why was he surprised, he thought?

The scanner started to bleep. A.D. was completely disconcerted at this and looked at Laurie and shrugged.

'I don't understand it,' said A.D. He stood back waiting for Laurie to go through the contents. 'This hasn't happened before.' A.D. added to Chris.

'This is just protocol, Archdeacon sir.' Laurie explained as he started taking items out of the satchel and laying them on the desk. In the bag search, he pulled out a Swiss Army knife.

'That's not mine. How did that get in there?' A.D. looked shocked.

'A very good question.' Laurie agreed. 'You can have it back when you leave, Archdeacon sir.'

'I don't really want it, it's not mine.' A.D. said.

'Protocol says I have to give it back to you, Archdeacon sir, as it came from your bag. I cannot keep it, it would look odd me having a Swiss Army knife at the desk.'

'Oh, very well. Hang on to it until I come back then.' A.D. stood back as Laurie did a sweep of Chris's bag and then waved him through.

A.D. and Chris walked through the reception hall towards the lifts. Both were out of order, leaving them with five flights of stairs to climb. On the first floor landing they passed a "break out space" being used as a prayer room and watched two colleagues walk in with their coffee.

A.D. looked at his watch and frowned. 'Look at that, eleven thirty in the morning!'

'Yeah, great,' said Chris, with enthusiasm. 'People praying!'

'You add up the smoking and praying breaks in here and they're getting an extra lunch break effectively.'

'I think you're irritated more by the bag search and the lifts not working A.D.' said Chris, risking an opinion.

A.D. looked like a small child who had been disciplined unfairly.

Chris thought he might as well go for it. He said: 'They may see prayer as being productive. Do you remember that old evangelist, Smith Wigglesworth? What he said about not praying for more than fifteen minutes and never letting more than fifteen minutes go by without praying?'

A.D. was a little shocked that his normally withdrawn curate had so much to say on the matter. He looked at Chris over his glasses, wondering from where he had got this sudden burst of information.

'You aren't suggesting that we should see a trail of employees every fifteen minutes heading into "break out spaces" to join each other for prayer surely? I thought the point was one could silently and contemplatively pray wherever one happened to be. There's too much making coffee, eating cereal, and catching up at coffee points in this place as it is, without encouraging them to meet up and pray together! Nothing would get done.'

'Depends on your point of view about prayer.' Chris said. A.D. frowned and pursed his lips. 'Are you the type of prayer that sits quietly in a room?'

'Yes.' Chris said.

'Ha. Right. I'm not. I pray while I walk the dogs in the morning. We're all different, you see.'

'That's why we should have a prayer room, then A.D.' Chris said.

A.D. sensed he was beaten. Out of breath at the fifth floor, he leant against the wall unable to make another point while recovering from the climb. He ushered Chris to go ahead of him and touched his pass against the reader to gain access to the offices. It did not work. He took his mobile out and punched in a number. Chris opened a window to let oxygen into A.D's lungs.

Jenny's voice answered the call and Chris heard her say, 'A.D. I've been trying to get hold of you.'

'Jenny, bring my laptop to the stairwell will you. The pass is dead.' He hung up before any further explanation could be given to her. Gasping still, he said to Chris, 'Got to control who gets through on my phone today, we've got enough on.'

Jenny, A.D's secretary, arrived on the office side of the stairwell door. Chris could see her outline through the opaque glass. The door opened and the lady that he and Storm had thrown soil at when they were six years old beamed at him. Now his mother's old friend from Colyton lived in Surrey and quietly managed the Archdeacon. She was dressed in brown from head to foot. Chris found a fascination in counting how many shades of the colour she was wearing. Her shoes looked like the flattest pair she could have found. The heel was solid though and would have dealt a serious injury if it came into contact with a set of toes. Jenny held A.D's laptop out to him with one foot against the door to keep it open.

'Ah, A.D,' she said, 'HQ is after you before the meeting this afternoon. How did breakfast go?'

'It was a stupendous breakfast but not here! By HQ you mean, who?' He waited but only received a shrug. 'Do you know who was chasing me?'

'I couldn't get a name.' Jenny adopted her look that was not giving anything away, even to the Archdeacon. 'My contact said she thought it was about five grades down, I think she said it was an "Honorary" something or other. I didn't quite catch it.'

'Your contact being who?' A.D. asked hopefully.

'Just a contact.' Jenny replied, obtusely. Chris thought she was wasted in Church House.

A.D. made a decision. He said: 'If the person is five grades down the call is not urgent then. Bishop Rob would have got through if it was.'

Jenny nodded and then turned her attention to Chris, her tone softening as she remembered him as a child she had liked, despite the soil incident. She and his mother went a long way back to their own university days. She smiled and he felt himself starting to relax as he had over breakfast.

'How's mum?' Jenny asked.

Before Chris could reply A.D's mobile rang. He looked at it to check the caller, and moved away to answer it. Chris leant against the doorpost and said: 'I spoke to her at the weekend. She's fine, busy at school and with the usual number of meetings. She sent her love when I mentioned I would see you.'

Jenny nodded. 'Is she due to come up to London soon?'

'No, not really,' said Chris. 'I'm due to do a visit down there. Storm is here, but you probably know that.'

'Yes, I did know. I spoke to him and his boss yesterday. It'll be good for you to get out of London and go back home and get some sea air, maybe do some biking across the hills?' She nodded enthusiastically at him as a way of encouragement.

A.D. had finished taking the call and had turned back towards them. Jenny raised her eyebrows to enquire about the caller.

A.D. said: 'It's Eve, she's downstairs.'

Chris breathed the name, 'Eve.' He had said it before he could stop himself. Jenny looked at him, then across to A.D. waiting to see what his reaction was, and then when her boss only raised the smallest movement of his eyebrows she looked back at Chris with a straight face.

A.D. coughed and continued, 'We're off to St John's Smith Square for lunch. I'm not sure I can stomach lunch after that breakfast actually. Ah well, just a salad I think. Jenny try and find out what HQ was after and who was behind the call. I should get back there about 5pm, I think, all being well.'

'Will do A.D.'

Chris gave Jenny a hug. 'Bye Jenny,' he said. 'See you probably later in the week. I'll be here more often now Rafe is at Purley. Don't forget if you are down Colyton way over the summer let mum and dad know as they would love to see you.'

'I will. Thanks Chris. When are you in precisely? Just in case there're messages,' asked Jenny. With a glance at the disappearing A.D. she said quietly: 'I'll make sure you have an office,' and she winked at him.

Chris gave her a thumbs up and started the walk downstairs. A.D. paused at the "break out" space and checked his watch. The same people were still in there.

Chris could not help himself. 'A.D, they probably see prayer as part of the job.'

'What else needs saying except "help" or "thanks!" A.D. said grumpily. If the truth be told he was a little rattled by someone chasing him from Lambeth. 'What takes this long?' he added. 'A bit of self-indulgence if you ask me.'

In reception, Eve, A.D's eldest daughter, was sitting chatting to Laurie. It struck Chris again how extraordinary it was that a child could be so little like a parent. Her dark hair was loose and long and strands fell across her shoulders. Her eyes were direct pools of blue that saw into his soul. He averted his gaze, sensing he was a drowning man and there would be no one to save him if she did not want him. Eve had stood up as they walked towards the desk. A.D. kissed her on the cheek and patted her arm.

'Hello darling, I'm sorry if you've been waiting.'

'Don't worry, dad, I've only just got here and I've been having a very interesting chat with Laurie. Hi Chris, nice to see you. I didn't know you'd been in Sierra Leone.'

Chris looked at her, surprised Laurie had told her. He felt himself tense and lowered his eyes in case they gave him away. He said: 'Yes, Laurie and I did some major drives together.' He glanced at her briefly, 'Nice to see you too, Eve.' The body language was in danger of giving him away and he felt a fool at not being able to carry off the attempted nonchalance.

A.D. gave them both a brief glance, catching Laurie's eye in the process. Laurie responded with a wink. A.D. turned his attention to Eve. 'I've had a huge breakfast so nothing more than a salad for me or mum will skin me! Especially, after that do last night. Laurie, the door pass didn't work on the fifth floor and we had problems with both lifts.'

Laurie held his hand out for the pass and A.D. gave it to him. He ran it across a machine under the desk and said: 'No Archdeacon, sir, the fact you brought a knife into the building meant I had to cancel your pass. Just following protocol.'

Eve laughed and looked askance at Laurie. 'Dad! What are you doing with a knife?'

'It's not mine! Really Laurie, this is ridiculous! You know me.' A.D. was turning pink with frustration.

'Just protocol, Archdeacon sir. I'll restore your pass as soon as I give you back the knife as you leave the building. Are you about to leave the building, Archdeacon sir?'

A.D. looked exasperated. Begrudgingly he said: 'Yes, I am about to leave the building.'

82

Laurie held out the Swiss army knife, A.D. ignored it. Laurie proffered it again with very definite body language. A.D. looked at him and ignored the knife. Eve took it and turned it over. She showed her father the inscription on the back and laughed: 'Look, dad, it's Jude's! The monkey! She must have put it in your bag for a joke.'

'That child! What's she doing with a Swiss army knife? Where would she get it from?' A.D. wiped his hand across his brow.

Eve was trying to control the laughter that was bubbling up inside her. She said: 'It's probably something that she's got to have for that taster course for the Duke of Edinburgh award that she was interested in.' She put the knife away in her bag.

Chris changed the subject in the hope of creating a distraction: 'How did the tie go down last night?'

A.D. put his hand up to his collar, momentarily forgetting what he was wearing. He said: 'You know what these city do's are like.'

Chris shook his head at A.D. to show he did not have any idea of what a city do would be like.

A.D. looked frustrated at the effort of explaining: 'As soon as you tell them what you do for a living they walk around you. I enjoyed wearing it and it was a nice place so I just appreciated the ambience.'

Eve was still smiling at her younger sister's hoax. She turned the full force of it onto Chris: 'You're welcome to come with us for lunch, Chris.'

****

Five

Chris had half turned away to avoid the impact of Eve's smile and invitation. Aware he was coming across as churlish he adopted a more open position.

Chris said: 'Thanks, I'd love to another time but I've got to get back across to the flat to change for the BBC. I'll see you at Langham Place, A.D.'

A.D. spotted the attempted withdrawal of his assistant and thought he would hit home with a double whammy.

'Oh, Chris, I forgot to mention, with your interest in Africa, that Eve's off to Kenya for a year, working with an NGO like you did.' A.D. allowed a little smile to play around the corners of his mouth.

'Oh, wonderful,' Chris was a lost man. 'Great. I'll be off then.' Wrong-footed, Chris realised he should express more interest instead of trying to escape. He stopped and turned back looking into the face of a smiling Laurie. Ignoring him and the triumphant expression on A.D'S face he knew there was nothing for it but to concentrate on Eve. And there was the problem. He smiled into the eyes and the response was so spontaneous he felt the sweat start. He said: 'Hope your trip goes well. When do you go?'

'In a couple of months,' said Eve. 'I'd welcome any tips you can give me.'

'Yes, of course.' Chris looked at her open smile. He heard himself say. 'I'm over on Sunday if you have time to chat then.'

A.D. and Laurie were looking from one to the other, this being the most that Chris had ever said to Eve. It dried up though and her disappointment was visible.

A.D intervened: 'Oh, lots of time to discuss Kenya on Sunday. And we're having a do, lunch at the house after the service so all you young fellahs must come back. We thought it would combine with Rafe being introduced to the church. You could all stay over on Sunday night so there's no rush for you. I was meaning to mention it this morning to you all.'

Lost, thought Chris, I'm really lost. His hand went up to check his hair. Eve saw his uneasy response and wished that just sometimes, her dad would be more backward in coming forward.

Eve said: 'You don't have to come to the lunch or stay over. At the moment, I'm due to go out at the end of August and there will be a send-off before that. Not that you have to come to that either but it would be lovely to have friends there, otherwise it will be mum and dad's networking and a load of rellies. If you're around on Sunday I'd love to chat if you have the time.'

Laurie picked up the thread and said, 'You must give the lady a send-off! And Eve, he has so much advice he can give you from his time in Africa. He was in Kenya too you know, weren't you Chris?

'Yes, I wish I was still there!' Chris disconsolately looked at the floor.

A.D. patted his arm. 'All right dear boy you get off now and I'll see you at 1.45 ready for the BBC.'

'Yes,' said Chris. Looking again into the eyes he paused just a little too long.

Eve said: 'Bye then Chris.'

'Bye,' said Chris. 'See you soon Laurie. See you later A.D.' He went through the doors and down the steps to cross the green.

Eve fell silent as she watched Chris reach the arch in Dean's Yard, his shoulders slumped. Laurie and A.D. exchanged a look and A.D. raised his eyebrows towards heaven with a sigh in his own prayer moment.

'Young men today,' said Laurie, quietly.

'I know,' said A.D. 'We were different.' He turned to Eve and suggested: 'Shall we make a move down to St John's? We can cut through into Great Smith Street.' Adopting enthusiasm that he did not feel A.D. started to walk across the hall and Eve followed, giving Laurie a small disconsolate wave goodbye. Laurie gave her his best smile and just stopped himself from blowing a kiss, making a mental note to have a fatherly chat with Chris next time he was in. Eve caught her father up and linked arms. Together they walked through the ground floor to the other exit.

'Dad, that was too pushy of you. I don't have to make it any more obvious to him. I think he'll get there in his own time if you just back off a bit,' Eve said.

'Ah well, that may yet happen! Give it time darling. I've noticed sometimes he needs a bit of steering. Then again, he's surrounded by over keen women trying to catch a curate. Goodness knows why, the money's rubbish!'

****

Ravi read out the text in a flat tone. He had just finished googling what appeared to be a string of words around a monument and he ran it all together. Ellie and he had decided to try and do some sightseeing of their own around the Langham Place area while they waited to go to the BBC and they had seen the glass sculpture ten metres above a roof of the new wing. The words were winding around the glass.

'Oh, it's a poem!' said Ellie as she craned her neck and shaded her eyes so she could distinguish the words in the now bright sunshine of this late part of May.

'It's apparently a memorial, to news people killed in a conflict zone, that's what the write-up says,' explained Ravi. 'It's called "Breathing." Oh, and it's a third spire.'

'Right, thanks, how clever,' said Ellie. 'Does it say where the other two spires are?'

'The mast and the spire of the church.' Ravi hesitated as he looked around. 'And the church is All Souls.'

'I've walked along here but never looked up. Mainly as far as the church but I didn't go on.' Ellie did a look up and down the road and then checked her map.

'How are we doing for time?' Ravi asked.

Ellie glanced at the time on her mobile, 'Still early.'

Ravi nodded towards a large building opposite All Souls. 'The Langham,' he said. 'Shall we stick our heads in the door of that hotel and maybe sit for a bit?'

Ellie had no compunction in refusing the silver dish being proffered, but Ravi was seduced by the food on it and accepted a small taster. He knew it would be costly both to his wallet and to his weight. The waiter was delighted, bringing to Ravi within minutes a plate, condiments and napkin. A bottle of wine was placed at his elbow, just in case, "Sir" wished to partake.

'Thank you so much,' Ravi said to him as the man retreated, 'I won't have the wine and I had better have the bill now as we have a meeting shortly.'

'You make me feel ill just watching you tuck in to all that.' Ellie pulled a face. 'I don't know where you put it. After that breakfast too that we had.'

'Oh well, I didn't have the extra toast, and it will keep me going through the meeting.' Ravi took a bite and then closed his eyes. 'Taste is such a gift. We have to eat but the fact that we taste it is like a blessing. You know finding these places makes it such a pleasure in the city centre. Thank God for taste buds! I don't care what it costs, this is my kind of tourism in London.'

****

The bag scan at the entrance to the BBC set off an alarm with A.D's bag being put through the scanner three times. He was taken on one side by a stocky security man, totally devoid of expression, with "Ken" on his badge, while another went through his bag.

Inside an inner recess of the bag was a screwdriver.

'Doing some DIY in the church are we sir?' Ken asked.

'I don't know how that got in there, it's not mine! What is happening today?' A.D. was genuinely shocked.

There was little expression on the second man's face as well. He took firm hold of the screwdriver. 'I'll just hang onto it 'til you've finished sir. Come back to the desk on your way out and you can have it back.' He also gave A.D. a look and stood holding the screwdriver aloft like a prize.

A.D. heard someone calling to him. It was Mike, with a sympathetic expression on his face standing with Storm and Ravi. They had not witnessed the bag search at Church House earlier. The latter two were doubled up laughing as A.D. was also about to be frisked by the second security guard called "Damien." He seemed unhappy about the "frock" AD was wearing in case he was secreting weapons. Chris had stood to one side in the entrance and had not yet attracted their attention, although he was similarly dressed.

'It's my youngest daughter,' said A.D. The screwdriver I mean.'

Ken looked unconvinced.

'She's going through a funny stage. That's the second time today.' A.D. groaned.

The two security men stayed put to help each other in case things turned nasty. They exchanged a look between them. The one with the deadpan expression, Ken, was now holding the screw driver and he was producing a plastic bag.

He attached a ticket to it but did not offer the other half with the number on it to A.D.

'Done this before have you, sir?' asked Ken.

'Not here, said A.D. 'Somewhere else, but that was a Swiss army knife and I left that in the office.'

'What sort of religion are you, sir?'

'Christian. Surely you can tell by what I'm wearing.' A.D. said, unhappily.

'Some sort of protest, is it?' asked Damien.

Chris decided he had heard enough and moved forward. Ken and Damien took a step back as the second man in religious garb was tall and young. They positioned themselves for trouble. The two security men were uncomfortable that another one, also wearing a "frock," had moved towards them and decided they had better treat him the same as the first one. Chris and A.D. were asked to go behind a screen. There was a pause while they disrobed and then emerged again pulling their black coats back over their heads.

Ellie went to the table and asked to speak to a manager about the way her colleagues were being treated. Ravi joined, but was unable to suppress the humour he felt so he went back to Storm and they doubled up again. Giving them both a look Ellie explained to Ken that she was an ordained Minister of the Anglican Church as well, and then was followed by Mike who decided to explain he was licensed by the Bishop as a Youth Minister.

The two security guards looked at Ellie first and had problems giving Mike the time of day, so stunned were they by the apparition of loveliness before them. They finally paid some attention to Mike when he stood in front of Ellie and smiled into their faces saying, 'It's just a uniform.'

But A.D. interrupted, 'No, no, a symbol.'

'Digging a hole,' gasped Storm to Ravi, and they started laughing again.

'Oh yeah. We've had a few of those in here. Symbolic stuff. Put them through the scanner again Damien. Just make doubly sure. Now ,Miss,' Ken the security guard turned all his charm onto Ellie, 'If you'd like to just stand over here next to me we'll sort your friends out. What religion did you say you are?'

Ellie's hands went onto the hips, which only served to wow Ken all the more. He felt like he could just about convert to whatever she was representing.

'Actually,' Ellie said firmly. 'I'd like you to look at my face while I'm talking to you. My title is Reverend Doctor, actually, and the religion's the same as them. Come on, you must have seen vicars before?'

'Not seen nothing like you before Miss, er, I mean Dr Miss, er....'

Storm moved forward and held out his hand to Ken. 'Hey mate,' he said. There was no response so Storm dropped his hand but kept smiling.

He continued: 'These friends of ours are here for a religious affairs programme. Upstairs obviously didn't keep you in the loop. Sorry about that and you might want to mention it to your union rep. We really do apologise for our friends looking like something out of the middle ages. It's a bit antiquated but they mean well, sort of symbolic so people recognise that they hang out round Cathedrals. Means a lot to them, you see, and it's like a costume today so that the folks upstairs get a flavour of the different ways vicars can look. That's why the stunning blonde looks like she does. Take the make-up off, scrape back the hair and stick her in a dog collar and you wouldn't notice her. OK to go through now if the Archdeacon leaves the offensive weapon with you? Might come in handy for you fixing stuff, so hang onto it here as he doesn't need it back given how much sharp stuff he obviously has at home.'

'They didn't tell us.' Damien said, standing back and letting them through. They watched the team pass one by one through the gate. Ravi was still having problems controlling himself and Chris was starting to lose it as well after Storm's explanation to Ken. Ellie gave Storm a punch in his side once she was through.

'Wouldn't notice me eh?' she said.

'Just to get us through. I'm sure your church is packed to the gunnels with men with their tongues hanging out.' Storm grinned at her and avoided another punch.

Mike had registered that the cause of the problem was Jude.

The same child that had sent her friends round to the flat the day before.

He made a mental note to be very wary of too much contact with her in order to avoid getting accused of being a terrorist.

However, what she was putting her dad through was pretty entertaining, and he acknowledged to himself that the kid had a great sense of humour.

As they were now through the barrier, A.D. leant against the wall already looking exhausted. Chris looked at the two men he was standing next to. They had also been checked before being allowed in. As was normal to him, his eyes went to their hair as both had a studied builder's look of expensive scruff, with grey stubble and grey cropped hair. Chris's hand automatically strayed to his own hair and he looked round for a mirror.

The first man leant against the wall and Chris heard him say: 'Are you here for this religious programming thing?'

The second man was giving the Archdeacon a look over. 'Interesting face, that guy. They must be the team we're meeting. Yes, I guess you're directing, but it'd be like the kiss of death to one's career to get stuck in religious programming for too long.'

Both laughed. The Director looked at his phone. 'It will be good to have you on board as Editor. Who's the writer going to be?'

The other man tried to control himself. He said: 'Rumour has it, it's God.'

Both laughed almost hysterically and then realised that Chris was scrutinising them. They controlled themselves and their faces straightened. But to no use as they collapsed with hysterics again. Chris, with a grin saw the irony of what they had said and thought they were absolutely right, despite the fact that they did not know it. His grin widened at the joke being the reality. Gradually the Director returned to his phone, and nudged the Editor. He was scrolling through something and occasionally they both looked from one to the other of the team and then at each other. Chris realised they were probably into "Linked in." He heard the Director's question.

'Any thoughts about where to put the pilot?'

Yes, thought Chris. I wonder where they'll put us. Could be anywhere. I stupidly assumed it would be in a church but we could end up hand gliding in the Chilterns.

The lift doors opened and two women came out into reception, preoccupied with the first woman's monologue:

'I said to her ,you've slapped me in the face! I was raging. I mean who does that! I could have turned around on November the first and said "get out" but I'm not that kind of person. She and Jaimie had fallen out. Never mind - its families.' Seeing the Archdeacon, the first woman out of the lift enthusiastically headed straight for him.

'Oh, hello, clergy people! I'm Sarah and I'm coordinating the meeting. This is my intern, Steph. You must be the Archdeacon. Are your team all here?' she said, looking at Chris. "I thought there were more of you.'

A.D. and Sarah shook hands. A.D. turned to the team and ushered them across to join him. Sarah beckoned to the Director and the Editor and they moved reluctantly over.

Sarah leaned into A.D's space and said: 'Looking forward to getting your leadership on this venture Archdeacon. This is the Director and Editor.'

A.D. was at his most charming. 'Call me A.D. everyone does. As to leadership, will it be good or bad?' He looked at the ceiling and launched into a quote:

"When degenerates take charge, crime runs wild,
 but the righteous will eventually observe their collapse"

Continuing to stare at the ceiling, A.D. then raised a finger. 'Whereas:

(everyone waited)

"Leadership gains authority and respect
 when the voiceless poor are treated fairly."

Mike gave Chris a look and then shrugged. Chris wanted the floor to swallow him up. A.D. was not finished, he was starting the introductions. He said: 'This is the team.' He waved a hand towards the five, "Shall I save introductions 'til we're upstairs?'

Confused by his quote, although she was not alone in that, Sarah went into her air hostess routine, motioning with a hand towards the lift, while starting to walk towards it.

Taller than A.D. she inclined her head down towards him again. 'Was that your own, Archdeacon, or the Bible?'

A.D. smiled graciously as to the uninitiated. 'Proverbs. A modern version to bring the rhythms, and idioms of the original Greek into English: It's called The Message.'

'Ah! We must use it.' Sarah looked no less clear.

'Yes,' said A.D. 'You should!'

Storm and Chris hung back while the others started to try and fit into the one lift. Storm turned his back on the others so that they did not hear him speak to Chris.

Storm asked: 'What's he on about?'

Chris said quietly out of the corner of his mouth, 'I think he's chucking references to leadership out when he can. Apparently, it's very trendy at the moment and he said yesterday it attracts funding. We'd better try and squeeze in.'

There were mutual smiles but everyone was far too close to each other in the lift. Ravi noted that the lift was supposed to take twelve people. He wondered how small those who had tested it had been. He also noted that Ellie and the intern were not in the lift. The Director and Editor managed to get in last and stand with their backs to the rest. And then, with a completely controlled face, Storm said to Mike: 'How's your wind?' Mike closed his eyes and his shoulders started to shake as the laughter overtook him.

On the fourth floor, they were shown into a meeting room by a breathless intern who had run up forty stairs to make it to the right floor and had waited at the lift for it to arrive.

Ellie had followed her up the stairs and was now seated in the meeting room. Coffee and tea were on the side table and Steph ushered them towards it while she gave Ravi the once-over with some appreciation. She was a pretty girl, clearly bright with a penetrating stare, and she liked the look of him. Religion however meant nothing to her. She handed him a black tea with two sugars. He thought she was about nineteen or twenty.

'What do you all do?' Steph asked.

Ravi registered the interest and moved slightly away. 'We all work in the church in different ways, but I am here in the UK for a year doing different placements and then I go back to India.'

Steph looked round the group, taking in the differences. 'Why aren't you dressed like these two? I thought you had to wear a uniform?'

'No, we don't wear it all the time. Some do, but not everyone. Other times if I've got it on people approach me for help. Mike and Storm have a different job to me. A.D. thought it would be good if we were more casually dressed today with the exception of him and Chris.'

'But I suppose you're celibate?' Her question made him slop the water he was pouring. Steph smiled at the fact she had hit home and moved closer to help him clean it up. Sarah was motioning to her to sit down as they were about to start and she took up her seat at Sarah's side.

Everyone was seated but A.D. as he had moved Mike so that he could sit between Storm and Ellie. His gut was telling him that he could not predict their responses.

Sarah pushed the iPad towards Steph. 'Make notes,' she said under her breath. Then she turned her smile onto A.D. and those at the table and said: 'Would you go round the group, A.D, and make the introductions?'

A.D. extended his arm towards the group. 'Certainly, this is the team we are putting forward: Chris Duncan is ordained and will be our main man but to reach a younger set of viewers you need youth aspects, and that's where Mike Briggs comes in from the Skateboard Church, based on the South Bank.' A.D. paused and took a sip of water and then picked up his theme again. 'And this is Giles Downing, or Storm, to use his surfer name, and he is with us from the Surfer Church in North Devon. There is potential for a lot of international link ups there with the surfing.'

Storm's face set and he looked at Chris. He was realising that much more was going on that he had bargained for. Storm was working things out. Chris knew, however, that A.D. was thinking on his feet. Storm gave just a hint of an eyebrow movement to indicate that the international link up was news to him. Chris did not move a muscle. A.D. was continuing with his sales pitch.

'The Reverend Doctor Ellen Beech is six months into a placement here from a church in Melbourne and is very innovative, worked with the homeless there.' A.D cleared his throat:

'And as you can tell from her title is an intellectual heavyweight, lecturing in London.

She will be advising on theology with a backroom role as a result. She does also have a great presence with her personality.' A.D. took another sip of water. Chris registered he was nervous. A.D. looked at Ravi, who braced himself: 'Ravindra Acharya here, or Ravi, also on a placement, is from India, Oxford graduate, keen interest in the Slum community and is a very dynamic curate, full of entrepreneurial verve from research papers that he has written and a great ideas man. I think these two bring "today" into the set up.'

The Director was nodding starting to look interested. He said: 'Great possibilities for scenes and international links, you're right about that Archdeacon.' He turned to Ellie, 'You surf, right? Being Australian.'

Ellie opened her mouth to speak but A.D. coughed, the Editor was leaning forward enthusiastically and Sarah joined him, clasping her hands together, eyes shining she said, 'How do you see it going with this team then, A.D? I mean how do we make it ebullient?'

'Ebullient?' Mike almost spat the word out. He had not heard that one before. He laughed despite himself.

'Yes,' Sarah continued enthusiastically. 'We want the brand to be an ebullient style....different locations, like, you, Mike, on your skateboard, for example, preaching, while you do a flip.'

Mike kept his face straight and nodded sagely. 'In church? Down the aisle? Or external in a skate park?'

****

Six

Ravi switched his accent to heavy Delhi. 'I could sing while cooking a curry and do the pat the dog, twist the light bulb routine. Ellie, you could cuddle a Koala, or use Storm's rain maker for background effect while leading prayer. Chris, you could do a wheelie over the South Downs while doing the blessing...'

A.D. seeing the dangers, said under his breath, 'Let's bring it back shall we.'

Ravi sat back in his chair, face straight, eyes fixed on a spot on the window, but Chris frowned and knew his friend's humour was going to surface again through the afternoon if they were stereotyped.

A.D. turned his gaze with a smile to Sarah. 'Where were we, ah, yes! Ebullient. Chris, you're the English graduate, how do you see this brand?'

Chris was keying the word into his app. He said: 'Just a mo.'

The Director looked at A.D. and said: 'No, seriously, there's some good ideas there. I like the idea of the cycling on the South Downs. But it would be better if it's in the same area as the surfing in North Devon.'

Chris looked like doom was pending.

Ravi looked at him and mouthed: 'Sorry.'

'So, let me summarise what I'm picking up here,' the Director began.

'Your front man is a sort of adventurous type, eh? Make a note Sarah...we need to get him into the gym though, get him into cycle gear and see how he looks... maybe do a bare-chested shot of the Surfer guy, Storm, here. There's humour from the man from Oxford pretending to have a strong Delhi accent. So, here's how I see it. Storm on the beach with his surfer group, emerging from his wet suit down to waist level....

'Semi nudity? Sells a programme, does it?' Ellie was in battling form.

'What is it? What bothers you about that?' The Director and Ellie locked eyes as he gave a sardonic smile. 'Yes, it's worked on other programmes and your guy here has the physique. It's only what people do on beaches, take off wet suits. It's normal. But I was forgetting, of course we're dealing with churches aren't we and the denial of the body.'

Ellie let the side swipe go. 'It's not the point of the programme.'

But the Director carried on. 'And you, with the connection with Melbourne... it would fit with the surfer theme here, wouldn't it? I mean you would not be wearing your cassock on the beach, would you? Get the Australian surfers in who have a church connection...get the programme out of those gloomy buildings into God's creation, eh?'

'Let's keep any garbage ideas out. Ow!' said Ellie as A.D. gripped her hand on the table in his panic. His hand was unconsciously tight. He loosened it immediately and said quietly: 'I'm sorry, it was panic,'

Ellie saw the concern in his eyes, 'Alright A.D. but sort this will you.'

A.D. was sitting so far forward on his chair with the tension that it tipped. Storm and Ellie helped him up from the carpet.

The Director turned to Ravi and handed him a sheet from the file in front of him. It was Ravi's C.V. and particularly focussed on his research. Ravi looked at it and realised with some apprehension, that the man was thorough and quite serious.

'Where did you get this from? Ravi asked. 'Would you like me to go into the research now?'

'No, I wanted you to know we don't underestimate you, ' the Director smiled as he had got Ravi's full attention at last. 'But it means we can get a good angle on the work in the slums and digital transformation, start-ups, and how you see it coming into your calling to transform the lot of the poor. Better than pat the dog, twist the light bulb, eh?'

'Sorry,' said Ravi.

The Director turned to Ellie who was just sitting back down again. He said: 'And I think, Reverend Doctor, that there is a good link with your University in Melbourne and the slums in the west of Delhi?' They locked eyes again, and Ellie looked over at Ravi. Ravi passed a hand over his brow. He felt himself being convinced as the humour drained and the realisation came that this man was not to be trifled with. It was also potentially the opportunity he had been praying for, to promote the ideas, and get work going in the slums, to help people lift themselves out of poverty.

'Ebullient! Got it.' Chris exclaimed and he broke the tension, triumphantly sliding his phone into the middle of the table, 'It means jaunty, chirpy, elated, excited.'

'That's it,' said Sarah, 'so stick them on a beach with clips cutting in from time to time of the work being done. It's perfect.'

A.D. had recovered his calm exterior although it did feel like trying to control a runaway horse. He inclined his head slightly to the side, raised his eyebrows to show interest.

Mike had been very quiet during all the exchanges, watching each one, not doing too well where there was conflict developing. It was his background, he knew. He waited to see if A.D. was going to bring the control back, but the man was silent. Mike had seen him stagger a bit after slipping from the chair and was concerned. He heard himself asking a question without any previous thought.

'How do you do all this filming outside without studios in these places?' He hoped he was asking a relevant question that did not sound too stupid.

The Editor appreciated the exception in a session that had proved more difficult than he had expected. Some of this team had clearly come in thinking the whole thing was a joke. They've probably had been made to come, he thought. He leant forward with some enthusiasm, warming to Mike's interest.

'Right, this is how it works: We can make it that every programme is really a specialist one, and if we utilise the technology we're using now with radio we can use the small digital desks instead of studios, so, we can set up anywhere.'

He paused and sipped water before continuing: 'They've been rolling out in the UK for radio in the last few years as regional stations closed. We've got camera in radio studios too as you'll know if you listen to radio 1, so we can do that and get you in. It means we can hit the public where we already have good audiences and it ceases to be so UK focussed.'

'So, it's "Digital or Death." Have you really got a good size of audience?' Mike continued to feed a question.

The Editor smiled at him. 'Yes, it's beautiful, we can do it just anywhere. If we start with world figures, 2019 BBC analysis showed 426 million people each week tuning into the BBC. That had risen 13 per cent in a year. The target will be 500 million weekly next year.'

'Wow,' said Chris.

"And the Oxford English graduate says it all,' said Storm, grinning at Chris.

'Indeed,' said the Editor. 'India, Kenya and the USA saw the most gains.'

'There's also the syndication through partner T.V. and radio stations around the world as well as digital platforms like YouTube and Facebook. That all adds up to about 60 per cent of audience reach,' said Sarah.

A.D. had recovered and was following the size of the potential undertaking, finally understanding why these two men were at the meeting. He drew a mind map on the sheet in front of him.

'Perfect,' said A.D. 'So, the headline is that a lot of people are consuming the BBC weekly. Yes?'

'Exactly, a lot to be ebullient about,' said Sarah.

'Dead right,' said Chris.

'And we are talking radio and a pilot in August on television. I'd like to talk to you in detail about the content. Can we monitor the responses?' A.D. asked.

'Of course,' said the Director, 'no point otherwise.'

Finally, the group were starting to function constructively as far as he was concerned. He added: 'Editors tend to put their personality into it and decide on the content but I'm happy to liaise with you, A.D. on this, given the specialist nature of the focus.'

'And the responses?' A.D. re-emphasised his point.

The Editor looked pleased at the engagement, he leant forward and answered A.D's question: 'We can use the software to connect with Facebook and Twitter. There are companies that are recording all the time so we can constantly go in and out of it and check it.' The Editor sat back as Mike passed a diagram to A.D. outlining the social media aspect.

'Excellent,' said A.D. looking it over and putting it next to his own diagram. He pushed them across the table to the Editor. The others apart from Chris and Mike were a little lost after the realisation that the BBC team were not to be toyed with. It was serious and the pace was moving. They had come in thinking they were being stereotyped but the opposite was true. These people wanted something different as did they.

'Yes, exactly,' the Editor said, his eyes crinkling with appreciation of the buy-in. 'Easy! It's beautiful - we can take the programme just anywhere.'

Sarah was appraising Storm and Chris. Storm met her gaze and Chris looked away while the Director made a final attempt to engage Ellie.

'Look, we don't want you to think that we are being disrespectful about your faith, and what is, effectively, a programme to help people explore belief and do some worship. It's true we are looking at this from a particular point of view as we are used to presentation, but there is also the point of what people relate to.' The programming has an aging population, nothing wrong in that but this is an opportunity to add new viewers. Most people don't understand why "church" is anything other than a building. You can show them what it is.'

He looked round the table at all of them. 'The team you've put up A.D. are all "lookers," that's all. You two guys, for example,' he said to Chris and Storm. 'I'm sure you're already used to the fact that you'll attract attention. You've good hair and a good look, and you,' he said specifically to Storm, 'have a good build.'

Storm stared at the man. He said: 'Swimming.'

The Director stared at Storm. 'You may not like this but you look like what people will think of as a typical surfer. But there's more to you than the stereotype so let's show that. The look gets you taken seriously with a certain market. You know that or you wouldn't look like you do.' He looked round the team before continuing:

'Chris looks very unlike the stereotype of a vicar and that's going to be interesting to people. Cycling's also big now and surfing links in well with Australia and the USA. That plays to all the interest that was triggered by the "Songs of Praise" final with that Melbourne school.'

Sarah continued to stare at Storm in a rather self-indulgent way.

Storm fixed her with a clear gaze. 'You should come down for Sunday and try surfing. I can fix you up with an instructor called Mary.'

A.D. turned his head to Storm and gave him a stern look as Sarah was becoming flustered. 'Stop,' A.D. muttered quietly.

The Director was clearly taken with the idea of a quick visit to North Devon and interrupted. He said: 'Exactly! Fix it up! We can suss out the area Sarah and what they do with church.'

Storm pulled a face at Chris.

A.D. said: 'I think I can be down there if that would be helpful Director?' There goes the diary thought A.D. but he sensed that Storm had a tendency to create a state of embarrassing confusion with the opposite sex. A.D. was determined not to lose control, despite feeling like he would like to leave the building. However, he was determined not to show his team that he was rattled. He said: 'Perhaps we could fix up it being in two Sundays time as we all have commitments this week. Perhaps we can get Chris and Mike down there next week to work on some ideas as well?' he suggested.

The Director liked the suggestion. 'Look this is good A.D. We could try something out, broadcast it on the Sunday morning with local radio. Normally it's a service at 6.30 am on a Sunday in Devon but we could try something fresh and link into face book and twitter. Let's treat it as a pilot using radio first and we can take a few days to film in North Devon. We'd need to link to London and maybe the youth side with the skateboarder could come in there, Sarah. Try and get it on campus ready for an infill on student life. We can have multiple uses for this so these guys are starting to become familiar to the younger crowd when the pilot goes out in August. Sarah check the schedule, will you?'

Sarah looked at Ellie, 'And the Dr? It would be a shame if you weren't in it.'

A.D. looked at Ellie's face and gave her a reassuring nod. He said: 'As I said, the Dr. is background only.'

Sarah, however, was not sure if Ellie was being serious, so to her cost she pursued an idea. 'You would look great in a wet suit...we could feed you in...an intellectual woman with looks as well and a faith ... can't you see the ratings? How about an opening shot with Chris and A.D. as they're dressed now with Exeter Cathedral in the background, and then cut to Chris cycling and Storm...'

'A.D.' Ellie said fiercely, 'Please deal with this or I will have to.'

'There will be nothing that you are uncomfortable with.' A.D. looked firmly at her.

He then turned to Sarah and smiled: 'As I did explain, the Reverend Dr. was an advisor only and would be in the background.'

The Director gave the Editor a barely visible wink. 'Cut to surfer boy here riding the waves.'

Storm for the first time in the meeting was irritated. 'Excuse me?' Storm said.

The Director though was on a roll. 'Then fade to the guy with the hair on his bike on the coast road, assuming there is one.'

Chris felt the desire to put his head into his hands but sat on them instead.

'Just messing with you.' The Director grinned, but Storm's face was like stone.

Mike looked across at Chris, gave a half wink and said:

'Shame about the leg injury isn't it mate.'

****

The team walked from the building as if they had shell shock. A.D. was watched by Ken and Damien as he entered the lobby until he was out of the building. They did not offer to give him back his screwdriver. A.D. led his colleagues out towards the hotel that Ravi and Ellie had enjoyed earlier. He had booked a table for afternoon tea at the Langham. It was meant as a celebration, but now it felt more like a therapy session.

It was drizzling and grey but the golden lights of the Langham were like beacons bringing the team home.

The Hotel had uniformed staff on the entrance who were decidedly unsure that Storm and Mike should be admitted. As usual AD invited a grovelling response just by appearing as himself. Ravi and Ellie were recognised from earlier, which caused great confusion for their friends. The rotating doors at the entrance jammed with Mike in the middle, despite him not having touched them. The uniformed type who undid them to let Mike out thought it was par for the course with this sort.

'That was scary," said Mike, in an attempt to joke with the staff. Safely on the other side of the door Mike took A.D. on one side.

'It's a bit too posh for the way I'm dressed A.D. I deliberately dressed it down for the BBC, so I looked like I was at the skater park.'

'Nonsense, Mike, you look fine. It's the way you are that matters.' A.D. patted him on the shoulder.

A.D. appeared to grow in stature himself as he moved through the reception area, admiring the blooms and the décor. Chris disappeared to change out of his black coat. A.D. gave him a surprised look, feeling comfortable at remaining in his own clerical garb.

'Might as well change,' Chris said to A.D. with a wan smile. 'It's been an exhausting afternoon and I just feel better out of it.'

Their table was in the Palm Court which was immaculately furnished and a grand piano playing. A.D. led the way in, chatting with the staff as the group were shown to the table.

The environment was working its magic on A.D. He had thought the meeting would be hard but it had surpassed any difficulties he had imagined. The tea was meant to be a treat and a team builder for them all. Although thoroughly exhausted himself the environment was so different for them all it provided an excellent distraction. A.D. began to feel they had pulled it round and was grateful to Mike for the way he had been. He just had not anticipated the sense of chaos in the way the rest of the team had initially behaved. He felt bad about it as he knew he had forced their involvement. A voice to his right brought him out of his reverie.

'Good afternoon sir, madam. How nice to see you back with us.' A waiter had spoken to Ravi and Ellie.

Ravi quickly explained to A.D: 'We were doing some sightseeing earlier as we had some time to kill. It's Ellie they remember really.'

Ellie looked askance, 'You're the one who gave them business, Ravi. I was just soaking up the atmosphere. Anyway, nice to be remembered.'

'Yeah, Ellie, and you've got your heels on.' Chris said, trying to be complimentary.

Storm nudged Mike, laughing he said: 'There you are Mike, that's how to get the right attention at the door, get your heels on!'

'The Langham is quite an historic place, you know,' said A.D. deliberately trying to change the subject. 'Its famous for being the place where afternoon tea began. They call it Tiffin here.'

Ravi nodded: 'As usual the British borrow good ideas from India.'

'Did it mean tea?' asked Ellie.

'It was a type of meal,' explained Ravi. 'A light one and depends where you are in India as to what it is. It could be around 3pm or it could be a light breakfast. Some places use the word instead of lunch and it would not be light then. It's true the British brought the idea back of replacing afternoon tea with the Indian practice of having a light meal instead. 'Tiffin' meant having a little drink to the British.'

****

It was a quiet tea initially, but slowly, as the food hit the spot, the natural energy in the conversation returned.

'That feels better.' Chris said, after his second cup of tea. 'How are you feeling A.D. now? You looked quite low when we came in. I'm sorry I let you down in there. I don't think any of us knew what to expect, really.'

'I can tell I'm warming to the ambience of the place Chris, and the excellent food helps. I think I need to apologise to you all. I've forced your involvement and also underestimated what we were going into. They had bought much more into the sort of team we are than I expected and it just shows one should never underestimate the situation.'

'That's alright, A.D. we're all new to this," said Mike.

'You did the best job in there, Mike,' said Chris.

'No, not really,' said Mike.

"Yes, you did,' said Ellie. 'You had by far the most focused discussion with them and showed you knew your stuff. You had a much better impact than I had with my reactions.'

'We're getting through these sandwiches I see rather quickly. I think I'll order more,' said A.D. deliberately moving the subject away from the meeting as everyone was exhausted. The exchange had helped everyone but he was sure it shouldn't go on. Faces relaxed more visibly and he thought they would cope better next time. A.D. waved a hand and a man was at his side in moments. Ellie put her hand on her stomach and tried to breathe in, hoping it would produce her usual flat stomach.

Ellie said: 'Where do you guys put it?' The men shrugged and chewed. Her colleagues continued to devour the last few remaining sandwiches. A new supply arrived and the men moved seamlessly through the new plate.

'With me,' Chris swallowed, 'it's nervous tension.'

'I'm a growing lad,' Mike grinned.

The tea progressed and they all moved naturally onto the selection of warm scones with clotted cream and strawberry jam.

'Good as this is,' Storm said, 'the cream never tastes quite like it does at home.'

'No, quite true,' Chris agreed and helped himself to another scone. 'But by the sound of it we shall be all down in Devon next week and then we can do a check of our usual places and make sure they're keeping up the standard.' His expression was one of sheer pleasure for the first time all afternoon.

Ellie pushed her plate away. 'Today has been quite strange, but the highlight has definitely been the food, from the wonderful breakfast to this tea and this place. I must bring Joel here. I can't do pastries so you guys have mine.' She sat back and breathed out.

'Thank you so much,' A.D. said to the waitress, as fresh tea was put down and some of the debris was cleared away. He looked at Ellie. 'And when is Joel coming?'

'Not sure, I've got a call with him shortly and hopefully I'll have more of an idea then,' said Ellie.

A.D looked round and asked: 'More tea I think?'

Ravi nodded, but as regards the food he reluctantly put his napkin onto the table as a final sign that he was done. He said: 'Tea yes, but I'm done as regards the food. I was saying to Ellie when we were in here before the meeting, that I think the fact we can taste food is a sort of gift.'

'Yes Ravi, I agree.' A.D. said. 'From the first chip with salt and vinegar to smoked salmon, it is a revelation.'

'You eat fish and chips A.D?' Mike had his mouth full but was so surprised he forgot himself. His Gran would not have approved. 'Behave like you're with the Queen,' she had told him as he was growing up.

'Of course, Mike. Every Friday where I grew up, regardless of where you lived down our way, you joined the queue outside the fish and chippy.' A.D. smiled with the memory.

'Where was that actually A.D? You said Midlands to Laurie earlier.' Chris realised he knew very little about his boss.

'A town on the edge of the Black Country.' A.D. said, as he poured himself a third cup of tea, relishing the colour of the steaming liquid as it swirled into the china. He caught the puzzled look on Chris's face and added a further explanation. 'It's complicated which parts come under that title and to do with the coal seam.'

Chris looked more puzzled.

'Dudley,' A.D. said finally.

'That's what I can hear in your accent! Not normally, but I hear it when you pray aloud,' Chris said.

A.D. laughed and said: ' Ah I relax, you see with God. Louise teases me that as soon as I get back into the area I revert. Like it's in the air! Funny, I was thinking, about the way fish and chips are viewed. When we were at an occasion put on by Louise's company some years ago I was chatting to a woman dripping with expensive pearls. Wife of some big wig, went to school with practically every woman in the room, you know the sort of thing. I happened to mention that we'd taken the children away down to the sea side the previous weekend and picked up fish and chips to eat in the car on the way. She said: "How common." I thought it very funny, partly because she was being rude but didn't recognise it in herself. I laughed unfortunately before I realised she was serious. I felt like blowing my nose on the curtains to see how she would react to that.' A.D. threw his head back and laughed.

'So, on the important topic of fish and chips where are we going to get them from when we come down to North Devon, Storm?' Mike asked, still chewing and savouring, and now eyeing Ellie's share of the pastries.

Storm thought, and chewed. 'Woolacombe,' he said. 'And, if we go down towards Chris's, then we must do Beer.' Turning to Chris he asked: 'How do you feel after the day, cycle boy? You looked like you were struggling with the whole thing in there until the end.'

Chris nodded. He said: 'Frankly? Yes, I was, but I get the bit about it being ebullient, funnily enough. It's what's developing and the profile we're likely to receive that worries me. I think we're in danger of being unable to control what they do. I just don't want it, for myself. The highlight will be going down to Devon though next week.'

'Well we did get through it today and we showed them we had engaged. Admittedly the technical and digital side of it is so huge we will never have a handle on it but we can influence the content.' A.D. said, his indomitable spirit surfacing with the food and the atmosphere. He checked his watch.

'I need to go back to Lambeth shortly to pick up the luggage and the car. You can carry on here though as I've taken care of the bill. I've got some calls to make first so I'll pop out into the Artesian Bar just near reception as it looked quieter at this time of the day than in here. I'll be back shortly to say goodbye.'

A.D. looked at Chris as a thought struck him. Chris saw the change of expression and braced himself: 'Chris,' said A.D. 'why don't you come with me to Lambeth when I leave and we'll chat through on the journey how you feel the meeting really went. I'll leave you all to relax and enjoy the ambience. There's no rush to go.'

****

Seven

A.D. shook his head when offered the list of cocktails. He had dialled his wife's mobile and waited for her answer.

'Just a water,' he said to the waiter.

Louise was answering: 'Mark? Where are you? I thought you were coming back for 4pm so we could make a quick getaway to get home for dinner.'

'Yes, I'm sorry Louise, everything went on much longer than we expected and the team's only just finishing tea. I forgot to ask Jenny to let you know as well as Lambeth. I'll be on my way shortly to the flat and Chris Duncan is coming with me. Thought it might do him good to have some time to debrief. You sound a bit flat, are you alright? How did *your* meeting go?' A.D. paused.

"A few difficult things,' said Louise. Her feedback on board meetings never told A.D. anything. 'I'd had enough by the time it was over and thought I'd work from the flat.'

'I might give Chris the long walk through the rooms at Lambeth as a point of interest as he's not been before,' said A.D.

'So long as we're not too late leaving. I'll tell you later about my stuff. How did it go at the BBC?' Louise asked.

'The Beeb? Pretty awful really, it was difficult to control the direction and the team were reacting all over the place. I think we pulled it together in the end. I'm trying to be upbeat with them as everyone's exhausted. Sounds like we both need a quiet evening.'

'That won't be easy,' Louise said, and then she paused. A.D. could almost hear that her strategic brain was still in the meeting.

'They're lucky to have you, so remember that. You're so clever.' A.D. said in his most affirming tone.

'You're wonderful. Do you ever feel like just going back to accepting a small parish instead of trying these ideas you get? I'm sorry I was feeling it shouldn't be this hard for us both now. I'm tempted to go back into practice in a small rural Accountancy firm, accepting jobs which arrive in a carrier bag.'

'Louise, you'd hate it, you'd be bored in a week. Maybe we need to get away for a while and take a spontaneous holiday.' A.D's mind was whirring away with a germ of an idea about the West Country for a long weekend.

'Yes, you're probably right,' said Louise. 'Sounds like I'll see you shortly then if the team's finishing tea. Where are you if you're not with them? Can you give me an idea of when you're leaving and we'll get the bags to the car?'

'I'm in that interesting Artesian bar in the hotel. You said we. Is Eve still there?' A.D. asked, another idea forming in his mind.

'Yes, she's coming home with us. I told you this morning.'

'Excellent, as I'm bringing Chris. I should be on my way in about thirty minutes, I've just got some more calls to make. I may need to be away tomorrow night and also a couple of nights next week down in North Devon. Will you be alright with that?'

'Sounds rather nice. What are you up to down there?' Louise asked.

'I want to get to know one of the young guys from the Surfer Church down there better by going back with him tomorrow. He's a bit of a dark horse and I need to understand where he's coming from. I could do with meeting his boss anyway and seeing how the whole thing down there works with ministry. A long rail journey is a good opportunity. The BBC were quite keen on the surfing link and photo opportunities in Devon.'

'Is this the one with the funny name?' Louise asked.

'Storm. Yes, it's a surfing nickname I gather. He doesn't use his real name. I've upset him a couple of times as I forgot. Goes by Storm Downing.'

'Oh, Storm's not that funny, quite imaginative really.' There was a pause at Louise's end. Then she asked: 'He's not a relative to Paul Downing, is he?'

'The Paul from university? No idea really. He grew up with Chris. Not sure I want to ask that question given how obnoxious the guy was. I'll get to know him first so I don't become jaundiced if he is a relative. You sound tired.'

'Well, yes, I am. Issues in meetings are always so exhausting when you get a character that kicks off and tries to sabotage things. Looking forward to getting home and having a relaxing evening. Nothing challenging and some comedy on TV. See you shortly, love.' And she was gone.

A.D. thought about the prospect of a quiet evening and watched it float away in his mind as he remembered that their youngest daughter would have arrived home from her school trip to Paris and they would have to listen to her exploits. He dialled Louise again.

She answered immediately: 'What's up?'

'Jude's back tonight, isn't she?' A.D. asked.

'Yes, I asked Charis to throw something together in a pan for us all as it would be late when we eat. I doubt she'll want to stay in, she'll be desperate to tell her friends about Paris. Why, was there something you need to talk to her about?'

'Oh, just a couple of practical jokes she's played on me. Lucky I wasn't arrested.' A.D. waved away a waiter who was hovering in case he wanted anything else.

'Oh dear, hope they didn't cause a problem? What did she do?' Louise asked.

'I'll fill you in later. I suppose I should be grateful that she thinks I've got a sense of humour. At least it's not boys I'm having to sort her out over.' A.D. said.

'Not yet, but that day will come. See you at the Lambeth flat then.' Louise hung up and A.D. hit his office number.

'Jenny, glad you're still there, it's A.D.' He always said this although he knew his name had come up on her screen. A.D. just felt he should always introduce himself. 'Any messages come through?' he asked.

'How did it go A.D? Are we going to see you in a starring role?' Jenny's sense of humour was well established between them.

'Ha! Not if I can help it, Jenny,' said A.D. 'It was rather unpredictable and therefore thoroughly exhausting. I'm just checking in with you before I go back to the flat. Are there any more messages from that source at Lambeth?'

'No, we can't trace them and in fact A.D. we've come to the conclusion that the person doesn't seem to exist. We think it may have been a reporter.' Jenny dropped her voice to give her idea an air of mystery.

'How very odd. Oh well, it's good you sorted that one out then before we end up in a scandal sheet.'

'I don't think it would be in a sheet anymore A.D. Digital has moved on a bit from there.' He heard the laughter in her voice. 'They'd have a job finding any scandal in our office, A.D.'

'Well I suppose they could always make it up.'

'I'd rather not go down that route. Yes, I suppose so. I can see the headlines AD. "The scandal around the tea point." I don't think finance are investing in time shares anywhere.' Jenny laughed as her imagination worked over time.

'Don't even go there Jenny. Look while you're on, I think I'm going to go back to North Devon with Chris's friend, Storm tomorrow. How is the diary?'

'The diary is full. There's no capacity for you to disappear A.D.' Jenny's tone held a warning.

'Can't be helped, Jenny,' said A.D. 'You and I can have a chat while I'm on the train in the morning and I can try and deal with anything from a distance.' He paused but Jenny was silent.

A.D. continued: 'I think understanding the ministry these guys have to the surfers is quite important as the BBC will hone in on it. There's a lot of potential in the Director's mind with international links. It'll make good television both from a photographic angle and they can roll it out across the world. Ravi's going to get picked up by them as well by the sound of it with his interest in the slum poor work. The Director had done his homework on the links with Melbourne University as well as Ravi's areas of interest.'

'How amazing but vaguely terrifying,' said Jenny. 'Bit different from watching all those people singing hymns from Ancient and Modern isn't it? Sounds very interesting though A.D. Amazing the talent in the team you've got. How is Storm getting on? Does he know he's coming under your scrutiny tomorrow?'

'Seems very altogether. Yes, of course, you know him, don't you?' A.D. remembered the story of the soil over the hedge and two little six-year olds in Colyton. He ignored her question and asked: 'Anything I need to know there?'

'Yes, probably. Bit of a sad background in some ways. He was a lovely little boy, mischievous though and a bit unpredictable. Maureen, Chris's mum, started picking Storm up to go to school with Chris to help his father out after the wife left. She had cancer treatment by the way. Then he seemed to be always with them except for weekends.' Jenny paused to make sure her memory was not playing tricks.

'It was the time when Storm's father was promoted and needed to be in London so the boy basically stayed with the Duncan family through the week,' Jenny said. 'I came to London then so lost touch a bit. Those two boys as children were a right couple of roamers and they knew every bit of beach as teenagers on that North Devon coast with the surfing. They were completely inseparable.'

'Ah interesting. Thank you. So, our Chris is also a surfer. Hiding his light under a bushel I think. So, have you had any contact with Storm since his school days, Jenny?'

'Oh yes. I was at a family wedding last December. Storm's got a large number of half brothers and sisters. His father married three times, first wife, Storm's mum, had a terrible battle with cancer and died by the time he was five. His dad's had children with each wife. Got a bit of a death wish with the amount of alimony he must be paying.' Jenny saw the funny side of how much money was going out and the inability to stay in a marriage.

A.D. did not laugh. A cold wind from the past was blowing around his ankles. He ran his hand across his brow and asked: 'Not Paul Downing is it? The father I mean?'

Jenny paused briefly. 'Yes, that's right. Do you know him then?'

'Yes,' said A.D, remembering the humiliation. 'Long time ago.'

Jenny stopped again for a few seconds as though a memory had just come to her. She carried on confidently as the memory cleared. 'He had some sort of arrangement with John and Maureen Duncan to look after Storm. John, Chris's dad, had it out with Paul Downing. Big row one day. I moved shortly after so not sure what happened then. I guess eventually the University years came along and Chris and Storm went their separate ways.' Jenny tailed off with the recollection of so much time going by.

So, there it was, thought A.D. Storm was Paul's son. He pulled himself back to the call with Jenny. 'And whose was the wedding you were at?' A.D. asked.

'A younger sister,' Jenny said

'And you think Storm's alright?' A.D. asked.

'Solid as a rock I thought last December. From what I remember in Maureen's Christmas card news he doesn't get on with his dad, but that's not really surprising. Hard to have a stream of step mothers paraded before you as a child. I think Maureen said a few years ago that Storm sees the work with the Surfer Church as a mission. I think he runs his own surf school too, A.D. Oh, and he came into a trust from his mum when he was twenty-five. He's got a house, and a mortgage. Pretty good really, I think. I suspect it's the effect of John and Maureen. I'm looking forward to seeing him again. Storm understands our Chris thoroughly. I've had a look at the webpage of his church. Don't let the bleached surfer appearance fool you, it's a trendy look down there.'

'Thank you, Jenny. As always, you've dealt with the concerns I had. It was his behaviour in the meeting actually with one of the women. I just had alarm bells going off,' A.D. said kicking himself as he knew the bias was seeping into his soul as if it was like a blood transfusion.

'Ah *girls*. Well with those two boys in their teens! Maureen's stories in her cards did make me laugh. Well, I noticed at the wedding, like Chris, Storm's a babe magnet, but very on top of it.' She laughed. 'Sorry A.D. I didn't mean it like that.' There was a trill of high-pitched laughter from Jenny and A.D. moved the phone away from his ear. He exhaled and thought of his student days trying to avoid Storm's dad.

'Are you there?' said Jenny loudly.

'I am,' said A.D. trying not to feel depressed.

' What I meant was is he is very chilled about women and not playing the field at all, but accepts he does attract them. He seems to walk away. Might be his dad's behaviour perhaps that worries you but I definitely think Storm overcompensates for his history. He's extremely focused on his faith but I did get the impression, thinking about it, that his dad's behaviour was a problem to him. Storm came across very cynical about his dad at the wedding. As to our Chris, he has never coped with being at the centre of attention and has always headed for the hills.'

'Right. I'll see how it goes tomorrow,' said A.D. flatly.

He added: 'Jenny, could you do one more thing before you go for me? I'll get the train time Storm is likely to travel on tomorrow for you and if you could book "First" for us both that would be a better environment to get some work done. I'll cover the difference in the cost of course, but I think it will be a better use of time to work.'

'Of course, A.D. I'll get you an open return now and speak to you tomorrow morning. I'll re-jig the diary and perhaps Chris can pick some things up tomorrow now he's at Church House more? Have a good evening.' And she was gone.

Putting his phone away A.D. stared at his own reflection in the mirror behind the bar. He muttered: 'Paul Downing resurfaces. Storm is Paul Downing's son. The Paul who was everything I was not. Probably still is.' He caught sight of himself in the mirror over the bar. ' But,' he said with determination. 'According to Louise, I was everything he was not. And I got the girl, praise God.' A.D. beamed to the consternation of a passing waiter and said loudly: 'Body and soul I am marvellously made!'

****

A.D. had tried to get through to his daughter but had only been able to leave a voice mail. However, she rang him back almost as soon as he had finished his message.

'Eve,' he said, 'How's it going, darling?'

'It's been a good afternoon actually, thanks dad. How was the Beeb?'

'Pretty awful really. I'll tell you later. Are you still at work?'

'About to leave and run for the tube to get to the flat,' said Eve. 'Where are you?'

'In a beautiful bar in the Langham,' said A.D, adding, so she was in no doubts, 'on the water in case you think I'm having a tipple. Thought I'd just let you know I'm bringing Chris back to the flat with me and wondered if you could give him a walk through the gardens before we head home?'

'Oh, good grief, dad, he'll flip.' Eve said, slightly cross at her dad's meddling.

'No, he'll be fine once alone with you. Probably time with you is what he needs to get his mind off the BBC. Anyway, it's a good opportunity for you both to spend time together. That way it starts to become normal for him and he'll feel the emptiness of each day without you.'

'Mum is right, you're like a Victorian mother match-making! Mum was expecting you back at the flat by now I think,' Eve said.

'Yes, I've just spoken to her. We're pretty much finished with tea now but I'm more or less on the way with Chris. The others can stay and enjoy the place. I'm just letting the guys finish their tea. Everything has run on longer than I thought it would. *More food,* Eve, you should have seen what everyone has eaten today, including me.'

'Bread and water for you then, dad.'

'Ha! I don't think so. Glad you're coming back with us tonight. It will be great to have all three of my girls at home for a night. Will you travel into Victoria tomorrow for work?'

'No, I can work at home tomorrow,' Eve said

'The other two will like you being home as well,' A.D. said.

'It means they get less time in the bathroom. Although I'm not sure Jude is that interested yet in hours in the bathroom yet. Are you working at home tomorrow dad?' asked Eve.

'No, I'm going to have to go down to Devon for a night to meet some people from a Surfer Church down there. I'll be off early and back probably on Thursday, although it might run to another day. Look, I'll get going. See you back at the flat shortly,' said A.D. ringing off.

****

A.D. looked at the number that was calling him and did not recognise it. It certainly was not one he had in his contacts. He put his bottom lip over his top one and debated about letting it go to answer phone. Part of him was curious, especially as Jenny had not been able to track down the mystery caller earlier at the office. Changing his mind, he thought, why not?

'Yes?' A.D. said, withholding his identity.

'Archdeacon? Is that the Archdeacon Mark Wilkinson? This is Adeniji the Bishop's executive assistant. The Bishop has left a communication for you that he would like to be informed of the developments this afternoon with the BBC.'

'Ah yes, hello.' A.D. did not recall an Adeniji on the staff. 'We haven't met, have we?' A.D. had raised one eyebrow at the officious tone.

He was also not aware that Bishop Rob had an executive assistant. 'The Bishop is away at present and would not be expecting an update.'

'But I shall be here in the morning and we will meet then. I am making a time for you to attend the Bishop and an appointment with me first in order to go through the detail with you that the Bishop requires.'

Not likely, thought A.D. Where have you turned up from? He made a mental note to get Jenny onto the task of finding out about this character.

'Really? Well unfortunately for all your arrangements I usually communicate directly with the Bishop on his private line so I think as I will not be in London tomorrow that will continue to be the best way for me to brief the Bishop on the meeting we had with the BBC. Nice of you to offer though.' A.D. used his silkiest voice.

'What line is that?' Adeniji asked.

'His private line,' A.D. said, as a statement of fact.

'I would be grateful for that number Archdeacon.'

I bet you would, thought A.D. He continued: 'Yes and I'm sure that the Bishop will eventually get around to giving it to you but I don't have his permission to pass it on.'

'It is most important that you understand the detail the Bishop requires from you.'

Amazing the forcefulness in the voice, thought A.D. He said: 'Thank you for being so concerned. Bishop Rob is very clear in his communications ...'

A.D. screwed up his bill by the mouthpiece.

'Oh, dear the line is breaking up, I can hardly hear you.' A.D. dropped his phone, moved it about with his foot a bit, and then bent down and hit the button to end the call.

He sent Jenny a text message:

'Cracked the mystery contact: Check out an Adeniji with Bishop Rob's lot.'

****

A.D. gave it five minutes, exploring the reception, taking the time to study the chandeliers in that area of the hotel, admiring the flowers, chatting briefly to a doorman. He glanced at his watch and thought that was enough time to have waited to see if Adeniji phoned back. Walking back to the Palm Court his phone rang. Bracing himself A.D. answered it: it was Jenny.

'*Jenny*, good, You've just caught me before I go. I think I've solved who the mystery caller was. A self-styled Executive Assistant to Bishop Rob, called Adeniji. Sounds officious, check him out will you and find out where he's appeared from.'

'Will do A.D. I'm just off but will do it when I get to Victoria,' Jenny ended the call.

That was quite enough for one day A.D. decided and mulled over the idea of turning his phone off. It was time now to get back to the team. One more call had come through during the afternoon. He looked at the number. It was she who, of all his daughters was most like himself: Jude. The practical joker who had recently had her thirteenth birthday. He hit the answerphone for her message:

'Dad this is Jude. I'm back from Paris! I thought you might have finished work today but I'll leave you a message instead. I know you're busy but I wondered if you could get that youth bloke, Mike, that you mentioned, to book us all into some sort of camp in July or August. It's not a churchy thing necessarily, but we could go somewhere that's fairly close and it would mean we do get to go away as a sort of youth group. It would be cool. I know you're working on it but it's going on a bit and we're all getting pretty fed up with boring services so please, please, please, *HELP US*. To go to camp, we need a youth leader to take us, and there's got to be a woman as well. I know we haven't got one yet but maybe Mike can help us. You don't want all the youth pushing off, do you, because there's nothing at church. The Baptist church has got a great youth group and everyone will end up leaving and going there, except for me, 'cos I won't be allowed to go, 'cos I never am. I'll be alone with a load of old people and end up becoming a Buddhist or something as a reaction. *I can't stand it.* I'm trying to help you out here so it seems to the congregation you have a supportive family but there's only *so much I can take.*' She had rung off. The answer machine beeped and she was there again.

'Oh, your phone has just beeped and said I've got 15 seconds left. That's very short for messages these days, dad, you need to change that. Anyway, you can google "Campsites" and I'll talk to you later when you get home. Did you like my jokes today? Love you.... I brought you French chocolate...'

It was the "Love you," that did it.

132

All was forgiven. A.D. walked back to the Palm Court and did an about-turn as his phone vibrated. The call was from Jenny as she was trying to make the train home from Victoria.

'A.D. I've got a lot of background noise as I'm already on Victoria. Can you hear me alright?'

'Yes, I can hear you fine but you don't need to shout as the noise is your end.' A.D. said to no avail. Jenny carried on at full volume:

'I've got some information for you on this assistant the Bishop has got. He's from a diocese in Nigeria. I think Bishop Rob is trying to avoid him most of the time but has to give him some stuff to do so he keeps busy. The Bishop's away but has left an itinerary for Adeniji. That's what my contact on the Bishop's staff said. The man doesn't seem to be following it though and is a little bit of a loose cannon. He's turned up at various departments at Church House and is back tomorrow apparently. I guess you'll end up handling things.'

'Who's your contact, Jenny?'

'Just a contact,' Jenny said evasively. A.D. had never managed to crack this. She moved on:

'I gather there's a bit of a risk with him because he's inclined to make decisions and then communicate them as being the Bishop's. You can imagine what could happen, especially if he starts giving interviews to the press,' Jenny said.

'What a nightmare, especially if people start communicating with him instead of Rob and he enjoys the publicity,' A.D. said.

There was an exasperated noise from Jenny.

"Hang on I'm at the barrier and can't hear you very well. I'll call you back in a minute,' she said, before her line went dead.

AD continued looking round the hotel hall that he had wandered into while speaking to Jenny. There were perfect marble pillars, and gorgeous displays of roses on stands. He fingered a petal to make sure they were real. And was surprised that they were. He smiled as he could almost hear the Finance Director he was married to comment about the hotel's flower bill and the effect on the profit margin. That was the trouble with Accountants, he thought, they interfered with the aesthetic. A.D. thought of all the restaurants he had left where double the number of tables had been crammed in after number crunchers had had their way. He looked up at the chandeliers again and imagined getting those down to clean them, then peered through the wrought iron doors that divided the afternoon tea area from the hall and gave a wave to the group so that they realised he had not forgotten them. Mike was still tucking in much to A.D's surprise but that was fine. His phone went again and Jenny was back.

'A.D. it's me, I'm on the train now so I can talk better.'

'Ah, Jenny does your contact know how Rob has come to have Adeniji?'

'Some Diocesan thing the Bishop went on in Nigeria.'

'Right Jenny, thanks for that. I shall do my best to handle him without upsetting anyone.' She laughed and A.D. smiled at the trill of the noise. Her laugh was so infectious.

'Politics!' Jenny said. After a station announcement at Clapham Jenny said: 'Goodnight AD, have a good evening, and I'll call you around nine-thirty tomorrow, when you're on the train. I've sent you a text with the ticket collection reference. I'll touch base with Chris tomorrow?'

'Yes, good,' said A.D. ringing off. To himself he added: 'I haven't told him yet.'

****

Eight

Ellie called the waiter over and he came hotfoot to the side of his most favourite guest that day. She half-turned her head away from the others so that she could speak quietly into his ear.

'I have a conference call to take in about thirty minutes and we are running late leaving. Is there anywhere like a business centre here I could take it confidentially?'

'I'm sure we can help Madam, I'll just go and check what we have available.'

'What are you up to Ellie?' Mike asked as he had finished the last pastry he could manage.

'A.D's taking so long I need to take Joel's call and now can't get home in time, so I've asked if the hotel has a business centre. Otherwise because of the time difference I'll miss it.'

'I guess its Melbourne, of course?' Mike asked. She nodded and he grinned at her.

'Yes. I thought we'd be finished ages ago and I could be back at the flat. I'm realising that the "food" thing is all part of A.D.'s life. Nice, but adds so much more time on to a meeting. At least I'll know next time and can plan in time for these gastronomic experiences.' Ellie realised that the waiter had returned and was indicating for her to follow him. 'Look I'll see you guys at home later. It looks like the hotel has got a room I can use.'

Ellie was shown into a room and slipped behind the desk.

Waiting for the internet to connect she thought that this was the life in the middle of a city. Then her attention was on her screen. There was the city suit, the tan, and her businessman calling from Melbourne: Joel Rivers behind a smile. He said: 'How's it going Els? You're looking gorgeous, where are you?'

Ellie relaxed and 'Aw Joel, such a relief to hear your Aussie tones, darl! The UK is living up to its reputation and soaking up the global precipitation right now. It was lovely earlier but it's just started raining again.'

'I don't recognize the background, that's not your room, where are you, beautiful?'

'I'm in a hotel across the road from the BBC. We're running late and have just finished tea. The Archdeacon went to take some calls, and I've missed getting home in time for you. So, I asked the hotel if they could help me out and they've given me a room. I hope it's free.'

'Sure, in a place like that he's picking up some bill so I think you'll find they're being gracious. Is that the place you've sent me the photos from? The weather's living up to its usual rep there eh? Now I'm acting like a Brit and asking about the weather!' Joel said, laughing.

'Not a top day as you can probably hear on the windows. How's my fav city, Joel?'

'It's sticky and hot, and I'm working up a good sweat in the lack of air con in this room. But it's raining here you know. Just think of all that travel experience when you notice the drizzle, Els.'

Ellie thought that Joel's grin was so good to see.

'It's great to see you but I always get that ache that I can't hold you. Talking like this satisfies a couple of senses but not all. It's only been a week since we were together but it feels like longer,' Ellie said.

Joel blew her a kiss. He said: 'Not long now. I'm pretty good and about to buy in to a big bit of froth on the top of the glass and swap leave dates with Jez so, I can make that trip over. If he agrees I'll be there next week. I can work from the office in Canary Wharf for a couple of weeks, take a bit of time off at the start of the trip, and then a week off at the end for our trip to Spain. I may be heading off across the world in search of my lady and adventure. San Miguel here we come!'

'That's soo exciting Joel. I'm made up now – I feel like I can knock those hours of marking on the head later. I'll book the holiday for Spain then?' Ellie asked.

'Any chance of you booking an extra day off Els, for when I land in the big smoke and you can show me your soggy London?' asked Joel.

'Aw, yes, I've got a church retreat to help with this week so I've got next Monday and Tuesday off anyway,' explained Ellie. 'It's so exciting that you'll be here in a week's time. I'd better check I can still take it now, as A.D. has walked all over my schedule. There's just a chance I'll be working on a religious TV programme that goes out.'

'Why would you do that?' Joel asked, his eyes going wide.

'It's about getting the ratings up for the BBC religious programming as far as media are concerned. But, watch this space darl, this one is gonna make some changes with how the church is portrayed in the media,' Ellie said.

'Woah, that sounds a job, but you're the woman to do it Els,' Joel said.

'I'll tell you more tomorrow, I need to switch that side of my brain off now, it was a hard meeting and I'm not sure A.D. can control them. Oh, you know Chris I share with?' Ellie said.

'Sure.'

'A.D. got his mate up from Croyde, his name's Storm, it's a nickname not his real name, but it's a surfer thing here that they try and sound less British, and it sounds like we may all be in Devon to do some filming. If it's still going on when you get here Storm has invited us to Croyde, so we can hit the chilly waves.'

'Sweet, definitely but where is it?' Joel asked.

'It's a village in North Devon, Joel. They call it the West Country here. There's a couple of swanky hotels there, but remember the weather's not exactly Byron Bay. Neither's the surf, but we can warm up in Spain. I was thinking about that West Country link with my family and wondering, if we went, if you were up for me trying to link up with any relatives if I can find them?' Ellie asked.

'Sure. I'll pack my thermal wet suit and my thongs.' Joel stifled a yawn. 'Look it's one a.m. here and I think I'd better get home for some sleep.'

'Joel, thongs here are underwear. You need to call them flip flops or people will think you're strange. Where are you tomorrow, or today I mean?' Ellie asked.

'Reviewing a company that owns nearly forty restaurants and bars, and there's a hotel as well. The guy's got a real work ethic. Not exactly the stereotype of an Aussie there in the UK, I guess,' Joel said.

'I don't think that's true anymore. Well looking like, you do tonight darl, neither are you.' Ellie said.

Joel laughed. 'I'll break them in gradually over there, and bring my hat with the bobbing corks. I won't look like this when I get off the plane after a twenty-two-hour flight. You alright if I set up some meetings in the City while I'm there? I can add on the time which means we're together longer if I do.'

'So, you'll be my bit of rough eh? We'll have to work out where you stay while you're in London. Chris's flat is a bit full,' Ellie said.

'Look, don't worry on that score about accommodation, I can work it out with the office for when we're in London,' said Joel. 'The rest of the time it sounds like we'll be either in Devon or Spain so, no probs. Love and kisses Els. Speak tomorrow as usual?'

****

The team had dispersed by six o'clock and Chris and A.D. were on their way to a medieval world from the fourteenth century.

The tube was too crowded to hope for a conversation on the way. Chris was relieved that A.D. had changed out of his black coat and donned a jacket before they left for the Tube. Being of the persuasion that believed his dog collar would mean someone could approach him if they needed help, A.D. left his visible. At Lambeth Palace the two men went through the gate in Morton's Tower and A.D. led him through the Guard and gave Chris a quick walk past the portraits of the Archbishops from 1602 to 1783.

'Of course, it's all so different when the rooms are full of people at a function. You must come to something here to see it,' said A.D. enthusiastically. 'There's a reception here soon. Eve will be with us and I'm sure she'd prefer a chat with you than her boring old parents.'

Chris's eyes had gone wide but A.D. carried on: 'It always strikes me as quite odd standing under all these old pictures, making small talk, and eating prawns on a stick.'

'It would be nice to see it in use,' Chris said, taking in the room. He frowned and said: 'It would be good to spend time with Eve.'

A.D. turned away to move to the door, his face a picture at the response. He said: 'Let me walk you through to the library quickly and then I'll show you the flat. We are later than we'd all wanted to be but it's a good opportunity to show you something as you've not been before. At least we're on the south side of the river now so the traffic home for us won't be too bad. You'll miss the worst of rush hour.'

While A.D. and Chris had travelled from Oxford Circus, it was too crowded to hope for anything like confidentiality if they had a discussion. Their conversation on the tube had been mainly about Colyton in East Devon and his parent's home. A.D. thought it was time now as they walked into the library and looked at the collection, to do a basic debrief of the BBC meeting.

'What did you think went well this afternoon?' asked A.D.

'Well, frankly, I thought at the end you and Mike were on top of it. Until then it was going anywhere. A bit of a nightmare,' Chris said.

'Interesting you thought that. I did too. I must admit Mike's question got that Editor engaging with us. Amazing the tech and digital side of things. I didn't realise how flexible it all was.'

'No, I didn't fully either. I suppose my view of the BBC is that it's reach was smaller. If we can do what you hope it will make it real for people and I suppose it will show them we are flesh and blood and not just people in black coats and dog collars. There's a good connection through Ravi's work potentially too, and Ellie's.'

'What did you least enjoy Chris?' asked A.D.

Chris remembered his debriefings in aid work and smiled at A.D. He said: 'I like your style A.D. this reminds me of overseas' debriefing. I think it was all those ridiculous references to Storm getting his kit off and getting me into the gym. I thought Ellie was going to blow a gasket.

She was right to challenge it because the objective for us is about worship after all. I know she worried you but it's because you don't really know her yet. She gets a lot of flack, being a woman in ministry, and a good-looking woman as well. People are inclined to write her off. I think that's one reason why she pushed to get the Ph.D.'

By now they were at the side of the red brick Tudor gatehouse called Morton's Tower by a smaller building that had been converted into several flats. These were restricted access and some were commercially let. A.D. pulled out his key and explained, 'I'll just open up and then it's up to the first floor.'

They climbed the stairs and A.D. let them both into a small hall which had three doors off it. One opened into a lounge that doubled as a dining area as well. At one end, there was a door into a galley kitchen and from this Louise popped her head round the door to greet Chris and her husband. She gave a wave as she was in the middle of packing the milk and a few other items in the fridge, which were likely to go off before they were back there. But sitting in an arm chair facing him with eyes he could drown in, was Eve.

'Eve's here!' said A.D. sounding surprised. He turned to Chris as if he was giving him a Christmas present. Eve gave her father a look as he bent to give her a peck on the cheek. He said: 'Hello, darling, been here long?'

'Is your memory alright, dad?' asked Eve.

A.D. laughed and Chris looked confused. A.D walked into the kitchen and Chris heard him say; 'I'll give mum a hand in the kitchen.'

'Do you get to stay?' asked Chris.

'Sometimes,' said Eve. 'The put-up bed isn't too good actually. I came over to get a lift home. How did the afternoon go with the BBC?'

'It was a challenging meeting. Hanging on to what the BBC team were up to was out of all expectation for me. but A.D. no doubt will fill you in. Great day on the food front, though. Ever been to the Palm Court for tea?' asked Chris.

'No, it sounds very nice from dad's description though,' said Eve. 'I should probably move and get some things down to the car.'

'Do you want a hand?' asked Chris, desperate for something to do instead of standing like a sunflower with his head following the sun, which was Eve.

'That would be great. Mum and dad's overnight bags are ready. They leave most of the stuff here but last night was a special do so all that clobber has to go home. It's just through here.'

A.D. had hovered in the doorway of the kitchen glancing back, delighted at the natural exchange. Eve moved to the hall and Chris took a deep breath. A.D called to Chris: 'It's a one bedroom flat but we've devised a crafty technique with a screen here to create a guest area with a sofa bed so the girls occasionally stay if one of them needs to.'

'So, the other two doors off the hall were your bedroom and …?' Chris asked.

'Bathroom,' said Louise, coming into the room. 'That's the fridge done. Good to see you again, Chris. How's my husband's long-suffering assistant?'

'Glad today's over actually.' Chris said, and thought how like her mother Eve was.

'Sounds like you've had a bit of a day all of you. You must be shattered and I guess you'd rather be home by now instead of having a guided tour around the old Palace. Can we get you some tea?'

'I'm alright, thanks Louise. It's nice to come into something cosy, like this. I've had more than enough food and drink today. A.D. has really looked after us well. And I'm meeting Storm at Waterloo later to have another night out in the Cut. He's been doing the tourist thing all day despite everything else. It's some years since he was in London.'

'Storm, that's a Downing isn't it?' asked Louise.

'Yeah, that's right,' said Chris.

'His father's not called Paul, by any chance, is he?' asked Louise.

'Yes, he is.' Chris looked interested and then the light dawned. He said: 'Of course, he's a finance director too. I guess you've come across him in the city.'

'Yes, I've run across him a few times in meetings in the last few years,' said Louise.

A.D. looked thoughtful, but dismissed it. He said: 'Yes I must call Storm as I'm going back with him tomorrow.'

'*What?*' Chris said, forgetting himself, his main thought being for his friend. Regaining control, he added: 'I mean, why?'

A.D. shrugged as if his decision was the most natural thing in the world. He said: 'Get to know him and see the sort of work Storm does in the next twenty-four hours. We've got about fifteen minutes haven't we Louise? Just enough time for Eve to show Chris that tree in the grounds after they've carried down the bags. It's been here for ever. Funny to think of all the changes at Lambeth since it was a sapling. Ask Eve to show you that old fig tree in the garden on your way back up. When it was planted the Archbishop of Canterbury would have been catholic.'

****

There was one more call to make and A.D. would wait until he was home to do so. Their journey was slower than Louise would have liked after a long day but A.D. was more interested at this point in knowing how Eve had got on with Chris. He asked: 'Did you have a nice time with Chris in the garden?'

Eve looked thoughtful, but before she could answer her mother cut in: 'Really Mark, you belong in a Jane Austen novel.'

Eve said: 'Yes, thanks,' and she continued staring out of the side window.'

A.D. glanced at his daughter in the rear-view mirror. He tried to think of an open question and asked: 'Whereabouts did you walk?'

146

'I just took him to see the old tree as you suggested and a few rose beds. He's probably the only guy I know who can make a pass without realising he's doing it.'

And that was all she said, taking pleasure in watching her father's eyes go wide in the rear-view mirror.'

Louise laughed: 'Touché, Eve,' she said.

****

Although it was a clear evening as they had left Lambeth it was already chilling down in the way that late May could do by the evening. The sky was rosy as they entered Purley, which augured well for tomorrow, and Louise felt the chill wrap itself around her as they emptied the car on the drive, with their two Spaniels dancing around them. A.D. was already in the house reaching for his phone. The call went through to answer machine.

'Mike, it's A.D. I'm sorry not to get you but I'm leaving a message about the accommodation issue for you. Before I do I want to say again thank-you for your input. You really made a difference to the whole meeting. The thing is, Louise and I have a bit of a concern about the way Youth Workers can get treated generally with the accommodation as they're not clergy. Look.... to cut it short, as I'm not sure how much space your phone has for a message...we have a flat above a garage which the previous owners called a granny flat. It's a bit more than that actually as it's a 3-car garage. It's one bedroom, which is en-suite, and a separate loo, a kitchen/lounge type arrangement....but a nice sized room. Anyway, it's yours under a lodger type of arrangement.... I think about £90 or something a week.... Louise says we wouldn't pay tax on it for that under the rent a room scheme. What I'm saying is we don't need to make money out of it. Anyway, have a think about it and you can have a look over it on Sunday when you and Chris come to do the service. No pressure from our side.' A.D. finished the call as Louise set her case down and she smiled at him.

****

By the time A.D. had changed into a pair of jeans and checked his bag for work for the following day Mike had called back: 'A.D. it's Mike here. I only just found your message as I've had a group tonight. What can I say? It's amazing of you and your wife. I'd love to look at it on Sunday but I can't imagine turning it down. I checked with Chris and he says it's unfurnished, but there's an IKEA in Croyden, so he thinks I could probably furnish it within a budget. So, at this point, yes, yes! Amazing offer....and many thanks.... and.... bless you for your kindness. See you Sunday.'

****

Nine

Tomorrow would be a "working at home day" and although Louise had never felt, as F. D. that she could hit the laptop at 7.30 am still in pyjamas, it was good to lose the commute. It was a mind-set that she dressed as if she was about to arrive at the office when she worked at home. The focus was something the family noted. No one A.D. knew remained at a computer screen for hours as Louise did. One of the seven percent of all new executives appointed to FTSE 250 companies in 2011 Louise was an advocate for levelling the playing field, her main skills being strategic vision and detail and A.D. had realised that she could see the message in a set of published accounts within a matter of minutes. A.D. had asked her once at just such a time: 'Is it saying anything to you?'

'Oh yes,' Louise had answered. 'Singing, loud and clear.'

But first the rest of the evening would involve a reunion with Jude back from the school trip to Paris and a short catch up between Charis and Eve. The girls were interested in the day's events and while Charis dished up the concoction which looked decidedly like student food, they were coming up with different strategies A.D. could have used for his time with the BBC. He loved these evenings when they were all together. Such opportunities were becoming rare since Eve had graduated and spent much of her time working in London to earn money towards her gap year in Kenya.

Charis was now into her finals for the B.A. at Oxford Brookes to gain her exemption from the part one of the Royal Institute of British Architects. Assuming all would be well with the outcome of her exams she had applied so that she could become professionally qualified in the UK. A.D. wondered how much longer these meals would happen with all of their three children around the table at the same time.

He listened and chewed without commenting as his three daughters discussed how to play the BBC. Indeed, with his four females at a table it could be quite difficult to get "his six pennath in," as his dad would have described it. However, he waited, "keeping his powder dry," and smiled as he recalled his mother's phrase. A.D. waited, spying his chance for the cacophony to subside.

'I wouldn't have gone along with it in the first place.' Charis commented, with her view on life shaped by clean lines, endlessly dreaming of different ways to build in space.

Jude, the sports fanatic in the house and part of the debating team at school, cut in with: 'It doesn't mean that they are going to go away because you choose not to engage with them, or worse they rubbish you because you didn't engage and then they make stuff up, or even worse than that, they go to someone else and the whole thing takes a nose dive and dies...and it would have been all your fault dad because you didn't try.'

A.D. had lost all the points she had made and knew it was a strategy designed to blitz the listener.

Louise said: 'Jude, don't run each idea together. You'll lose your audience if you're not careful.'

Jude snorted as that was exactly her intention. She partially heard the suggestion but was already on her way into the kitchen.

'Have we finished dinner?' Louise called after her. 'Where are you going? We're still eating.'

A.D. put his knife and fork together in the centre of his plate and decided that his nerves could not take much more of the advice. He zoned out of the conversation and thought of a chess move. But as he glanced back down the table he looked at his two oldest daughters, glad again that they looked like their mother and in no way resembled him in looks.

'Just to change the subject slightly,' he said in a brief pause, 'I'm going to North Devon quite early in the morning to visit the Surfer Church down there. I'll be away a night. Will you both be around over the weekend by any chance?' A.D. asked, looking from Eve to Charis.

'I will. Are you going to try a board dad? Eve giggled at the idea. Before A.D. could answer Charis said:

'I'm back at Brookes on Thursday. I can come back if there's a need, say Saturday evening? Is something happening? You don't usually ask us to be around unless there's a three-line whip on.' Charis put her head on one side, looking at her father, wondering what he was up to. Instead he focused on what she was doing on her weekend. He asked: 'What have you got planned?'

'It's a birthday weekend as my flatmate's 21st is on Tuesday, so we were having a party in the afternoon, down at Christchurch Meadow,' said Charis.

A.D. looked at his daughter. 'Very nice,' he said. Yes, so coming back here Saturday evening is convenient?'

'Yes, I can do, I just wondered what the big deal is to have to be here Saturday evening?' Charis asked, determined not to let her dad get away without an explanation.

'It's more for Sunday. I've got a couple of the team for the BBC coming out. Chris, you know, but there's likely to be Mike the youth worker to do a slot for Jude and her posse at church. How was that system going that you were testing?'

'Fine,' said Charis. 'You're being evasive which means you're up to something. I can now do anything with an extension with that system. I can show you the model. What are you up to dad?'

'Oh, Mum and I are thinking of letting the granny flat as lodgings to Mike. He lost his home as it was in his Gran's name and she didn't get around to trying to assign it to him. The diocese doesn't usually house youth workers so he's effectively homeless. My assistant Chris, who you know, is letting him have a bed. Just wanted everyone to meet him on Sunday over lunch to make sure you think he's OK before we go ahead.' A.D. looked at Charis innocently.

'I'd suspect you're up to the eligible men routine, if it wasn't a youth worker. It's not that again is it?' Charis sat back in her chair and moved the butter that was left on her plate around.

She gave her father a considered look. A.D. looked back and there was a pause while he waited to see how she would deal with him. He enjoyed the mind battles especially when one of the girls beat him. He waited.

'Yes, sure I can be here.' Charis said, after due consideration.

'And can you make it Eve, as Chris is coming with him?' A.D. asked, avoiding Louise's eyes, which were boring into his head.

'Is he definitely coming? I'll be here anyway so, yes, Dad.' Eve said.

A.D. waited for more but nothing else was forthcoming. He decided not to pursue it, but gave Louise a meaningful look. He got one back but hers meant a warning.

Jude shot back in from the kitchen carrying dessert. It made it onto the mat in the middle of the table with a slide as she clattered into her chair. A.D. looked at the Tarte au Citron and his stomach went into revolt following a day of gastronomic over indulgence. Louise saw his expression and sent Jude back for low fat Greek yoghurt and the honey. Once back at the table having plonked the two-litre yoghurt container down in front of her father she gave him a poke in the ribs. He was grateful the lid was on.

'Low fat food for gutsy!' Jude giggled.

Louise got up, collected the yoghurt and carried it back to the kitchen. She returned with a small glass dish with yoghurt and honey and a sprinkling of blueberries on the top.

She took her seat again and A.D. thought it was perfect. He smiled gratefully and asked Jude about her school trip to Paris. She had returned after lunch on Eurostar and they had all gone straight to school. She had been away from Monday morning and as her father always packed his bag on a Sunday night, had secreted the love gifts of her Swiss Army Knife and a screwdriver, just in case he missed her.

'Did you see the golden lady?' A.D. winked at Louise, waiting to see if Jude could work it out.

'Yes, if you mean the Eiffel Tower. We saw it from Montmartre,' Jude said.

'Ah, so you didn't get to go up it? What a shame,' A.D. said.

'No, we were only there for twenty-four hours really and we had to do museums and stuff. I didn't like Montmartre,' Jude said, as her brow furrowed.

'You probably were rushing through everywhere with a whistle stop tour. No time for sitting at a café with a crêpe and savouring Paris' said A.D. with a faraway look.

'No, we just didn't feel very safe,' Jude said.

'Because of what happened in the city?' A.D. knew the expression, and continued to dig to get at the real reason. 'Too many gilets jaunes around?'

'Oh no, not really, it was a bit deserted round the Sacré-Coeur and there was this large group of men selling bracelets they'd made. They were very pushy and we got scared,'

Louise put her hand on Jude's back and barely perceptibly rubbed it. 'What were they doing?' she asked.

Jude explained: 'Well they got hold of Amy's arm and tied one of the bracelets on it. She didn't ask them to and they kept shouting at us to buy it. There were a lot of them'

'Were the teachers there?' A.D's tone had changed.

'One of them was: Miss Carols. We'd split up you see so some had gone in the church with the rest of the group. So, there was just her. She was good though. Stood right in front of Amy and shouted at the man to take it off. Then Mr Evans came out of the church, and saw it all going on, and came over. He got Amy and the rest of us to walk away but we didn't know what was going to happen, dad, especially after seeing so much stuff on the telly. Miss Carols said it was a scam. But it was scary.'

Louise was looking at A.D. with the expression that she wore when she shut down a division. 'Perhaps I should call the school.' It was said with a tone that meant it was not a question.

A.D. took a spoonful of yoghurt, controlling his face.

'How about if I offer any help the children might need to talk about it as a group with their teachers there so it gets aired. I'll call Miss Carols in the morning. They're used to me going in for assembly every so often aren't they.'

Jude exploded: 'Oh, don't make a fuss. It's bad enough you turning up in a frock,' Jude said referring to what she called her father's medieval dress. She threw her spoon down. 'I wish I hadn't said anything now.'

'It's good you did.' Eve put an arm round her younger sister. 'It's a nasty situation and although you were all OK, it's a shock. Dad is just offering to help give everyone chance to talk about it. The teachers will soon tell him to get lost if they don't want him to do it.'

A.D. was quite determined anyway that he was going to offer help. He could make the call on the train. He said: 'Of course, tourists will stop and talk, because we're all trying to show we aren't discriminating and we're reasonable. Mr Evans did the right thing getting you all to walk away. Difficult though when you're in the moment.'

Charis had gone to the coffee table and picked up the iPad.

'Look, I put in the search "Begging in Paris." There's a video on you-tube someone has done of the bracelet scam on the steps of the Sacré-Coeur. It says that groups of four to five men block any access point to the steps and stop female tourists, tying a bracelet onto the wrist, or round a finger. Then they get hostile and demand money. And others come and manhandle the person and take their wallet and their phone if they can. The police chase them away every so often. There're other scams as well. Good grief!' She played the video for them.

Jude said, 'So, it's not just us, and we didn't do anything wrong by standing still and not going quickly. We didn't know what to do.'

'No, you didn't, it wasn't your fault it happened. It would be very quick and you would be being polite.' Eve gave her a hug and a kiss.

'Perhaps if I promise not to wear a "frock," as you called it. I could tell your teacher about the you-tube?' A.D. asked, waiting to see how the suggestion went down with Jude.

'Yes dad, great idea. I'll tell everyone in the morning that we did some research and found it happens to others and we think it would help everyone to see what's on You-tube. You don't think it's fake news, do you? I'm really hungry is there any more pud?' Jude had suddenly found her appetite.

Charis picked up Jude's plate and cut her another slice of the Tarte Citron. A.D. changed the subject.

'Jude, that youth worker, you mentioned in your message on my phone called Mike, is coming on Sunday. I was just telling the others about an idea mum and I had about him living in the granny flat and then he could help a bit more, perhaps. Your friends met him yesterday I gather. I promise I'll talk to him about the youth group.'

'Oh cool, is he doing something in the service for us?' Jude asked.

'Yes, he's going to do a slot for you. And Chris will be in the service too. I think your friends met him as well in your secret mission sending them to his flat.' A.D. gave her a look so that she understood he knew she had gone into confidential files to find the Rosary Gardens address. He carried on as she dropped her eyes onto her pudding. Tonight, was not the night to labour that one.

'Your friends are going into the skateboard church on Friday night this week.... Because you've been away you won't know yet. You can go as well if you like. We just have to sign a form. Louise why are you looking at me like that?' A.D. had caught sight of the grimace Louise had made at him with the mention of skateboarding. He said: 'Mike asks they just have a helmet that fits, he can supply the rest.' A.D. waited,

All eyes were on their mother who controlled her expression and gave her set smile.

****

'Shall we risk outside for coffee?' A.D. asked Louise as the three girls had set up a film to watch together. He got up to look at the sky and put the outside light on as the dusk was settling in, while the rest of the family dispersed.

'Yes, but I'll need a fleece,' said Louise. 'It's in the hall cupboard. Do you want one as well?'

'Probably, it's still got that late Spring chill,' said A.D.

Louise made decaf for A.D. more to give him a or the taste of coffee than anything else and they went out to the patio. Evenings in early summer were special to them both as they tended to get time alone. In the winter when the family were all home they would pack into the lounge. An early summer evening would often find A.D. and Louise reading outside, well wrapped up as the air cooled. Tonight, they were chewing over the conversations at dinner.

'You got off lightly without making that announcement in front of Jude,' Louise said.

'Which one?' A.D. looked at her, trying to remember.

'That you're going to North Devon tomorrow. Meeting a surfer, can you imagine the howl there would have been about coming with you from her?' Louise said. 'There will be a right furore when she finds out tomorrow where you've gone. I suppose you're going to tell her tonight?'

A.D pulled a face and said: 'Not sure.' He added: 'I'm still waiting for her to bring up the issue of the youth group going on a camp. I had a long, pleading message about them going locally for a night. I've got to speak to Mike. What she's suggested is possible but we need reinforcements to go with Mike. Safeguarding stuff will have to be done as well now. I think they need to go to a proper, organized, youth event. I need women.'

Louise raised her eyebrows but A.D. ploughed on with his thoughts.

'At present that probably means linking up with another group,' he said. 'Oh, and Mike sounds quite keen about the flat. Was even talking of IKEA and furniture so I thought that was encouraging.'

'He needs to come and have a look at it first and see what he's going to encounter on the drive every day.' Louise poured the peppermint tea for herself.

'What's the matter with the drive?' asked A.D.

'Nothing,' Louise laughed. 'I mean what will be on it standing outside to ambush him. Young Jude and her cohort of friends hanging out round the garage. We'll have to have some rules with her if he moves in, so she leaves the man alone.'

'Well, maybe he could have occasional meals with us. He's a nice lad and I thought Charis and he might hit it off.'

'Yes, I had worked that one out. Mark, really, you are dreadful. That's why you want her back here, of course. Charis isn't a fool, she's worked it out too. The girls will find their own partners, you know,' Louise said.

'Doesn't hurt to put a few good men their way.' A.D. said sheepishly.

'Good men in the sense of their faith?' Louise asked.

'Well, yes, what else? But he's a solid lad anyway. Some of those architecture students she's been knocking around with worry me a good deal more,' said A.D. poking the sugar.

'You don't need sugar,' said Louise removing it from his grasp. 'Your system's getting hooked on sweet stuff. So, you're lining up penniless curates and youth workers for our girls, are you?' persisted Louise.

'It didn't seem to matter to us, Louise.' A.D said.

'No, and it didn't, and it hasn't, but that's because of the salary I have,' Louise sighed. 'Young love and all that – I see things a little differently now. Charis will be all right if she qualifies but Eve? She's probably heading for a service-based job in overseas aid work if that training contract with Kimper Mann doesn't come through. She still hasn't heard from the firm. Of course, she'll be alright but can't you keep your eyes open for investment bankers, or stock brokers at church. Their future just concerns me.'

A.D. leaned forward and put his cup down on the table in front of them. He had turned and looked at her. Louise slipped her hand into the crook of his arm. He took it in his left hand and encircled her shoulders with his other arm. She leant her head on his shoulder.

She relaxed with the contact. 'It's alright, I just get a bit worried about the future for them. But we'll be in a position to help them probably if it's needed.'

A.D. kissed the top of Louise's head. 'I haven't heard you talk like this before,' he said, concerned.

'It's harder for that generation than it was for us, Mark,' said Louise. 'After years of austerity its tough finding a career at all. There are so many well qualified young people who can only get temporary contracts. Everything could get harder after the talks with the E.U.'

'Keep talking to me when you get bothered won't you? I don't want to sound like I'm brushing it off but we can and should be praying things through.' Then, remembering the prayer room, A.D. suddenly moved and Louise sat up. 'Oh, and talking of prayer, you have no idea how long people at the office are spending in the prayer room in the middle of the working day. There's bean bags and throws in there as well for comfort! It's turning into another version of the fag break. You'd have a fit about productivity!'

Louise laughed at his explosion seeing the similarity between him and their youngest daughter. 'What was it you were going to talk to Jude about ...I thought you said something about jokes on the phone with a potential consequence?'

'Yes, I was going to talk to her, but then I found a message from her and the last thing she said in it was: "love you," so I think I'll just have to take it that this is a game she's playing with her dad, which I hope won't get me arrested for terrorism. I'd better go and pack an overnight bag and check my briefcase for hatchets and hammers.'

****

An hour after he had left Lambeth, Chris had met up with Storm and the two were walking up from Waterloo station to the Cut while Chris googled where to eat.

'What sort of food do you fancy?' Chris asked. 'I'd quite like something different from last night's meal, but given the amount of grub we've packed away today I probably shouldn't eat until breakfast.'

'Nah, you'll have burned that off with the stress of the day. Best thing for us mate is a good dinner.' Storm clapped Chris on the back as they turned into the Blackfriars Road.

'What's that one? Polish?' Storm passed his mobile to Chris so he could have a look at the suggested restaurants. 'Let's give it a go, I've never tried Polish. What's the write up like?'

'Really good.' Chris showed him the reviews. 'Its Eastern European food not just one area. I'm up for trying that.'

Service in the restaurant was unhurried, but efficient and they had hit the end of the pre-theatre time so the restaurant started to empty. A waiter brought them a mix of breads while they chose from a main course from the menu. They tried Pogacha from the Balkans, which was beautifully soft, and a Russian Potato bread which was also delicious. The Polish Rye bread was a lighter texture than the rye breads they had had elsewhere as the rye flour had been mixed with the same proportion of white flour. Chris turned the subject to Storm going back in the morning. As Storm had not mentioned it, Chris brought up A.D's intention to go back to North Devon with him.

'Oh yes, don't worry, I know about it. I had a message from A.D. and then a call from Gareth who was having a panic attack, to say that A.D. was coming down for a couple of days, going back on Thursday or Friday, but seeing as much as he could in that time. Then I picked up a message on my phone that he was booking First-class for us both. Good stuff!' Storm was savouring the breads, as he explained.

Chris looked surprised at his friend's casual acceptance of A.D's decisions. He said: 'It doesn't bother you that he's just decided to come down, and goes ahead and arranges it?'

'Well, it will be fine,' said Storm, 'and when you think about it, it makes sense for him to spend some time with me and see what we do. It goes both ways you know, we have to get to know the old cove as well, especially if we're going to be part of this programming. I'll wind him up a bit, see how he copes with a surfer. I sense he's stereotyped me already.'

'You mean like you have with the "old cove"? He's no fool Storm,' Chris said as a warning.

Storm gave Chris a rueful smile. 'I guessed that. But we'll have some fun in the morning. How was Lambeth by the way?'

Chris told him about his time with Eve in the garden at Lambeth Palace.

'She told me about her gap year that's coming up. Her enthusiasm about it was really infectious and we chatted about Africa. She asked for advice and I told her some funny stories about my time in Kenya, which is where she's going to be. Actually, in Nairobi, like I was with Uncle Colin. We ended up laughing and it felt so easy and natural with her.' Chris stopped and stared at the table embarrassed about opening up.

Storm waited and then flicked some bread at him. 'Yeah, then what?'

'I told her I thought she was wonderful and I'd be thinking of her all the time in the areas I knew. Now I feel a fool,' Chris dried up again.

'*You* actually said that? I'm impressed.' Storm sat back on his chair and gave Chris a thoughtful look.

'What do you think of the food?' Chris asked, trying to change the subject.

'Bread's great but I'm not playing Chris.' Storm said.

'What do you mean?'

'You're trying to change the subject. How was Eve after you said that?'

Chris went quiet and stared at his plate. Storm waited, and looked around the restaurant. Then, turning back to Chris, he asked, 'How were *you* after you said it?'

'Don't know. I'm so embarrassed now.'

'Just chill my friend, said Storm. 'Probably should have followed it with a kiss but no worries, its progress. Look no need to be embarrassed if you really feel that. She's not going to be offended by someone telling her that she's wonderful.'

'She'll be away so long and there's nothing between us anyway. There'll be other people she'll meet and it will mean nothing,' said Chris, still staring at his plate.

'Nah, I'm not so sure that's the way girls work. You need to follow it up now. Are you likely to see her soon?' Storm asked.

'There's Sunday,' explained Chris. 'Mike and I are helping A.D. with a service at the village church where he lives. We're invited back to lunch. I got a WhatsApp from Mike that A.D's offered him a flat so I'll go look it over with him,'

Storm's eyes went wide. He said: 'Sounds good for Mike. Look Chris, lose Mike while he's looking at the flat and go for a walk with Eve. Mike will understand.'

They were both quiet for a minute, then Chris said in a woeful voice. 'Where's it heading though?'

'Heading? Chris, if it's good there's only one direction it can, my friend, for you,' said Storm. 'But there may be no long term. Just enjoy it and get to know her.' Storm waved, trying to catch a waiter's eye to place a further order.

'Yes, but A.D's her dad.' Chris put his hands down on the table so hard that the glasses rattled.

'Look at me mate,' said Storm. He leant forward and his face was serious. 'You're family as far as I'm concerned. I'll tell you if I think you're making a mistake. You haven't even made a move with her yet and you're having a breakdown about her dad. Do you know the wife?'

'Louise? Yes, she's great. But A.D? ...'

Storm laughed. He said: 'Well if the mum's alright don't worry about him. You'll end up a Bishop with that connection. I thought he was an OK sort of bloke, he looked after us today, didn't he? He paid for us to have tea in a five-star hotel.'

'There's something else Storm. I'm not sure I want to carry on, with the job,' Chris said.

****

Ten

'What?' Storm sat back in his chair, a look of incredulity growing. He searched Chris's face for a minute.

'When you started after Africa you were very clear about a calling. That's not something you imagined. What's behind this?' Storm asked.

'No, it's this particular job. I should never have gone for it. A.D's like a whirlwind at times. His ideas frighten me. It's the way this BBC thing is going as well. It feels out of control and I don't want the raised profile.' Chris crumbled his bread between his fingers onto the plate.

'Are you going to eat some of that?' asked Storm.

Chris pushed the basket of bread across the table and Storm selected a roll. He said with his mouth full: 'Well, we take control man and anyway, that's no reason to withdraw from something you felt very clear about. Can't you give A.D. notice?' Storm asked.

'It doesn't work like that Storm,' said Chris.

'And the girl, Eve, she sounds worth the trouble. Look, why don't you take some time off, or go home. Let's hit the waves like we used to and stop thinking for a while Chris.'

Chris had put his head in his hands, his elbows on the table. His hair was standing up on end as a result, the product in it stiffening it into an electric shock look.

The waiter, who had appeared at the side of the table, nodded sagely at Storm's advice and smiled sympathetically at Chris. He said: 'Woman trouble, isn't it? You might want to check a mirror sir, it's not a good look. Are we ready to order guys?' Chris scraped his chair back and headed for the gents.

'Give us five minutes,' Storm said to the waiter and leant back so his chair was precariously balanced on the two back legs. He looked at the dishes on other tables and inhaled the food carried past him. In a few minutes Chris was back, his hair style destroyed for the night. His attempt at repair had not worked for him. Storm sat on the amusement he felt at the way Chris looked and instead focused on the menu.

The ordering was eventually done, and Storm smiled in an attempt to be encouraging. He said: 'Look I'm going to be with the guy all day tomorrow. I'll tell you if I think you should head for the hills. But this girl, what's she like? Got a photo?'

****

At Paddington Station, A.D. and Storm approached the platform for the 7.30am train to Bristol. A.D. looked at his watch, then up at the board, then at his watch again, and said to Storm: 'Espresso, dear boy? We have time! Look there's a place, the Emperor's Choice!'

A.D. waved his arm and moved vigorously towards the coffee shop. Storm rubbed his eyes, being seriously short of sleep since he had arrived in London two days before. He followed, trying to work out how anyone could drink anything more than green tea at this time of the day.

'Right, A.D.' Storm called after him. A lady who had been weighing up the vicar and the surfer had stared just a little too long for Storm to ignore her. He grinned and said: 'Vicar's got an addiction.'

Storm nudged up his back pack. Unfortunately, as far as Chris had been concerned, Storm had brought the rainmaker with him. He had originally brought it to London to get a second opinion about using it in services as an instrument. Chris had told him to pick his congregations. With that in mind Storm had seen the funny side of introducing it into the journey he and A.D. were to make.

Perched on the high-level stools in the coffee shop, A.D. had already ordered for himself. Storm sat with his backpack still on and the rainmaker spread out across the coffee bar. A.D. sipped his Espresso and Storm talked to the Barista.

'Green tea, ... cheers bud,' Storm said.

A.D. thought he should start trying to understand Storm. In the back of his mind was the fact that he was, after all, Paul Downing's son. Bombastic, ambitious, highly intellectual Paul, good looking to boot, no faith and a hard businessman by all accounts. However, he should give the lad a chance. A.D. was at his smoothest: 'Tell me where the rainmaker fits in?' he asked.

Storm suddenly seemed to wake up and gave himself a shake with mock excitement.

'Oh man, this rain conjuring pole is transforming worship. Ah, yeah, yeah, as well as being constructed with natural materials such as being stacked with rice and lentils, ancient Mayans are said to have used it to brown-nose their weather god, it makes a bomb of a noise!'

A.D. kept his face deadpan. He asked: Tell me. In terms of our God of all Creation what's it for?'

Storm's expression remained enthusiastic knowing that A.D. thought he was dodgy.

'OK, man, yeah we don't manipulate God for anything, right? I mean is God really God if we can twist his arm!' He took a sip of his green tea and looked briefly thoughtful.' Storm continued: 'Nah, this beaut of an instrument, it's metaphorical. It acts as a reminder that God rains down his goodness.' He tilted his head to the side and stared into space. 'Imagine, a whole room of these sticks ...' Storm picked it up and gave a demonstration. Heads turned and he smiled back at his fellow travelers. He confirmed to them that they were right to be wary of religious cranks and vicars generally.

A.D. ran a hand across his forehead. Storm continued to move the rain stick, hands in front of him, waving it from side to side. He looked round the room and said to everyone, 'The booming loudness of God's goodness, in rice and lentils!' Storm pulled a wide grin at A.D. still nodding but A.D's face remained dead pan.

'Right, right dear boy, I can't get beyond a guitar at the moment but I will think about it as an instrument for the worship group. Leave it at that for now.' A.D looked at his watch, and suggested: 'Right, as its 7.15, we'd better hot foot it for the 7.30, platform 3, first class carriage J!'

A.D. picked up his Fossil bag and Storm the Rainmaker, giving it a little shake with an eager expression at A.D. A well-meaning city type passed him a card as Storm walked past and said: 'Try an Alpha course.'

Storm laughed despite himself. He slapped the man on the shoulder, winked and said: 'Nice one.'

A.D. led the way to platform three and Storm let the "old cove" go ahead, following him two steps behind. He thought A.D. obviously liked to think he was in charge. The rainmaker's rice and lentils made a constant noise and Storm grinned to himself that just maybe, maybe, he had got A.D. rattled.

In their carriage, they settled into their seats. A.D. went to a small fridge and got out two bottles of still mineral water for them. Storm adjusted his seat for his long legs and stretched them out into the aisle so that he would not cramp A.D. Then he made the fatal mistake as he found his copy of the Economist on his iPad. A small smile played around A.D's lips: Gotcha, he thought. A.D. started reading a hard copy of the Times. Storm from time to time played some tune with his hands drumming the table. It was very un-first class behaviour. A couple approached and looked at their tickets and the seat numbers above where A.D. and Storm were sitting. The woman leant forward and smiled at A.D. He seemed the safer one, being in a dog collar, whereas the young man opposite him looked a little dubious.

'Is it me or are you both sitting in our seats?' she asked, with a smile.

Storm answered: 'Definitely you, love.'

A.D. raised his eyebrows to her, opening his eyes wide. Storm continued to play the table. A.D said 'Let's have a look.'

He examined his tickets and looked at Storm's. 'No,' he said, 'it seems we are in the right seats, J24, J26.'

The man laughed and waved his own tickets in A.D's face.

'What a cock-up, our tickets also say, J24, J26. Anyone would think there's two sets!'

The woman started to look around and peered out of the window. 'Are we on the right train, do you think?' she asked her husband.

The man chuckled, "I made quite sure dear, it is the 7.35 am cross-country to Bristol, isn't it?'

A.D. smiled with relief. "Ah! There you have it. This is the fast 7.30am to Exeter. You've got a matter of minutes to get off.

Storm was up and helping get the bags off the train.

Gotcha again, thought A.D.

****

Wednesday morning weather did not live up to the promise of the night before. How it was in Purley, in comparison to South Kensington, the travellers heading for the West Country would discuss later. Chris had seen Storm off at Gloucester Road Tube for Paddington very early and he was in A.D's office for eight o'clock. There was no Laurie today on the front desk when he arrived and Jenny would not arrive until nine thirty. Chris logged into the diary for A.D. as he was covering for him. There were the usual calls around the parish in Purley, to make and one note marked in red with capital letters: "ADENIJI: IGNORE."

Chris decided that Rafe Ackland could make the parish calls. He sent Rafe a text with the numbers and names to call, and a suggestion that he introduce himself that way.

There was also an eleven o'clock appointment in the diary and Jenny had written next to it, "Turn down?" It was a pre-wedding meeting to do with a request for use of a church. The note said to meet in the Caxton Street Hotel. Chris was interested to find it was a Victorian hotel that had originally been built on the site of a fifteenth century chapel and apparently had been used for clandestine meetings by spies in the cold war. He was, however, none the wiser who he was to see. There were no names given, or any background for the couple that Chris was to meet at the hotel. He felt his heart sink as the very fact it was given to A.D. to have the meeting implied it was a difficult one. A.D. had been asked to be the hatchet man on many occasions and Chris was going into it blind without a briefing. He hoped that Jenny was in the know as she would arrive by nine-thirty.

'I'm in no better position than you, Chris,' Jenny said.

By eleven fifteen, Chris left Church House and walked up Broadway towards the Caxton Hotel. A.D. could really pick his meeting places, Chris decided. He would enjoy the

---

173

environment at least and he hoped that the meeting would go well. As he walked into the hotel Chris saw, waiting in the lounge area, a young, smartly dressed, and attractive couple. The tension between them as Chris shook hands was so apparent it could have been cut with a knife. The lady was called Tatiana, and she had a Russian Orthodox background, the man with her was her fiancé, but the information was unclear as to his background. So, this is what I'm "picking up" for A.D, thought Chris, due to his sudden decision to go down to Devon with Storm. Chris was completely fed up and it was not helping his doubts about carrying on. Five minutes in, and the couple were arguing every point. Chris started to zone out as he could not take the stress. He forced himself to concentrate and entered the row about the reception and alcohol.

'My relatives will expect alcohol at a wedding,' Tatiana said and rolled her eyes. Chris stared ahead trying not to get sucked in to taking a side on details, but the comment had pulled him back from his thoughts about his job.

'My parents will be offended if there's alcohol,' the man said. Chris nodded but thought it was time he was told a name at least. He was about to ask when Tatiana glared at her fiancé and said: 'They don't have to drink it.'

'Actually, the reception, isn't why we're here.' Chris intervened. They looked briefly at him and then were off again, this time on fine details of dress for the wedding.

'I want more of a cultural presence in the ceremony,' the man said.

'I'm not wearing anything but a "normal" bride's dress,' Tatiana retorted. 'And I want a wedding on a beach. Just a blessing in a church.'

'Beach is good,' Chris said, hopefully turning to Tatiana's fiancé.

'I want a ceremony in a Mosque as well as a Church,' the man stated. 'We just need someone to officiate.'

'Do you?' Chris opened his eyes wide. 'Wow! Tough one. Is that your background then? It's just I don't have any details for you, not even a name.' Chris waited but nothing was offered. Chris ran his hands over his knees and made a decision. He said: 'Erm, why do you both want to do this? I'm seriously tempted to tell you to forget it, or to start the way you mean to go on with your families as their expectations are only going to get stronger.'

The man stared ahead and ignored Chris. He launched into a put down and told his fiancée she was being "silly."

Chris felt his eyes going wider. However, Tatiana would not be put down. Chris heard the word "silly" several times more, sat with them for another thirty minutes attempting to explain the "love and cherishing" bit but got no-where. There was no give on either side. He wondered how this relationship was ever going to work and decided to bring it to a close. Chris waved at a waiter for the bill.

'This is on me,' Chris said, offering a card. Once the bill was paid he said to the couple: 'Look, frankly, this isn't going anywhere.'

'What?' the man turned his angry eyes on Chris. 'You're

supposed to be helping us.'

Tatiana started to go over again what she wanted. Chris had had enough and got up.

'I can't see why you're bothering trying to find a ceremony in either a church or a mosque. The last hour between you has been like World War Three. Look, it's clear the problems between you are not really about where you hold the wedding. There are fundamental things you need to work out. Have the marriage on your own without a load of drunken relatives, or overly critical ones, push off on a great honeymoon, and forget dresses, or trying to placate them all. You can't even agree to meet me at the church so this isn't working is it? Never mind working out what his lot or her lot are going to be happy with. Try and look at why you both want to be together as a beginning. I don't even see you've got a viable relationship to get married frankly, and that is me putting my neck on the line as you will no doubt think it's none of my business. I can't recommend to the church there is a ceremony of some sort at this point, having spent an hour listening to how you are with each other. You're people with such different backgrounds but you're not being open, mate, as you won't even tell me your name. Neither of you is meeting the other, working things out without hurting each other. I shouldn't be hearing the word "silly" to this lady either, mate. Now I've got other things to do today and need to get off. So, take care.'

Chris picked up his bag. The waiter had beaten a hasty retreat as the staff had been able to hear the row going on.

'They're destroying your character, now, sir,' said the waiter as he opened the door for Chris.

Chris smiled at him. He said: 'Well, at least they agree on something.'

He thought to himself as he walked down the hotel steps, that no doubt now there would be a complaint. The Rottweiler that was A.D. had been given that job for a reason. Outside he felt a mixture of panic but also the relief started to make him want to laugh. Two extremes starting to alternate as he walked down the road back to Church House. Chris stopped and stared into a shop window and attempted to adjust his hair while he looked at his reflection.

'I think I'm beyond caring. That was ridiculous. But is what I'm doing ridiculous?' he asked his reflection.

Not for the first time in the last few days he found himself wondering what he was doing in the job. Personal faith aside he was doubting he had made the right decision in working for A.D. He needed to think. Storm was right, he needed to get some space, take a few days off and get away from London. He thought about building in a couple of days at home around the visit to Woolacombe next week. He pulled his mobile from his bag and called Jenny. She answered after a few rings.

'Oh Chris, what happened?'

'Pretty awful scenario, Jenny. I feel sorry for them both really. But I had all the wrong reactions with the way the guy was behaving with his woman and he'll probably need counselling after it! Anyway, I said no. But could you do me a favour? Jenny, what are the chances of me taking a few days off next week when we all go down to North Devon with the

BBC thing? I'd like to see mum and dad and get some surfing in with Storm.'

'I'll book it in for you. You're all due to travel down on Wednesday and return Friday but I'll book you off from Thursday evening 'til Tuesday morning, if you like? Do you good.'

'Great. Thanks - what would we do without you?'

'Hire someone else - no one is indispensable Chris.'

'I think they are actually because each one is unique,' said Chris. 'I'll call mum and make sure they're going to be around. Could you check for me nothing else has cropped up in A.D's internal emails since I left,' said Chris, as he walked in to Dean's Yard.

'Of course, hold on Chris, I'll go in now.' Jenny said.

'I'm on my way back Jenny so should be with you in about five minutes.'

****

Eleven

'Mum, its Chris,' he knew it was obvious but he always said it.

"Mum," or Maureen Duncan to the rest of the world, was on her break at the school. She had glanced at her phone before pursuing a gaggle of girls into the toilets to drive them to a lesson. It had rung on while she registered that it was unusual for her son to call her in the middle of a working day. Alarm bells had started to go off in her brain. She said: 'Yes, I know. Nice to hear you but you don't normally ring on a working day. What's up?'

'Just fancy a break and seeing you and Dad,' explained Chris.

A cold hand clutched at Maureen's vitals.

Chris continued: 'We're coming down to Devon as a team on Wednesday night next week to so some work with the BBC. I've booked Friday and Monday off so wondered if I could bowl up on the Friday, probably late?'

'Marvellous, of course. Are you seeing Storm at all?' Maureen asked entering the staff room. She glanced at the clock while juggling her phone as she reached for a mug. Ten minutes, thought Maureen.

'Storm's been with me in London the last couple of days. He's part of the work we'll be doing in Devon. We thought we could hang out a bit, maybe bring a mate who's a youth worker with us, called Mike?'

'I'll get the rooms ready. How are you travelling?'

'It'll be train from Barnstaple,' Chris said.

'Fine, let us know where you're coming into, and times, and we'll meet you. Lovely news - looking forward to it. Look, I need to go Chris, break is ending,' Maureen said. Her waters told her things were not good with her son.

****

By nine minutes past ten the train pulled into Exeter St David's. It was cloudy and there was a smell of impending rain. A.D. pulled his waterproof round him even closer. He was all for hailing a cab but Storm wanted to walk to Exeter Central. They had been sitting for several hours and never usually still for long, Storm's body needed to move. So, hitching up their bags, they walked for the connection at nineteen minutes past eleven for Barnstaple.

A.D. was his usual enthusiastic self and quite ecstatic about the scenery on the Tarka line as they travelled towards Barnstaple. Storm was warming more to the old guy, and his attempts to wind him up were lessening. A.D's irrepressible enthusiasm and thirst for life was infectious. Having become accustomed to the frustratingly slow rail journey of thirty-nine miles from Exeter, Storm enjoyed the journey afresh as he watched A.D. move from one side of the compartment to the other, taking in the views of the valleys of the Yeo and the Taw.

At Barnstaple, ever mindful of comfort, A.D. suggested: 'Let's get a taxi to Croyde.'

'I can call a mate to come and collect us,' said Storm. A.D. had been googling the market town and was keen to see the historic hotel in Boutport St.

'A little "Elevenses," first eh?' A.D. suggested. 'Then a taxi. Your friend has got to get here so it's about the same time to pop into the hotel.'

'Alright,' said Storm, resigning himself to delay. 'I can see you want a bout of unplanned sight-seeing. I'll just have to let my boss, Gareth, know we'll be later than planned. Maybe lunch with him in Croyde?'

'Excellent,' said A.D. seeing another gourmet opportunity.

A.D. was captivated by the Georgian hotel and sniffed his way through the two restaurants and cocktail bar. They settled in the lounge, the rainmaker propped into a corner. Storm's renown in the area started to come home to A.D. as he was recognized by fellow guests having coffee and a surfer behind the bar. One of the waitresses came over to give Storm a hug and they chatted while A.D. took his seat. A.D. was finally seeing the real man. He noted the respect Storm drew from those he knew and again the easy way his travelling companion greeted and related to the staff.

The barman, Stefan, turned to be introduced to A.D. and nudged him. 'You should have seen this man in April at the championships.'

A.D. nodded. 'Yes, I wish I had. Perhaps there's something later in the year?'

'If you're interested, A.D.' said Storm.

Stefan slapped Storm on the shoulder.

'He's good, is he?' A.D. asked.

'The word good is an understatement,' Stefan said. ' If he'd leave that church of his and travel he would be big.'

'I suspect it's a calling,' said A.D. his eyes twinkling. 'Is this something I could do?' A.D. asked Storm.

Storm's head jerked back and he and A.D. looked at each other. The realization that A.D. was quite serious hit Storm.

'Sure, I can take you on a short board later if you really want to give it a try. Maybe at Woolacombe, and as I'm getting the idea that you like to sample the local fare, there's a good hotel I can show you at the back of the beach. We can get some time in.'

'Excellent. Now let's get coffee. And, yes, a little toast I think.' A.D. glanced quickly at the menu. 'Ah, toasted tea cakes. How about one of those instead.'

'Working with you is definitely a foodie experience A.D. Tea cake for me, but no coffee thanks. They know what I like here. Let me choose for you. They have a special you won't get anywhere else.' Storm waved to Stefan, who started to come back across to their table. 'Could you bring the Archdeacon a pot of the dark with the double cream Stefan? I'll have my usual, and two toasted tea cakes with butter. Ta, mate.'

****

'Can you grab, that one, Mike?' Ellie called, as she flung the hold-all out of the boot and exhaled with a guttural power. Mike added the large bag to the four others, which were all at different points of his arms, lean muscles protruding.

'That's the last one, I can manage, Doc, you got it from here?' Mike waited for her to give him a sign she was alright.

Ellie nodded wondering why Mike had started calling her "Doc." Mike stepped onto the skateboard, the bags balanced but he had to concentrate to slowly travel along the un-kempt slope to the hut.

Ellie tipped her baseball cap down, hoping it would cover up the grumpy attitude that she was battling with. Hoody and baseball cap were usually the signs that she was not happy. She picked up the large box of custard creams, the "Jammie Dodgers" and the supermarket basic tea bags, and following him, pushed forward through her mood and entered the hut. Someone had named it: The "Lads' Place."

Oh goody, thought Ellie.

The place was in a shabby state, as if it had the mark of recession on it. However, it was apparently the choice place to book, compared to other venues, for St Mark's to have their reflection and "fellowship break."

It was the choice of Ellie's supervisor and the church had agreed. Ellie thought that it would look better in the bush back home, with sun shining all around it, not to mention the fact that there would be no need to sleep inside as the climate would ensure these four walls were irrelevant. She opened the door and wondered if Mike noticed the state of it.

'Mike, do you think that smell is alright? I can't get my hunch on what it is.'

Mike looked serious as he explained: 'That's the damp, Christian Centre smell, Doc. A common experience. Churches excel at selecting places with it.'

'Never noticed it back home.' Ellie sniffed again.

'Probably because you don't have damp.... or they make a better choice. Or maybe they don't have that philosophy of grot being good for their soul.' Mike grinned at her.

Ellie literally dumped the box on the kitchen hatch counter and started to launch into every room, opening windows. She was a-tuned and perfectly comfortable camping with the most basic amenities, even with only a bush toilet. But, somehow, the mix of the cloudy sky, the wet and cold weather, made this seem worse. Even so, she had put her mind to it that this was just a few nights in her life. She thought that she would not run a retreat like this if the selection was down to her. Why this venue?

But it was not down to her.

The plan was to settle, then muck in, and once her supervisor arrived all she had to do was to run one session on the theology of equality, something she could get her teeth into, and drum into people's minds the centrality of it to the gospel. At least Mike was there now, although he would be back in London for the Friday night skateboard session on the Southbank.

'Mike, you're in room two, and I'm in room five, just down the corridor. Let's get unpacked and then I'm going to run through my talk for ten mins, before Rev. Deidre arrives.'

Walking into her room, she examined the conditions in which she would be a prisoner for the next few nights. Ellie asked herself again why they were there.

'I'm going to need several days off after this. What does it take to run a hoover over the floor? What's the process of cleaning between guests? Is there one?' Ellie said aloud. She realised that she was talking to herself and decided to clam up. There must be no more voicing her questions aloud as to do so with no one else there would reflect desperation. So, instead she pushed out her hands and turned her head, as if she wanted to stop something approaching her: 'the hygiene in this place is not my battle, today!'

But as she caught sight of herself in the mirror on the wall, she did comment aloud.

A large wood spider hung loosely from the ceiling, as if the race from cob-web to cob-web would arouse opposition from any guest. He was biding his time until Ellie turned her back. He clearly had no distaste at his lodgings. Ellie and the spider waited and then he moved and his antics were so in her face that Ellie made the decision that he would have to go.

'Well, you're too big mate for this Aussie to live with, so, you're dead,' Ellie called out.

Having dealt with the wildlife she looked at the shower.

'Toe thongs in the shower tonight or won't bother until I get home.'

She wondered when the toilets had last been cleaned with industrial strength, eco-friendly of course, but definitely a maximum strength stain remover … something she would bug Rev. Deidre about in her de-brief.

'I guess, putting us in here is taking the mick with people's worth,' Ellie said to the girl in the mirror who was not looking too impressed with the experience.

'Ah well, only a few nights, girl.' Ellie's reflection said back.

Mike's head appeared round the door and he said: 'They're supposed to be a friend, you know.'

'Who are?' Ellie asked.

'Spiders,' said Mike.

'Dream on, Mike,' said Ellie. 'Not in Australia. Ever heard of the Red Back on the Bum?'

****

Ellie strolled out having laid her sheets over the mud-stained duvet. She had been drilling into her mind that it was boy-scout mud, as they trailed the duvet near their muddy trainers, instead of another type of brown stain. She'd sniffed it while Mike skateboarded across the hut floor in the long corridor, practicing tricks and oblivious to the looming black clouds that hung threateningly over the unstable hut.

'What will you do, Mike, if the sky explodes, will it screw over your skateboarding workshop?'

'Depends how heavy it is, I'm sure drizzle won't dull the kids' enthusiasm.' Mike grinned at the thought of cancelling.

At that point, screeching tyres from a car heralded the coming of the Reverend Deidre Pullman. She stopped right outside the front entrance and revved the engine a few times just to show the car could do it. Ellie's supervisor while in the UK, and the senior lecturer on the Gnostics, turned off the car engine. Several black puffs from the exhaust slowly followed as the car coughed. Ellie and Mike found themselves spluttering too, as they walked to the driver's door.

As the smoke lifted, the Reverend Deidre stepped out of the car and with a big grin on a mouth full of re-worked teeth, lifted her hands to the sky and proclaimed: 'It all starts here!'

Mike waited for what it was that would start, feeling personally he would need a revelation to overcome the discomfort he had felt when he had tried out his bunk. Ellie walked forward to give her supervisor the hug that Rev. Deidre always expected.

'So, good to see you both. Ready for your nights in the English outback, Eleanor?'

'Ellen, it's not Eleanor.' This was for the sixth time of stating since Ellie's arrival in the UK.

In front of Mike and Ellie, stood a tall and slender lady in her early 70's, with wispy, curly, bobbed hair. She had red bifocals on and a midi-skirt that had seen the best of 1980's florals. Over a white shirt, she wore a tarnished brown leather jacket, which had the odd bit of stitching frayed at the edges. On her feet were brown loafers, with red leather tips. Colour coordination had at least been attempted.

Rev. Deidre's body language was energetic, and Ellie had never seen her sit down for more than ten minutes, as if she had an over-active thyroid. Ellie, unable to help having deep admiration for her supervisor's individuality, showed in her eyes the affection as she watched Rev. Deidre lean into the back door of her car and pull out a tennis racket, which she dropped onto the gravel path. Mike bent to retrieve it for her and Rev Deidre started to giggle at his chivalry.

'I think you've blown a gasket, Rev,' Mike spluttered still affected by the smoke as it continued to lift.

'Cheeky chap,' said Rev. Deidre as she patted her car. 'I've had my service, nothing wrong with this old gal.'

'I meant the car,' Mike said, and he received a bony elbow into his side making him cough with the impact.

Rev. Deidre carried on chuckling while she pulled out an old army hold-all from the back seat and briskly walked into the hut. Dropping the bag and waving the tennis racket in the air she turned back to them and exclaimed with great satisfaction: 'OoooooooOHHHH, we've had some good times here, since 1976.'

Ellie pulled her cap lower and rolled her eyes, accepting that her placement was not to persuade her supervisor to relocate church trips. She would be gone by the next one. Perhaps the church members would give feedback which would prevent them spending another getaway in sub-standard conditions. Mike took the issue up with Rev. Deidre.

'Myself, I think this place has seen better days, Rev.'

'We've all seen better days, my boy,' she replied.

Mike nodded, he couldn't disagree with that. Instead of pursuing it further he decided to quit on the state of the Lads' Place. He said: 'Well I'll go and get ready for the session with the skateboarders. You know I'm off on Sunday morning Doc, as I've got to get to the service at Purley?'

Ellie partially turned away and said sotto voce. 'So, long as you don't leave me before then, Mike. I need you to keep me sane here.'

'I can give you a lift Sunday morning back to the rail head.' Reverend Deidre pulled out a tatty diary. 'I'm leaving at 6am on the dot.'

Mike thought about it too long to appear enthusiastic.

****

In London Ravi looked at his phone with an unknown caller. He really needed to concentrate, and usually let calls go to answer phone when he was working. Most didn't leave a message and were frequently someone trying to sell him something when they did. He decided to ignore it and went back to his calculations.

Ravi's phone rang again ten minutes later. Feeling it was time for a break he left it ringing on the desk and walked to the coffee point. The noise bothered him and he thought he should switch it off. Back at his desk he picked up the phone and turned to its settings about to hit the airplane mode.

Working out how far wages had risen in the south and west of India in relation to the north required focus. The phone rang before he hit the button and, feeling cross with it, he answered sharply: 'Ravi.'

'Hi, it's Steph from the BBC. You sound different today.'

'Oh, hello, Steph. You were at the meeting weren't you. I'm concentrating and the phone's been going and I was about to switch it off. What did you want me for?'

There was a pause. 'I guess you're in the middle of a sermon preparation,' Steph said, patiently.

Unable to control a sense of irritation at being interrupted by the girl from the BBC, but also having a mix of pride in the work he was doing, Ravi felt an irrational need to let her know the level of work he was doing on the paper. She bothered him and the fact that part of him liked the attention also bothered him. It was a strange mix of wanting to be important and yet not to be contacted by her. Steph's patient tone had had an irrational effect. Ravi said: 'Lady, you are being patronising. I am not preparing a sermon. I'm actually involved in calculating the impact of a battery-operated cotton picker on the wage structure in the south and west of India. I didn't feel like answering an unknown number. Now if it's about the BBC, I think you would be better addressing your enquiries to the Archdeacon.'

There was another pause before Steph spoke. 'I thought you were quite charming in the meeting. First impressions in your case are obviously wrong.'

'I'm sorry. Look what is it I can help you with?' Ravi asked.

'I had wondered if we could meet up for coffee and you can tell me about that work you're doing.'

'Why?' Ravi barked out.

'Huh? I can't believe I'm doing this, you're just not interested, are you?' Steph said.

'I mean why are you wanting to meet me? You obviously don't want anything other than a physical relationship and I'm not into playing that game given my job.' Ravi waited for her answer but there was a long pause again. The line had cleared. She had hung up. Irritating as Ravi found the disturbance in the middle of the work, part of him wanted the attention. That fact bothered him as well. Ego, he told himself. His irritation was not really caused by Steph. Ravi threw his phone on to the desk and glowered at it, knowing that the fault was his. A past he was not happy with, which surfaced at times, and linked to it the associations of his conversion and the dishonour his family felt that he had brought them. Conflicted he was angry with himself.

****

Ellie's Skype depended on her driving for half a mile to a truckers' stop with a cafe. The "Lads' Place" was in a black hole and although there was enough internet to check an email (although it took an age to download) there was insufficient speed for a Skype with Joel. The signal was intermittent as well, at times only showing GPRS.

The facilities meant that it would not be private but no one present in the trucker's stop was really interested in her. She had dressed down further and was wearing the baggiest hoodie she possessed in order to hide her shape. Ellie's expectation of trucker stops was not too encouraging.

Ordering a tea as a way of paying a rent for the table, Ellie looked at the time. He was nine hours ahead so Joel would be up at six in the morning and they had booked a regular slot while she was at the centre so they could still see each other on Skype and speak each day. Nine in the evening was clear for her but she had not banked on having to leave the retreat.

Ellie hit Joel's Skype call and plugged in her earphones. There he was, still sleepy in bed and bare chested, with a smile at the sight of her. Ellie drew in a breath.

'Hey my girl, what have you got on your head?'

Ellie pushed the baseball cap back. 'Don't look at me Joel.'

'I thought that was the point of this. Where are you? It looks dodgy. What's that noise in the background?' Joel sat up and peered at the little background he could see on the screen.

'I'm in a truckers' stop - it's the only place I can get a good signal in these hills. The noise is the radio,' Ellie said.

'Are you safe there?' Joel asked, concerned.

'Oh yeah, there's a few blokes around but they're not paying me any attention.'

'No wonder, you look mean and nasty,' Joel screwed up his face.

'Thanks.' Ellie glowered at him from under her cap.

Joel grinned and then yawned as he was still waking up. 'I thought you wanted to have that effect.'

'Yes, I do, but not with you. Could you put a shirt on? It's really difficult looking at you like that,' said Ellie.

Tea arrived, and the lady who brought it over stopped behind Ellie and looked at the screen. She let out a high-pitched squeal, which made Ellie jump and pull out her ear phones. The lady leant over Ellie's shoulder so that she appeared in the Skype. Joel gave a wave and a grin. 'Hello there,' he came through the speaker.

'You're worth sitting here for. Have you got a friend?'

'I could probably find one for you.' Joel grinned and waved at her again.

Ellie turned and smiled at her, noticed the name badge, Paula. 'There's no signal at the place I'm staying in, Paula, you don't mind, do you?'

'No that's alright love, it's made my night. Australian, is he? You're welcome.'

'Born and bred, love,' Joel said, grinning.

'Put a shirt on.' Ellie repeated, under her breath.

Paula carried on leaning over Ellie's shoulder, one hand on her hip, grinning at Joel. She said: 'I haven't seen anything like that working here for years. 'Thinking about it I don't think I've ever seen anything like it.'

Ellie pressed disconnect. 'Whoops,' she said.

'Ah well, too much of a good thing. I'll get back to sloppy and grouchy overt here,' said Paula, nodding towards two truckers.

Ellie re-dialled. This time a shirted Joel was on screen.

'Ellie, can we get a date in the diary for when I arrive so we can go see a specific garden?' Joel asked, stifling a yawn.

'Garden? When did you get interested in gardening?' asked Ellie.

'Oh, it's a geological garden.' Joel dissembled innocence.

'In London? Oh, do you mean the Chelsea flower show? I think that's over now. I guess so, but we'll need tickets. Is it important for work or something?'

'It's certainly an investment opportunity and I'd like your opinion on some specimens.'

'Yes sure. I really don't mind what we do and I know there's so much you'll want to see. I just want to be with you.' Ellie said.

'Same here darl. OK, let's do it nice and early in the visit.' Joel did yawn this time.

'You'll need time for jet lag you know.' Ellie said.

'That's alright, I'll just nod off where ever I am,' said Joel. I'm going to have to get ready for work now love. Same time tomorrow?'

****

Twelve

A.D. was very enthusiastic about getting to the beach and the taxi dropped them in the main street in Woolacombe. They walked to the "Shed," off Beach Rd, and Storm unlocked his shop. Inside was an area displaying wet suits and other gear, and a set of changing areas towards the back of the shop.

'The report said it was fair to good today and the swell's a good level for you to start,' Storm said, moving outside and assessing a report on an app. Their bags were safely stowed away and Storm locked up ready for them to walk down to the sands.

'Beautiful, beautiful, beautiful,' A.D. said as he did a sweep of the wide bay, shading his eyes in the bright sun. There were a few other people down at the water's edge but it was pretty deserted, just a dog or two running around their owners.

'I should apologise to you if you've lost business over the last couple of days,' said A.D.

Storm looked at A.D. and said: 'No, that's alright. Mary usually covers those days but she's a magistrate and had to be at Barnstaple while I was in London. We usually don't have a clash but there was nothing we could do this time.'

'And Mary is?' asked A.D. as usual looking for the love interest.

'One of the Christian Surfers, but she's a lawyer by training and became a magistrate recently, moved out of London and came down here. She works part time in the shop and does a stint at Exeter Community Law Clinic.'

'Excellent I bet the BBC would love to meet her,' said A.D.

'But I bet Mary won't want to meet them,' said Storm. A.D. looked confused and Storm realised he had been a little short. 'Mary gets enough stereotyping as it is, as a black magistrate. People are always doing the positive discrimination thing with her.' He scanned the horizon, taking in the clean, but fairly gentle waves. 'Let's do the preliminary stuff on-shore now. It'll be better later this afternoon and early evening because there's a pushing tide so we would get the best of it then. We can start now and get another session in later before the evening. It's a great sunny day, A.D. and will be like this for hours. Let's get you suited and booted, shall we? Then you'd better do some stretches as this is potentially going to hurt otherwise.'

The change in Storm since they had broken their journey in Barnstaple had been very apparent. A.D. had realised hours ago that he was being played with, or perhaps, tested. He decided it was time to get everything on the table. He turned and looked at Storm. The difference in height meant it was not exactly eye to eye. He said: 'Now young man. It's quite clear you were putting me through some sort of test on the journey. What was all that about?'

Storm gave him an apologetic grin. He said: 'Just working you out as a potential father-in-law.'

'What?' spat out A.D. He stepped back, initially seized with panic.

The whole concept of being related to Paul Downing if this young man before him became his son-in-law was testing.

Prayer required he told himself. Possibly counselling. He breathed and closed his eyes. Storm waited as thirty seconds went by, watching him with some concern. A.D. opened his eyes, calmer now. He tried to look pleasant. He set his face to the expression he always wore with the Purley Flower Committee. After all, having Paul as an in-law was not the lad's fault. Trying to smile between praying for strength he gave Storm a once over. A.D. said: 'How do you know my daughters? Which one is it?'

Storm grinned and said, 'I don't know them. It's for Chris.'

'Ah, I see. I'm the thing that's holding him back, am I? Interesting,' said A.D.

'Oh, don't take it personally A.D. he's always been neurotic. Look it's to do with being the boss more than anything. Anyway, for what it's worth we'd better get you kitted out with a suit and in for a go. if we're to get across to Croyde in time to see Gareth we should do it now.'

'Do you have a spare?' asked A.D.

Storm thought of the vast array he had hanging in his shop. 'Yeah, I've got a few. Let's try an O'Neill Psycho on you.'

They started walking back to change. 'What's the temperature of the water?' A.D. asked, as he was aware from the breeze that he was not in for warm temperatures.

'About forty-eight to fifty degrees F at this time of the year.' Storm had registered the size of the board needed as A.D. was not a tall man. They went into his shop and he put the starter board down for A.D.

'Looks a serious board that.' A.D. said, while he stared at it, uncertain that he really wanted to do this anymore.

'Yeah, it's a "Salt Rock Beginner Soft." It's a good one to get you started or if you just want to muck about through the summer. It's light so it won't be a pain dragging down the beach, but strong enough to take the abuse you're going to give it. If you're interested to get that young'un of yours started this sort is a good price. In comparison to other makes that is, or if you're only going to do it occasionally.'

'You know your stuff ,Storm.' A.D. gave his surf instructor an appreciative look.

'Have to A.D. It's a complex sport. No one's going to pay any attention to what I say about God if I'm naff at this. Just stay positive and patient and remember the surf changes. Right let's get those stretches done. Before and after, OK? I'm afraid you will find muscles you didn't know existed.'

****

'How we doing Storm?' Gareth Evans put his phone on loud speaker while he closed the door. He was working from home as his wife, Millie, was on duty at the hospital.

Their two small children, Sophie and William aged five and three, were banging saucepans in the kitchen with Grandma, who was also singing. The half-term break for Sophie had created the need to draft in reinforcements in the form of grandparents doing shifts.

Gareth had managed to delay leaving as a result of the change in arrangements that morning.

'Kids starting an orchestra?' Storm asked, holding the phone away from his ear momentarily. 'Should be with you in about an hour Gareth. A.D. is just changing. We plan on coming back later as it should be good this evening with the tide. This guy's probably going to want a coffee when we get there.'

'How's it going with him?' Gareth asked.

'Yeah, he's alright actually. I wound him up a bit this morning to see how he'd react, but he's got an irrepressible spirit and he's very enthusiastic. I'm looking out for a friend who seems to have a thing for the guy's daughter so, I thought I'd put him through his paces with the rainmaker.'

'Don't blow it, mate, will you? This could be quite an opportunity for us and could also be a good one economically for the area if the BBC get involved filming down here.'

'No, we're getting on fine,' Storm said.

'Alright, I'll see you at the café for pasties. I'll get back to work as we're much later than we had arranged.' Gareth was gone.

A.D. had concluded part way through his first lesson that he did want to live, that he must be mad to put himself through the pains he was experiencing, and at forty-five he was clearly too old to start something like this torture. However, he realised as they got further into it, that he found it wonderful. The fact that he was, in most eyes that were watching him on the shoreline, too old for this activity drove him on.

Storm spotted this always in his older pupils and told him about the records being set by surfers in their forties. A.D. clearly was not a man from the local gym. He walked around London and he walked his dogs, Max and Gus, or, rather they walked him. Apart from feeling he was going to drown at times, his focus pushed him on, realising that it was going to be the hardest possible sport for him to be any good at. He was worried that he would never stand on the board but Storm got him up. After the stretches, by the time they neared the end of the drive to Croyde, A.D. felt aches like he had never experienced before in his chest and across his shoulders. His legs would hardly move.

****

Once the taxi from Woolacombe dropped Storm and A.D. outside the Garden Tea room for the meeting with Gareth, A.D. was in to a full of set of stretches in the street. Storm slapped him on the back, said, 'Good man!' and decided to leave him to it. Storm went into the café, deciding that the very positive A.D. would be good for his overly reflective friend and probably a very faithful influence on Chris. That was providing Chris didn't screw up in the relationship. Storm could imagine that A.D. would not take any prisoners. But what was he worrying about? This was Chris they were talking about. All that remained before he gave Chris the thumbs up on a relationship with Eve was to check her out by meeting her. How to wangle it was another thing.

A.D .was now coming through the entrance into the café, his expert nose starting to go into its sniffing routine.

'How do you know this cafe?' A.D. asked Storm, while fighting feeling like a geriatric. He had hardly been able to get up the steps.

'It's a good place to go for coffee and a pasty and knowing from our experience how you like trying different things I thought it would be an interesting place to meet up.'

'Thoughtful of you, dear boy. We must bring Ravi when he comes down, he's quite a foodie. Hang on, I just have to stretch again. Am I supposed to feel like this?' asked A.D.

'You just will, so keep it up,' said Storm.

'So, time to sample a pasty eh. I don't recall ever having one. What do you recommend?' A.D. looked at the choices before him and started to salivate.

'About the stretches,' said Storm, 'People twenty years younger on their first surfing lesson feel the same. Don't worry about people looking at you, everyone here will know what you're doing. As regards a pasty, try a traditional but there's also others. Some of the surfers may be in so I can introduce you. Gareth should be here by now as well.' Storm looked round the room. 'There's a couple of surfers in the corner who're older than you A.D. so I'll take you over. You can be the new kid on the block.'

Storm left A.D. getting acquainted with two guys and he heard a guffaw in response to a remark from A.D. Good, thought Storm, the guy's fitting right in.

A.D. was already telling them what he did for a living. Storm chuckled as one of them said, 'No way, you look so normal.'

Storm checked at the counter if Gareth had arrived and he was out on the terrace at the back waiting for them. Storm interrupted the new surfing enthusiast in the middle of explaining a project he was over-seeing.

A.D. had already made arrangements to meet up for a drink with the two men at the "Barn" in Woolacombe later. Storm shook hands with the two men himself and then steered A.D. through the café to the terrace where Gareth waited. The introductions were made and Storm took their order and went back into the café to the counter.

'Two traditional and Gareth wants a cheese and bacon. Coffee all round. I've told our visitor your coffee's good. It's his fourth this morning so make it a single shot will you, Lesley.'

'Will do. Teaching him, are you?' Lesley asked.

'In a manner of speaking,' said Storm nodding.

'Poor man. Where's he from, he's got a funny accent? I'll make it a special coffee for him.'

Storm, knowing the jungle drums would start, leant conspiratorially across the counter and gave Lesley enough fuel to get the locals going.

'He's a big noise with the BBC and the church. The BBC are coming down next week for some filming. Better get a stock in.'

'Thanks, lovely, I will. Put in a good word for us, will you?'

'Don't I always?' Storm stood with arms wide open. Lesley threw a dishcloth at him and he dodged it.

The coffees were on the table in record time and A.D. realised that this was now his fourth. He decided this would be the last day for a while that he would have any coffee. 'Even I don't do more than two in a day,' A.D. said.

'You should bring your family down, A.D. How many children do you have?' Gareth asked. They were getting on well and Storm allowed his mind to wander onto the pressing issue of fixing Chris up with the eldest daughter. A.D. was about to do the proud father routine with photos.

'I have photos here,' said A.D. and he pulled out his phone and showed a screen saver of Louise and the girls. 'The eldest two are more or less independent now, Eve's about to take a gap year working in Kenya, and then start a training contract with a firm of accountants we hope, If it comes through. I suspect she'll follow in her mother's footsteps.' A.D. pointed to Charis next: 'Charis is more often or not at Oxford Brookes now than at home. Just finishing year three with her Architecture B.A. Then she'll carry on there for the second part of qualifying. It's just the youngest at home, really: Jude. But I think they would all love it down here so I'll keep my eyes open for something for a weekend I think. In fact, I was wondering Storm, about next week when the BBC finish down here. I'll call Louise later and see if there's any chance she can tear herself away from her study and do a "working from home" day round here. That would give us three nights if she came down late on Thursday.'

AD flicked through some more photos: Louise walking the dogs, a family group on the patio at the back of their home Park Lodge. A.D. said to Gareth: 'Storm's high on my list for lessons for the family and I do think it would be good while I'm here for them to see it all. Helps them understand the sort of thing I'm doing, you know. It's such a beautiful area too. I think Louise would love it and Jude especially will be up for a surf lesson or two.'

'Did you say Eve's off to Kenya?' Storm had waited for A.D. to finish showing his photos and latched onto Eve's gap year destination.

'Yes, have you been?' AD asked.

'I went out a couple of times when Chris was working there. He has an uncle in aid work and we stayed with him in Nairobi. I did some volunteering in a school in the area Chris was in. It was good experience. Sort of helped him settle having someone who was a mate there. You should get Chris to chat the lady through.'

'Yes thanks, I was rather hoping that Chris would spend a bit of time with her on that,' said A.D.

'Well, I can encourage him A.D. Chris can give her a lot of pointers. When does she go?' Storm asked just as the food arrived. There was a brief pause while it was put down in front of them smells savoured and the first bite taken. A.D. closed his eyes and nodded while he chewed.

'Good?' Gareth asked.

'Excellent! To answer your question Storm, at the moment Eve doesn't go 'til August, but she's getting restless and feels there's nothing for her to stay for. I think she'll go earlier. If I can get hold of a flat round here that's big enough for us all I can get them all down.'

'Look, A.D.' said Storm, ' I can set up a group lesson for your girls and get Mary over. Chris will be here and he's a good surfer. Not in my league of course, but good enough and as Eve knows him that could be an ice breaker with your girls meeting Mary and I if Chris joined in the coaching.'

'Brilliant!' said A.D. 'If I can find something large enough to stay in for us all, maybe something with a garden so we could do a barbecue and you could all come over. Gareth, you could bring your family and we could spend a bit of time socially. Staying over the weekend would give us opportunity to come to a service as well.' A.D. chewed and thought. 'We'd better have a chat about next week's visitation by the BBC.'

'Exactly what I'd hoped A.D.' agreed Gareth. 'Look if you're staying down for most of tomorrow, the pressure is off. You and I could meet up with my team tomorrow and check out another stretch of coast in between sorting out the game plan. We don't need to try and get through it all this afternoon, just do an outline.'

They went over the strategy on the back of a serviette and also the more practical needs of where A.D.'s team would stay. Gareth said: 'Millie and I can put a couple of the team up. Storm, you could take two, couldn't you?'

'Yes, of course,' agreed Storm. 'You'll see my place later A.D. You're in my spare bedroom tonight.'

'As regards your family coming down as the BBC shoot finishes have a look at the Woolacombe Bay Hotel, they have self-catering places,' suggested Gareth, 'You're going back to Woolacombe, aren't you Storm later, to try the surf again? Why don't you both go and have a look at what's available. It's a bit cheaper next week as half term is over so there may be something available.'

'Excellent!' A.D. glanced at the time. 'I'd better check in with Jenny, my secretary in London, in a couple of minutes if you don't mind or she'll be sending out a search party for me.' A.D. pulled out his mobile and headed for the street.

****

There was nothing he had to deal with as far as Jenny was concerned and she offered to square it with Chris that he would cover for A.D. on Thursday as well. Friday would have been a day off for Chris and there was no reason why that should not still happen.

A.D. made the call to Louise. He went through to her answer phone and then remembered she was in a senior management meeting all afternoon. He left a message eulogising about the area and suggesting his idea. Then he decided on mustering the reinforcements and in turn called Eve and Charis.

They were keen on it all, especially private surf lessons. Charis offered to do the research on the train costs/car costs and Eve would be on standby to talk mum through later. Also, the idea of the family all going away together before she went to Kenya really appealed to Eve.

The force majeure of his strategy was to leave a message on Jude's phone. Knowing full well his younger daughter's personality it would be a done deal by the time Louise found the message.

****

There were patches of blue sky above Croyde Bay as Storm picked up his car from the office and drove A.D. along the Croyde Rd, stopping at the point where it morphed into the Saunton Rd. There Storm turned around and they headed back towards Woolacombe.

'So, there's no through road from here?' A.D. asked.

'Only through Georgeham, or back to Braunton, and up through Knowle. We're going the scenic route, giving you a flavour of the joys of driving round Devon lanes in the tourist season. Place your bets A.D. on how often I have to stop and reverse.'

A.D. chuckled. 'Tell me how long you've known Chris?' A.D. wanted to hear Storm's version and still had not broached the fact that he had been at the same university as Storm's father, Paul Downing.

'Since junior school.'

'And where's your family living?'

'Down in Colyton, like the Duncans. Dad's in London during the week. Look A.D. family is a bit of a moving concept for me. I have many step mothers, and step brothers and sisters. My dad believes in serial monogamy. He moves on to a newer model and then always seems to have some utopia in his mind involving having more children. It never works. Needless to explain that he doesn't believe in God. That is a source of tension between him and I. The welcome isn't too warm for me as he sees me as a failure after my degree. Dad sees what I do as a waste of an education but he's coming round to understanding I see it as a calling. However, he's driven with different values.' Storm's tone had hardened while he talked and A.D. noted it.

Remembering the student version of Paul Downing A.D. could see that the student he and Louise had known had not changed. He asked a question: 'The BBC profile may help there then?'

Storm thought for some seconds. 'Maybe. I'm not sure. There're no big bucks forthcoming and he's a businessman, and is of the sort that will die with his boots on. Mum died of cancer when I was three. I'm the eldest of all his numerous progeny so he takes a failure, as he perceives it, hard.'

And hard for you, thought A.D. He realised that Storm was asking him about his own background.

'What about you A.D? How did you end up in all this church stuff that you do?'

'Ah, University. Met Louise, became a Christian. She was gorgeous, I wasn't. Thought she'd never look twice at me. Charis, my middle daughter, calls it the 'Great Christian Equalizer. She explains it as: "mediocre men ending up with fabulous women." True in my case. Then I felt it was a calling to go into the ministry, and Louise believed it was something she should support me in, and she was happy to bring home the bacon, as she calls it, in the years of training and early Curacies. I just didn't expect such a successful career for her and the benefits financially that it has produced.'

'Really?' said Storm.

'No, but she's very clever,' added A.D.

They had reached Putsborough and the tide was rising. There were clear sets of surf pushing through and the surfers were gathering. Further out on the horizon there was a gloom which indicated a squall. It was four thirty now and the water would be waist to shoulder high. Storm felt that there would probably be a good chance of an extra foot or two shortly but that this was not ideal conditions for A.D. at this point. He turned the car round and drove back along Marine Drive to the village of Woolacombe.

Once changed they were down to the beach.

'The wind's light and onshore,' said Storm. 'The sea temperature won't be any higher than earlier. Best to do what you do best before you go in.'

'As in stretching I take it?' There were more aches evident as A.D. walked into the water.

'How good are the conditions Storm?' A.D. asked after a couple of minutes.

'Well, its fair, the best conditions here would be a west/south west swell at about three to eight feet in height and a wind in the east. It's a bit messy now. Check that App you showed me that your daughter downloaded for you. You'll start to pick up good and bad. Look out at the horizon A.D. You can see the darker clouds and the showers out there. You've done well. Another fifteen minutes I think and then let's call it a day. Are you still meeting those two guys?'

'If there's time, yes. I arranged to meet them at the Barn near the front.'

****

Later the evening sky showed blue between the gaps of rippling clouds as A.D. walked back towards South Street from the Barn. A "Mackerel" sky, he thought, looking at the cloud. He stopped at a few places on the way to read the menus and his world started to crash about him as he could not face the fried food. Worse still he was expecting any minute that Storm might offer to cook, with whale song as background music. A.D. told himself to get a grip and that he was being rude. Turning into Storm's small front garden A.D. had decided they would have to return to Barnstaple for dinner. Storm came out of his front door and laughed at the suggestion.

'No way, A.D. look let me show you the Woolacombe Hotel. We're going in anyway about accommodation for you and the family.'

They walked back down South Street towards the village and Storm pointed to the green lawns and gardens in front of a building which was set back from the beach. At the side of the grounds were tennis courts and a putting green.

'Let's cut through the gardens to the reception. I need to get my 'Fuchsia' fix.'

'As in flowers? You like fuchsias. What a strange mix you are,' said A.D.

'Fuchsias are beautiful. There're beds full of them. Wait 'til you see them. They're my favourite and I miss them every time I leave the area. I thought about dinner here as you're so into the gastronomic delights A.D.' Storm showed him the menu on the gate.

'Guinea fowl, the breast wrapped in pancetta, royal jersey potatoes and veg,' A.D. read out. 'Now that is interesting as I think of it as an autumn dish. I would like to try that and see how it is. Oh, and Chablis, this looks good!'

Storm led A.D. by the arm through the revolving doors. A smile spread on A.D's face. He felt he had come home.

****

They made it as far as the entrance to the dining room. Neither of them was dressed as the manager would prefer, so Storm said he would run home and get a tie for both of them.

'Do you actually possess ties?' A.D. was surprised.

'Yes, I have actually been known to wear one as well. And I know how to tie one without it looking like I was taught by a footballer,' said Storm. 'Let's cut back through the hotel to the bar and I'll go out the side door. You get the drinks in, A.D. and I'll be back in a few minutes.'

A.D. waited at the veranda instead, taking photos of the grounds from the windows, and out across the sea towards Lundy Island. He walked through the reception back towards the lounges and went into a room on the right that had the evening light pouring in through the windows. He liked it, especially the dark wood fireplace and soft furnishings. He took more photos for Louise and the girls and a brief explanation of each location in the hotel. These were sent on the family WhatsApp and then AD returned to the entrance of the dining room and amused himself by reading some of the quotes that were beautifully etched onto its walls. He imagined where he and Louise would sit when she came down. It was a done deal in his mind that she would. Perhaps on the Friday night, or Saturday, they would have dinner without the girls. Then Storm was back, with ties which were a little dubious, but they were ties. So, A.D. put on the orange and blue horizontal stripe, thin as a 1960's style, which even he could not remember, and Storm sported a bright yellow with blue dots.

Oysters on ice, with a vinaigrette and chopped onion, followed by the guinea fowl. Storm allowed himself to be guided by his new pupil, and in turn was tutored.

A.D. closed his eyes as the sea entered his mouth and turned into silk. The day had turned out so much better than he had expected.

****

Thirteen

As they finished the guinea fowl two Americans at the next table started up the focused conversation which was clearly the real reason for their meeting that night. There was an older man in a sports jacket, and "Bing Crosby" trousers, and a younger man, less well dressed but wearing the requisite tie.

The subject matter brought Storm and A.D. up sharp. A.D. looked round the room. The two tables were now in a fairly isolated part of the dining room, most of their near neighbours having adjourned to the lounge for their tea and coffee.

'So, you'll help us out?' asked the older man.

'Sure,' replied the younger man.' How much do you have to work on?'

'About $200,000. So that's five to recruit. How much do they pay you now?' The older man asked.

'$52k.'

'We need to get going with the numbers.' The older man crumbled the bits of bread on his side plate.

'I don't see that. I don't think now's the time to iterate. You know if you look at what the Obama $5-dollar campaign did, it had more going than Sanders.'

A.D. and Storm froze and they were barely breathing. A.D. looked down at the table avoiding Storm's wide eyes.

'So, we can rely on you?' The older man asked.

'I said so.'

'Thanks for the tour round here, I would never have thought it was like this.'

'No problem. Let's get coffee.' The younger man dropped his damask napkin on his chair as he stood. He led the way out of the dining room.

Storm had managed to control his face after the initial wide-eyed shock he had displayed. Now he was a study of nonchalance. That is until the two men had left the room, then he leaned forward and with eyebrows hitting his hairline whispered, 'A.D. do you think the place is bugged? Do you think we should follow for the next instalment?'

Here they were in a North Devon hotel and the world had just crowded in. A.D. inclined his head and leaned forward so Storm could hear him.

'No,' A.D. said. He thought for a few moments. 'No, I don't think we should move at present.'

'Give them privacy you mean?' Storm was still wide eyed.

'No.... they chose to discuss whatever that was really about in a public place. Something about the Democrat campaign I would think given who they mentioned. I don't want to shatter the illusion of being away from it all here.' He paused. 'Have you any idea what 'iterate' means?'

'Yeah man. It's a maths and computer science thing re repetition and algorithms.'

'Ah,' said A.D. as he looked at the wall. He read a quote from Ecclesiastes and thought it was interesting that it was there.

'Who do you think they were talking about A.D?' asked Storm. 'I mean given they've started primaries and things.'

'One could assume things, dear boy.'

'Dead right you could.' Storm's eyebrows had all but disappeared into his mop of sun and sea bleached hair. He was waiting for the older man to enlighten him. When it came, it was unexpected but afterwards, as he reflected, Storm realised that if the place was bugged it was the best suggestion. It was wisdom.

'Let's have dessert, shall we?' A.D. said.

****

They didn't see the men again, and A.D. and Storm left through the front entrance of the hotel to walk through the fading light across the grounds for a final look at the sea. Storm had come up with a good place for dinner A.D. reflected, and what a dinner. A.D. excused himself as he heard his ringtone. He could see it was Louise's number. Storm walked away diplomatically to allow space for A.D. to talk to his wife. They got the initial catch up over and A.D. prepared himself to go into sales mode on his idea of Louise working from Woolacombe on a Friday.

'Mark, the photos look beautiful. You like it there, I can tell. Where are you Mark, right now?'

'In the hotel grounds, down to the beach. I'll do a video for you after we've finished talking. Yes, I do like it very much. It's been a good day, marvellous food, and I've actually managed to stand on a surf board. As a result, I'm in such pain I can't believe it. But you will love it here.'

'I'm coming, am I?' asked Louise.

'I thought the girls. ..'

'Just teasing,' Louise laughed. 'Yes, I've been press-ganged by the three of them this evening over dinner. You will have about six calls in your messages from Jude, she's so excited. Have you any ideas about where we can stay? I just thought it may be fully booked at this time of the year. Plus, having an eye for costs.'

'I need to sort accommodation,' said A.D. 'I'll go back in to the hotel and get on with it after we finish. Gareth mentioned self-catering accommodation attached to the hotel. With the food and the atmosphere, I relaxed so much.... sorry, I'll get onto it now.'

Louise laughed again. 'We've done it. Relax, I'm teasing you. It's across the road from the hotel and big enough for all of us. Called after some character of Dickens but I can't remember which one! You can probably see it tomorrow if you want.'

'You've booked it! That's wonderful. And you're really alright with coming? Will you still be able to work on Friday from here?' A.D. was so pleased he was beaming.

'I think it will be fine as I can do a couple of hours on the journey both ways, and I'll get dinner on Thursday night in first, so apart from how I get to you from Barnstaple? I guess there's a taxi service?' Louise paused.

'I'll sort that.' A.D. said quickly.

'So, tell me about surfing,' asked Louise.

'Marvellous and Storm is good, bit odd at times this morning – wound me up to see how I'd react to things. But once we sorted that out it's been a good start to get to know him. He's a good instructor. I really do hurt now though and my legs don't want to move every time I get up. Most of the time I spent on my stomach on the board but I managed to stand and kept my balance.'

Louise asked: 'Let's have a photo of you in your wet suit then.'

'Oh, no, hardly James Bond. I'll get one done tomorrow and send it.' A.D. laughed, slightly embarrassed.

'Where are you staying?' Louise asked

'Storm has a very nice place actually. I did wonder on the way down here this morning what I was in for but he was putting me through my paces to see what I was like. It was all about Chris and Eve and apparently, I'm the reason Chris hasn't followed through. I'll have to talk to him next week about what's going on.'

A.D. explained about the afternoon meeting, his idea about a social time with Gareth, where the team would stay down there, and the families getting together on the Sunday.

He was clear that Louise didn't need to do anything, he was sure they could do a barbecue if there was some outdoor space. There was a pause and he waited briefly, realising that he had run so many themes together that he may not have been clear. He noticed Storm walking back towards him.

Louise picked up the theme of A.D's match making. 'You know Eve will make her own mind, up don't you? She'll talk to Chris herself.'

'Yes, I suppose so. I only want to help. I think I'd better go if you don't mind as Storm is on his way back from the beach and we need to doss down soon. I'll send you a message about the pick-up from Barnstaple. Can you send me the times of your train?'

'*Doss down* that's surfer talk rubbing off. I'll forward the train booking to you.' Louise laughed, liking how relaxed he sounded. 'Enjoy darling,' she said and she was gone before he could respond.

He searched through the emoticons and found the heart that Charis had shown him. She had found some sort of setting that made it larger and also throb. A.D. selected it for Louise and hit "send."

****

By Thursday morning Chris felt he was coasting at work and looking forward to his day off on Friday. Ahead lay the weekend with Sunday at Purley, followed by a church social over lunch at A.D's home.

He should have been relaxed but he had slept fitfully, waking early. In the back of his mind was concern as Ravi had been withdrawn on Wednesday evening. His friend had kept to his room, eating alone. The silence in the flat was probably more marked for Chris with Ellie and Mike being away.

Ravi and Chris had been friends since they were in their second year at Oxford. They had shared accommodation in a flat off the Cowley Road and it had been a comfortable relationship, both often talking into the night or working on comfy sofas in the Upper Gladstone Link as it was the most relaxed library. Chris was aware that at times Ravi went through a "dark night of the soul," as his past re-remerged with all the hurt and to some extent guilt that he felt about his conversion to Christianity. The exclusion by his family was painful. At those times, he also lost his cheerfulness and became withdrawn. Ravi usually did not want anyone to see his pain and would carry on working hard but with an intensity that showed he was trying to cover the turmoil by the focus. He was a younger son in a wealthy family and in his late teens Ravi had displayed all the behaviour of a spoilt son. His father had been forgiving, providing he towed the line after Oxford and accepted the arrangements his parents had made for a business life and wife. His course was set for the future and the good of his family and business. However, Ravi's conversion at Oxford meant things were not easy for him when he returned home.

Since ordination they had both revisited the outcome on many occasions through the night. Often it was enough Chris was there, silently keeping a vigil with his friend. But last night there had been no response when he had tapped at the door. Of course, Ravi probably just had his head phones on and Chris had drawn back and spent time praying. But Chris had slept fitfully, alert to small noises in case his friend was up and about in the middle of the night. By 7.30am there was no sign of Ravi. Chris knocked on his door. There was no answer and Chris cautiously opened the door. The bed was made and Ravi's laptop was gone. Ravi had clearly left early for work. Chris ate breakfast and then stacked the dishwasher. He looked at his phone and saw there was a message. But it was not from Ravi. Chris put the phone down and walked away from a call back. Adeniji: A.D's instructions were very clear: Chris was not to return any calls from the man.

****

Ravi had gone into Church House before 7am and was working hard but his peace was shattered. The attention from Steph was unwanted, but it was not just that which had kept him awake late and woke him early. He regretted his earlier years and his behaviour. His father had despaired of him in his late teens. Then the conversion from being a Hindu to Christianity and the disowning that followed.

To be in danger from one's own family was a hard thing to explain and he had needed to leave. Ravi had walked away from family, a potential marriage and his heritage. It was only the joy with Christ he had experienced that helped.

It was all years ago but it had re-surfaced with the attention from Steph, memories, desires, hurts. He felt confused about his past and his family and was fighting the sense of loss, of being alone, and struggling with faith, fact and feeling. He also knew he had been rude to her. He knew he was the problem and he was too aware that he was not strong enough to have the contact and could so easily slip into a physical relationship with little else involved as a desperate measure.

Ravi knew he had been short with Chris last night too and so he had chosen to keep to his room instead of having their usual easy banter over a meal. He knew Chris would be working it out. Better to be out of there today and to focus, push it all down again, get a perspective before he went home tonight. A call from his diocese stopped his reflection.

Ravi was still working on the impact of the "cotton picker" and seeing the number come up on his office phone hesitated before taking the call. It was Doctor Laurence, A.D's equivalent, who was calling him from New Delhi. He took the call and heard a voice he knew well, the voice of a friend.

'Ravi? Laurence here. I know you've put in to come back with a focus on the slum community work. It sounds like something has triggered this sudden change though. What has been going on for you? You are a good man to have here and there is an opening that's come through if you want it. I can send the details to you by email.'

'Yes, thank-you. I think it's time to come back, Doctor,' Ravi said.

'I'd like you to think it through perhaps with A.D. there. Look at the details but knowing you as I do I suspect you are trying to jump because of your past.'

'Has there been any contact from...?' Ravi stopped before he said the word.

'No,' replied Laurence, 'Your father hasn't been involved with this. He hasn't contacted us. It's still silent from your family I'm afraid. I don't want to wound you by telling you this but neither do I want to raise your hopes. It's your email to me that I'm responding to. But I sense in it that there are things which are driving you to run away from London now. You will need to be at peace my friend to live anywhere and especially returning to an area that has been traumatic for you. Of course, you will work hard and be invaluable. I am concerned about the 'you' behind the work and the things that still need facing to get peace in your life.'

'Then coming back may be the way forward to get there.' Ravi said firmly.

'Maybe, or not,' said Doctor Laurence. 'One day many years to come it may be right but as they say, it takes two to tango Ravi. There has been no response from your family.

As regards the work you've expressed interest in, take a look at the details and pray and think it through. You are a young man, this may be a post you could do well but the personal life may be overwhelming. Talk to people you trust, listen to them. Get back to me by Tuesday, will you? I just want to know what your real intentions are and then we can think through how best to support you. Take care, my friend, will you?' Laurence waited.

'I will. I will do as you suggest. Thank-you for your wisdom,' said Ravi.

'Good, we'll speak on Tuesday then,' Laurence ended the call.

Ravi looked at the back of the Abbey that dominated the view from the window in front of his desk. The opportunity to apply his skill base and the intellectual discipline it involved had prompted him to put out a feeler to the Slum Community project after seeing an advert. It was a challenge. He knew he would need a support team though. He would have to talk to Chris. Ravi decided that he would follow through with Dr Laurence's suggestion of speaking to A.D. soon. He thought about sending a message to Chris, but after waiting briefly he walked up a couple of floors to find him instead. Chris looked up as Ravi stick his head round the office door and asked:

'Do you fancy lunch somewhere off site?'

He and Chris walked from Church House along the Embankment, skirting past the tourists around the Houses of Parliament and jumping onto a Thames Clipper heading to London Bridge. They sat at the back of the boat outside while Ravi explained his idea with Chris listening. Then it was Chris who talked.

Ravi, aware of Chris's experience in aid work, had explained that he wanted Chris to come with him to work in the Slum Community.

Chris smiled and thanked him for asking: 'I'm glad to be asked but I feel I've got enough doubts about what I'm doing at present. I probably should stay and work a few things out. I'm not sure that I should leave yet, Ravi. And then there's, well, there's Eve.' Chris gave an apologetic smile at mentioning that he had feelings for someone while his friend was in torture.

'I'm glad for you, Chris. Does she know?' asked Ravi.

'I just about told her that she's wonderful. But that's it,' Chris explained, and shrugged.

'Doctor Laurence said that I have to find peace wherever I am. He's right but it doesn't come. I'm so unsure about this, if I should take the job in case it's too much, or going back is too much. It feels like I have a pain here.' He clenched his fist and thumped his chest. 'It's in the heart. I want to beat the fact that I keep feeling like this, Chris. It fades and then seems to come back.' He looked so affected that Chris sat silently next to him. They both stared at the Tower of London as the boat slipped into the mooring.

As they watched people disembarking Chris felt it was time to made a suggestion: 'How about we get off and walk for a bit? Grab a coffee and then we can go back.'

Ravi agreed and they followed the tourists off the boat and walked towards Tower Bridge which was starting to lift to let a small cruise ship through.

Chris and Ravi joined the many people standing, watching the process of the two sides being raised and then starting to lower, which took all of five minutes from start to finish. The distraction was a good one as Ravi had not seen Tower Bridge open and close before.

'What an amazing city this is,' Ravi said to Chris with the first smile of the day.

Taking advantage of the distraction Chris led them towards a coffee stall and they collected drinks for themselves. He said: 'I know I can't understand everything you are dealing with because I haven't gone through it, Ravi. But you aren't alone spiritually, and you don't have to go through this emotionally alone. I can't undo the hurts but I can be your brother and you can even share my mum and dad if you want to. They'd love you to meet you. They're pretty good on lost boys. As regards the history you mention and physical desire, well you're just a bloke. Especially in this culture where it's so in your face. You are a new creation Ravi, the old has gone.' Chris paused as Ravi grinned at him.

'You shouldn't have any doubts about your calling, Chris, you're such a vicar!'

Chris winced but moved on and thought of a point he had meant to mention: 'Do you know any of the people on the Slum project?'

'No, I don't, except for their reputations. I'd have the support of the church of course and I've got to go through the job description more thoroughly yet,' Ravi said.

'I can go through it with you from an aid perspective, if that helps. We could have a look this afternoon if you like?' Chris offered.

'I'd value that, having your development overview,' Ravi said.

Chris saw a clipper that was going back to Westminster. It would be leaving shortly so he suggested they hop on. He said: 'Let's go back and go through the job spec at the office. We can think about details like where you'd stay and who's involved. Once you're there you would work at it as you're not the type to let something you take on go downhill. I could come out and visit if you like and see what the work is that the Slum Community does.'

'It's a long way from the BBC religious programming,' Ravi gave a brief smile.

Chris smiled and said: 'Actually I think they'd be really keen to come and see it.' To himself he wondered if that might be a way of protecting Ravi by getting international interest via the BBC in the project. The work out in the Slum Community was famous already but if Ravi became involved there would be a new angle.

****

Much to A.D's surprise Storm's spare bed was a double so he had a lot of room to spread out his aching limbs. When he lay on it he groaned with pleasure.

He had reconciled himself that he would cope with whatever he had to lay on for the next few nights if only he could go back to that wonderful hotel for dinner each evening. As he woke on Thursday morning he could barely move and he partially fell out of the bed by rolling like a stiff log. He had slept to the time of the alarm and there was a knock on the bedroom door with Storm, poking his head round the door, with a cup of tea. He had let A.D. sleep as long as he could but now they needed to move.

Thursday went well and after a long session with Gareth and Storm, A.D. met a few more of the team as they drifted in. He especially warmed to Mary thinking she had a good deal of spunk. The strategy for when the BBC arrived was clear: they would include as much of the community in Croyde and the surrounding areas as possible. It was also agreed that Storm would have his colleagues, Mary and Cheng, with him for the mock-up of the lesson he was suggesting could be filmed. Storm's idea was that the more of the clergy team that would surf the better. He was roping in Chris in his absence, and thought Mike would be willing to try and adapt from a skateboard to a surf board. A.D. was nervous about putting himself forward but with Storm's enthusiasm that the BBC would love it if an Archdeacon went surfing he eventually agreed.

The routes around Croyde, Putsborough and Woolacombe, were mapped out and A.D. was happy that they had a mutually agreed strategy to put up to the BBC. Gareth hit the send option, having offered to do the voice over if needed, should the BBC want to film the proposed group session. He emphasised the coastline, the villages, the ministry, and came up with a couple of suggestions near the beach in Croyde where the whole BBC team could stay. The email went off to Sarah. As an afterthought A.D. asked Gareth to forward a copy to Jenny.

The rain had battered the oval windows in Gareth's office and kept them indoors longer than they had hoped. By the time A.D. and Storm got down to the shore it was late afternoon and the gloom had settled in. There would be another memorable dinner at the Woolacombe Bay but this time in the Brasserie. A.D. settled for the Crab linguine with lime and chilli, making noises all through it that reminded Storm of a cat purring. Eventually Storm couldn't help himself and he laughed. A.D. met his amused look and apologised:

'Sorry, I'm making noises, aren't I? First time Louise took me home her mother had cooked pork chops with three different sauces. There was apple, onion and a bread sauce. Apparently, I purred my way through the dinner without realising. Her mother was sorry for me, thought it was the only proper dinner I'd had all week. It was wonderful.'

'It must have been if you've remembered it that clearly,' said Storm.

'That and the double scotch her father gave me to see if I could handle it like a man. I had problems concentrating,' said A.D.

'Did you pass?' asked Storm.

'Must have done. Now dessert!' A.D. reached for the menu. 'I'm sad to go in some ways from this beautiful place, But we will be back next week, and the family too. We've firmed up on those lessons for them, haven't we?'

'Well, yes, thanks A.D. everything helps. You've booked a lot of lessons for the girls. I just want to make sure you understand the costs involved. I've got to confirm that Mary can be with us for the lesson with the girls on Friday evening next week, if you're involving me. Mary will do the rest of the lessons, if she's free on Saturday, as I'll go off with Chris to Colyton. You're in the diary and I'll let you know definitely as soon as I hear from her. What time's your train from Exeter tomorrow?' Storm asked.

'I just need to check.' A.D. brought his Trainline booking up. 'Here we are, 16.03. So, I guess we work back from then as to what we can do in the morning?'

****

Fourteen

On Friday morning A.D. woke late to find he had slept through his alarm With all the fresh air, exercise and the good food from the night before his snores could be heard on the landing. Officially it was his day off and Storm let him sleep until nine o'clock before A.D. came to as there was a knock at the door.

'Breakfast's ready, A.D.' Storm called from the other side of the door.

The only problem A.D. had as he reached to check the time on his mobile was that his body was in revolt at the attempt to move.

'Ow,' A.D. called out. 'I can't believe how I hurt. I have aches in places you would not believe.'

'Bet you I would.' Storm said from the landing. 'You know what to do A.D. It's the only way.'

A.D. made it out of bed onto his knees. Holding onto the bedside table he pulled himself up. Pain in his groin brought an 'aaah,' from him. He hobbled to the bedroom door, which he opened to find Storm poised on the top step of the stairs as he had been about to go down. He was waiting for the tortured apparition to appear and he grinned at the contortions on A.D's face.

'I haven't exercised this much for years. About twenty years actually.' A.D. admitted. 'I feel good though.' He frowned, cleared his throat, and then raised his eyebrows at Storm.

'Who are you trying to convince?' Storm asked. 'You're doing different exercise to what you're used to. You might find building some strength in the gym, and doing some swimming, will help the fitness. Have a chat with a trainer when you get back and get an exercise programme going. You can only gain, you know. Then, when you come back, you'll see the difference the strength makes. See you downstairs when you're ready.'

'Right, I'll just have a shower,' A.D. said adding, 'If I can ever get up.'

Storm left A.D. on the landing, holding the banister rails trying to get off his knees.

****

'We should leave here about half past one I think, in case of Friday traffic around Barnstaple,' said Storm, as he dished up porridge and sprinkled chia and pumpkin seeds on the top. He shoved the honey across the table towards A.D. and gave his pupil a meaningful look. A.D. sighed and picked up a spoon.

'We might have a bit of a wait for the train but better to get there early than you miss your connection at Exeter. We'll have good time for your final lesson this week then!'

'Can we fit one in?' A.D. had written off the idea of any more surfing until the following week.

'I think so. Give it a bit of time from now. It's a bit messy this morning and the winds are blustery and on shore. It should ease off and be a bit cleaner later. The water will be cold today so keep going with the stretches. Do you run at all?'

'Why would I run?' AD asked.

Storm laughed. 'Running will build stamina. You could talk to your trainer when you get back.'

'I don't have one Storm.'

'But you will A.D.' Storm looked at him and nodded. 'Competitive as you are you will want to get one.'

A.D. looked over his glasses at his surf instructor realising Storm had got the measure of him. It was a new experience.

'Yes, I suppose I will,' A.D. said. 'I was thinking about some shopping before I go actually. That surf shop has a yellow hoodie I quite like the look of. The two guys I had a drink with mentioned some t-shirts by a brand called "Old Guys," in there as well.'

Storm thought how different AD would look in a yellow hoodie. 'A lesson followed by shop 'til you drop. You can always get it online, you know. Your missus may not speak to me next week if you go back looking too different A.D.'

'No, I like to feel the fabric, test the quality, once I know it, and trust it, I can order online. I quite like the fact that I'm in a small, quiet street and the assistants have time for me. They're all very chilled here. I'm into forming a relationship with them so they remember me when I'm back here. My girls will like some of the stuff in the shops as well. Totally different experience from central London. Right! Stretches!' A.D. was up and on the floor. Storm thought he had to admire the man's commitment.

By the time they got down at the shore, A.D. was itching to get onto a board again. Storm thought that he had to give it to the old guy, he was keen and determined. A.D. had the bit between his teeth and Storm was impressed with him. The balance was improving and he still wanted to go out despite the fairly poor conditions.

'You'll really cash in by doing a third day and it will feel more natural by the time you come back next week for the BBC shoot,' said Storm.

There were the usual dog walkers at the beach and the sea was only ankle to knee deep as high tide would not be until later that afternoon. They would not make that time but Storm was going to help A.D. as much as he could before they had to leave for the train.

****

Midday at the bay the clouds were progressing across the sky, keeping in step with each other. The squall on the horizon meant the rain would be with them within fifteen minutes according to Storm, who did not seem at all deterred by a threatened downpour, as he and A.D. moved from shop to shop along West Road. A.D. decided he would just go with Storm's mood. The light started to dim and the colour of the sea was grey.

Such a contrast to Wednesday, his first day, A.D. thought. It seemed longer to him. He could not believe that he could get on a board now. It just showed what a good instructor could do and the fact that he had one to himself.

'The missus was alright with you staying down an extra night?' Storm asked.

'Oh yes. Quite happy, and she said she would enjoy the mussels.'

Storm pulled a face and stopped walking. 'Way too much information man!'

A.D. laughed at the thought of himself with muscles. He said: 'No, not body muscles, shell fish mussels. I did an order from that shop over there yesterday for an express delivery of mussels and also a clotted cream tea. They should have had it this morning. They are going to love it down here.'

Storm was distracted by the start of the rain. He suggested: 'I think we'd better head for the car. You mentioned lunch in Barnstaple and time's moving on. I don't want you having problems with connections after I drop you at the station.'

The two men turned for South Street. Once in the car, his purchases and the rain maker for Purley stowed on the back seat, A.D. came out with a question that caught Storm by surprise. 'Will I ever be good enough for a competition?'

Storm momentarily took his eyes off the road and stared at A.D. The rain was getting heavier and Storm slowed and looked into the rear-view mirror as they climbed the hill out of Woolacombe.

'There are senior classes - guys over forty-five...but most of them have been doing it longer than you. It will depend how much time you manage to get in. You might find Bournemouth easier to get to from your way of the world to practice. But I don't see why you shouldn't have a go eventually. Most of it's in the head and you don't have a problem with your age. You will need to do some more exercise every week though to build the strength up.' Storm grinned and an idea hit him: "The surfing Archdeacon" eh. I bet the BBC would love it if we got your name down for a competition.'

'Fill me in on what I need to do to enter over lunch, which is on me by the way,' said A.D.

****

A.D. pulled out his mobile when he was finally on the train from Exeter. Yes, it was technically a day off but Jenny might need support as Chris was also off that day.

Jenny's response was to whisper into the phone that she was not alone and 'A' was there. A.D. caught the hint that she could not talk openly but Jenny started to speak at normal volume. She was using her "dealing with a marketing call," tone.

'Thank you for your call but I'm afraid I can't talk with you now as I'm with a colleague and will be tied up for a couple of hours.' Jenny ended the call and A.D. was left staring at his phone resisting the desire to shout at it.

He resorted to text messaging a list of points: 'Jenny. What is going on? Can you get a message to the worship leader about using a rainmaker for Sunday? I'm bringing one back from Storm.

Can you also get a message to Rafe, so that he can introduce himself to the congregation on Sunday – no more than ten minutes or he'll rabbit on about his background and Eton.'

A couple of minutes later three texts pinged in one after the other. They were all from Jenny:

'Adeniji,' was all the first text said. A.D. hoped he had remembered to lock his filing cabinet and desk.

Jenny's second text read: ' No crisis.'

The third text: 'There's an answer machine message from a man called Joel. It's not a good line. Think some details are missing. He says he wants to talk to you next week about a special licence. Nothing more.'

Jenny had put an emoticon of a surfer at the end of her text. A.D. smiled at his new persona.

****

Flopping down onto the tea-stained sofa, greasy haired and in want of a shower, Ellie drew breath as she had all, but five minutes ago, finished delivering her talk titled: "Gender Equality in the Church." Rev Diedre had drawn a breath at that one and absented herself.

Ellie took a sip of her slightly stewed tea, having fully adapted now to the Supermarket basic brand of brown liquid that, at the start of the fellowship time away, had tasted like she was drinking rust. Ellie reflected on the session that she had run and shrugged.

It was not a shock that a middle-aged man, with a wine tinted nose, had made a comment about her appearance as she positioned her notes on the lectern in front of the fifty participants. It happened all too often.

'Always dazzling us with your Aussie blonde hair, dear,' he had said. 'What are you speaking on?'

Ellie had flinched at the use of the word 'dear,' synonymous in her experience of being patronised since she had entered the ministry. She had fixed him with a long, hard stare and said in a monotone voice: 'How we can be more Gender Equal in our Church, Roger.'

This had obviously puzzled the man, as he paused and looked vacant. He suggested: 'Wouldn't it be more suitable to talk to us about how we can care for the children of the church?'

She assessed if there was a better way of responding than what she had said. Nothing occurred unless she was to sweep the issue under the carpet. Ellie had fixed him with a gaze that normally reduced the students in her lectures to complete silence. She had said: 'I know nothing about the discipleship of children. You are better qualified for that, as you have four kids and eight grandchildren. Now let's start, shall we?'

Mike had loudly sniggered as he played with the projector. 1990's technology in the centre was all they had available. He had offered to run a presentation but the internet was poor. Still at least there was a projector. Ellie concluded as regards Roger that there was no better way with those comments. It was blunt, but not too rude hopefully, although she expected that she would get an ear-wigging in a very patient tone from Rev Deidre next week. Still it was done and hopefully it had got him thinking.

The negatives out of the way, Ellie moved her mind onto evaluating the positives. Everyone had listened and contributed to her questions. The had seemed engaged and had come up with a good amount of empowering suggestions in the activity at the end: all suggesting how to work at looking at the effect of culturally based gender roles in their church and at home. So, in balance, the problem was just probably going to be the fact that she always felt irritated by the issue and knew it showed. Ellie glanced at herself in the mirror and said: 'Roger isn't really the problem, you are.'

The starting point she hoped she had got across was that they each had to look at how God accepted each person. The ground each one stood on was level ground at the Cross. She took another sip of her tea as Mike bounded up, skateboard in hand, smiling broadly at her.

'Good job in there, Doc! Looks like people engaged. Maybe we can grill Roger another time?' He smirked and winked all at the same time. Ellie smiled but his comments were confirming that she had overdone it.

'Cheers, Mike. The humour is therapeutic.'

'I'm heading out with the skaters for an hour on the equipment we set up on the basketball court and then will pack ready for that early morning hitch with Rev. Deidre. I'm into the Southbank with my usual group tonight and won't be back 'til late by the time I make Tring, and get a taxi out here. See you at breakfast tomorrow and maybe we can hatch the plan for the 'counter Roger revolution.' He went into a fist pump action.

Ellie stared at him but did respond. She said: 'Think I'll go for a jog, while the clouds are sleeping.' They left the building and stared into the grey sky while it threatened to drop its load across the Chiltern Hills.

****

'Louise, it's Mark, when you pick this up I'm on my way back but I've decided to call in at the Skateboard Church on the Southbank before I get the train from Victoria. I'll bring the youth all back with me on the train. I want to catch Mike with the group and have a chat about Jude. Also make sure he is alright with the idea of the flat and isn't just being polite. So, you just relax about collecting them all on your way through as I think they are due to finish by 7pm.' A.D. hung up from the recorded message he had left and picked up his bags ready to leave the train.

****

A.D. arrived on the Southbank in time to see Mike teaching the group how to fall off a skateboard. It struck him as odd at first, and then as sensible, that they should know how to fall. Jude fell anyway as she enthusiastically waved at him. He caught Mike's eye and decided to withdraw to one of the stalls on the embankment gesturing to Mike as he went where he would be. The set of stairs and the ledges they would try eventually were making his stomach turn. A.D. decided his face would give his concern away to Jude and that he must be out of sight. Mike gave him a thumbs up briefly and then turned back to the group.

A.D. ordered a rooibos with milk and honey, having drunk too much coffee over the last few days. It was also a sign that he was becoming Storm's disciple as he had tried different teas in the little house in South Street and decided that he quite liked them. He sat at a counter and picked up a paper left by a previous customer. Occasionally he lifted his eyes from the pages and looked across the river to the Victoria Embankment and the Savoy, grateful for the water and the space, but struck by the contrast of this city to the world he had been in over the last few days. By seven, the group was packing up and he walked across to them. A.D. was starting to ache again and he longed to lay down on a good mattress.

'How did it go, down there with Storm?' asked Mike as he was packing up to return to the Lad's Place. He had one more coaching session to do on Saturday there.

A.D. said: 'It was a brilliant time, we've put a good plan together and I met Gareth and quite a few of the surfers. Great job they're doing there. And, I may add, I spent some time on a board myself thanks to Storm's great tuition. Feeling pretty stiff though now.'

'You'll need to....' Mike started.

'Stretch?' A.D. got the word in, 'Yes, I know.' A.D. smiled and patted Mike on the arm. 'Look, thanks for this tonight. It means a lot to them. Their faces are really happy and it's helping them as a group doing things like this.' He paused and Mike was aware that there was more to come.

'Before you go, can I play a quick recorded message to you?'

Mike was a bit surprised. 'Yeah, of course. What is it?'

'I don't want you to feel this has anything to do with the flat. Think of me not as A.D. when you listen to this but as a desperate father.'

'Jude?' asked Mike.

'How did you work that out?' asked A.D.

'She leaves quite a trail.' Mike grinned.

'Yes, I suppose she does. Jokes and everything aside she has such a heart.' A.D. said.

Mike nodded: 'Let me hear it,' he said.

A.D. gave him the phone and Mike listened to Jude's message about the group and the camping. He gave A.D. his phone back.

'Look that's quite easy to fix but we would need a local venue as a one off, also female volunteers who've been cleared with the CRB check, a safeguarding policy and funding. That would take some time but we might be able to do something by the end of July or in August.' Mike paused and debated in his mind whether or not to say it.

A.D. waited, sensing the bomb about to drop. Mike said:

'Alternatively, why don't you just get them all down to the Baptist church? If they just attach themselves to a group that's already off to a good event it's easier. There's gear I can bring but the practicalities of it aren't hard. I could talk it through with the group after church on Sunday if they can hang on after the service.'

'That's wonderful of you, you have no idea, what a relief. After the service on Sunday. I'll tell them to hang on then and what it's about. Marvellous!' A.D. beamed from ear to ear but added: 'By the way that suggestion is not something I can encourage. The politics of it, you have no idea!'

'Well, I'd better make a move and get this lot home. You're back to the Lad's Place aren't you tonight?' A.D. asked.

'Yes, 'til early Sunday morning. I'm getting a lift in to London and should be with you without too much of a problem,' Mike said.

'Dreadful place when I was there. Never again I said. Who's running the time away?' A.D. asked.

'Rev. Deidre,' Mike tried to look positive.,

'Ah. Say no more. How's Ellie coping?'

'No shower and hasn't taken a baseball cap off since she got there. Did a good session though today. Her bloke flies in on Tuesday.'

'Really?' A.D. looked surprised. 'She's only just got back from Melbourne though. What's his name?'

'Joel. She's been skyping him every night from a Trucker's stop up the road.'

'Ah, that sounds serious.' A.D. looked thoughtful. Remembering Jude and her friends he took his leave of Mike and spent the last few minutes happily being inundated by their excitement. With the news about Mike Sunday could not come quickly enough for any of them. Even the three cool girls were bouncing up and down.

Mike reached the bridge over the Thames and looked down on the group chatting to each other and he noticed the easy relationship with A.D. He smiled to himself: he decided that A.D. was alright.

****

Fifteen

Mike had set the alarm for five o'clock on Sunday morning. He threw it across the room when it went off and turned over. Five more minutes he told himself but it was to no avail as there was a banging on his door and a contralto was singing his name in time to the birdsong. Rev. Deidre was up and at 'em:

'Michael, Michael, your steed awaits.'

Still with his eyes closed he slipped his feet into his trainers and stuck his head under the cold-water tap. Purley awaited him and a nightmare journey at the hands of the Rev. Deidre. What was it his Gran used to say about the dentist? Ah yes, that was it: 'Soon be over love.'

Several hours later at Victoria Chris caught the 7.34 train to Purley by a hair's breadth. He had found the text from A.D. earlier but hadn't managed to respond. His thumbs were now working. He wrote: 'Yes, Jenny told Rafe to watch the apocryphal stories and to keep off his background.' He hit send and it was gone. This new curate at Purley was obviously causing A.D. some grief.

There had been no sign of Mike on Victoria but Chris had collected two coffees just in case. He had wrongly assumed that Mike was coming in to Euston by train and had probably been delayed getting across London. The trains were regular enough and he was not needed until the family service. Chris was trying to make the early communion to help AD and should just do it but the other curate, Rafe, would be there anyway.

Chris looked round the carriage which was full. There was a group of seven to eight-year olds with mums and helpers, all in brightly coloured t-shirts so they did not get lost. It was the age, his mother insisted, that was the most exciting to teach. The children were being good and as the train pulled in to Clapham the group got off. Chris told a little girl who passed him to tell her mum they were all very good. He was rewarded as the train pulled out by the children smiling and waving to him at the carriage window from the platform with the adults joining in. Spontaneously he laughed. The trust in the eyes had hit him. Those faces would live with him. It had made his morning.

Ravi had been persuaded to come out and would follow later getting to Purley for the start of the family service. Chris had cleared Ravi lending a hand with A.D. who was frankly delighted. He had suggested that Ravi explain a little of the work of the Slum Community to the congregation and then would join them for lunch of course. Chris wondered how Louise and the family coped as A.D. was very into church socials and barbecues. One thing was certain, with A.D. there would be plenty of food for all.

'Bring and share.' A.D. had said to Chris, who pushed away the memories of his old Baptist church bring and share family gatherings and every type of quiche imaginable.

His coffee finished, Chris came out of his reverie to see they were pulling into Purley. Now to find Eve who was collecting him at the station. He walked out to the cramped collection area at the front of Purley station.

There she was at the wheel, looking through the windscreen and smiling as she saw him. She wound down a window and looked up at him as he reached the car. In his mind, he saw himself bending down through the open window and kissing her. She would respond and ... The reality was that he simply stood still and grinned inanely.

****

Mike was at the point of leaning against a wall outside Victoria trying to fight the motion sickness brought on by Rev. Deidre's driving. They had left the Lads' Place in good time but, as her car would not go over sixty on the motorway the journey had taken longer than he had imagined in his time management. He had hoped to join Chris on Victoria but had realised, after Watford, that that was out of the question. In fact, it turned out that sixty was her speed regardless of where she drove. This included central London and she had driven up Victoria Street like a bullet out of a gun.

'Watch the speed limit,' Mike tried to tell her, shouting quite a lot above the engine noise. 'You'll get your photo taken.'

Which was exactly what happened, several times but she shouted back: 'They've got to catch me first.'

'Too late,' said Mike covering his eyes. 'It will be fine,' he muttered. 'Please, Lord, let me live a little longer.'

The world seemed to be on Victoria Station and he needed a quiet place to pull himself together. Still undergoing development Victoria seemed more packed than usual.

Mike checked the board for the next train. There was one that would get him into Purley shortly after nine and then he could get a bus up the hill. What was that hotel A.D. had mentioned, the one he knew on Victoria? Mike saw the sign at the side of the station and entered the convenient world of the Archdeacon. The lobby was beautiful of course. A.D. knew how to pick them, loads of marble and red furnishings. Despite the early hour hotel staff were laying up for afternoon tea in the lounge but Mike negotiated a small table in the bar by a window, just for some tea and cold water. He had thirty minutes. He closed his eyes to stop the motion sickness and breathed in and out slowly.

****

Rafe Ackland introduced himself first to Eve as she walked in with Chris through the vestry door. Chris got the measure of him while this game play was on as overconfident with the opposite sex, conscious of his looks. Alarm bells were ringing as he heard Eve giggle. She excused herself and disappeared as A.D. arrived.

'Ah, Chris, well done getting here in good time. You've met Rafe of course.'

'Yes, only by phone A.D. Good to meet you in person Rafe,' said Chris, feeling a hypocrite.

'Good to meet you too. Where did you say you were from?' Rafe asked.

A.D. was quick to respond as he saw Chris hesitate. 'Chris is an Oxford man, worked overseas in aid and development before he was ordained.'

'Oh, Oxford. I was at Cambridge, of course, after Eton.'

There it was again, Chris thought, this leaning into one's background. Chris had no time for it and almost despised the social reliance it brought. However, he thought he was really overreacting because of the muscles before him. A.D. glanced at them both and led Rafe into the church. A.D. was back in a moment, and gave Chris an involuntary shrug. He said: 'Of course, Rafe's a complete plonker, but if we get through the morning without him mentioning Eton and the Princes, we'll have done well. Keep an eye on him through his talk will you Chris, he's inclined to forget what he's supposed to be saying. You might have to prompt. I've had to stop him reading out his talks. How he got through Eton and Cambridge I just don't know.'

'Probably was allowed to read everything out,' muttered Chris. 'How did you end up with him here A.D?' Chris asked.

'He's someone's Godson, mum's the word,' A.D. tapped the side of his nose. 'Mentioning no names.' There was the shrug again. Chris ran some names through his mind. Surely not...... Oh well, he was probably wrong. No one he could think of, he decided, was likely to have friends who could afford Eton.

Chris realised he was being rude and had not asked A.D. about his reconnoitre to Woolacombe. He asked: 'How was the trip?'

'Brilliant, dear boy, and what a deep chap that Storm is,' said A.D. 'Covers his abilities up a bit at first but once we got going on a board Storm opened up quite a bit. I thought he was a little odd at first. But a beautiful area. I'm getting the family down next weekend.'

'Did you say you got going on a board?' asked Chris, eyes widening.

'Oh yes, I'm up for competition and Storm is going to coach me,' said A.D.

'Is he?'

'Yes, fee paying of course,' explained A.D. 'Once I've got the exercise sorted and had a chat with a personal trainer. Those breakfasts will have to stop, unfortunately.'

Chris let it go. There was another point A.D. had mentioned that was burning a hole in his brain.

'The family? Did you say you were getting the family down next weekend?' Chris waited.

A.D. was peering round the vestry door. 'That's right. Did you let the worship leader know about the rain maker?'

'Yes,' said Chris. 'Is that all the family, A.D or just some of them? I don't think there was a problem with the rainmaker. I spoke to the worship leader for this morning and he thought he could use it. He was well impressed it was your suggestion.'

'All the family,' A.D. said, firmly. 'I put the rainmaker next to the drums. Can't see it now.'

'They've probably got it in a side room having a practice. When are all the family arriving?'

A.D. suppressed the desire to cheer at the interest. Instead he gave a simple answer: 'Friday.'

The service moved along quite well. The youth got the giggles with the rain maker at first. Part way through Rafe's talk Mike and Ravi entered the back of the church having met up on the train. Mike mouthed a, "sorry," at Chris and he and Ravi sat down at the back.

Ravi nudged Mike and half pointed at Rafe, who had dressed "down," as he put it for the family service, in an overly tight t-shirt that he had decided to wear. This was marked with sweat stains under the arms as his nerves at speaking without notes took over. Muscles bulged but the effect on the females in the congregation was killed through sweat. All with the exception of the local right honourable, Letitia Simpkins-Blyth, who ran a stud farm that covered an area across the Surrey/Sussex boundary line.

'*Tremendous*,' Letitia said quite audibly when Rafe stood up to start his talk.

However, Rafe was clearly not coping with trying to remember what he had to say and was looking at A.D. for a clue. A.D. had his eyes closed and was refusing to play. He had given Chris the talk that Rafe had written out and was switching off hoping for a damage limitation with Chris's help. Rafe, however, was not looking at Chris. It was a fumbling attempt at a talk. Eton, of course had been mentioned, as had the Princes and the tuck shop but now he was struggling to recall the points he had to make.

'Archdeacon,' said Rafe, 'Help me out.'

A.D's eyes were wide open now and the eyes of the congregation were moving from him to Rafe, and then back again. Chris was sitting slightly to the side of Rafe, parked behind a pillar unseen. A bodiless voice echoed in the acoustic, which was unfortunately very good in that church. To give him his due, Rafe picked it up and finished quite well. A.D's mind, however, was fixed on a transfer. He was less than impressed at the standard of dress as well. Louise had shaken with stifled laughter through most of it, made worse by the look on A.D's face.

The youth had started to comment on the stains of sweat, and Jude was giggling so much and holding her nose. A.D. turned to seek Mike and Ravi out, spotted them and, with relief, beckoned them forward. They were up in an instant aware they had a job to do to pull the standard up. People would be kind, of course, as it was the man's first time. However, A.D. was not ' people.'

Chris resigned himself to the task of giving the new man an earwigging. He wondered why Rafe was putting himself through this. A sense of calling perhaps?

After the service, while A.D. and Chris changed in the vestry, Mike filled A.D. in on the time away at the Lads' Place but A.D. was distracted by the overly quiet Ravi, who quietly had smiled at him before he went back into the church for coffee.

'He's a bit quiet' A.D. said cutting across Mike's feedback on the retreat. 'What's going on?'

'Yeah, with being away I don't know what's happened,' said Mike, looking at Chris.

'We need to lift him out of this struggle Chris,' said A.D.

'He's better than he was a few days ago, A.D,' explained Chris. 'This happens at times and it's usually triggered by something. He thinks that he needs to go back to Delhi to help the emotion inside and that working on a project may help him.'

'That might be disastrous to go back,' said A.D.

Mike remained silent, aware that something had developed that was too involved for a quick explanation. There was a click of the door handle and Ravi reappeared with three coffees for them.

'I haven't seen Rafe, is he still mingling?' A.D. asked.

Ravi said: 'He's talking to Charis, and I think your wife has just organised a lift back to the house for him with her.'

'What? No! Mike, come on.' A.D. was through the door like a greyhound, ignoring the coffee Ravi held out to him.

Mike looked surprised, 'Since when was I the heavy?'

'What's that about?' Ravi asked Chris.

'I don't think A.D. is over keen on the idea of Rafe for lunch,' said Chris, and the funny side of the sweaty armpits and lunch started him laughing.

A.D. came back into the vestry. He said: 'I'm not having that man anywhere near Charis. Come on, Mike!'

Mike looked at Chris. 'Which one is Charis?'

Ravi grinned. 'She's the pretty one.'

'No, that's Eve.' Chris corrected him and Ravi's grin turned into a laugh at the giveaway comment.

'Listen to you. There are two lovely girls, Mike, and looks like you're earmarked for Charis. You see nothing really different re arranged marriages here either.' Ravi said, starting to laugh. It was good to see.

'Yes, there is Ravi. We can walk away. Worth exploring an opportunity if she doesn't look like her dad. Doubtful she'd give me a second look though. I'll go see what is winding A.D. up,' Mike said.

A.D. had continued to call Mike from the aisle, with some urgency. Once Mike caught up with him A.D's intention was to introduce Mike to Charis and head off the lift for Rafe that Louise had organised.

'Did you see the size of the rucksack Mike brought with him today?' Ravi asked Chris. 'Looks like he's off somewhere.'

'Yes,' said Chris and smiled. 'He's packed everything he's got. I don't think he'll be coming back to London with us. It's too good an opportunity to miss and I'm glad for him. He's had it hard losing his Gran and his home. She was all he'd got.'

'It will be odd without the little guy and his strange choice of T-shirts. The beard grooming kit smelling of mango and apple will finally be out of the bathroom and no more black bits from his socks on the carpet. No more guitar in the garden either,' Ravi said.

They stared up the aisle to the area where Mike was being introduced to Charis.

'I suspect he'll be over often enough,' Chris said.

He nudged Ravi as they both watched A.D. take hold of Rafe's arm and steer him to the side of the church to meet the right honourable Letitia Simpkins-Blythe.

Ravi started to laugh as well. He said: 'Chris, look at A.D. He could make a fortune if he charged a fee.'

Chris looked across to where Mike was now talking to Charis, a big smile on the youth worker's face.

'Mike will still be working on the Southbank and I was going to offer him space to work in Rosary Gardens if he needed it. Shall we go over?'

Carrying their own coffees plus one for Mike, Chris and Ravi went into the church. Ravi briefly appeared at Mike's side and handed him his coffee, introducing himself to Charis. Ravi thought she had her father's assessing look as she asked him where he worked. Mike took the coffee but barely noticed Ravi's presence. Ravi walked back to join Chris and the two men stood at one side of the church watching the proceedings.

Having removed Rafe from the proximity of his daughters A.D. had joined Louise and they were now in a corner having a heavy discussion. The cause of the disquiet between the Wilkinson couple was because Louise had invited Rafe to join them all for lunch. She did not understand what the problem was and thought A.D. was being unreasonable as so many other people were coming.

However, at the back of both of their minds were intentions about their daughters. For Louise, a young man with a "preferred" background had come on the scene.

However, for A.D. he was more interested in the potential for his second daughter with the most inspirational youth worker that he had ever met.

Unknown to either parent, their two eligible daughters had already carved up the available talent between them. Eve would give Chris a lift to the house and Charis would drive Mike.

****

Sixteen

Eve drove Chris and Rafe past the High School and down Riddles Way until they came to Park Lodge and its four acres. Charis had taken Mike and Ravi, the latter diplomatically taking the back seat while enjoying listening to the two in the front getting to know each other. Mike, Ravi thought, was very good on the emotional intelligence.

Eve parked next to her sister by the garage flat entrance and she and Charis took Mike through the side door of the garage and into the flat above it. Chris got out of Eve's car while Rafe collected his bag from the boot. Ravi raised his eyebrows expectantly at Chris in case there was progress as regards Eve. Chris smiled at him and almost imperceptibly shook his head. Not much he could do with Rafe in the car.

Ravi stuck his head into the entrance of the flat and called up the stairs about coming up. He wanted to support his friend, Mike. Whatever discussions went on once they were inside Chris could only guess at, but he and Rafe, had other business to do. Chris thought the only way with this curate was to say it as it was. The time was ripe as they were alone and he did so, noticing a stubborn chin jutting out while Rafe listened. Chris thought that A.D's mention of the fact that he was an "Oxford man" had been deliberate so that Rafe would give Chris some credence and respect. Background clearly mattered to this man because, at this point in his life, it was where he was at. Chris thought that there were rough edges on them all.

Mike was down within ten minutes and collected his rucksack from Charis's car. Chris was heavily into a response from Rafe, but noted that Mike intended to stay. A.D. was walking down the drive towards them having changed into jeans and a yellow hoodie that he had obviously picked up at a surf shop during his time with Storm. Chris had never seen A.D. dressed like that in the six months that he had worked for him. A.D. looked completely different and with the wind tan he had acquired in Woolacombe he had shed years.

'Are we ready, gents, to start a barbecue?' A.D. asked in a tone that would not take a no for an answer.

'Happy to help,' said Rafe, who was putting a good face on it. 'I appreciate being here A.D.'

'Good, good.' A.D. beamed at the two men. 'You two have gone over this morning I take it?'

Chris and Rafe both nodded, although Rafe gave a stiff nod and set his face to show it would not happen again, while Chris showed with his eyes that the points had hit home to the man. A.D. changed the subject and suggested that Rafe might like to go and give Louise a hand with the barbecue and asked him to let her know he and Chris would be along in about ten minutes. Rafe set off in the direction of the patio at the side of the house.

Once out of earshot A.D. said: 'Louise needs to get to know him.' A.D. put his hands in his pockets and rocked back on his heels. 'Right, where are the others?'

'They went straight up to the flat A.D. I think it's a hit as Mike came down for his stuff.'

'Let's go up then. If he wants to stay that's fine, Eve and Charis picked up enough flat packs yesterday for him to cope tonight.'

'If he wants to do this, A.D. I'd like to help him tonight, you know, put them together, if that's alright with you, sort of settle him in,' said Chris. 'He'll work on it 'til it's done otherwise. It's such a great thing for him to have a home of his own, even though it's not actually his, if you see what I mean. I wouldn't want him suddenly to feel alone to begin with.'

'Of course, you and Ravi stay if you want to. We'll find room, or something you can crash on in there tonight. No problem, dear boy, good idea.' A.D. said and patted Chris's arm.

Chris looked at his boss realising that something had affected A.D's mood since he and Louise had been talking intently in a corner of the church. The hard edges from an argument with her about choice for the girls were however starting to go. A.D. hated disagreeing with Louise. In fact, it was impossible to argue with her, but whenever they were at odds on a subject he felt like it was the end. She was so rational, always weighed everything up, whereas he was the one that would be spontaneous and emotional.

'I can go up and get them if you need to go back and help your wife,' Chris offered.

'Thanks, but I'll come up and formalise everything with Mike and then leave you all to it. We could probably do with one of the girls and perhaps you coming and helping for a while as people arrive,' A.D. said.

In the flat Ravi was already bolting a chest of drawers together, finding the activity therapeutic. Mike, Charis, and Eve were laying the different sections of a bed frame out in the bedroom. Mike emerged from under plastic wrapping to come and shake A.D. by the hand. Although smiling, the young man was silent with emotion.

A.D. pumped Mike's hand up and down. 'It looks like we have a lodger, dear boy. It will do then for you?'

'Wonderful. Thank you so much A.D.' Mike lowered his head so the emotion did not show and purposefully strode back into the bedroom.

A.D. put some papers on a window sill. He called: 'I'll leave the Lodger's agreement for you to have a look at Mike.' Looking around he said: 'I think I need to take some reinforcements to the barbecue. Eve could you come back with me and maybe Chris? Three of you up here 'til lunch should get the bed and enough furniture up for tonight. Ravi, you and Chris are welcome to stay tonight. I think we can find a couple of futons if you can manage on those. Mike, don't forget in your enthusiasm to stop for food.'

A.D. had walked back part way to the house when he was joined by Eve and Chris. Suddenly remembering he had to collect equipment from the shed A.D. excused himself. Glancing back, he paused briefly to watch Chris and Eve continuing the walk alone. One side of his mouth went up in a lop-sided smile.

****

The sun was already high with a clear blue sky and the hint of a breeze. People were arriving and, on the drive, Jude was meeting and greeting, directing parishioners to where the barbecue was set up. Louise thought how like her father she was becoming, all easy conversation and goodwill. A.D. himself was full of bonhomie and was officiating with the drinks. Louise, who was now circulating having escaped from Rafe and his early history at Eton, touched her husband on the arm, and said quietly:

'You win on that one'

A.D. glanced at her, and then dismissed the disagreement forever with a wave of the hand. 'Did he get on to the Princes?'

'Copiously. Where's Charis?' Louise asked looking around for her middle daughter.

'Bolting together a bedframe with Mike and Ravi.' A.D. said.

Louise looked thoughtful. She said: 'I'll wander over with some food and drink. I'd better have a look at the youth worker. Eve?'

'Don't know,' said A.D. 'I thought she and Chris had come back to help you. We left the flat together but I had to go to the shed so they were on their way over here.'

Louise closed her eyes briefly and inhaled, she turned to her husband but he was already starting a conversation with an elderly parishioner. Her good nature prevailed and she shrugged, doing a scan of the garden.

Louise could see Chris and Eve under the Oak tree talking, smiling, unaware of the crowd filling the garden. She caught A.D's eye and nodded in their direction. He looked across towards the Oak tree and then back at Louise, clearly delighted. Beaming at his wife he resumed the conversation with his parishioner with great enthusiasm.

****

Chris and Eve had sat on a conversation chair under the oak tree. They were unaware of the time chatting freely about the work Eve was doing. Chris told her about the couple of days filling in for A.D. while her dad had been in Woolacombe. Conversation was easy between them once Chris forgot himself. Eve looked so happy and Chris caught the fragrance of her hair as it mixed with the scent from early summer flowers near-by.

They were not to be alone for long as the youth group, unable to find Mike, were bearing down on them with Jude in the lead. Zack was a few steps behind her. Chris looked at them both deciding that Zack may be CEO potential but Jude was definitely the Chairman.

The youth had organised trays of food from the buffet and each member of the youth group was carrying one. They had clearly decided to optimise a networking opportunity with Chris as the next best thing to finding Mike. Zack had grabbed an ice box full of soft drinks and the group were set up for the afternoon.

'How's it going?' Chris called to approaching group.

'Alright but we wanted to talk to Mike about the camping as we didn't get the chance after church. Dad grabbed him for something. Oh yes, it was called Charis.' Jude said, with a giggle. Even Chris could not resist laughing at her sense of humour and general giggling broke out amongst her friends. Eve attempted a stern look but it was like water off a duck's back. Chris shook his head and thought what a nightmare Jude would be in a couple of years. She was already showing signs at times of that transition from gangly teenager to the young woman. He pitied the boys in the group in three years' time. Jude laid the groundsheet and Zack put the ice box on it and the others settled down. Jude held out a burger to Chris, who took it and joined them in eating and then one to her sister who was standing to go.

Eve shook her head and said to Chris: 'If you're fine with this lot I'll go and help at the house?' She ran her hands through her hair pushing the curls back from her face in a fight with the breeze.

'I'm fine,' Chris said. He thought that he would be fine forever if the future was full of Eve.

'See you later then, when this has all cleared. I'll go down to the kitchen to see what I can do.' And Eve was gone, walking up the slope towards the house.

Zack had taken her seat, sitting on its edge, waiting for Chris to give him attention.

Chris became aware of the boy staring at him.

'How did the skateboarding go on Friday?' Chris asked. The group were full of nervous excitement. There was a chorus of 'brilliant,' 'really hard,' 'so many bruises,' all at the same time.

Chris zoned out of the chatter and watched Eve's figure get smaller. Jude with her sharp eye spotted the direction he was looking in and did a 'tick' on a checklist that she carried in her mind about potential brothers-in-law. Dad liked him and having another vicar in the family would keep dad occupied so he wouldn't notice what Jude got up to so much. Jude called Chris back from his thoughts. She said: 'We're going down for the surfing next week to Devon. You're going, aren't you? Do you surf?'

'I do.' Chris answered. 'I usually surf with Storm, who I hear is going to give you lessons.'

Jude's street cred had just soared in the eyes of the future CEO. Zack coughed to get her attention. However, Jude merely glanced at him.

'I surf.' Zack said.

'Whatever,' Jude said, dismissively. Without looking at the boy Jude put her head slightly on one side like a younger version of A.D. She said to Chris: 'You'd better hurry if you're going to catch her.'

Chris looked at Jude who was genuinely smiling at him without any artifice.

Chris got up from his seat and grinned at Jude, recognising an ally. The thirteen-year-old was fully in charge of the ice box, and therefore holding the attention from three thirsty boys.

She was more than a match for the male of the species and Chris wondered, if he was still around to see the family in the next three years, if he would see her in the future sorting out Zack.

****

A.D's study was a warm room with curtains that were made from designs and fabrics in 1952 by the Edinburgh weavers. He had talked about them endlessly when they had been put up a few months ago and Chris had tried to look as if he would have known about the company. The study was off the hall and there were still about fifteen people for the lunch who had gathered in the space by the front door after trying to escape the cooling, early, June wind in the garden. Chris had slipped in through the open French window of the study to try and avoid them. He also had a love affair with libraries and studies and this one was no exception. The shelves were lined with books, but the desk was a shock, being completely of glass. A comfortable sofa was in a corner of the room behind a glass coffee table. There were photographs of skiing holidays of the family, various elderly relatives in their youth in black and white, A.D. being ordained, received at Number 10 by a Prime Minister or two, and a photo of Louise and A.D. at a garden party somewhere. Then Chris had it: 'Could it be Buck House?' he asked aloud.

Chris opened the door slightly to get his bearings of where the kitchen may be from the hall. He thought he could just do it without encountering any parishioners. He was wrong.

'Oh Vicar, can I have a word.' There before him was an elderly man, Doctor Matthews, a retired doctor who had made a successful career since the 1960's. Chris understood from previous conversations that the doctor was still providing consultancy on the pathology front. Today his breath smelled of the wine provided with the lunch.

The doctor said: 'I've been looking for my Archdeacon, but you will sort me out.'

Hoping to avoid whatever it was that needed sorting out, Chris said: 'I'm on kitchen duty Doctor Matthews, I'm afraid. I think the Archdeacon is just outside the front door, saying goodbye to a couple of people.'

'I liked the service this morning. I really enjoyed hearing about the work going on in the Slum Community as well. I was out in India for a year after I qualified. That new young man who gave the sermon needs to see someone about that sweat problem he's got though. Off to the kitchen, are you? I've just been in there. Some very pretty women in there.' He tapped his nose, 'Mums the word young Vicar, you get down there and do your "kitchen duty." I won't tell the Archdeacon.'

Chris gave him a rueful grin and the doctor held his hand out for Chris to shake. He gripped Chris's hand and they both laughed, with Chris realising he was that transparent about his intentions in heading for the kitchen.

By late afternoon the peace was disturbed by a small Mini coming up the drive. Most of the family, apart from the daughter that had stayed to help their new lodger in the flat above the garage, were all lazing on the patio with the remains of the lunch and large mugs of tea.

A.D. was dozing in a hammock, breathing heavily and occasionally swatting a fly as it settled on his nose. The two spaniels, Max and Gus, were harmonising with his breathing, one at his feet in the hammock and the other underneath it. Louise had disappeared to their bedroom and was having her usual catch up sleep on a Sunday afternoon after the long days and short nights of her working week.

Mike looked at the view from his new flat as a Mini went by. He assumed it was a parishioner and turned back to the rest of the flat pack furniture still to be built. The others were having a break and the plan forming in Mike's mind was they were all going to christen his new place later with a takeaway. He was able to pick up the internet from the house so he was, to quote his Gran: "living like a king." With some poignancy he thought of how she would react if she could see the place he was in.

Jude and her friends had ferreted for some of the bunting and flags which the church had last used when it was the Queen's 90th birthday bash. Zack was up a ladder putting it around the front of the garage. A home-made banner said:

"Welcome home Mike, Youth Worker Extraordinaire."

Despite there being too many Chiefs and not enough Indians in the youth group, their attempts to organise each other were sufficiently far away from the patio to blend with the noise of inquisitive bees, snoring Spaniels and the somnambulant A.D. So, things were peaceful at the house, and everything felt like it should.

Until the Mini arrived at the front door with Jude running along behind it, shouting to let them know Aunty was here. The dogs went wild and both tore down the garden barking, finally disappearing into the woody bit that grew wild behind the Oak tree. Moments later they were belting up the drive and chasing each other in circles around the lawn. Despite the row created by Max and Gus it was the sound of the mini that brought A.D. out of his nap.

Charis had been at the door of the flat about to start helping on the flat pack furniture again. She called up the stairs: 'That's it, guys for me for now. It's a three-line whip when Aunty turns up. I'll come back later.'

Mike put the instructions he was holding down and shouted: 'That's OK, I could do with a break.'

Auntie's mini had slowed, jerked forward, then stopped and an Octogenarian, a little overweight to be in the passenger seat, swung the car door open and managed to get a leg out onto the drive. He heaved himself up with the aid of the car door and stood resting his arms along the top of the door while his arthritic legs adjusted to his weight again.

Finally, able to move away he pulled the back of the front passenger seat down towards the dashboard and yanked both suitcases out of the car. These had seen better days and some epic journeys from Auntie's airline stickers. Pulling both of them the man went in through the open front door and was met by Louise as she came down the stairs. Somewhere in the recesses of her brain, like A.D. the engine had sounded familiar. Louise weighed up the size of the cases, hearing an exclamation as A.D. rolled out of the hammock onto his back on the patio.

Aunty was in through the front door after her friend and, arms akimbo, gave her great niece a big smile. She said: 'Don't worry Louise, we're here for the night if you can have us, and we're off in the morning. Thought a catch up would be nicer than a motel at Gatwick.'

'Are you off on an expedition?' asked Louise, giving her elderly relative a hug. As a child, her great aunt had always called their outings "expeditions." Louise turned to shake hands with the travelling companion.

'I'm Louise the great niece, and this surf dude is my husband, Mark.' A.D. who had made it into the hall, limped slightly after landing on his back and with the stiffness that was still evident from his surfing.

'Wills.' Auntie's friend said. 'The original one, not the Prince.' He snorted with a laugh and they all shook hands.

'Good grief, Mark, what are you wearing?' said Aunty staring at the yellow hoodie.

Without waiting for the explanation, she was off through the house towards the patio where she could hear chatter. A.D. fixed his expression and Louise recognised it had "flower committee," written all over it.

'Do leave the cases,' Louise said to Wills, 'We'll sort out rooms later and get them upstairs. Everyone's on the patio, and I daresay you could do with some lunch.'

'That's kind, don't want to put you out,' said Wills.

'No problem, we had a parish barbecue and there's loads left,' Louise explained.

'Ah yes, Elspeth said you were a vicar,' said Wills.

'In a manner of speaking,' said A.D. 'The bishop delegates ....' he started to explain but that was as far as he got as Louise and Wills disappeared into the garden. A.D. shrugged and followed.

He arrived on the patio as Aunty was taking in the crowd.

'Rather a houseful Louise. Who are these *delicious* young men? Forgive me dear, at my age I get away with it,' chortled Aunty as she pulled up a free garden chair.

'Don't bank on it,' said A.D. under his breath.

Aunty spotted a glass of white wine on the side table, still untouched by human hand. Casually she held out her hand. Mike who had sat down next to the table passed it to her.

'We're a bit of an item actually, although at times you wouldn't think it,' Wills said, as an explanation to A.D.

Aunty waited for the hug she expected from the three girls. Jude was first, and then Eve and Charis resisting the whispers about the young men present. Aunty picked up the glass again and had a noisy slurp while she took in the scene.

'Darlings!' she exclaimed to everyone there, scrunching up her face with passion. 'Any grub left?'

Jude was off on a mission to bring some offering from the kitchen. Aunty turned her attention to A.D.

'Mark, that colour makes you look jaundiced. Not trying to compete with the young men, are you?'

'I've been surfing. I picked up the hoodie down in Devon.' A.D. left standing, attempted to get back into the hammock. This time he had to get Gus to leave it before he could get his legs up. The dog was back up as soon as A.D. lay back onto his cushion. Not wanting to appear to be inhospitable but feeling irritated at the number of times Aunty dropped in A.D. looked at the recent arrivals and said: 'What are you doing here Auntie?'

'Breaking my intrepid voyage to New Zealand, and, as I will be gone for six weeks, thought I'd come and see you all. Hope you don't mind Wills, he can sleep anywhere, but not with me. Silly prune keeps telling people we're an item. As if! I'm not likely to start washing shirts at my age and cooking meals. Haven't the time. What did you say about surfing? I didn't know you could do it round here.'

As a way of a quick explanation Louise interrupted her elderly relative. She said: 'Mark has been to Devon to look at a link with a church down there. He had a couple of surfing lessons.'

Jude returned with plates piled high for Wills and Aunty and Louise gave up for a while. Neither of them was listening to her. She tried again about the accommodation. 'We're a bit tight for space actually as you can see.'

'Yes.' A.D. closed his eyes again and said: 'Try a different weekend.'

Charis was on the case. 'It's OK dad, Eve and I can move in with Jude tonight. Aunty can have my room. We'll sort ourselves out.'

'We can go back to London if that helps,' Ravi offered.

'You guys can crash with me' said Mike. Aunty gave Mike her full attention. He carried on trying to ignore the scrutiny. 'I did bring a crash mat in case I was on a floor tonight not in a brand-new bed.'

'Fine then. Wills can have the bed settee in the study.' A.D. pronounced, realising that he was not going to win this as far as his daughters were concerned and so it was settled.

Aunty was taking in the baseball cap that Mike was wearing as it was on backwards to protect his neck from the sun. His check shirt was slung across the back of his chair and the short-sleeved t-shirt he was wearing emphasised the muscles in the arms and chest.

Aunty gave him the once over and took him for the gardener. He stood up, wiped his hand on his jeans and held it out to shake her hand. She looked at him dubiously.

'Letting the gardener stay here now are you Mark? Probably your church stuff going too far.'

'Now, now Aunty, this is a colleague of mine and he is lodging with us in the flat over the garage,' said A.D. raising his eyebrows at her. 'They've been putting furniture together which is why they're all dusty. These others are young curates I work with, Chris and Ravi, and the girls' friends.' Aunty offered her own hand reluctantly.

Charis was laughing at her elderly Aunt's distaste at the hand. 'This is Mike, a youth leader,' she said enunciating the words into her elderly relative's ear,

'I'm not deaf dear.' Aunty looked at Charis's animated face. 'Boyfriend?' Aunty said in a stage whisper.

'Not yet.' Mike said, laughing. 'But I'm living in hope of filling the job.' He and Charis exchanged looks and she smiled, raised an eyebrow, and put one hand on her hip.

'You haven't asked me yet.' Charis said.

Mike took off his cap and swept it down in an exaggerated bow. Smiling from ear to ear he looked up at her from midway in his bow and said. 'Lady Charis, will you be my girl?'

The proverbial pin dropped as the play between them continued.

'Good-oh,' Aunty said and sucked her teeth. No one gave the relative any attention though, as Charis dropped a mock curtsey and looked into Mike's eyes.

A.D. despite being delighted at the interplay, decided that there was now too much of an audience for this to develop as he hoped it would. He struggled out of the hammock, Gus getting wrapped in it.

'Come on everyone, time for an aperitif.' A.D. attempted to usher everyone away into the hall. Nothing was shifting. Jude looked to her dog whose paws were caught up in the holes of the hammock. However, as she untangled him and Gus joined Max in rounding the members of the family up, her mouth hit her boots at the exchange between her sister and her youth leader. Jude was not going anywhere and managed to wriggle round her dad. Louise wore a resigned look but A.D. put his arm around his wife and moved her towards the house. Quietly he said: 'You like him, you know you do.'

The dogs retuned to the patio being aware not everyone was where they expected their human friends to be at this time. Mike was in the process of experimentally picking up Charis's hand to see if she would leave it in his, dust and all. He swallowed hard. Charis left her hand in Mike's and the two dogs danced and leaped.

Jude, deciding that nothing else other than her sister and youth leader standing staring at each other was going to happen of any interest, followed the rest of her family into the lounge and announced: 'One down, one to go.'

'Stop it,' mouthed Eve.

'Do you think we should go back out there?' Chris muttered to Ravi.

'I think that is the last place we should be, Chris. Mike's fine. He's beaten you to it, man. I thought you might have got your act together this afternoon as well.'

****

Seventeen

Aunty was Great Aunt Elspeth to Louise Wilkinson, and "twice great" to the girls, as she was inclined to remind Eve, Charis and Jude. On her visits to Park Lodge she always insisted on a new bottle of Jerez being opened. A.D. was pouring a glass of it for her. Everyone was finally seated in the lounge with the exception of Mike and Charis.

'It's meant to be opened and drunk like a bottle of wine, not kept for six months and wheeled out when the elderly come to stay,' said Aunty, lifting her glass to the light in appreciation of its rich colour. The rest of it would get poured into the cooking when she'd gone as A.D. loathed the stuff.

Jude nudged Eve and pointed to Auntie's feet. She had a regular pedicure and in summer sported her open toed sandals, wearing a brilliant red throughout the season while the warmer months lasted. Sure enough, in anticipation of her six weeks in New Zealand, her toes gleamed. The girls found it fascinating that despite conforming in so many ways to their idea of an octogenarian she broke out in various ways.

Dancing twice a week, volunteering and travelling, she led, as she described it, a useful and active life. And now there was a man in tow, although Aunty was completely disinterested in him other than as a useful travelling companion.

Holding out her glass for a top up, Aunty said: 'you can come and see me off for the first leg of my tour in the morning.'

'Sadly Aunty, we are all at work,' said A.D.

'But Charis is a student.'

'Not that sort of student.' A.D. said, firmly. 'And she is still doing finals this summer. Architecture is a little more demanding re the timetable. She will be back at Brookes for her day to start before 9am tomorrow morning.'

Aunty sipped her sherry and then turned in her chair to face Chris who was standing behind it, raising a cup to his mouth. The cup hovered in mid motion while she gave him an inspection. Chris put the cup down on the saucer very slowly and quietly and gave her a smile that he reserved for congregations. Ravi stuffed his fist into his mouth to stifle the laugh, waiting for her punch line.

'Jude,' said Aunty, 'you said when you came in, one down, one to go. Which one is which?'

Jude was up before Eve could stop her, and at her Auntie's side. The room was completely silent and A.D. passed a hand across his eyes waiting for the embarrassment. Only the dogs could be heard barking in the distance as Mike and Charis had taken them for a walk. Jude put her hand to her Auntie's ear and whispered into it.

The eyes began to sparkle and the smile went wide again revealing a full set of dentures. Chris had the benefit of it. She sized him up, the eyes, height, build, and said: '*Hello*.' Her tone scaled and descended octaves.

****

Late afternoon asparagus with home-made Hollandaise had materialised from the kitchen. Chris stared up at the cloudy sky and remained unimpressed by the local weather. Poached eggs appeared from the direction of the kitchen followed by a large plate of smoked salmon. Idyllic it was supposed to be and he could so easily be seduced by it all if it had not been for his own doubts about his boss. Chris was brought out of his reverie as A.D. was speaking to him while he handed him a plate:

'We have another of these in a month, you must come. You could always swap your day off on the Friday for Monday and stay over. Mike would probably be delighted.'

There was the steel in his bosses' eyes. Eve, Chris glanced across at Eve and could see she was obviously pleased by her father's suggestion.

'If it was only just her,' Chris thought.

Someone was saying that it was his birthday, which could not be right as he knew when his birthday was. With horror Chris realised it was him. It was the most ridiculous excuse to avoid giving up his day off. More than that though he was in avoidance mode. How weak of him, how stupid, how spineless to lie instead of just saying, no. Better still why not tell Eve the real problem. Her father, not her, and his own doubts about working for A.D. now. Too late, Eve's expression had melted and she actually linked her arm through his. His brain died at the touch and her perfume.

'Oh Chris, you can't spend your birthday on your own.'

Louise intervened. 'Perhaps he already has plans Eve.'

Again, Chris answered politely that he had nothing arranged. Idiot! Chris thought to himself that there was no way out now. Ravi looked confused, remembering a time a few years ago when they had both organised a joint party as Ravi's birthday was in the same month. Chris entered a tortured state made worse by freezing physically at Eve's touch. Instead of acting like Mike and picking up the situation he was coming across like a frozen cod.

A.D. stared at him, as did Ravi. Of course, his staff file would have his birthday on it. Chris knew he was dead in the water as A.D. would check. Ravi knew. The expression said it all.

'How old this year, Chris?' Ravi asked, his eyes had hardened.

What to do? Again, the hesitation instead of the truth.

A.D. was looking at him knowingly. Here it comes, Chris thought. Disgrace. I'm fired. Oh God, forgive me, he thought, what have I done! The hand went to the hair.

'Now, I think I know.' A.D. was nodding, narrowing his eyes. 'Thirty isn't it. Yes, it's a special one.'

Ravi was up, slapping Chris on the back, trying to create the distraction. He said: 'I didn't know you were older than me. I thought we were both twenty-eight this year.'

A.D. looked at Louise and she knew the look. They were about to throw a party as a technical surprise and of course it would be a networking opportunity for A.D. and his team.

She put her head back and closed her eyes, feeling some sympathy for this nervous young man who was definitely wriggling on the hook trying to get free. She momentarily thought about getting Chris alone and offering him a cheque to kidnap Eve and run off. But she knew her daughter and there was sufficient of A.D. in Eve to want a party and a big wedding. How to help him? Louise tried following logic and said: 'I should think he probably already has made arrangements with his own parents as it's a big year.'

There it was, dissension in the ranks. A.D. was at first shocked and then looked flat as his idea floated away with the wind. It was in danger of blowing as far away as the waving branches of the Oak tree. He recalled the forecast for a chance of showers by six o'clock that evening. How to turn this round before everyone agreed with Louise? Then the rain started and everyone stared at the windows. Chris hoped the issue would be dropped but Jude offered a comment to break the silence.

'Ooh thirty, he's ancient. I wouldn't touch him with a barge pole.' Aunty raised her glass to the youngest there, deciding she was a chip off the old block. However, it appeared Eve was not pleased.

'Don't be such a child,' Eve said.

Jude knew her eldest sister was dead in the water, Charis and now Eve. Soon she would be the last one and things would never be the same again. Her parents complete focus would be on her and what sort of a life would that be?

Jude looked at Chris and saw the words: 'Brother in law,' tattooed on his forehead again.

Still ruminating on the potential of a "do," and whether he could get the BBC team up here to film Purley, A.D. slipped away into his study while everyone else was distracted by the food.

Lifting the lid of his iPad A.D. found the file he was looking for and inserted a name in the search box. There it was: the next of kin contacts Jenny had put together, only in case of emergency. Well a thirtieth birthday without a party was a pretty big emergency to A.D. He picked up his phone. He could do it while they were all eating. He was sure Chris's parents would not mind a call even though it was a Sunday. Best to do a double check that they did not have a surprise planned on the same day as A.D's target date.

****

The 01297 number rang out in the hall of the Georgian home in Colyton. 'Two Chimneys,' where Chris had grown up with his blood brother Storm, resounded on that Sunday evening to the sounds of John Duncan stacking the dishwasher. John paused as he decided whether to bother answering the landline. It was nearly time for their church service and their small Terrier, Mags, got in the way as always and slid down the parquet flooring, legs spreading to the four corners of the house as John moved into the hall to pick up the receiver.

No one called the landline anymore, thought John. The other canine resident of the Duncan home, the partner in crime to the boisterous Terrier was Pitch, a black, elderly Labrador. He opened his eyes but did not move and John felt deep empathy with the dog.

'Good dog, Mags, calm down and let's see who this is,' John said.

John Duncan, about to retire from the civil service felt he had aged, as he said, another ten years since 2016, picked up the landline and said: 'Duncan.' The tone rang with the manner of a permanent secretary.

'Ah, so good to speak to you Mr Duncan. We have met briefly at your son's ordination. This is Mark Wilkinson, the Archdeacon, and I'm sorry to call unexpectedly.'

A brief pause as John's mind recalled the small man with the interesting prayers at the service. 'Hello, yes I remember you. Is everything alright?' asked John steeling himself for news of a crash on the M25.

'Oh yes, there's nothing wrong, didn't mean to alarm you by calling. It's just that we've realised Chris is due a big birthday in a few weeks. With his usual humility and hesitation, he's tried to play it down. I'm ringing as we've found out today that it's his birthday on the third of July.'

'Right, I see. He's told you that has he?' John said to establish the main issue.

'Absolutely. It's just that as it's his thirtieth and he doesn't seem to be having a do that he's confessing to, I thought I would ring you and your wife and check before we organised anything here. It was also, just a thought and no pressure at all, that there is already a garden party here on the third, and I thought I could get the Bishop down and it would be a good networking opportunity for Chris with all this BBC stuff that's happening. The BBC may come actually. Taking it from there, I wanted to check we wouldn't be messing up any arrangements you may have with him?' A.D. waited.

'No, no arrangements on the third. And he's thirty this year he's said? Almost inviting a work's do isn't he telling you that.' John thought he had better establish exact criteria for one of his son's cock-ups.

A.D. thought this was a bit odd but carried on. 'Yes, although I had to drag it out of him give him his due. Thirty's a big birthday. I wondered if there was any chance of you both coming across. I have a flat in Lambeth you could use if you wanted to make a weekend of it or you would be welcome to stay here.'

'Lambeth? That's interesting. Not sure where you are Archdeacon.'

'Do call me Mark. We're in Purley,' said A.D.

'I'm John. Nice spot Purley, with the Downs and all,' John said.

'Yes, beautiful. You're Devon I believe?'

'Yes, we are, in Colyton. Do you know it?' asked John.

'No. I was in the Woolacombe and Croyde areas last week with a young man you know well, that is, so I gather from my secretary, Jenny. It's Storm.'

'Oh, Storm. Yes, he's like a second son to us. Chris and he were inseparable 'til University.'

The conversation lapsed a little. John Duncan cleared his throat and picked up the point for the call.

'The third you said. I'll have to check with my wife Maureen, but I don't think there's anything on other than the usual village fete. We had assumed Chris would be working as he hadn't said anything,' said John, truthfully. 'We were celebrating his birthday a little later in the year.' In November when his actual birthday is, thought John, and his twenty-eighth birthday, which is his actual age. He carried on: 'It would depend on whether she's involved or not. I could tie in a meeting or two on the Friday if we came down. The ministry is trying to get me to stay on with everything that's happening in the next year.'

'Ah, you're involved in the trade negotiations,' said A.D. with enthusiasm. What larks, thought A.D. and what interesting snippets he would gather from this new contact.

'Not if I can help it. Rather do 18 holes,' said John. The conversation lapsed again.

'Still, if your country needs you ...' said A.D.

Again, a lapse in response. Typical ministry man, thought A.D. never committing himself.

John Duncan had, however, signed the Official Secrets Act and silence had become second nature.

There was no way he was going to let slip a piece of information to his son's chatty boss. Apart from which it was Sunday and he didn't work on a Sunday for anyone.

A.D. felt quite sorry for Chris at the lack of enthusiasm in the father's voice. Strange reaction about a son's thirtieth, and an only son as well. Still one never knew the full story. He pressed on with his invitation. 'And you would be welcome to stay.'

'Thanks, er … Mark, but dare say there are people we could stay with and have a bit of a catch-up time. We have friends out in Cheam actually. Members of the Baptist Church there. However, I am sorely tempted by the offer of the flat in Lambeth. Sounds an interesting opportunity to stay there and it would be good to meet you and your family properly.' John stared at the ceiling, noting an area in the corner that he needed to touch up. His dogs sat at his feet looking admiringly at their master.

'Excellent. I'll go ahead and get the organising done this end then. Make it a surprise for him you coming,' said A.D.

'Yes, it will be quite a surprise. Let me know the cost and I'll meet you halfway. Jenny has my email.' John Duncan couldn't think of anything else to say. Seemed the only decent thing to do.

This was more like it as far as A.D. was concerned. Not a bad bloke after all, just a little restrained. Civil Service so was not giving anything away. A.D. said: 'Excellent, and we should meet up for an evening in London. I'm a member of the Royal Academy Friends so we could have a drink in the bar.'

'Interesting,' said John, liking the new possibilities he was being offered despite his son's mess. 'I've often wondered what it was like in there. Can you get tickets?'

'For the summer exhibition? Yes, are you interested?' asked A.D.

'Maureen would love it and I'm just up the road. I could get her up to London for a few nights and we could do the theatre as well.'

'Excellent idea. I'll send dates via Jenny with all the other details re the party,' said A.D.

John's face never moved, 'Yes,' he said, and inhaled deeply. How one's children complicated things. He said: 'Good to chat and look forward to hearing from you.'

They made their goodbyes and John went back to stacking the dishwasher. He was thoughtful about the conversation and assumed he had not blown whatever Chris was up to. Years of working with Government ministers of both sides of the political divide had made it a second instinct.

'Who was that, and what's happening on the third of July? Did I hear you say Archdeacon? Is Chris alright?' Maureen Duncan came into the kitchen, still with the two Sunday papers in her hands, which she had been devouring for the last hour. They were now heading for the recycling. John glanced at the clock, and noted it was time to get ready for the evening service.

'Yes, Mu,' he said, using the pet name for his wife of forty years. 'At least I think he's alright. Well I don't really know.'

John closed the dishwasher door and pushed the ECO switch to start. 'The call was about Chris's thirtieth birthday.'

'What in three years. Bit early isn't it to be talking about his thirtieth birthday?'

'I wasn't. That chap he works for had phoned to check if we could join in the celebrations he's planning. Do you remember the date?'

Maureen gave him a look wondering if this was the beginning of him losing it. She said: 'I should know, and you should too, given that Cabinet meeting you missed. It's November four. We were both there .... remember!'

'Yes, I do. Mark, the chap Chris works for, you know the Archdeacon, seems to be under the illusion that Chris is thirty on the third of July. They're throwing him a birthday party as a surprise and wondered if we didn't have anything planned whether we would like to go. Nice chap, offered us his flat at Lambeth Palace, which would be interesting as I've never been, or we could stay with them out in Purley. I thought that would be a bit intense actually so wondered about old Graham and Julie in Cheam as we haven't seen them for a while.'

'John, John, slow down. Chris is twenty-eight this year.'

'I know that.' John said, and they both stood looking at each other. Mags decided that it was time to play ball and to have John's full attention. John duly picked the ball up and moved it round and round while the dog pursued it.

Maureen broke the silence: 'What's going on?'

'Goodness knows,' answered John.

He stared out into the garden and the only sound was the dishwasher and a gush of water as the programme started. John looked at Maureen and said: 'He's clearly dropped himself in it, Chris I mean. Probably tried to wriggle out of something the Archdeacon wants him to do on July 3rd. Either that or there's obviously a mix up. I thought he was in mortal dread of the man, calls him the Rottweiler, doesn't he? Introduced himself as Mark and sounded alright to me. Decent thing to offer to throw your employee a special party and invite the parents. I said I'd meet him halfway on the cost.'

'What? John, you don't actually think this is going to happen. We need to speak to Chris,' said Maureen.

'Why?' John looked genuinely surprised at the idea of interfering. He said: 'No, you can't ruin the surprise. It may just be a mistake or he's doing a wriggle. Either way he's not a child, Mu. If something else is going on we have to wait for him to tell us. He'll be here on Friday, won't he? And anyway, we should be there as he obviously needs our help. He's got himself into a stupid situation by the sound of it.' John thought for a couple of moments, while his wife pulled a couple of dead begonias off the plant on the kitchen window sill with some force. Watching the process John realised that sooner or later her frustration was going to surface and there would be no peace.

'Tell you what,' said John, picking up his mobile, 'Actually, I'll ring Storm. If anyone knows what's going on he will.' And he walked into the garden.

****

There was ten minutes before the service started. They were going to be late. The dial tone rang out and John remembered that Storm would already be well into his own evening service in Croyde. He was about to hang up without leaving a message and was already striding back into the house. Then he heard Storm's voice say: "Uncle John, good to hear you. I've just stepped out of the service as it was you and you don't normally call. What's happening?'

'We're both fine, don't worry it was only going to be quick. We're leaving for our service in a couple of minutes. We're wondering if there is anything we should know about Chris as I've had a call from the Archdeacon, who seems to be under the illusion that Chris has his 30th in a few weeks and want's to include a birthday celebration in some Bishop's bash he's already holding. As it's unusual and you were with him last week I thought you may be able to shed some light on what is going on.'

Storm inhaled and then let the breath out slowly. He had no idea what was happening regarding a birthday but as the Archdeacon was involved it must be Chris in crisis.

'To put it bluntly Chris has the hots for Eve, A.D's eldest daughter, doesn't want to have because he can't stand the thought of A.D. long-term, as in father-in-law. Chris is also having a down time on whether or not he made the right decision about taking the job, which I've told him is a bit late now. It's triggered by some BBC programming A.D. has got us all involved with and Chris hates the idea of a raised profile.

That's it in a nutshell. It sounds like he's avoiding a date if he's told A.D. the third of July is his birthday.'

'I see, thanks, Storm. We'll be prepared if we hear from Chris then. Anyway, I've more or less accepted the invitation for the third of July,' said John.

'WHAT?' spluttered Storm.

'I get to stay in Lambeth Palace. Mark has a flat there,' said John.

'Uncle John, you're colluding,' said Storm.

John Duncan thought this was an interesting concept for a senior Civil Servant. Ignoring the issue, he moved on with: 'Wasn't the Archdeacon's family at the Cathedral? They looked nice enough. I had a chat with one of the daughters, clever I thought. Struck me as a "good'un." Only talked to her briefly, of course, but I liked her. We're seeing you Friday night, I think, aren't we?'

'Yup. The BBC is down in Woolacombe and Croyde on Wednesday night and the shoot is Thursday, providing the surf's OK. Then we're coming over in the evening on Friday. From the photos I've seen John, the daughter was called Eve.'

'That's the name. Looked lovely at the Cathedral. What's the issue I wonder?' mused John.

'The issue's A.D. John. I think he's alright, actually. You know how Chris has been besieged with women since he became a curate. His head says something different to his heart but I think it's mainly the doubts about being in the job with A.D. that's doing it. Chris feels a mess and not fit for purpose as far as getting involved with someone.

Thing is he is involved emotionally anyway but it probably wouldn't have mattered if she wasn't A.D's daughter. I think I should go, John. Good to hear you, and love to aunty Mu.'

'And you, thanks for the chat Storm. See you later in the week.' John Duncan ended the call and stood watching the roses bend in the wind. He must put in fresh stakes or they would snap. Momentarily he reflected his concern about his son in a prayer, which A.D. would have thought of as a Smith Wigglesworth moment. Maureen knew he would be praying and left him to it. Five minutes more and she would prompt him as they must go out themselves.

****

Eighteen

Night had come down suddenly across the garden and Ravi and Mike had been setting up the kitchen. Chris was in a tortured state as one lie, which had not been pre-meditated, was growing in significance with A.D's arrangements. Mike now sat on the flat roof of the garage outside his new bedroom and played the sweet-sounding classical guitar softly so that the night air carried the music along the drive and across the gardens to the family in the house. Charis, silent in her surprise that Mike could play so well, sat with her eyes closed knowing where she wanted to be. Wisdom, however, told her to leave the guitarist to his music and his new home.

On a newly put together table in the flat above the garage sat the remains of the takeaway. Ravi rose to start wrapping it up. He was feeling pleased for Mike and the day had also helped him out of his own reflective state. There had been a good deal of constructive laughter and Ravi was grateful for the time in the service to share the vision about the work with the slum community. Chris had asked him to wait a few weeks before he made a final decision and Ravi was almost persuaded to come to Devon with them rather than jump and return to Delhi. He glanced across at Chris as the hair clutching had started again. Ravi hoped that his friend was not going to go through the night in such a state. He sat on a kitchen stool and said: 'Chris, you are all over the place, what's wrong?'

With the tone of a hedge fund analyst watching all gains evaporating, Chris flopped back on the new Chaise Longue. He said: 'Ravi, I've done a terrible thing.'

****

By the time their service was over and they were walking back through the village to home, Maureen Duncan was fully appraised of her son's avoidance tactics. This was because he had called John's number and left a message. At first Maureen thought that her husband had misheard the sorry story but John was adamant that years of taking strange calls from Government Ministers, on both sides of the political divide, meant he rarely misinterpreted a message. It was, after all, a question of which fan the proverbial was going to hit.

'I have not misheard,' John had said firmly. 'It's here, you have a listen.' And he had handed the phone to her.

Maureen waited while she listened to her large son, soon to be aged twenty-eight and not thirty, as he rabbited on. Her face had the look of a teacher who had approached the classroom to find her class had wedged the door slightly ajar in order to place a bucket of water on the top of it. To walk into the situation or not? she debated.

****

Mike was now in on the deception too and the three of them were out on the flat roof. Ravi was firm that no matter what the consequence Chris must tell A.D. the truth tonight. Tomorrow would be too late as A.D. would get going on invitations very fast with a touch of a button.

'You know what he's like, it's all action and reflection afterwards,' said Ravi, ' A.D. will see it as a networking opportunity not to be missed. You must go down there and put it right.'

Chris sat with his head in his hands and said nothing. Mike reached for his phone. He had found Charis on WhatsApp and wrote:

'Come quick. Need your help. Chris has dropped himself right in it. xxxxx'

This sent, Mike put his phone down and looked at Chris and Ravi.

'The thing is, Ravi, that we don't know how the guy will react. It's late, it's been a really tiring day with all those people, and we saw how he went off on one when he thought Rafe was onto Charis. I've just sent for reinforcements.'

The phone buzzed: 'And the marines are on their way over,' said Mike, with a grin.

****

A.D. had lovingly picked up his Alistair Cooke copy of a book he had first read as a student. Clergyman as he was he thought he saw things pretty clearly about the human mess, but in thinking about the presidential election to come in the USA, he remembered that Cooke had referred somewhere to the American's tendency to elect a businessman when they perceived a crisis. He could not remember if it was in the book or a talk. His memory told him Cooke had said it seemed they always went for an academic or a businessman. Well there we are, thought A.D. that's Obama and Trump.

At the time, A.D. had first come across the reference, the emphasis was on a business 'man.' The logic, in Cooke's opinion, was that the businessman had been successful. So, Americans, at that time of the talk assumed the skills were transferable.

A.D's memory was unclear but he thought he recalled in a different episode of "Letter from America," that Alistair Cooke had said the Americans would never elect a woman. Of course, the journalist had said it all those decades ago. A.D. thought he would ask Cooke his opinion now if he had had the privilege of sharing a meal with him tonight.

His musings stopped as the bedroom door opened slightly and Charis tapped gently so as not to wake her mother. She diplomatically waited for her father to come to the door.

Slipping his feet into slippers A.D. picked up a dressing gown and went to the bedroom door.

'Sorry,' Charis apologised. 'I know you're trying to switch off, but I need to talk to you about a big mistake that's happened.'

'Oh dear, are you alright? I'm sure the boy will understand,' A.D. patted her arm.

'Sorry dad?' Charis stared at her dad.

'Mike.' A.D. said. 'I like him a lot, but I guess apart from the obvious you haven't got much in common and it did all happen as a bit of fun.'

'Dad, stop, if you mean what I think you do. Mike isn't a mistake. He's the most real man I've been out with. It's this silly birthday thing I'm on about that everyone got carried away with this afternoon. Chris mumbled something and I think it was misheard. It isn't his birthday until November and he isn't thirty this year, he'll be twenty-eight. You have to stop assuming everyone is fine with you taking over their lives and organising events around them. Mike got me over to the flat as he's a total mess about it.'

'Mike's a total mess?' A.D. asked. He had been slightly wrong-footed at the reference to a "real man." Un-nerved, A.D. was hoping it didn't mean what it might. He missed part of Charis's explanation as a result.

Charis paused while she tried to hold on to her rapidly evaporating patience. She said: 'No, Chris is a total mess. Mike's fine. Chris doesn't know what to do now as you've probably started organising everything in your mind. I've told him he's been stupid for not talking up and just going to brain death when Eve put her arm through his this afternoon. Goodness, *men*.'

Charis took another deep breath before she continued: 'Anyway, I've told him the consequence of not speaking up is that he has to come to the do anyway and network. That's it!'

A.D. was impressed. 'Well done Charis. What a mess indeed. You'll make a great business woman. And yes, I think that's a good consequence. I keep telling him to speak up in his talks. Ah well.' A.D. remembered his call to John Duncan. He looked sheepish. Charis looked at her father and knew he had inevitably dabbled too soon.

A.D. came clean: 'Ah, but I rang his parents. John Duncan sounds an interesting fellah, civil servant you know. I offered them the flat at Lambeth, which he sounded quite interested in and then there's the summer exhibition at the Royal Academy I've got tickets for. He was very keen. Your mother hates it and I'm sure she......'

'Dad, stop. You actually phoned his mum and dad? Are you nuts?' Charis's eyes had gone wide and she forgot to be quiet. They both glanced at the sleeping mound under the duvet which was Louise.

A.D. looked sheepish. He said: 'Yes, too soon? Ah well, another consequence but I accept I was a bit fast off the block. Funny thing though John didn't say anything about it being the wrong date. He must be a bit vague not to remember his son's birthday. Even offered to pay half the cost of the do. Are you going back over?'

'No, not now. I'm up early so I've had it after all that. I'll let Mike know it's alright and the networking do is on regardless and Chris has to be there. You are fine about the mistake, aren't you?'

'Yes, think so,' A.D. thought about it briefly. 'Yes, I suppose I am but we will have to talk about what is going on. I'll see him in the morning anyway. What time are you off?'

'Six-thirty. I'm giving Mike a lift as he's never been to Oxford and he's got some toil after last week.'

'Charis.'

'Yes dad?'

'Did you say Chris's brain went to mush when Eve put her arm through his?'

'Oh yes, apparently he's nuts about her but something's holding him back.'

'Yes, I'm afraid it's probably me. Well, worth all this just to find out that's how he feels about her.'

'Dad, you do need to back off,' said Charis, and she leant forward and gave him a peck on the cheek.

A.D. returned to Alistair Cooke but before long a cold hand gripped his vitals. He swung his legs out of bed forgetting Louise was soundly asleep. She stirred slightly but her breathing settled back and A.D. slipped quietly to the door.

'Charis,' he hissed up the landing towards his daughter's bedroom, 'Charis.'

It was useless. A form of punishment for his over-activity on the match making front.

A.D. would have to face a disturbed night pondering the fact that his middle daughter was running off with a youth worker to Oxford for a few days.

****

Full of guilt when he woke from an exhausted sleep on Monday morning, Chris felt flat with the realisation that he still had A.D. to face and they were travelling in to work together. The borrowed sleeping bag was in a knot around his legs and the pillow drenched with his sweat. There was no time for a long shower as he had turned off the alarm and fallen asleep again. He also realised that he had not been the strength for Mike last night that he had intended and that his friends had bailed him out because they hadn't actually heard what he had muttered about his birthday. However, they had also insisted that he did attend the next occasion that was being organised at A.D's home and that he did network it. That was the consequence for him and he would do it. But he had to be honest with A.D. and not hide behind a lie.

The only friend he thought had heard him properly in his lie was Eve and he needed to come clean with her or probably lose the potential of any relationship with her in the future. Chris also realised he needed to speak to his parents before Friday but now he had a train to make and a journey to do with A.D. into Westminster.

He set his face for a confrontation practising a more cheerful expression in the mirror, while plastering his hair.

It was too wet to take the product and gave him the look of a damp dog.

A.D. was on the drive looking at his watch, just back from dropping Jude at school. A white-faced young curate came from the garage and joined him by the car.

'Morning,' said Chris.

A.D. smiled a brief welcome and Chris thought the man hated him. In reality A.D. had been texting Charis without any response. Texts were not a medium anyone in the family used, with the exception of A.D. He was so stressed he had forgotten. But here was another opportunity before him and he was truly ready to forgive anything as long as this young man gave his heart to Eve.

'Good night?' asked A.D.

'Bit mixed,' said Chris.

'Joys of sleeping on a futon no doubt,' A.D. said.

Eve's message to her dad said she had left early and gone back into London with Louise. A.D's thoughts were interrupted by a ruction from the side of the house as the dogs had decided that Wills was unwelcome. Aunty had spent breakfast giving the dogs what she thought of as a treat. She was poisoning them with chocolate to quieten them down and A.D. had had the delight of his wife's elderly relative and her friend over breakfast. He clearly wanted to get off to the station before he became embroiled with them again. But he needed to save his dogs.

He whistled and Max and Gus were round to him like lightening.

To keep the dogs safe from any more delicacies he excused him to Chris and walked the dogs down to the area behind the Oak tree where there was a quarter of an acre, a shed with their beds in, which the spaniels could use for shelter while the family were out. Putting them down there would keep them away from Aunty, stop imminent canine death from chocolate and give Wills some peace. He just had to fill two containers with water down there. Chris leant against the car and pondered a lack of a future.

A.D. was distracted by messages on his phone as he and Chris found seats in a crowded carriage for London. But the messages were not the only distraction. The fact that Charis and Mike were in Oxford for a few days niggled at a fatherly area of his brain. Irrationally he would admit to himself, but it was happening, so when Chris started to speak to him he only listened with half an ear. Half an ear, that is, until the word "resign," registered. He jerked his head up and looked at the earnest young man opposite him.

'But why, dear boy?' A.D. asked, all thoughts of Oxford evaporating.

They were sitting crammed in by the window on two of six seats. Buttocks were rammed into the corner to avoid those who were next to them. Dressed as both he and Chris were it was not the best place to choose to have such a discussion but Chris had started and was seeing it through. He was sitting on his hands so he controlled the tendency to clutch his hair.

The woman next to Chris had stopped typing on her phone to listen and there was a rustle of a paper from the man sitting next to A.D.

Chris shrugged: 'I have doubts that I should be doing this. I may have made a mistake. I think I shouldn't have left aid work. I don't agree with this BBC project. I hate the raised profile it'll give me. Also, I have feelings for your daughter, and that won't happen if I'm working for you. But there is something else I have to tell you about last night.'

A.D. distracted again, recalled General George Marshall's advice to listen to the other person's full story, first. He had come across it last night while searching through his podcasts looking for the Alistair Cook reference. Listening did not come easily to A.D. He was fighting the desire to butt in, and had heard all he needed to which was the reference to having feelings for his daughter. Instead he adopted his most open expression, working hard at sitting on himself. Chris had paused and the pause was so long that A.D's imagination was starting to work overtime. Confession, it sounded like.

To Chris, what he had to say was frank, and a mess. It was time he stopped the mess he was in. Apart from that he was becoming what he most despised: a hypocrite.

'Last night,' Chris started again suddenly.

The passengers were attentive.

'I blurted out that I wasn't available that weekend because it was my birthday. It happened because I panicked about losing my weekend off. But worse still I added to the lie by letting you believe it was my thirtieth birthday. That was a lie too.

You would find out eventually anyway because it's in the staff records. It doesn't matter why, A.D. I did it to get out of another weekend. The only person who heard me say it was Eve I think, and what is worse, I haven't been able to put it right with her because I stupidly turned the alarm off this morning and went back to sleep. So, I missed her. And she'll hate me because she'll know what Charis and Mike and Ravi then did to bale me out with you. So that's it. That's this curate for you. So, I need to go because of that alone.'

It took ten seconds for A.D. to realise that Chris had stopped. The paper rustler next to A.D. was in full agreement with Chris that he needed to go, and had looked at Chris over the top of his paper with a firm expression. The man turned his head and looked at A.D. who met the gaze with a friendly expression. The man stared back and raised his eyebrows and nodded briefly. A.D. gave him a rather tight smile and then half turned his body so that he was twisted away. He knew the type. The hatchet man in the office. The people on the seats opposite were also looking at A.D. waiting to see how he would react. Well they would wait, while A.D. stared through the window at suburbia while the train rolled past it. Chris had dropped his eyes and was staring at the floor. A.D. wished his curate had waited until they were in the office. Time went by and they were coming into Victoria and the train drew to its stop. The exodus began but man of faith as he was A.D. was waiting for the answer and he carried on sitting while the carriage emptied. Chris had the look of an adolescent caught shoplifting.

Finally, A.D. spoke: 'Let's get off and walk up to your cafe shall we. I'll let Jenny know we'll be a bit late.'

Chris mechanically picked up his bag and stood, respectfully allowing A.D. to go first. A.D. sent Jenny a text as he walked to the door of the train. It read: "We'll be late. Chris in melt-down."

Chris followed the Archdeacon blindly, feeling wretched but at the same time like he had fallen off a wall. That was it. He had left his watch and was falling off the wall. Soldier down, he thought. Chris looked at A.D. who was walking a little ahead and thought of Eve. Irrationally he imagined her running off with Rafe, or that director she was working for or never returning from her year in Kenya. The torture he felt deepened.

A.D. was through the barrier and concentrating on his phone. Chris followed blindly but got stuck in the barrier gates. Walking too slowly his backpack became trapped and a mammoth task ensued to open them or pull him through. A.D. looked up from his message to Eve, hitting send. It said:

'Chris has come clean re the birthday - full confession - good man - all will be well. He wanted to see you to explain but overslept.'

Two members of Southern Rail were extracting his assistant who had parted company with the backpack. On his front screen, A.D. saw that there was a response from Jenny and a surfeit of exclamation marks.

'Got a quick call from his (Chris's) mum this morning. Apparently, you rang their home!!!!!! She's very worried about him. Don't come in 'til 10. 'A' is here again!!!!!'

Ah, thought A.D. a good reason for a second breakfast. He scrolled down and found a notification from Eve with an emoticon of a kiss. That was good.

There were texts from Rafe about the church flower committee. A.D. grunted and decided these were not going to be read at present. He put the phone in his pocket.

Chris got his backpack on again and glanced at A.D. Despite the smile Chris thought A.D. must despise him. He duly followed walking several steps behind. From Victoria on a work day morning they passed the smokers huddled in chairs outside the cafes in the cool of early June and Chris, in his silence, wondered if he would ever be able to start a normal conversation again. They made a left turn through Christchurch Gardens, then towards Lucya's cafe and St James's tube. A.D. would see to the well-being of the man his eldest daughter loved.

To A.D. it was all feeling very positive and despite the silent gloom of the man trailing behind him up Victoria Street there was an honesty between them: so, there was a way back. Charis had hit home last night about taking over people's lives. However, it would not be quick and Chris must have space. A.D. liked the honesty. They could build from here. And Chris had finally come clean about Eve. Yes, it was all going well.

A.D. smiled as they turned into Lucya's. She glanced past him at Chris, her usual customer, who had not spoken to her. Chris had sat in a corner by the window and stared at the wall.

'Two full English for Chris and I this morning Lucya. Lovely morning, isn't it? Still got that early summer freshness.

Let me pay you now and I just have to pop outside to make some calls.' A.D. wrote on a napkin his mobile number and an explanation for her.

'Chris not too good, think he might have shock,' the note said.

'Thank you, where will you be?' Lucya asked. They exchanged a look and she glanced across at Chris. He had been a regular there for years and A.D. thought he could trust her.

'Just by the paper shop,' said A.D. and kept his smile for her. Once outside on the pavement he called Jenny. She answered, but before he could speak A.D. got her full officious tone, which he knew meant that she was not alone. Then there was a silence as she waited.

A.D. said: 'I'm just feeding the man. I think he's in shock actually. I'm not sure he'll cope with ringing his parents at the moment, Jenny. I shouldn't have called them last night. Do you mind playing go between?'

Her response was like an answer machine message:

'I've heard your message and noted your call. Absolutely. Good morning,' and Jenny was gone.

A.D. registered that she was still fending off Adiniji. In fact, he had been standing behind her as she took A.D's call.

A.D. tossed up if he needed to check Rafe's texts.

Finally deciding that he could not avoid them any longer he hit the first looking out on to Palmer street from his position by the paper shop.

Rafe was to go on a parish visit that morning and had been invited early to see the horses training at the stud farm of the wealthy young widow, the Right Honourable Letitia. A.D. knew how that would go. She wouldn't mind the sweat and the Eton background would appeal. A.D. doubted that Rafe would escape especially if she got him into the barn. Probably Letitia could be good for Rafe's career. Somewhere in the recesses of A.D's memory was a note that Letitia was related to a number of Bishops. It might encourage a few of them to show up at Purley if Rafe and Letitia became an item.

'Yes, she and Rafe may hit it off. Ah well that's Rafe sorted out,' A.D. said aloud, as he bought a paper.

Rafe's second text however, had clearly forgotten the flower committee. It was a cry for help as the Right Honourable was getting amorous.

'You're a grown man,' A.D. said to his phone despite the fact that no one was on the other end. But he softened: 'Oh well, I'd better give him a call.' A.D. hit Rafe's number and the dial tone rang out. The call ended and he sent a text which suggested: 'Don't go into the barn.'

That should do it A.D. thought and moved onto a new message that had just popped up on his screen from Jenny: 'Will call Maureen later. 'A' not being fobbed off this morning.'

He typed a reply, his thumbs working overtime: 'Keep him there, I'll be in shortly. Give him a cupboard or something to search through.'

A.D. thought that it was time to sort this bloke out.

****

The rain had started as they walked from Broadway, up Tothill Street, working their way through the tourists making an early visit to the Abbey. The rain had a despondent feel about it as it was heavy and there was no variation in its direction. A.D. and Chris turned into the lush green of Dean's Yard, the smell of the wet foliage striking the senses after the fumes of the buses and taxis.

As the two men walked towards the entrance to the cloisters Chris thought how incongruous it was to have a post box there in Dean's Yard.

The harmony of the boys from the school who were singing in the Abbey rose as they entered. A.D's face lit up and he hummed along before briefly stopping to chat to the assistant to the minor canons who had appeared from his right. Chris walked to some stone seating by the plaque that commemorated the work of "the men and women of your race." Chris looked onto the green of the cloisters opposite and sat beneath a memorial to Anne Gawen. He had often stared at it, knowing he would remember the name forever

Chris still had not spoken since the train, leaving his responses to just nods, once a half smile, when A.D. had suggested they go into the cloisters. The breakfast had helped, and Chris had started thinking again. It felt like the world had slowed down in its orbit, heaven had gulped and there was a ripple of the shock he felt after initiating a resignation from his job with A.D.

Chris had said: 'help,' a few times during breakfast, just in case God was still interested.

A.D. joined him on the stone seat and followed Chris's line of sight. Clearing his throat, A.D. said: 'I need to apologise to you Chris on a number of points. Charis, last night, pointed out to me my propensity for taking over other people's lives. I am sorry, Chris, because I suspect that my driving projects on hasn't taken into account that I have a co-driver. I haven't listened to you, which is strange, because when I recruited you as my assistant, I was very struck with the evident strength of your faith. You were the right choice, definitely. I've been operating like things were a done deal and just communicating decisions made alone, well not alone if you get my drift but feeling sure of direction should not have been to exclude you.'

This was a surprise and Chris spoke a sentence for the first time from the train.

'Of course, you would make decisions. It's only natural,' Chris said, feeling disarmed by A.D's frank honesty.

A.D. stared at the plaques along the walls and registered the polite response. It was too polite. Auto pilot type of polite and not the response from the gut which was produced by the honesty he wanted to get to with Chris today if the two of them were to move forward with a working relationship.

'I think I'm going to suggest a change of direction for a while because you were very firm that you felt called into the ministry. I'm taking the calling as a fact. If there are aspects of working with me that you are uncomfortable about we can talk it through. I'd like you to take six months, perhaps returning to Africa and doing some work with a charity or that uncle you have, take some time for a break as well, rest, eat, and sleep. Think about what you really believe you should be doing. I would like you with us though this week and down in Devon with the BBC though. You do matter in this venture Chris. But, if you feel you've had enough that is your decision in six months' time. Think about it and let me know.'

Chris stared out through the glassless, arched, window of the cloisters and noted how neatly the green was tended. He thought about the number of people that had sat where he was sitting in the Abbey over the centuries, in states of turmoil like him.

'I can't even pray properly.' Chris said, staring ahead. 'All that comes out is, help.'

A.D. leaned forward, his hands on his knees. He chuckled and said: 'What was your point to me last week about Smith Wigglesworth moments? I took that on board, you know but remember what I said at the prayer room as well. There's only two words you need at times: "Help" and "Thanks." God hasn't changed this morning, regardless of how you feel now. And where did you get the idea that as a clergyman you would be perfect?' A.D. stood up and stretched. He turned around to face Chris who had remained seated. For once A.D. had the advantage of height. 'Now, to the other thing that has come up this morning that I must mention. You said on the train, that you have feelings for Eve, and that working for me meant that that couldn't go anywhere. I'm assuming that was due to my propensity to interfere?'

'Yes,' Chris said the word quietly but it had all the resonance of a shout.

'Good,' A.D. said and his face relaxed. 'We have honesty between us at last. Look, don't go walking away from Eve because of me. I'll back off, I promise, and if I forget just tell me. Honesty works with me, seriously.' A.D. thought for a second and then added: 'Louise does it all the time. At least you know that I think you're fine for my daughter, for what it's worth. More than that. I'd be delighted for you both. Anyway, that's all part of what you're working through I know. All I can say, to encourage you, is that Eve feels the same, so if I was in your shoes I'd be inclined to follow young Mike's example and go for it. Now, I'm going to see if that cafe outside is open as its ten o'clock, and get a coffee. Want one?'

'Yes, to both points. But I feel such a mess and I can't put that on Eve,' Chris said.

A.D. sat on his sense of exasperation.

He said: 'That's up to Eve. Let her have the choice. If she doesn't want you she'll tell you. That's the risk we all take about love. But at least you'll have acted, Chris, instead of letting it fester. The risk you also take by not telling her, of course, is that she'll go away for a year without you addressing how you both feel. She may then meet someone else who will tell her. Actually, I've told you she feels the same so you can go for it. Telling her may help with the sense of mess.' A.D. looked at his watch. 'I'm going for a coffee, what will you have, this is on me.'

'But you paid for breakfast.' Chris looked up at him.

AD smiled as Chris had managed a very small challenge. 'Quite right.' A.D. said. 'You pay. Then I'm going in to sort this character, Adeniji, out. He's turned up again and seems to be adopting the unofficial role of auditor/hatchet man. Want to come?'

'I feel quite sorry for him if he's decided to take you on,' said Chris. 'Yes, I want to come. I'll get those coffees and follow you in.' Chris stood up and A.D. started to walk back towards the archway into Dean's Yard. He paused and pulled his phone from his pocket and held it out to Chris.

'Have a look at these texts from Rafe,' said A.D. 'He's with an amorous parishioner this morning.'

Chris screwed up his face as he read the cry for help. He said: 'Did you set that up? I think Charis is right about you taking over people's lives. What on earth possessed you to send him round there?'

A.D. beamed at the frankness, glad they were making progress.

****

Nineteen

Tuesday at Heathrow saw an elegant blonde at Arrivals, neatly attired in jeans and silk top and her hair curled and silky having spent far too much time to achieve that effect as far as she was concerned. The Emirates flight had already landed and Ellie was walking rapidly to meet Joel. The Piccadilly line from Hammersmith had been delayed and she had lost fifteen minutes. Ellie was in good time though as Joel would be only just off the plane and heading to Passports. After her time at the Lad's place, Ellie had lost track of how long she had soaked in a bath. The baseball cap that she had worn for the previous five days had bitten the dust in the rubbish. This was therapy following days and nights at Rev. Deidre's church break.

Her man, Joel, had sent a WhatsApp that he was disembarking now and she was that funny mix of tension and excitement. She had effectively all of today, with him. Then there would be most of tomorrow that they would be alone together, albeit on a mainline train to Exeter. Ellie knew Joel had work to do, as did she. He had said something about "innovation imperative, and the digital age and finance," but they would have the first two days without her work until Wednesday evening.

Ellie had also booked tickets weeks ago, for Covent Garden for tonight, with a champagne package. It was part of giving Joel the London experience. He would probably fall asleep in the performance but she did not care.

Ellie ordered a cappuccino and sat on a stool in the coffee bar facing the doors Joel would come through. Since he had come to Melbourne for work and joined the hundreds of fund and investment managers in the city Joel had met Ellie following an Alpha course. She thought of how he had wandered into her day centre for the homeless one Sunday, joking that he had got the wrong entrance and stayed to help wash up. Joel had changed so much since then as he had lived for wealth and material gain, girls, and having a good time. But it was an inner emptiness that took him to Alpha. After a few weeks of Joel turning up at the centre Ellie had given in and finally agreed to have dinner with him. In the days that followed Joel had sent flowers and showered her with expensive gifts. Ellie had given them back. Instead, she asked Joel to spend a day with her at the shelter and for her to spend a couple of hours in his office so that they could understand each other's work. The sacrifice of taking a whole day seeing the full work of the homeless shelter was the most expensive gift that Joel could give Ellie.

With him, Ellie knew this one was going full term. Her life had been in the small suburb of Melbourne as a child with her three younger sisters. Family barbecues in the back garden and playing amongst Eucalyptus trees formed her earliest memories. She had not associated high finance with her version of Melbourne.

Joel made money for other people. The result had been massive bonuses. Now he was impacted by God.

He was a new man but like everyone, including herself, a work in progress spiritually. Ellie suggested to him he try an experiment of giving his money away. He had started doing that and found he was making more. At first Joel thought God was playing with him but realised he was being taught that God was interested in him not his money. It was a dilemma for him. Joel owned a five-bedroomed house in Melbourne, and lived alone. Or rather he slept there, crashing out on his bed or the sofa as soon as he got in, working on average twelve to sixteen hours a day.

After she had finished her coffee Ellie picked up a paper left by another customer. And then the doors opened and she got off her stool and joined the row of people holding cards up with names on. Five minutes went by, and her phone pinged. A message that he was: "through passport and collecting bags."

Ellie went back to the coffee area and carried on reading, checking her watch fifteen minutes later. As she did so a tall, scruffy looking man, sporting a five o'clock shadow and a fresh white t-shirt which he had pulled from his hand luggage over his jeans, was standing by her side with a broad smile.

'Well how chilled is this Reverend Dr! I come all this way....' The rest of his sentence was lost in a mass of hair as Ellie wrapped her arms around his neck and they kissed.

Joel stood back and looked at her, holding her arms out. 'Let me take in the fact you are real, girl. Sorry about the wait, we had police come on board and remove someone.'

'Good grief, what for?' Ellie asked.

'Probably immigration. It was all very calm and I think she was expecting it. But you never know these days.'

Ellie looked at the bags under his eyes. 'You must be shattered. Did you sleep at all?'

'Yes, in business class I got six hours. And I've gained a day, so, I fully intend to make the most of the extra day in my life, with you. Look, I've got Heathrow Express booked so we can pick you up a ticket and head over to the hotel. And then I want to go and sort out these rocks before anything else.'

'Why do you want to do that today? I thought you'd want to chill and have dinner, maybe nap and I've got us tickets for Covent Garden tonight.' Ellie was a little taken aback at the topic of the geological specimens again.

'Perfect. Nah, I'm fine and need to get on with this task,' Joel smiled, as he looked at her.

'Where are you booked into?' Ellie asked.

'Somewhere round Canary Wharf,' replied Joel. 'The office thought half way between the City and the office there made sense but I'm not sure where it is.' Joel fished out his phone and found the booking from his office. He showed Ellie and said: 'It's a Hilton, on Marsh Wall.'

'OK, we need to work out the route to that,' said Ellie. 'It's not an area I know at all. 'That's going to take a bit of time to get across to but if we get you settled in first, lose the luggage, we can grab some food and get to the geology place you want to go to? We're free 'til about six-thirty tonight, and then need to be in Covent Garden to pick up tonight's tickets.'

Joel laughed. He said: 'Ha, two gardens today. I'll work out where the first garden is on the train.' Joel paused and looked around the arrival's hall for signs. 'Do you know where we get the train? I can see a sign for underground but this train I'm booked on is different isn't it?'

****

While Ellie was at Heathrow, A.D. had had his second morning of Adeniji at Church House. Second guessing where the man would go next was an art. A.D. had, by mid Tuesday morning, dispatched him by introducing him to Finance. There would be much more for the man to get stuck into a load of spreadsheets. Jenny had done her best to deflect Adeniji but to no avail. Giving up she had turned to her answering machine and had found further calls from the Australian called Joel. A.D. had dismissed the issue when she tried to tell him earlier. The calls appeared to be about a question of a special licence. Jenny was replaying the messages over again as A.D. reappeared from Finance.

A.D. pushed open the office door rubbing his hands together with a satisfied smile. He said: 'That should keep him busy for a couple of days.'

'What have you done with him?' Jenny asked.

'Parked him in Finance,' said A.D. heading for his own office.

'You haven't left him with Angela?' Jenny called after him, looking horrified.

'Yes, who else?' said A.D.

'Oh no! Poor woman. I'd better collect her for a coffee in a bit to get her away. Honestly A.D. I don't know what the Bishop was thinking inviting him here,' Jenny said.

'Oh, I don't think it was by invitation. The man's on a mission. We all needing saving apparently. Where's Chris? A.D. asked, looking round, 'I need to line him up for this afternoon or I'll get nothing done before we leave for Woolacombe,'

'He's down the hall in a meeting room with the blinds down, hiding from Adeniji. He's been working on that strategy you wanted. I don't think he's really concentrating but I said there was a deadline so that he focuses a bit more. Better his mind is on something. I called the Duncans last night and explained that you had made a mistake and that was it really. I'm not sure Maureen believed me. She muttered something about one of Chris's cock-ups. But Chris is due there over the weekend so he'll probably tell them more then.'

Jenny paused and A.D. waited, sensing more was coming.

'There are lots of calls on your extension again, A.D. from that man called Joel. He's very pushy and I don't know how he got the number. He's left messages and he says there is an urgent issue of a special licence while he's in the UK. He flies in today apparently from Australia. He says he will see you on Thursday in North Devon? Can you give him a ring? Here's the number.' Jenny put the number down in front of him and waited for him to work out what it was about.

'Oh, must be someone from the BBC. Why call me about special licences?' said A.D. 'I would have thought they were used to sorting out whatever they need to arrange for filming.' A.D. turned the paper over in his hand. 'I'll call that woman who's arranging everything, what's her name?'

'Sarah isn't it?' said Jenny.

'Or I can probably talk to him on Thursday, as goodness knows where he's calling from. Save the bill a bit. I can't be ringing Australia as there's an international dialling code in front of the number. Who on earth are they flying in I wonder?' A.D. pointed to the number. 'Do they need special licences to film in a church?'

'Perhaps it depends on what they want to do? If they're stopping traffic, for example. Maybe there's different council rules, or something like that, A.D.' Jenny decided not to enlighten him about her suspicions as to what Joel was after as A.D. had enough on his plate between Adeniji, Chris and the BBC.

****

At the Hilton, Joel left Ellie in the lounge searching on her iPad while he went to settle in his room and have a shower. When he reappeared, Joel had changed into a Hugo Boss suit. He looked, Ellie thought, breathtakingly good in it. Joel explained that he needed to check in with the bank in Canary Wharf before he could do anything else but after that the time was his own until next Monday.

They were going to pick up the Docklands Light Railway, from South Quay to Heron Quays, but Ellie suggested that they could walk to his office by crossing a bridge over a wharf, she could go and sight see all the glass and steel of Canary Wharf and wait for him to finish. An hour later Joel joined her outside Carluccio's. He had worked out just where the "garden' was that he wanted to go to in EC1. He said: 'Els, there's a street market around the corner from the garden called Leather Lane and an old church, St Etheldreda's, which goes back to the 1300's. Wow! How about we have a look? I know how much you love history.'

Ellie, it was true, really enjoyed finding such old buildings in the UK. The reality was that Leather Lane was close to the jewellery area of Hatton Garden, which was really Joel's intended destination. He showed her the map and she saw Hatton Garden. Ellie worked out that this was a personal investment and not for work.

'Have you had a bonus or something?' Ellie asked.

'Yeah, a big one,' said Joel. 'I'd appreciate your overview on the selection though if you don't mind tagging along on this.'

'I was just surprised you wanted to do it today. Will the price go up or something?' Ellie asked.

'Could well do, Els,' said Joel. 'We're also away from Thursday in the wilds of Devon, and when I get back I'm straight into things at the bank. I think there's quite a lot of history around the area, and I guess you haven't been over that way yet?'

'No, I haven't. I did want to see St Pauls at some point, but we don't have to do that today. How did you find out about this place?'

'Oh, a bloke at work. He did some research on Trip Advisor and said it was five stars,' said Joel.

'Sounds odd,' Ellie said, frowning at him but Joel kept a straight face.

The black cab they had picked up dropped Joel and Ellie at the end of the road in Greville Street. Ellie looked around expecting a London garden or an inner-city centre for conservation. Instead there were only jewellers and people outside the shops vying for the trade.

Joel took her hand and they walked into the shop that had been recommended. He had made an appointment and as the shop admitted them Ellie said: 'You're investing in diamonds?'

'Maybe, or some other rock,' Joel shrugged.

'Why didn't you tell me, darl, you said geological specimens.'

'Well that's exactly what they are, aren't they?' Joel said grinning at her. The door was locked behind them and Joel waited for Ellie to go ahead. He added: 'Besides, if I'd said I was looking to buy a diamond or two you might have headed for the hills.' Joel said.

'No, because I would imagine you would have asked me something first.' Ellie walked into the shop, leaving Joel working through the potential that he may just have blown the negotiation. He'd assumed he had to get her into the shop and then propose.

Sensing the potential of a wrong approach with this independent woman he decided he just had to go with it now.

All sorts of different shapes and sizes and percentages of carats were put in front of them, one by one. Ellie stifled a yawn as Joel asked her opinion. Being honest she said it was completely out of her field and quite overwhelming that so much money could be spent on these pieces of carbon.

She pointed to a couple of shapes and said they were beautifully done. Joel gave the jeweller, who had been briefed, a look and the man pulled out some styles of ring. Ellie thought she had better put the poor man straight and that she was just here as a second opinion.

The jeweller smiled and maintained the facade. 'Quite, Miss, they're worth more if they're mounted though. Could "Miss" assist by showing "Sir" how it looks on? Has to be a lady's finger in my opinion.'

The jeweller picked up her left hand and the ring slid over her third finger. 'It looks a lovely piece of jewellery, and very good on "Miss," if I may say so.'

This was the way they had planned over the phone. Joel turned to Ellie preparing to drop on one knee. She took the ring off and gave it back to the jeweller, who looked at Joel. Joel was looking at Ellie trying to work out how he could have got it so wrong.

'Yes, it's very nice,' Ellie said but then held her hands up and grimaced. 'Not that I would ever wear anything like that given my work, but it's a beautiful stone. You could hardly go on the tube with that thing on your finger.'

Ellie laughed at the idea of anyone wearing something that size and walking around London. She smiled at the jeweller. 'Sorry that sounded rude of me, but you'd need a body guard to walk around London wearing that.'

Joel straightened up again, wearing his best poker face that he reserved at points when negotiations were not going the way the game plan had suggested.

'Something smaller then with a better carat?' Joel asked.

'Bit more tasteful but I couldn't possibly say,' Ellie laughed. 'I don't move in the situations where that stuff would be worn. It would feel wrong dealing with the situations I deal with. It's all too in your face. I can understand the desire to use your money in such a way that you grow an asset as a form of stewardship in the long term, which is where I assume you're going with this, but not to actually wear the thing. No, a simple band, definitely.'

'Would "Miss" think it should have a few diamonds?' The jeweller was making his pitch.

'Probably one, if it was discrete. Inlaid. Much nicer don't you think?' said Ellie, turning to Joel.

The jeweller and Joel exchanged a look. "Miss" had dealt an unexpected whammy. Not only that but "Miss" was moving towards the door.

'I'll pop out and have a quick look at the street market, Joel. Message me when you're through, darl,' The door was unlocked, she passed through and it closed behind her.

Joel, unusually, was stuck for words. He leant on the counter and sucked in his top lip. The jeweller joined him and the two men watched the Reverend Doctor walk away.

The jeweller exhaled and said: 'Tough one to crack this. Am I right that she has no idea what you're about?'

'No, not a glimmer,' said Joel.

'Perhaps "Sir" could do a little preparation first? Maybe come back tomorrow? I can fit you in around two.'

'Nah, I don't think this is going to work. I've blown it,' said Joel. 'You have to know when to cut and run, mate. She's very equality minded you see. Not interested in money either. I thought if I got her in here and she tried on one she liked the look of I could do the proposal and that would be a done deal. Hadn't bargained with the fact she'd never wear the stuff.' Joel looked at the array of diamonds under the reinforced glass of the counter and wrinkled up his nose in distaste. They would not do.

'Sort of melt in your arms routine, you mean? Was that what you thought was going to happen?' The jeweller asked, pitying the man in the suit.

'Yeah, that's what I hoped,' said Joel. 'Have to admit it's rocked my confidence a bit. I can't believe I got it so wrong. Jewellery always worked in the past.'

'Done this before, have you?' The jeweller raised his eyebrows. He added: 'Presumably not the same girl though.'

'Not a proposal. I never did that before. Gifts, you know the thing. Still that's the past. New man now! She's a church minister you see, does a lot of work with the homeless.' Joel and the jeweller exchanged looks.

'Ah,' said the jeweller. There was a pause while both men stared through the window in case there was a chance Ellie was coming back. She was nowhere to be seen. The jeweller leant on the counter in the manner of an expert and said: 'I was right when I said this was a tough one to crack. When exactly do you think she's going to wear anything I sell?' The jeweller paused.

Joel shrugged. He said: 'Good point.' Time ticked by and then Joel carried on with his explanation.

'I'm a numbers man you see. Not too much dealing with people. I say: "you go there," and they go. "You do that," and they do it. Not too sure what to do now.' Joel moved a couple of the diamonds around on the black velvet that were still there. The jeweller removed them from Joel's reach. Just in case.

'Hard for the young men of today now,' the jeweller sympathised. 'Women want to be treated equally, but generally also they want the romance too. It was easier in my generation. I soon caught on that if I tried to open a door for my girlfriend, or pull out a chair for her, it was the end of the relationship. Now it's difficult to know how to get it right.' The jeweller shook his head.

'I don't quite get your drift mate.' Joel said, frowning. Then he paused and went back to staring at the door, wondering if Ellie would ever come back through it. 'It's difficult to know what to do now. I thought you see, if I asked her to be my wife I'd get clobbered with the whole: "viewing me as a possession," routine. But doing it this way would be romantic.'

The jeweller adopted his philosophical look. 'Quite so, but you have to face it there's one good thing that's come out of this.'

'What's that?' Joel asked.

'Miss just wants a piece of Schmuck. Cheap to keep. I suggest "Sir" gets going, before the trail goes cold and come clean with her. If she says, yes, I can sort you out with whatever she prefers. Not what we'd both hoped but in a spirit of comradeship I can do it for you.'

'Right, you think that might work?' Joel asked. 'The "down on one knee routine," putting myself in the vulnerable position?'

'Well we've gone this far. Shame to waste the opportunity.' The jeweller glanced at the clock as he started to lock the cabinets. 'I'm open 'til five.'

****

Joel found Ellie at the old church. She looked for the package she thought he would have and realised that he had not gone ahead with the investment.

'No good?' Ellie asked, surprised that Joel had come out empty handed.

'No. Not what I came here to do.' Joel knelt down.

'Joel, what are you doing? Your suit!' Ellie's concern was for the Hugo Boss on a London street.

'I actually came to propose Els, and hoped that if you saw the rings, that you would say, yes.' Joel reached forward to take a hand. It was removed from his potential grasp.

Her hands went onto her hips and she said in a forced whisper: 'I can't believe that you would really think *I* would want something the size of some of those stones. I'd have said, *yes*, without this. You don't really know me at all. What future are we going to have together if you think that's what I'm like?'

'It's not that. It's what I thought … well, never mind what I thought. I'm still learning. Alright girl, I got it wrong but I had hoped that I could spend the rest of my life getting to know you, and you, me. The aim was to ask you if you'd like to get married. That's why I'm here.' Joel did not whisper, and remained down on one knee. Pedestrians were starting to clap and a taxi sounded the horn. The Instagram photos were starting. Ellie scowled at the lack of privacy.

'Look Ellie,' Joel thought he might as well continue although the look was off-putting. 'I love you, and want to be with you forever. I don't know how to say it now for fear of getting it wrong and blowing this. Will you say yes? Can I be with you forever? I know it's got to be forever for us now, believing what we do and all. I can't imagine tomorrow without you. I hoped you might feel the same?'

He waited while Ellie processed his words. The desire to clobber him and walk away was dissipating.

Joel got his yes.

But the jeweller did not get any business.

****

Adeniji was back from Finance, stuffing a couple of fifty-pound notes into his wallet. A.D. had felt completely calm until he saw them having intended to behave as if he had just noticed something in the room that would not take him long to deal with. With the money, he now felt that he was on the wrong foot. Theft, falsifying expenses claims … all sorts of reasons why the man had the money went through his mind.

Adeniji fixed A.D. with a frosty stare. He was used to commanding respect immediately, with a frisson of terror thrown in for good measure. This Archdeacon was irritating.

'I have been through the cupboards.' As he said it, Adeniji, leaned forward.

'Tidying? Finding fifty-pound notes that Finance have been a little careless with?' asked A.D. resorting to sarcasm.

'No, that is my expenses. I was not referring to the cupboards in Finance. I was referring to your cupboards.'

A.D. shrugged and looked over his reading glasses, while walking to his desk. He had already checked that morning if his beard had the sheen it should. Now he made a downwards stroking action checking its softness.

He leant against his desk, adopting the open posture of someone who had nothing to hide. An idea was forming if Laurie at the desk would play ball.

'Ah, well very nice of you to try and tidy things but I tend to leave cupboards to Jenny. And have you signed a confidentiality agreement? No? *Shame.* Better pop back to the Bishop's and get that sorted out before you go through anything else. Nice lot in Finance, aren't they? Excuse me, won't you, I just need to go to a meeting.'

A.D. slipped past the tall man and made for Jennie's desk. Beckoning to her they both left the office. By the lift A.D. said: 'Jennie call Laurie and tell him I'm on my way down.'

'Laurie? Why Laurie?

'I'm going to suggest Laurie cancels A's pass,' said A.D. as the lift doors opened.

Jenny could imagine Laurie's big smile.

****

Chris was home at Rosary Gardens after seven that evening. It had been an exhausting day with trying to avoid Adeniji and complete the scenarios A.D. wanted. A.D. had got Laurie on side re the confidentiality issues and Adeniji had found himself denied access when he returned from lunch as his pass had been cancelled. Laurie had hooted as he told Chris later.

Chris picked the post up from the mat and sorted it into three piles according to name.

He found a card with a photo on the front of three figures sitting in a tent dressed in the Tuareg costume of Mali. Turning it over he smiled spontaneously for the first time since Sunday evening. The card was from Timbuktu, or Tombouctou as his Uncle Colin had spelt it. Chris read:

'Hi Chris (and flatmates) from Tombouctou. Thought your flat could do with a postcard from here. It's just as hot as usual but the dust makes everything white. Pastor Elijah is just the same and the team are as 'entertaining' as ever. There's some really interesting human rights promotion work being undertaken. The financial systems, well, perhaps there might be cause for an accountant rather than me out here! I guess that would take some persuasion though right now. Love to you all and catch up again sooner than last time. Uncle Colin.'

The postmark showed he had posted it three weeks ago. He may be back by now, Chris thought. He searched in his contacts, found the last UK mobile number his uncle had had and hit it. It rang out without an answer.

'Where in the world would you be right now, Uncle Colin?' said Chris to himself.

****

Twenty

The light through the glass roof at Paddington took Chris back to the descriptions of the station that had been written by P.G. Wodehouse. His mother, Maureen, had introduced the humorous Blanding's Castle stories to Chris as a small boy. They had been an excellent lead in to the history and locality of the areas as John worked off Piccadilly in London. Like the Wodehouse character, Twistleton, arriving on Paddington at the end of a stay in London was something of a relief to Chris. It was the first part of going home. He did however, wonder what Wodehouse would make of the station today.

An announcement punctured the station with its echo effect calling him back to the present as he, Ravi and Mike, walked towards the first-class lounge to find A.D. Their train, the 14.06 to Penzance, would leave them at Exeter St David's, and it was now being announced that it was at platform five, with first class accommodation at the rear of the train. A.D. was providing another treat for his team.

In the lounge A.D. rustled his paper and quickly glanced at the clock on the wall. He had been anticipating the group's arrival for the last thirty minutes. Just the three he was expecting, as Ellie and Joel were making their way down separately and would be staying with Storm. He took his glasses off and wiped his eyes, stifling a yawn.

He had spent a funny night, not because Chris had strong feelings at the strategy they were following but because Mike had not reappeared on Monday or Tuesday nights, leaving the flat over the garage in darkness.

A.D. stroked his beard.

In fact, A.D. had not seen his lodger since Charis had driven off with him in the passenger seat of her car on Monday morning, bound for Oxford. Louise, always the rational one, had been fine with Mike not being back, but A.D. had a "niggle" at the back of his fatherly brain. It was the part where, occasionally, the protective instinct manifested itself regarding his daughters. He was pushing down the desire to clobber the young man.

'Charis isn't a fool, Mark.' Louise had said as she kissed him goodbye. That had been as she left the house at half past six that morning for work.

'I know that.' A.D. had looked crestfallen. 'She's like you. All the same. The fact Mike hasn't reappeared worries me.'

'See you tomorrow night in Devon, surfer boy!' Louise had called as she opened her car door. At that comment a little smile had played about A.D's lips.

Now in the first-class lounge he saw his three team members walking in. A.D. tried not to focus on Mike for any sign of guilt. He greeted Ravi first, then Chris and was excessively jovial when he got round to Mike: 'Good time in Oxford, Mike?'

Mike ferreted through the free packets of biscuits on offer.

'Yeah, first time I've been,' Mike said, nodding.

He sat down opposite A.D and explained: 'I must have walked miles on those tours of the colleges. Great group of mates Charis has there. She said there'd be no problem with me staying over with someone and they were really kind to find a space for me.' Mike was full of life and offered A.D. one of his finds: a packet of bourbon biscuits. A.D. declined. Mike was grinning at being in the first-class lounge. True to his calling as a youth worker he was up again and already exploring the fridge for freebies. Chris helped himself and Ravi to coffee and they joined A.D. at his table.

A.D. said to Mike: 'Oh, that's good.' And just to make sure, he added: 'Who was that with?'

Somewhere in the back of A.D's mind there was an imagined rebuke from Louise starting to burn a hole. Still, he pressed on to know where Mike had stayed.

'Couple of blokes from one of the student churches,' said Mike with a mouth full of shortbread. 'Daniel and Kelvin, on her course I think, but they've got a third room in the house they're renting and it was OK to stay a couple of nights before the new guy moved in. Cool city Oxford, but the traffic! I couldn't believe it. Felt worse than London somehow. This is nice isn't it, this lounge. Makes a big difference getting off the station before we go for the train.' Mike looked around the lounge and then took his seat again.

The desire to clobber his lodger had retreated to the part of the brain he, as a father, had temporarily filed it in. A.D. was full of remorse at misjudging Mike.

Ravi picked up his cup to get a refill. 'I must go back for a day before I leave. You ready for this work in Devon, A.D?'

'I am, Ravi. Look we had better get going in a couple of minutes. We can chat on the train.'

Chris looked at his phone and then at A.D. He said: 'I've got a message from Rafe. Have you left him in charge at Purley? He says: "World War Three has broken out over the position of the flowers in church for Sunday." Then there's were a load of emojis and he says he moved the plinth they should be on.'

'Any dead or wounded?' A.D. asked, showing little interest. Realising he was being unhelpful he added: 'Tell him to apologise, Chris, and say he won't win, so put it back where it was.' A.D's attention was drawn to Mike who was stuffing packets in his bag. 'Mike, you don't need to load up with packets of biscuits for the train. It's all in the ticket and they will feed you. *Mike, put them back*,' hissed A.D. 'I assure you, you won't go *hungry*. Let's go, shall we?'

****

Storm had met them at Barnstaple in the VW. He dropped A.D. and Ravi at the Woolacombe hotel so A.D. could take possession of the house opposite and settle in for a couple of nights. A.D's daughters would be descending from London on Friday night as most of A.D's team left for the weekend. Louise was to travel down by train on Thursday evening and use Friday as a working day from the hotel.

Ravi was going to do some walking along the coast after Thursday as he wanted to make the most of his time in a place he thought he would probably never return to. But tonight, he was keeping A.D. company over dinner, and crashing on the bed settee in the lounge of the house A.D. and Louise had rented. Ravi and A.D. stood at the front of the hotel for a few minutes while A.D. pointed out the tennis court and the putting green and then went in through the revolving doors. There was a rather nice room in the hotel that A.D. had spotted as he had walked through with Storm. It had a bureau in the corner, and A.D. had had a word with reception to reserve it as working space for Louise for Friday.

His tasks done A.D. had decided it was time to get at what was bothering Ravi.

'A good dinner first and even better conversation,' beamed A.D.

'Perhaps a walk to the beach?' suggested Ravi. 'Chris said it's a wide bay and beautiful,'

'Good idea, let's cut through the grounds,' said A.D. 'it's been a very sedentary day.'

'This is beautiful,' said Ravi, taking in the view to the sea.

'It's pretty quiet at the moment,' said A.D. 'But a world away from Westminster.'

****

Storm drove off with Chris and Mike to Gareth and Millie's home in Croyde, where they would stay for a couple of nights. With a blast of the horn, he waved as he passed a couple of surfers he knew that were making their way down to the bay. It had been a fair morning but only knee-high surf. The afternoon had been brilliant, sunny and warm. There was still some good low water at Saunton for the evening and he wanted to get them across, so that he and Chris could get in and wait for some sets.

It was Mike's first time in Devon and he was quite staggered with the beauty of the area. Mike kept saying:

'Oh *WOW*,' with every corner they turned, as they wound their way up past Potter's Hill to Croyde. The silver path across the sea to Lundy was mounted by the white-hot orb above it, pouring out shafts of light to the heavens, and to the water below.

Storm pointed to the headland and explained: 'Mike, that's Baggy Point. If you turn around now, you'll get a good look up the coast towards Morte Point almost just above Woolacombe.'

'It's so rugged,' said Mike.

'Pretty typical of the area really,' explained Storm. 'It's the Atlantic so you can get a large swell which makes it good for surfing.'

'What's the land on the horizon?' asked Mike.

'Lundy,' said Chris, 'You can do a day trip if you want to.'

'Have you heard of Tarka the Otter Mike?' Chris gave Storm a wink.

'No Chris, are there otters here? I've never seen one,' Mike said.

'When we were on the train to Barnstaple that line is called the Tarka line. You probably saw signs. Tarka's out of a book I read years ago, but there is a trail called the Tarka trail you can walk and cycle. It's fictional about the Otter called Tarka, but the trail is the area it was supposed to use.'

'I don't think I'll ever go back to London.' Mike wound down the window and stuck his head out to get the smell of the sea.

'That's how everyone feels. The problem is work and affording somewhere to live. How're we doing about getting some time in the surf Storm?' Chris asked.

'It'll be tight and the best is over today but if we can just drop your stuff and grab keys for Gareth's, we'll do it before the light goes. Mike, there's a suit in the back for you. The water's low today so I thought you might like to get your balance as a practice.'

'Yeah, sure Storm. Thanks,' said Mike.

'What time do Joel and Ellie get here?' Chris asked.

'They're here, Chris.' Storm glanced at him quickly and then got his eyes back on the road. 'Already installed in South Street. Ellie's got the spare room and Joel is crashing in the lounge. I think they were going to have a meal in the Brasserie tonight, so I hope they can avoid A.D.'

'How was Joel bearing up with the jet lag?' asked Mike.

'He was dealing with it. Did you know they've got engaged?' asked Storm.

Chris and Mike momentarily took the news in and then made comments about, 'another one bites the dust,' and, 'not surprised, she's a great girl.'

'Joel's brought a winter wet suit with him.' Storm said, laughing.

'No! It's June here!' Chris looked astonished.

'Yeah. I don't blame him really,' said Storm. 'The water will be cold to him. We're going out in the morning if it's good enough. He'll probably beat us all hands down. The guy is used to Byron Bay. I told him where to go to avoid the BBC, but I don't think he's bothered. At least he'll be able to stay in a while but the water's not really that cold now. To us that is. Here we are.' Storm nodded at the house on the corner. It was a three bedroomed, terraced house. Chris and Mike got out and Gareth emerged onto the front red-tiled step. Storm made the introductions and greetings were made with Gareth and Millie Evans and their two little children, Sophie, who was cuddling the family cat, and William who decided to hide in Millie's skirt. Gareth gladly took their bags, and showed them the layout of the ground floor as the spare room was a converted outhouse.

'I'll get you a key so you can come and go,' said Gareth.

'We thought we'd hit the surf with Storm and then probably eat with him. Are we likely to disturb the children if we come back late?' asked Chris.

'No there's a gate from a passage that runs along the back of the gardens. I'll show you now. Come through that way later and let yourself into the kitchen. Perhaps we can grab a chat before bed after the children are down,' said Gareth.

Storm, Chris and Mike set off along the road to Saunton, and as they passed a set of detached white houses, they spotted the BBC vans which the crews were unloading. The BBC team had arrived in a very different type of vehicle to the one Storm was driving.

Chris shrank down in his seat, turning up an imaginary collar. 'Keep going, don't look,' he said and Mike ducked. Storm laughed and said: 'Too late, they saw the van earlier this afternoon.' He waved and some of the crew acknowledged him. 'They've been out this afternoon, sizing up the shots they're after and filming along the coast to get the intro done,' explained Storm. 'There's thirteen of them in two houses, and they've got their own catering team as well.'

Storm made a snap decision to stay in Croyde due to the time. He pulled round the back of the surf shack and parked behind the line of wet suits hanging from a line. Chris and Mike followed him out of the VW and Storm pulled out the Hyperfreak suit he had for Mike. Chris and Storm were into their own suits as quickly as possible.

'How're we doing with the tide, Storm?' Chris asked.

'I checked earlier, but only for Saunton. I'll just check with Eric.' Storm said.

'Who's Eric?' Mike asked.

'It's a report on an app,' Chris said, laughing.

'OK. The wind's a north-west direction and the tide's falling.' Storm locked their valuables away and the three men walked down to the water.

'The water's only knee to thigh high Mike,' Chris said.

'Your main challenge, Mike, is to see if you can stand at all on the board in the sea. I've got one for you. It's a given that it's about you adapting from a skateboard to a surfboard.' Storm said.

'My only worry is what impact the sea will have on my beard,' said Mike.

'You and A.D,' said Storm.

Chris was in and paddling out but Storm stayed close to Mike, talking him through while they waited for the next set. Storm explained that he felt so close to God as Creator in the surfing that he did. As they finished he showed Mike the tide chart and encouraged him to check the wind direction if he was going to surf. Chris came back to them having got up on his board quickly.

On the beach were four men and a camera. One of them was waving and shouting. The men had followed them down on the off chance of getting some footage once they saw the VW double back. Mike spotted them and decided he would avoid being seen to fall off. Storm and Chris were in the water together waiting for a set to develop, trying to ignore the potential of being filmed when they were trying to enjoy the moment. Then they were up and loving it, calling to each other into the waves, doing what they had done since they were boys together.

Mike, on the beach, was fending off questions, trying not to sound like what he was, a complete amateur. He could just about show them standing on the board. The questions were coming at him like rapid fire and all the time the film was running. Chris came out of the water and walked over, coming to the rescue, just as Mike was asked what surfing taught him about life.

Chris answered for him as Mike paused. With a reassuring smile he said: 'Perhaps I can answer that for myself. It's patience.'

****

Ravi survived the dinner with A.D. by keeping to the main topic of the Slum project. When it seemed that A.D. was starting to bring things round to a personal level Ravi deflected him onto the food. In short A.D. got no further than confirming in his mind that Ravi was dealing with a personal problem. The time they spent over the meal was relatively short for the two men as they were joined by Joel and Ellie in the Brasserie. They respected the couple's privacy over dinner but were at risk of appearing off hand without the inevitable invitation to celebrate and adjourn to a lounge for after dinner drinks. This was readily accepted and Joel visibly relaxed as he had been dying to talk to the Archdeacon about a special licence. A.D. had not linked the "Joel" from his discussion with Jenny to the man before him when Ellie introduced her boyfriend.

They had all avoided dessert but now with the announcement made to them that Joel and Ellie were engaged there had to be champagne, and sweet food to go with it. A.D. with all his enthusiasm, insisted on buying as the most senior there, despite Joel's income. So, a good bottle was produced and Ravi's problems receded with all the good humour from his new Australian friend.

'Look, Ravi,' Joel said, 'India's not far, you should come and stay and have some respite from the project when you go back. The beaches are great.'

'That's kind, Joel, but it takes quite a time if you check it out from Delhi. I wouldn't like to lose touch though and it would be a great way to see a part of the world I've never been to, so thank-you. When you are both back there and settled, I will come.' Ravi gave the beginnings of a smile at Joel's invitation.

A.D. was bemused at the lack of a ring for Ellie, and a little concerned, so he voiced his curiosity. Ellie laughed and gave Joel a nudge. She explained: 'There's a bit of a story about that A.D. I'm having one ring, which will be a wedding ring, with one diamond inlaid. It will be made because this man wants to spend money on junk no matter what I do to try and stop him.'

'But people will think he doesn't care.' Ravi looked quite at a loss at her reaction to her fiancé trying to give her a gift of a piece of jewellery. 'There's also the message to other men.'

'Exactly. Thank-you my friend,' said Joel.

'Oh, here we go with the "putting a mark on a woman as a "possession" thing,' said Ellie.

Ravi was concerned he had given her the wrong impression.

'No Ellie, please don't think that. I am not part of that way of thinking, although I know many who are. I fight this. Yes, it's true that to give a gift of love would be extraordinary as would be the jewel I would choose. It would contain all my hope and all my passion in its choice. But never to own a woman with such a gift. To love and cherish, to honour her.' Ravi looked so unhappy Ellie leant over and put her hand on his.

Joel registered that the romantic expression had affected Ellie. He said: 'Look never mind all that I'm quitting while I'm ahead mate. She said yes, to me, that's it. It's fine. Whatever way she wants to do it we'll do it. Anyway, she's more than capable of seeing other blokes off. I'm amazed *I* was allowed to get close.' He received a thump as Ellie's response.

'You should run a master class in proposals Ravi. You see how to do it Joel. Maybe I'm marrying the wrong man!' Ellie gave Joel a quizzical look.

'Yes, I noticed what he said had an effect. Quite a lady's man eh.' Joel raised his glass to Ravi.

It was, of course, exactly part of the issue he was struggling with. Ravi retreated further into the high-backed chair and A.D. saw the effect of Joel's words. A.D. pursed his lips and registered that there were more issues than he had thought.

However, A.D. covered it by scraping the cream off the plate in determined sections and moved the conversation directly to the couple to avert attention from the pain Ravi was in.

Realising the distance for the Australian couple which would separate them for some time A.D. asked: 'Where will you get married?'

'That's what I'd wanted to have a chat with you about A.D.' Joel took advantage of the opportunity and leant forward. 'I left a few messages for you at your office, but I know it's a bit of a week for you. It's this thing about getting a special licence to marry.'

A.D. looked at Joel while registering who the calls were from.

'Oh, you're the Joel. I thought it was tied up with the BBC. Ah...getting a *special licence*. You mean.... ah, I see. Marrying in a church where you don't live in the parish. Is there a time frame you had in mind?'

'Yeah, about fifteen days.' Joel said.

Ellie went into a minor nuclear explosion. 'What are you nuts? Will you talk to me about things? I would like to talk to my parents first and...' She stopped to slap A.D. on the back as he was choking with the mention of fifteen days.

'They're all on standby, darl.' Joel lent forward and joined in helping A.D. recover his breath. Once the coughing had stopped Joel continued: 'I went to see them. I was waiting to see A.D. here and then, if it was possible, to tell you. I was thinking of the Abbey AD.'

'Oh no, oh no, no, no, no, no, wrong diocese anyway. Probably could swing a small chapel in St Paul's. But not up to me, we need to go to the big guy.'

'You mean you want to pray about it?' Joel looked surprised.

'Well there is that but I'm assuming you've both been there and done that, knowing Ellie as I do.' A.D. looked over the top of his glasses and gave her an avuncular smile. 'No, I meant A.B.'

Who?' Joel asked.

Ellie gave Joel another thump, gentler this time, and said, 'The Archbish.'

'How much will he want?' Joel relaxed, money he could deal with.

This time Joel got the full elbow from Ellie. 'Joel, stop it,' she said. 'There's rules. Apart from which, you actually told *my* parents before you'd even asked me? It's like you did a deal. Is there anything else, right now, that you've worked out which I don't know like...? Honeymoon?'

'Your dad only wanted twenty-five cows for you so it was a bit pricey.' This time the cushion was thrown and Joel ducked. He picked it up and slipped it behind him so it was out of Ellie's reach. He picked up the theme of her question about the honeymoon.

'I thought if we can do it while I'm here then, Italy. Say, Venice, the Lakes and Sorrento.'

Ellie had opened her mouth ready to demolish him. It stayed open for a while and a small frown turned to a wide-eyed look as she stared at the wall opposite working out the fact that this was... 'Perfect,' she exhaled a little breathlessly.

A.D. gave him a high five for the honeymoon but his face was serious. He explained: 'However, Joel, it's highly unlikely in fifteen days.'

'But only unlikely. That means there's a possibility of a deal. How long have you been married A.D?' Joel asked while he topped up everyone's glass and waited for the answer.

'Twenty-four years.' A.D. looked at the champagne in the crystal against the light as the bubbles made their way to the surface. The colour, he decided, reflected his marriage.

****

A.D. emailed and hit send:

'Jenny, find out about the possibility of a special licence for Ellie and her fiancé Joel. They don't fit the legal requirements so it's a question of getting a special job from A.B. Get onto it quick as Joel's not here for long.'

When Jenny came into her office the following morning and found the message there was a little smile, because, as usual, she was already three steps ahead of him. Jenny had called a contact in the Faculty office on Tuesday.

****

Twenty-One

The day had dawned when the teams' lives would cease to be private and their faces would, if the BBC were right, soon be seen by millions.

A.D. was determined that they should start the day well and had booked a good breakfast in the hotel. Joel and Ellie came up to join A.D. and Ravi but Storm was away early across to Croyde to find Chris and Mike.

Apart from the cost, Ravi was not in the right state of mind to face the quantity of food on offer. But A.D. would have none of it. They were shown a table by an open window overlooking the sea but the light and sea mist deprived them of a perfect view. A cold night after a warm day had obscured the view.

Joel and Ellie pointed out the quotations on the walls of the dining room to each other and Ravi picked one he particularly liked: the Longfellow from the "Day is Done."

'It's the part about the cares of the day folding up like a tent. I wish it were true. Not a writer I really know, but it has a flavour of the time he wrote it I think, before OPEC.' Ravi smiled broadly at his own joke.

'Yes, and the financial crisis,' added Joel.

'Longfellow,' said A.D. 'I read "The Song of Hiawatha," at junior school, quite young. It made an impact on me and seemed a magical world, not sure why. Ah, now we can order anything you prefer from the menu too.'

'I could add one to the wall.' Ravi carried on looking round the room at the quotes. 'I don't know the author but it's a Chinese proverb: "If you want to get rich first build a road."'

'Seems very apt given the Chinese economy.' Ellie laughed.

A.D. joined in and said: 'It does indeed.'

Ravi had another task today to do and this had weighed on his mind and deprived him of sleep. It was the right course, but it was the memories that had plagued him and had taken his sleep.

The waiter for their table was a New Zealand student working over the summer. A.D. beamed at him. He took the order for poached eggs, which were for Ravi, and for A.D. an addition of smoked Haddock with them. Joel mentioned rugby and the "best team," and A.D. joined in the banter insisting this must be England.

****

Emerging from the houses on the Saunton Road, the BBC team were taking up positions after the call from Gareth. He had recommended the location as far as the surf was concerned. The Editor and the Director down for the sole purpose of seeing the area stood at the low wall in the front garden staring down the road towards the beach. Coffee was brought out to them while the sea mist drifted over the bay and they both knew that the visibility would be too poor for filming unless it lifted. Taking their mugs, they walked towards the beach. The Editor was not impressed by the weather.

'See how it goes in a couple of hours. We've got some footage from late yesterday and three of the men from the church lot went out last evening. We can have a look at it while we're waiting for the weather to lift.'

Steph walked over to them while the Director lit up a cigarette. He said: 'I suggested Croyde as it's convenient but we may need to move. That intern, Steph, says there are four potential spots we could film.'

'That's right,' replied Steph.

The Director asked: 'Have you a preference?'

'I had a look briefly from the road as we drove through,' explained the Editor. 'They've all got good points to them and it would be great if we can use more than one. Late afternoon and early evening yesterday, there was a quality to the light that was perfect so we have some good lead-in shots. The light now isn't good though, so we need to find out from that guy, Storm, where they can go today. He's due down here in an hour.' The Editor glanced at his watch, and took a sip of his coffee.

'Bit late, suppose we had wanted to start?' The Director looked mildly irritated.

'He's calling the shots due to safety reasons. I went with it because it's his turf.'

A crew member walked towards them waving a phone. 'I've got a message for you to listen to, from the surfer called Storm. It's about the weather.'

'Here we go.' The Director stubbed out his cigarette and took the phone he was being offered. He listened to Storm's message and then handed the phone back.

'Storm says the fog will lift in the next couple of hours but they're expecting sun and showers so it will be a bit mixed. The surf is messy, whatever that means. Best time at Croyde will be towards 4pm. The other places will be later. They'll come down if we want them to but he doesn't want to take people out because the visibility is poor and they need to take extra care. Some of the team don't know the area and as we're only here for one day there's not enough time to familiarise them. What do you think?'

The Editor nodded. 'We can do some work in Croyde. Interview Gareth perhaps, film thatched cottages, get the team talking. Find a cream tea. Helps the choice later. Steph, fix it up, would you? Then get them in this afternoon.'

Steph nodded and said: 'Storm's doing a lesson at three apparently. Some of the team as starters. He says the Archdeacon may be of interest to us as a veteran surfer!'

'Really?' said the Director. 'The old guy who's doing the liaising? Good.'

****

A.D. thought that there may be a way in to talk about Ravi's problems. Gently does it, he though as he cut into his second poached egg and watched the yoke ooze into the top of the smoked haddock.

Mouth-watering as he savoured the expected taste, he said: 'Oh, that is excellent. Just as it should be.'

'I'm going to take Joel over to Mortehoe, A.D. as we're not expected at Croyde until three pm according to the message from Storm,' said Ellie. 'We'll see you back here ready for the lift, shall we?'

A.D. mumbled and nodded as his mouth was full. Swallowing, he apologized. Joel pulled a serious looking camera from his bag and gave A.D. a thumbs up. He said:

'Enjoy your breakfast. See ya both later.' Pausing uncertainly, he added to Ravi: 'You're welcome to join us, we don't want to be exclusive.'

'Having just got engaged you should be *very* exclusive,' Ravi said with a smile.

'Quite right,' said A.D. 'I'd be interested to see your photos though, later.'

'You have been married a long time, A.D.' Ravi said it as a fact as Ellie and Joel left the breakfast room. A.D. smiled as he drew a knife through the handmade butter from Quicke's Dairy. This may be a way in to talk about Ravi's problems but gently does it, he thought. A.D. was onto his second poached egg on the top of the smoked haddock. He exploratively poked the tip of his knife into the top of it and the yolk oozed out. Mouth-watering as he savoured the anticipated taste, he said: 'Oh that is excellent. Just as it should be.' A.D. scooped up egg yolk and fish, eyes on Ravi as he looked over his glasses. He chewed, and unable to help himself closed his eyes for a moment and pondered the question he should ask. He had it:

'No doubt your parents are the same?' he asked.

Pain in the eyes: we have it, thought A.D. Not waiting for Ravi to answer he chattered on: 'Yes, indeed, we have been married a long time although it doesn't seem like that. I still think of Louise as about twenty-eight. What about you Ravi, any lady in your life?' A.D. dropped his eyes but sensed the hesitation from Ravi. Concentrating on his food A.D. registered by the silence that his instinct had been right. More than one problem there, thought A.D. He focussed steadily on the fish. Remembering from years of this sort of thing not to rush an answer. He generally counted to ten when facing a silence. A.D. counted as far as a slow nine and then the answer came.

'I don't.' Ravi said.

Short, but not very sweet, thought A.D. He decided to go for it. He said: 'Getting established in the ministry I suppose. And of course, I would hazard a guess that things were difficult for you as regards your family. Probably walked away from a marriage your parents were setting up with a good woman when you became a Christian. Would I be right?' A.D. glanced up.

Ravi's eyes held so much feeling as they gazed into wisps of mist floating in from the sea. A.D. could see there was mist in the eyes to match it.

Ravi said: 'There's a bit of a past. It's not a happy one from my late teens. I played the field as you say here and angered my father. I was a spoilt younger son. I am not proud of it now.

Yes, I walked away from a good marriage that my parents had carefully and lovingly chosen for me.' He paused.

――――
352

'I walked away from everything I had in order to inherit everything spiritually, if you see what I mean. But I also understand their reaction and would have been the same myself at one time.'

A.D. nodded and beckoned to the waiter for more coffee. He said: 'And now you can't go back, not safely, anyway according to your mentor,' said A.D.

Their cooked breakfast plates were cleared. He had followed Storm's advice to get a good breakfast and now A.D. moved onto his toast, restricting himself to one small round of butter, focusing on splitting it between the two pieces of toast on his plate.

Ravi said: 'So I am told.'

'A double grief,' said A.D. 'Yes indeed, I see what you mean, although I can't possibly understand the pain that there is for you. My decision for Christ didn't involve the costs you have had. I wasn't a 'lady's man' either, to quote Joel. I think my youngest daughter would describe me as having been a bit of a geek. But the stunning love we receive from God also carried with it for me the fact of meeting Louise. We fell in love, felt we should marry, both shared a faith and a sense of calling into ministry. This may happen for you here.' A.D. paused. 'The future then, if you go back?'

Ravi didn't answer this but went back to A.D's relationship with Louise.

'How did you know, to marry and all? Forgive me, I have no one else to ask how it works. My parents found love through their children. The fact you see your wife in the way you describe, after three children and years together. It's wonderful!'

'Passion, you mean? We're talking of passion, dear boy. Oh, yes there's passion. Forgive me, I don't mean to be embarrassing. It is stronger Ravi, now. On our twentieth wedding anniversary our parish, and our children, threw us a big party. Louise and I really wanted to run away together. Again, take this in the context in which it is meant, a long and loving relationship but one where we accepted a calling to ministry and Louise to working commercially to support us while I went through all the years of voluntary placements and then training. I don't mean to offend you by my story. By the evening of that party we actually left a note for the children, and ran off. The children aren't little anymore you see, the youngest one was old enough to understand our need to be together on a day like that. Looking at me it's difficult to grasp I know.' A.D. shrugged, smiled and lifted his hands to heaven. Ravi smiled at him.

'Our children were very embarrassed at their parents' behaviour.' A.D. continued. 'They're still telling us off about it from time to time. However, I hope in their own future relationships they will remember that passion for each other didn't diminish with dad's thinning hair!'

Ravi laughed and looked at the receding hairline.

'Your beard more than makes up for what you have lost on top. It would be an honour to talk to you more, A.D.'

'Well, we have hours before Storm will come roaring up with Joel and Ellie. Let's walk some of this breakfast off on the beach, shall we? I believe there's a good bit of scenery from here up to Putsborough.'

****

Gareth had set up breakfast outside in the back garden as the visit of their guests had had enough of a disruptive effect on the family. He decided to barbecue at half past seven and soon the aroma of sausages had woken the children who refused to be kept out of the garden.

Mike and Chris woke to the sound of small whispers outside their door. There was even some scratching as the family cat sought a way in. Chris opened the door and there was an invasion of a five and three-year-old led by the family pet. Squeals filled the room as all three landed on top of Mike's bed, excited at their new friends. Between petting the cat and allowing his bed to be bounced on, Mike's day started much as it was to continue.

Gareth had had the call from the intern Steph to set up background interviews in the village. The BBC team were keen to take advantage of the thatched cottages and the general scenery away from the beach.

She was also passing on the Director's suggestion that the "cyclist" bike over the hills with a camera following him. The crew had found a small skateboard compound at the back of a car park and thought it was perfect for the "skateboarder" do a stint so they could film that as well. They would wait for the afternoon regarding the surfing, so that the weather to lifted. Storm's lesson was pitched for three o'clock. It was Chris that they would like to bike over the hills.

'Would they.' Chris responded sharply, as Gareth explained the gist of the call. His face set and Gareth turned to look at him so unusual was the tone. Distracted Gareth missed seeing his five-year-old pick a sausage off the barbecue and feed it to the cat. Chris was not impressed at the suggestion of cycling. The emotion it produced inside surprised him. He was angry.

'They've got a bike, and will do a helmet fitting as soon as we get down there. They've got gear for you. They said they just make things happen. I just stopped myself from saying sarcastically that it was a miracle,' said Gareth and turned back to dishing up sausage, bacon and egg for the children. Millie removed them into the house despite the protest at her actions. Mike forced himself to go for a third rasher of bacon while thinking about the skate park. He doubted it would be very large from the size of the village.

'OK, I can suss out the skate park but how about suggesting that hill, what did you call it, Pot something?'

'Potter's Hill.' Chris said flatly.

'That's it, Potter's hill, you riding, me skating down. Make a good shot I think.'

'Fine,' replied Chris's sounding short-tempered. 'Let's see what they want first, Mike. Gareth, save me some bacon if you don't mind. I'm going for a swim to work off this mood.'

'Watch the visibility Chris. The other thing is that the BBC is all over the area like a virus,' Gareth called to him as Chris started to disappear into the house for his kit.

'I know where to avoid them, don't worry.' Chris called back. They heard the front door close a few minutes later after Chris had changed into his swimming shorts and pulled a pair of tracksuit bottoms over them. He walked through the damp air and the few moments of a promise of sun to go down to the beach. Chris cut across the sand hills at an angle and so avoided the BBC crews standing in the front garden of the houses they had occupied for the night. He was rarely affected by changes in weather. He swam hard and strong trying to lose the frustration he felt at what he found himself in. He was back at Gareth's in half-an-hour, more relaxed and devouring the bacon in a sandwich. Hunger satisfied, Chris briefly showered off the salt and changed into what would pass for cycling gear. They were ready.

Gareth, wore a t-shirt with, "Christ in a Surfer," across his chest, while Mike sported, "Work in Progress," across the back of his. A.D. and Ravi would maintain the visible evidence of their calling in clothing for when they arrived at the BBC houses. Then, Chris thought, whatever they had to wear would be worn and whatever was to come would come. He just had to get through the day.

Down at the beach in Croyde, Storm had the look of the hunter. His gaze was out to sea, not at the BBC crew, assessing where the horizon was hidden by the morning's sea mist. It was habitual for him to assess and wait and he was reading the signs for later.

****

Mike and Chris sat in the back of a Range-Rover, Chris had been kitted up with both a bike and gear. All the kit was following in the van behind. There was a brief stop at the main car park in the village and Mike and crew went into the skateboard compound. Being a school day and out of holiday season it was empty at that time of day. He had been right that it was small but he did a couple of tricks for the crew, repeated them as many times as they wanted with a level of skill he maintained each time. The crew registered his skill base was pretty impressive. Eventually, they were happy with the outcome and Mike joined Chris back in the Range Rover.

The BBC vehicles drove across country on the narrow road from Croyde to Woolacombe to find a stretch of road with which they were happy. Sarah and Steph were rapidly talking into their mobiles to the relevant departments for permission to do this ad-hoc piece of filming on a public road. They were about to stop traffic briefly. Both women were used to the vagaries of sudden decisions from the crew as to where filming was to happen and were completely un-phased at having to get permissions quickly.

Sarah put her hand over the phone and asked the cameraman: 'Are we about to film stately homes, museums, churches, shopping malls, railway stations/airports and council or government buildings.' She rolled her eyes.

'Not likely out here is it?' came the short response.

'Are we likely to film other people's children?'

An expletive from the front of the car was all her answer.

'Are we going to be considerate where people can expect privacy?' No response from the front of the car, so she answered that of course they would be.

'OK.' Sarah put her mobile away. 'Providing we don't block roads we're good to go. So different from London boroughs.' She explained to Mike: 'It can be a nightmare trying to film in London.'

Of course, blocking the road was precisely what they did do.

****

Chris suggested the area from the top of the hill as it wound its way down. Mike did a preliminary run on his skate board to look it over before they started the filmed descent. The film crew were pleased with Chris's background knowledge and were warming to them both. The Range-Rover brought Mike up and Chris started to put his helmet on. There would normally have been views across the bay towards Mortehoe, but the sea-mist was obscuring it.

Cyclist and skateboarder wound their way down the isolated route. Mike assumed they were both going to return to Croyde with the crew but Chris called over to Mike.

'I'm going to bike to Storm's and borrow some gear to walk to Mortehoe.'

'How long will that take?' asked Mike, thinking of the time.

'Not long, I'll get back to Croyde by twelve.'

Mike gave Chris a thumb's up and then Chris was gone, speeding down the hill, before the crew realised.

It was into the vehicle for Mike, and the BBC convoy headed back to Croyde. Mike had recognised the set expression on his friend's face and thought there was just a chance he might not return.

****

By twelve o'clock Joel had arrived suited up in the thermal wet suit that he had brought with him from Australia. Storm had got a message to Ellie for them to come early. They had stopped on the way back from Morthoe at another hotel, the Watersmeet, for coffee and were soon back at Storm's house. There Ellie changed into her clerical garb, just because she had decided to make the point. The sea-mist was clearing and there were some small waves with an onshore wind. Storm had been in and decided it was fair and they could do something out there within the next hour. He unzipped his wetsuit down to waist level and grabbed a hoodie.

'There's your bare-chested shot,' The cameraman said to Sarah.

'Did you get it?' Sarah asked.

'Yup. Guys like that always make me feel irritable.' He got a grunt as affirmation from another team member.

Storm walked to do the rest of his changing in the surf hut and came out to find a heavy discussion between Joel and Ellie underway. It was about her going in to surf as well. Ellie's objections had not changed since the meeting at Langham Place the previous week. She had no intention of allowing them to objectify her as a woman.

Storm was distracted by the catering crew with the offer of a cup of tea, which he declined, and missed some of the detail. To the side of where Storm stood, Mike was tucking in to a piece of watermelon, intent on removing the seeds. His feet were resting on his board, his tartan jacket slung over the back of his chair, and his guitar was propped against the bench. Mike was making the most of the down time. Chris was nowhere around. It registered with Storm that this was not good.

'How do you know the conditions?' A voice asked him. Storm looked round and the Director was behind him, lighting up. Storm's mouth twitched as he suppressed a grin.

'I ask Eric,' Storm answered.

'Can we meet him? Do an interview?'

Storm looked thoughtful, playing to the stereotype he knew they had given him.

'Where is Eric?' He nodded slowly and looked up at the sky. 'Eric is all around.'

'Like some sort of Guru?' The Director asked.

'More like a camera on a pole.' Storm said, walking away. A guffaw of laughter followed him. There was a gurgling sound behind them as A.D. stifled a laugh, having overheard the exchange as he paid the taxi driver. Ravi and he had decided to give the lift with Storm a miss in order to give the time for Ravi to confide in A.D. They had walked to a tea hut at Putsborough and begged a taxi firm's number. It had been an incongruous sight for two vicars, in trainers, scrabbling across rocks and avoiding the pools. A.D. had listened more than he had spoken, weighing the consequences of the potential return to Delhi. Then as it appeared Ravi had exhausted himself in his explanation about Steph, A.D. had agreed with Ravi that he must apologise to the intern. From all their conversation, A.D. had a glimmer of an idea forming about Ravi but first, he needed to talk to Chris.

Joel was calling over to Storm. 'What's the temp of the water?'

'About 48-50 degrees,' Storm called back. 'Another month and it will be warmer.'

'Good grief, winter suit was right. Come on Els, let's do this together.'

Ellie looked at Joel wondering why this man was so suddenly intent on ignoring everything she had explained to him.

'No, I'm not going to conform to their marketing strategy. What is it you don't understand about what I've said?' Ellie crossed her arms.

'You'll be in a wet suit, Els, and it's a fact that you should be out there.' Joel stopped and faced her.

'Joel...there is no "fact" involved. Don't try all your negotiation techniques on me.'

'What about the girls then?' Joel asked.

'What girls?' Ellie shouted back, exasperated with him. 'There are no girls here!'

'Exactly. The Christian surfer girls Ellie. All girls.'

'That's exactly why I'm not going in. They just get stereo-typed.'

'Help them then,' Joel took her hand. 'You can't do anything about what happens with men's brains, it happens anyway, you only need to show up and it's happening. I thought you were the best looker, despite the collar, when I first saw you. But they need leaders, out there, good surfers with a brain like you who have the message of the "ground being level at the foot of the cross," to quote you. Come on!' Joel gave her a pull towards him as he walked backwards.

'You just don't give up, do you?' Ellie swallowed hard. 'I don't have my gear.'

'I picked it up when I saw your parents. It's in the case in the back of Storm's V.W.'

****

Ravi and A.D. had agreed that Ravi would make amends with Steph first thing. He was waylaid though by the Editor who had footage of the Slum Project that he wanted to look at with Ravi. They would fix up an interview while they ran it and get his background on what they were watching. The lead in was to explain Ravi's presence in the UK and to ask him questions about the level of India's GDP from 1970 to date, the existence and causes of such poverty, despite the Rolls Royce passing the slums. They actually had one in the footage driving past. Ravi was given to a team member who ran the footage and asked the questions.

'It needs an edit it but it's good. Thanks for that.' The man was pleased and patted Ravi on the shoulder.

Ravi turned and almost walked into Steph. One by one the rest of the crew went outside to watch the surfing.

'Silence?' asked Steph while her eyes were hard as she spoke but her face had coloured at bumping into him.

'Just the sound of my conscience in my head telling me to apologise to you,' Ravi said.

'Ah, the charm is being switched back on. Do you have any idea of how you made me feel?'

'I am truly sorry. The problem is with me not you. It's from things about me not from anything about you.'

'Really? You were so offensive. You're dead right it's you and not because of me. I've done nothing to you except show I liked you. Is this cultural or something?' Steph asked.

Ravi frowned. 'No, why would you think the entire nation of Indian men would behave like me?'

'Actually, I'm not interested in your reasons. I wouldn't go anywhere near you now. You should be ashamed of yourself in that collar you wear.'

'I am.' Ravi said but Steph had gone through the door and stomped down the steps to the road. Ravi could have tried to explain it any way he could think of but he had done the damage not only in the way she viewed him but the collar he was wearing was tainted in her view as well. He could see that Steph would be wary of every Indian man she would ever meet because of him. Ravi felt like something lower than the fly crawling up the window opposite him, lower in consideration, position or importance: the least of them all.

****

Storm had kept an eye open for his friend around the beach, even walking back to the service road into the village in case Chris had slipped off for a break. A.D was walking towards him after a brief spell in the town. Storm called to him: 'Have you seen Chris, anywhere, A.D?'

'Mike saw him go off on the bike for a bit after the filming at Potters Hill,' replied A.D. 'He'll be back in time for your class. I think it was politic he should get away.' A.D. paused and then continued. 'Storm I wondered if I could ask your help tonight?'

'Sure, what's happening?'

'I have to hang around Croyde, with the Editor and Director, this evening and it's likely to overlap with Louise getting into Barnstaple.'

A.D. had only thought the problem through briefly but now the solution presented itself to him. He said: 'I wondered if you could pick her up and bring her over to the house in Woolacombe? She's due in at Barnstaple about ten past eight and it would be a more pleasant way to arrive to meet someone from the team collecting her than getting a taxi. I should get back to the house to coincide with you dropping her off.'

'Of course. I should be done here by about 4pm and I'm going back home straight away. Will she need dinner?' Storm asked.

'That's kind, but no, she'll get a meal on the train.' A.D. said under his breath. 'First class so she can work. I'll let her know to look for you.'

'A.D. are you still on to surf this afternoon? I've hinted at it with the crew.' Storm said.

'Yes,' A.D. said emphatically. 'Let's hit them, Storm.' A.D. held his hand up to do a high five. Storm grinned and returned the action. He thought the old guy was coming on apace. Storm left A.D. and walked over towards the catering van to get a drink. He heard his name being called.

'Storm, are you around tonight?' Joel was back from trying the sea temperatures and was cradling a hot mug of coffee in his hands. Going back into the sea held no appeal for him at all.

'Early evening,' Storm replied. 'I've got a late collection to do for A.D. so up to seven is fine. What's on your mind?' Storm asked.

'Ellie mentioned you'd been at the LSE for your degree. Economics, wasn't it? She said that this work you're doing here was supposed to be for a year. I wondered if you'd thought any further after what you do here, or had any business ideas ahead, given your degree and all?'

'Nah, that year was some time ago, mate. It's pretty much a ministry as I see it. That's why I'm still here.' Storm ordered a tea.

'Yeah, sure, I get that.' Joel thought briefly and then said, 'Look can I have a chat about an idea I've been mulling over for a few months with you? Perhaps later over a beer?'

'Ellie joining us?'

'Not tonight, she's supporting A.D. and Chris with the crew down here. Chris seems to have disappeared off. Ellie's a bit concerned about him today and the way he's behaving. I don't know him well enough but from what she said he's a bit short with everyone, like he's had a gutful. It was Ellie's suggestion I chat to you actually. Ravi's going off to Truro later on his way down to Cornwall, so she thought if she hung around with A.D. it would be a help.'

'Yeah, gutful is probably a good description of exactly how Chris feels. I can meet up about six? I'm driving later and I'm not a drinker so no beer for me, if you don't mind, but I'll enjoy meeting up. Are you prepared to come in this afternoon for the shoot?'

'I've squared it with A.D. and the Director if you don't mind. I thought I could probably persuade Ellie to go in if I did. She's wavering but it might just work. A.D. thought the Beeb would like the romantic connection of a love interest for Ellie.'

'Really? Unless you've got a death wish, Joel, I wouldn't mention that to her. The other surfers should be here soon. In fact, I can see Gareth's grey hair now. Come on over and I'll introduce you.' Storm waved towards the edge of the beach.

'Who else are you waiting for, Storm?' Joel asked.

'Two ladies who work as instructors from time to time. They all have other jobs. One's a magistrate which the Beeb love. They also love the fact that she's a black magistrate and comes from Brixton, originally. You'll spot the yellow t-shirt of the school they'll be wearing. What we're really waiting for is the weather.'

'Right, mate. I was going to ask you a key question,' Joel said.

'Sure. Anything you like.'

'Do you ever get any waves here?' Joel's face crinkled into a grin as Storm kicked sand at him.

****

Chris had stopped at Woolacombe and left the bike in Storm's back garden. He was going to change the biking gear for some of Storm's old clothes and pad out his feet with two pairs of walking socks to fit Storm's size thirteen boots. Chris let himself into Storm's kitchen and borrowed the binoculars that were always ready on a hook on the back door. With them he picked up Storm's small back rucksack also packed with a set of waterproofs. Then he turned out of the back gate for the general direction of the cliffs and the walk to Mortehoe. It would take him an hour and a half there and back if he went to the Point. There would be the ride back as well, so he would make Croyde shortly after midday.

There was a freedom in the walking he had not felt for a long time. It was so different from his walks in London. He could appreciate it because he was tasting salt and smelling something other than diesel fumes. Although he knew the area well, it highlighted the disparity in his existence. London had become an endurance test, set by himself, for himself. It was all mixed up and despite still believing in a sense of calling into the ministry, he doubted himself in his current role.

At Mortehoe he turned past the cemetery, and old St Mary's church, and went through the gates in the direction of Morte Point. He was on the grassy track downhill, slippery from the rain in the night and the damp mist in the early morning. He would not make the Point in the time but was feeling more alive than for a while. It was a hard walk to stop from slipping. Too many flat roads in London, he thought. The only time he climbed there was using the stairs on the underground.

He put the binoculars to his eyes and looked for the Atlantic grey seals. Sometimes they played close to the shore. He would need patience. Chris reached into the small rucksack for the waterproof trousers and laid them out on the grass. He sat down on them and waited.

'Chaos calls to chaos,' ran through his mind. What was the rest of it? Running away this afternoon to a place he knew had not been a state that he wanted to be in but Chris had felt that he needed this time alone. The crash of waves and the swirling water echoed the chaos within. His mind cleared into the full verse:

> 'Chaos calls to chaos,
> to the tune of white-water rapids.
> Your breaking surf, your
> thundering breakers
> crash and crush me.'

There it was. A sense of God meeting Chris where he was. In the middle of his own particular storm. He set his sights on the Point.

****

By mid-afternoon Chris had not arrived and Storm was worried. There were any numbers of places Chris may have gone. The mock-up of a lesson that the BBC had asked for was starting and everyone who was going in to surf had changed and were leaving the surf hut. Storm whirled round as the sound of a bike crashed down as the cyclist jumped off. The man ran into the hut. It was Chris.

Chris threw the helmet onto a bench as Storm stuck his head round the door and shouted to him: 'Your suit's in my locker. See you down at the shore.' Storm paused briefly in the doorway for a response.

'Yeah, fine. I'm sorry,' Chris said.

'You alright?' Storm asked.

'Yes, just unfit with the hills coming back. It took longer than I remembered.'

'Where did you go?'

'To the Point. Then I had to pick the bike up from your place and I'd forgotten some of the inclines on the way back across here.'

Storm registered that Chris was alright, although looking drained. 'Have you eaten anything?'

'I had a huge breakfast at Gareth's,' Chris said.

Storm noted the hours that had gone by and what Chris had already done, physically. He said: 'Well, it's not exactly demanding out there today. Get something to eat bro, when we finish, eh?'

Storm left Chris changing into his wet suit and went back to the group that were forming for the shoot.

A.D. had already emerged, to the delight of the BBC crew, in his wet suit with his board. A brief cheer went up from Mike and Ravi which A.D. had not expected.

'Let's see if I can balance, then you can cheer,' A.D. called across to them.

A BBC operative was already starting to take him on one side and A.D. was interviewed about the challenges of surfing at his age. Walking back to join the group, he muttered: 'What nonsense.'

Ellie had given in to Joel's persuasion and Joel was described as the "love interest," by the film crew.

Chris was out of the hut and walking down to join the rest of the team, but the Director only had interest in the potential of the surfing Archdeacon, the Reverend Dr. Ellie and her love interest in the form of an Australian merchant banker. Joel was an unexpected addition to the surfing team. Mary and Cheng had arrived from the surf school. Much was made of Mary from Brixton and the Director had not come across a Chinese surfer before, so Cheng was interviewed.

All the surfers were already on the water's edge, the yellow t-shirts displaying the name of the school. Mike was also there, playing the clown and falling off into the water. He had started to adapt to the fact that there was no solid ground under his board but decided to raise a laugh anyway.

Ravi stayed on the shore line as an observer, cheering, forgetting he was being filmed too. Gareth did the talk over, answering questions, providing the commentary and explaining about the Christian Surfers.

Twenty minutes later it was over. The team stayed in the water while the BBC withdrew back to their houses. The review of the footage from the morning and the surf lesson would begin. The Director and the Editor were about to spend hours working closely together on the finished sample ready for A.D. to view. Everything they had filmed would be condensed into approximately half of the pilot, which would go out later in the summer. A.D, it was planned, would see it with them next week, in order for them to potentially get more voice over. Then there was the question of what else would go into the pilot. The interviews that had already been done that morning were being planned to be used for the Sunday morning slot on local radio, with some careful monitoring of social media.

Walking back towards the surfer hut Storm had a word with Mary about the lesson booked for A.D's three daughters on Friday evening. She agreed to share the lesson with him and could be available to help with Saturday as well. The girls were coming down in time for the evening and if the weather held that would be the best of the day on Friday.

****

That evening the train arrived at Barnstaple at eight o'clock and the brakes on the car announced Storm's arrival in front of the station. He had overrun on his time with Joel and had risked being late to meet A.D's wife, changing not only the vehicle at the last minute from the team's V.W. to his car, but smartening himself up as well. He was managing first impressions because of what he had to discuss with her on the journey.

The chat with Joel, and his subsequent offer to Storm, had both excited and disturbed him. It was out of the blue and they had left it that Storm would sleep on it tonight and the two would have coffee at eleven on Friday morning to go over more details. Storm wanted to think it through, reflect and pray in case there was any mileage in the idea.

Storm sat in the car and watched the passengers as they exited the station. Some went over to cars that were waiting and others had booked taxis. An attractive, smart, woman in her mid-forties appeared from the platform carrying a laptop case and a piece of hand luggage. Storm was out of the car and walking over to greet her. Amongst the rest of the passengers this had to be Louise, a Finance Director of a FTSE 250 company, still in her business suit. She was very assured in her manner as she gazed around the car park. The woman stood out. With some interest Storm wondered how couples ended up together.

Storm held out his hand. 'Is it Louise?' he asked.

'Yes, hello, you must be Storm?' Louise replied.

Louise sized him up as he walked slightly ahead of her to the car. Storm talked over his shoulder about how good it was to meet her. Put him in a suit and with a different haircut he would dominate a board room with those eyes and the proficient polite manner.

From what A.D. had told her Louise had expected eccentricity, but there was no trace of it tonight. Storm also reminded her of the boy at university she had briefly dated before she realised he was a potential swine. She shrugged the memory off. Paul, she occasionally met across a board room table and her understanding of the personality meant she dealt with him to the benefit of her company. Storm's expression was different, it was open and he had a similar direct gaze but without the arrogance.

They got into the car and after some small talk about the journey Storm got straight down to business.

'I wanted to ask your help on something I think I have to do tomorrow.'

'Really? said Louise, a little surprised. 'I'll help you if I can. What is it?'

'It's about your daughter Eve and my mate Chris,' Storm said and then paused to give Louise time to absorb who was involved. Louise did not need time. It was something that she was never given in her work, and on the Richter scale this issue was not scoring very highly. There was no seismic wave at present, as far as he was concerned.

'Go on,' Louise said.

'You'll know by now I guess, that Chris has admitted to A.D. that he has feelings for Eve, and A.D. has confirmed that she has for him.'

A pause again.

So, the authority being cited for this piece of information was well chosen, thought Louise.

It also indicated that her own relationship with A.D. was intimate as the assumption was that they communicated. Therefore, he could continue without challenge. But he did not.

So, why is he waiting? Louise thought. Is it nerves?

'Go on.' She said gently, to encourage him.

'For some reason, none of us understand, he hasn't made a move. Chris and I grew up together, we went to school together and spent all our holidays mainly in the sea together. I know him well. So, with that all in mind I'm going to suggest a course of action to you to move him on so that he and Eve become an item.'

'Have you shared this with Mark, I mean A.D?' Louise asked.

'No, because I think he would stop me,' Storm said.

'I don't have secrets from my husband, Storm. Particularly where family are concerned. You tell me, you tell him. That's how it works. It's the concept of being one.'

Louise paused to let that sink in. It did, and Storm pulled his old car over and with a jerk of the handbrake, turned the engine off. He twisted round slightly towards her. The face was earnest and the eyes continued to remind her of that someone she had met before.

Louise softened her expression. 'What's your real name Storm?'

'Giles.'

'And your surname?'

'Oh, you'll have heard of dad, he's in your line of work. Does it matter?' Storm's tone had changed to mild irritation.

'Paul? Is it Paul Downing?' Louise adjusted her body posture to also reflect his. An open position she reminded herself, to encourage communication.

'You see I told you you'd met him. I know people think I'm like him in looks. Not in character though.' The reaction and the tone from the son of the man Louise had dated at university was interesting. It was flat, hard, almost dismissive. It was a statement of fact that Storm expected her to have met another Finance Director in her line of work. However, she could not help but wonder how Paul had adapted to fatherhood.

'I was at university with him. So was Mark, I mean A.D. We were on the same course. I have come across him in my work, you're quite right. So where did you get the nickname Storm from?'

'Oh, I think the Duncan family gave me the nick name as I would go out in anything, any weather. Aunty Mo used to say I was like the onset of a storm as well, brewing on the horizon and then it would suddenly hit.'

'Fearless, a hunter,' Louise said. She was describing a family trait, but Storm took it as a compliment to a surfer and smiled.

'So, I think your Aunty Mo is right,' Louise continued. 'What's the plan then?' Her face and tone remained deliberately soft. He did not need her to give him a hard time. He could go home to his dad for that.

'I'll brief Eve so she knows what's going on.' Storm started to explain. 'In the middle of the lesson tomorrow night, I'll make a move and Eve will play along. Chris will be there in the water as well and then he'll probably try and kill me, but it will make it obvious that he wants her, so hopefully he'll grab Eve and they'll get together.'

Louise was already drawing up the pros and cons. 'And the bit about him trying to kill you, this curate who works with my husband? How do we deal with that in the film in your head? And Eve being grabbed like a sack of spuds?'

'Oh, don't worry about the killing bit. I can always beat him. I know his moves, because I taught him to fight. Had to, he was losing his pocket money every day at school. No one had any respect for him. So, once he knew how to fight them, he was fine.'

'When did this happen?' Louise asked.

'When we were nine.' Storm said.

'Ah the glories of the English private school system!' Louise commented sarcastically but it was lost on Storm. 'Right,' she said, 'so we have some sort of a plan. And the fall-back position if it goes wrong?'

'Why would it go wrong?' Storm looked puzzled.

'I see. You don't plan in disaster. No risk analysis?' Louise paused, looked at him but did not read any potential double cross in the eyes. 'So, my role in this play is, what?'

'You're like the solicitor that the character in the film leaves the letter with just in case he gets killed. You know the truth. When I get rubbished you'll be the one who comes to my rescue,' Storm said, firmly.

'Right. And you expect death? Or are you using a metaphor?' Louise asked.

'It could affect my rep locally, a "death of reputation." Making a move on a girl so obviously being coached. If Chris really is in love with her he'll lose it. Always does. We're all a work in progress. I'll have to defend myself to a certain extent to control him. I doubt Gareth, my boss will be too impressed. Mary, another instructor, will know too, so she'll cover me. But I want you to know so someone squares it with the family. Especially A.D.' Storm was done and sat back in his seat and started the car.

'Why A.D,' asked Louise.

'Because I respect him. He's got guts on a board,' explained Storm.

Louise nodded. She asked: 'And when is Eve to know about all this?'

'I'll tell her just before I make a move on her, no time then for her to think about it,' explained Storm.

'And just pursuing the basic risk analysis here, have you thought about what happens if when you take Eve in your arms there's a connection between you both?'

'That won't happen,' Storm said with conviction.

'Really. You think?'

'No, it won't happen. I won't be doing it like that. There'll be no connection with me.' Storm gave a quick glance at Louise, a little uncertain now at why she was pursuing this line. He looked back at the road.

'No?' Louise continued with her line of questioning. 'Not in comparison to your geeky looking, neurotic friend who doesn't have the muscle, or the eyes, and who seems to be a mess about his job, his love life and his appearance?'

'No,' Storm answered. 'Because she loves him.'

'Right,' said Louise. 'You're pretty sure are you of that are you, never having met her?'

There was no answer from Storm. He moved in the driving seat, his eyes only on the road but a frown on his face at the very idea that Eve would prefer him to Chris.

Louise had her answer. She said: 'Well, that's everything covered then. So, when does this event happen, so I can prepare myself for the fallout?'

'Shortly after the girls arrive tomorrow evening. If the weather holds we'll do the lesson then. Mary's my back up when I do lessons with girls so that nothing happens and I don't get accused of anything. So, I'll fill Mary in otherwise she'll whack me with a surf board.'

Louise was laughing now, quite uncontrollably at the picture of a female instructor having to keep Storm in check. She gasped for breath and Storm looked at her trying to understand.

'You'll be on a beach, though. It's very public, isn't it? Won't your reputation be shot to pieces after this?' asked Louise.

'I'll work it out. He's my mate. We're like brothers. He needs her. A.D. showed me her photo. She's perfect for him. He's not the sort that plays around. If he seriously is in love with Eve, it will be for life.' Storm glanced quickly at Louise and then looked back at the road. He gave a brief smile trying to communicate to Eve's mother that Chris was alright.

Louise slowly nodded. 'So, Eve's getting a good'un! For your friend then and my daughter: Partners in crime!'

Storm took one hand off the steering wheel, grinned and shook her hand.

'And A.D?' Storm asked.

'Leave telling him to me. You're right he will try and stop it but I'll tell him at some point tomorrow. Storm, it has a bad feel to it, frankly, but I will be the person that's like the solicitor in the story for you. So, you leave the information with me and I know your good intentions and will try and put things right after you're dead. Not literally hopefully, but as regards your professional suicide job.' Louise sucked in a deep breath.

Storm gave her a quick glance again. He said: 'Thanks,' as he turned the corner and Woolacombe came into view. Louise took in the sun on the water and the wide expanse of the spectacular bay. Below her the Woolacombe Hotel sprawled across its grounds and the golden path across the water to Lundy beckoned. She decided she would wait to tell A.D. and not spoil such a beautiful night.

That was almost a year ago.

****

'Mark, have you finished?' asked Louise as she pushed open the door.

A.D. glanced at her, noting she had entered with a certain expression on her face that would brook no nonsense. He leant forward and pulled out the leads into the two laptops. A.D. had made a decision. His mobile rang. It was Sarah. A.D. switched it off and it went to voice mail but he could ignore that for a while.

'Right,' A.D. said, 'It's all yours. Do you want to do your meeting in here?'

'Aren't you doing the programme?' asked Louise, softening at his contorted face.

'No, I had a call come through from Storm, missed my slot again,' said A.D. He added: 'He's got as far as Geneva and Amy couldn't get a flight so she's staying put and liaising with her embassy. I'm picking Storm up from Heathrow around ten tonight. I'll have to bring him back here, hope that's going to be alright? Can't have him trying to make that journey to Devon at that time of the night and he'll want to be near Heathrow in case Amy gets back suddenly. He can have the flat over the garage. The furniture's there from Mike's stay and we can isolate if needed but give him some care. He probably shouldn't go near Maureen and John with them being older, just in case.'

'You might get stopped doing that journey,' said Louise.

'I'll wear my dog collar – errand of mercy etc. Sorry about the internet,' said A.D.

'It's fine about Storm, and thanks for the internet, now. What will you tell the beeb?' asked Louise.

'The truth, she'll make a story out of it knowing Sarah.'

'A.D. to the rescue?' said Louise.

****

Other Books by J Ewins and L Telfer

The Jack Sargent Historical Crime series:

The Faceless Woman: Jack Sargent's First Murder.
1872
Young labourer Jack Sargent leaves Sussex in 1872 to join the
Metropolitan Police. He enters a world of crime, murder and
love.

Cords of the Grave: a Jack Sargent mystery.
1873
Two major events in London and Sussex lure Jack into the
fight against organised crime with deadly consequences.

Printed in Great Britain
by Amazon

61429918R00219